SNOW IN SEATTLE

A NOVEL

AMY M. LE

*Joyce —
From one professional
daydreamer to another —
never give up!*

SNOW IN SEATTLE

First edition August 2020

Jacket design by Virginia McKevitt

Manufactured in the United States of America

ISBN: 978-1-7351194-1-0 (paperback)

ISBN: 978-1-7351194-0-3 (hardback)

ISBN: 978-1-7351194-2-7 (ebook)

DEDICATION

This book is dedicated to all the refugees who were forced to leave their homes to escape war, persecution, disasters, and conflicts. In honor of our fallen soldiers and war veterans, thank you with deep gratitude for your bravery and service.

PRAISE FOR SNOW IN SEATTLE

"Author Amy M. Le has written a powerful, heartwarming story of resilience and family that inspired me and kept me turning the page. I couldn't wait to find out what happened next as Snow, the protagonist, struggled to adjust to the American culture while retaining her Vietnamese heritage. Le sprinkled this novel with humor, romance, and drama, and I highly recommend it!"
—Staci Mauney, Editor, Prestige Prose

"*Snow in Seattle* is an astounding story bringing to life the complexities of adjusting to a new way of life for Vietnam refugees. It engulfs you in this family's reality and the struggles they faced. Written with such beautiful passion, I felt as if I was there with them. I am hopeful there will be another book to learn about the new adventures that await them."
—Tabitha Salom, Beta Reader

"*Snow in Seattle* has been one of the best books I've read in a long time. Snow, her daughter, and nephew had such difficulties getting to Seattle. This story will open your eyes to what refugees and our Vietnam Veterans went through during and after the war. This book will make you laugh, cry, and cheer on Snow and her family. Definitely worth the read!"
—Lori Kennedy, Beta Reader

"After reading *Snow in Seattle* I have a better understanding of how the Vietnamese refugees lived here in America in the '70s and '80s. The journey of learning our culture while still incorporating her culture in her daughter was so impressive. I cried, laughed, loved, hated, and lived with Snow. The description of the food and atmosphere of everywhere around her is phenomenal. I could not put this book down! I was there with Snow from the beginning and hope there is more to come."
—Bri Neighbors, Beta Reader

"*We humans can be adaptable and thrive if we have the strength and willpower to do so.*"
—Skyler Herrington

"It was an honor to be invited to be a beta reader for Amy Le's sophomore novel, *Snow in Seattle*. This is a sequel to her debut novel, *Snow in Vietnam*. The sequel picks up with Snow and Dolly's introduction to America via Seattle, Washington. *Snow in Seattle* takes us on the heartfelt journey of Snow and Dolly's acclamation and orientation to America. For Dolly, it is also about her pursuit of urgently needed medical care and lifelong good health.

For Snow, it is the trek to healing her soul of the wounds inflicted from a lifetime of war, basic survival, hunger, violence, loss, and heartache. It is about forgiveness and salvation. It is about building a community of loved ones and supporters."

"Remember that grit and tenacity will take you far in life, but love and forgiveness will carry you to the finish line."
—Snow

"There is a part of the book that will stay with me for a very long time. I won't spoil it for future readers, but let this quote from the book be a teaser. *"Like cobwebs or like honeycombs? Like glass or like horse?"* Nope, not just a very long time…maybe forever. You know that a story is well told when, days after completing it, you are still thinking about the amazing characters. Amy, while telling the fictionalized story of her mother, is really sharing the story of herself and how she became the strong woman that she is today. Like Snow, she is an amazing person, mother, wife, friend, and storyteller."
—Gina Richardson, Beta Reader

"How does the human spirit have the courage and willpower to overcome extreme obstacles in the fight for life, safety and security? Based on true events, *Snow in Seattle* is Amy Le's follow up to her exciting first book, *Snow in Vietnam*, where one determined woman's escape from the atrocities in her beloved war-torn country shows what a difference a chance friendship can make in the struggle to assimilate into a foreign culture in a strange new land on the other side of the world. When everything and almost everyone she knows and loves is so far away, how does Snow manage to learn and grow, understand, forgive and love again? *Snow in Seattle* will take you on an emotional journey of heartbreak, humor and self-discovery as she mourns the loss of her previous life while nurturing her little girl, encouraging her young nephew, and supporting their new life with surprising results. Amy Le's excellent dialogue in *Snow in Seattle* gives the reader fresh illumination into tumultuous events. She does this with well-developed characters dealing with authentic issues that have no easy solutions. This satisfying road trip will give you insightful observations into the critical problems that continue to be experienced by humans in today's world. I recommend this book to anyone who is interested in feeling like they shared a piece of their heart and made new friends that they grew to know and love."
—Diana LeBeau, Beta Reader

"Snow in Seattle" is a wonderful sequel to "Snow in Vietnam". The story touches all the emotions. Being a veteran myself, I can relate to the character Sky's story. Amy delves deeper than the typical boat person/refugee story. She demonstrates the power of family and faith, love and forgiveness. I also like it when an author expands my vocabulary. I had to look up a word. Friends are family that we choose. The main character "Snow" has her real family, but is soon surrounded by her chosen family. They help her adjust to her new life in America. Snow and Sky both learn that if you surround yourself with loving, caring people, you will be loving and caring, too. Unfortunately, the opposite is also true. Mean, hurtful people are usually miserable and want you to join them in their misery. That character at Disneyland showed his prejudice and misery when he harassed Snow. The phrase "forgive and forget" comes to mind. Snow tries to forget the past. She cannot live there or change it. Snow learns forgiveness. She first forgives herself. Then she forgives others that have brought her harm. Forgiveness really is divine. Amy also gives us a glimpse of Vietnamese culture. I have been to Saigon, Little Saigon in Seattle, Little Saigon in San Jose, and even found Little Saigon in Berlin, Germany when I was there. Hearing the singsong language, seeing the signage on the shops, and smelling the food always brings back good memories. I have always believed that love conquers all. Somehow Amy has made love the theme of this story. Consider me conquered.

—Michael Harmon, Vietnam War Veteran and Beta Reader

CONTENTS

Snow in Seattle (November 2015)

ACKNOWLEDGMENTS

To the military veterans who shared with me their personal stories of pain and hope, I thank you sincerely for your time. My gratitude to David Cruz, Dominic Dimino, Michael Doud, Michael Harmon, Joshua McGoveran, Charles Peters, and Greg Simpson. To my critique team "The Quixotics" (Ilene Birkwood, Keith Madsen, Frances Sonnabend, Tricia Corbett, and Mac MacCullough) I am in awe of your wisdom and perseverance. A special thanks to my editor, Staci Mauney at Prestige Prose, for her falcon eyes catching all the nits and nats of my work with peregrine speed. To my beta readers, you inspire me to write my best. Thank you, Michael Harmon, Lori Kennedy, Diana LeBeau, Brianna Neighbors, Gina Richardson, Tabitha Salom, and Lisa Schumann for your feedback. To Virginia McKevitt at Black Widow Books, thank you for designing my beautiful book cover. Finally, this book would not have been possible without the support and encouragement of my fans, who demanded a sequel to *Snow in Vietnam*. My biggest fans continue to be my husband, Joe, and son, Preston. I love you both.

Dolly and Snow in Vietnam together, February 2008
(Twenty-nine years after their escape as refugees)

Thủy-Tiên aka Dolly (Vietnam, 1974)

Dolly (Seattle, 1983)

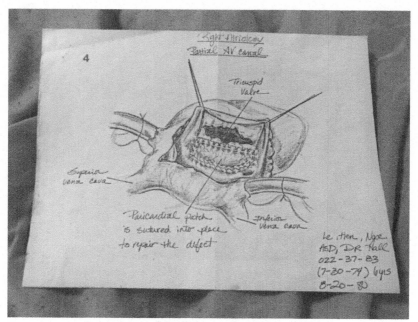

Drawings of Dolly's open-heart surgery
(Seattle Children's Hospital, August 1980)

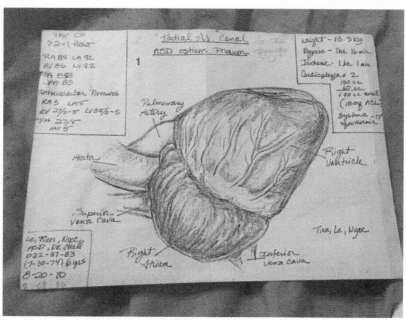

Drawings of Dolly's open-heart surgery
(Seattle Children's Hospital, August 1980)

1. ATRIAL SEPTAL DEFECT (AUGUST 1980)

Her face, both lionhearted and bitter, represents the willful baby I fought to keep alive and the hardened woman she may one day become. My daughter rests on the hospital bed with her small fingers squeezing the bedrails. Her eyes cast shurikens at the medical staff as if they are samurais coming for her. Ready for battle, Dolly accepts her fate and acknowledges that her chest will be cut open to fix the defect in her heart.

The fear inside me is parasitic. One would think the origin of the infestation came when Sài Gòn fell and communism blanketed Việt Nam. Perhaps it derived from abandonment and betrayal by my husband who left us in 1975. Or maybe the fear stemmed from the difficulties of escaping my country and facing uncertainties with forty-two other boat refugees on trawler 93752. I am certain my fears began the day I became a mother. That fear has evolved and today, it has a name: atrial septal defect.

"Snow, please step aside and let them do their job." Sky Herrington laces his calloused fingers through mine and leads me to the black upholstered chair with the yellow and red tribal designs. On the wall are pictures of Chief Seattle and David Swinson "Doc" Maynard. Their black eyes drill holes into my heart. They understand about uncertainties.

I watch helplessly as the nurses at Seattle Children's Hospital wheel my six-year-old, my little dolly, into surgery. She gives me a brave smile and waves. My nephew, Tree, stands by the window. His stare is vacant. A tear belies his strength. I ache to comfort him and erase his worries as I did when he was a child. A hug and the promise of some banana and coconut pudding was all it took back then to bring a smile to his face. He is seventeen years old now. My touch repels him and his recoil daggers my spirit. I have only Sky to comfort me.

Sergeant Skyler Herrington, my old friend who was in the US Army,

1

who did everything he could to deliver my freedom but also nothing to save the love of my life. At only thirty-six years old, his vibrant youth has been replaced by careworn senescence. The last time I saw him was eight years ago, in my hometown of Vĩnh Bình, where he stood shell-shocked over Sam's lifeless body. Sam, the soldier I was going to marry…the man who still haunts me when I close my eyes. The Việt Nam War took its toll on all of us, but perhaps in some ways, it robbed Sky of more than his peace of mind; it siphoned the essence of him, the embodiment of everything Skyler.

Still, a part of me resents him for not doing more. More of what, I cannot say. Just more. Can I forgive him for Sam's death?

"Aunt Eight," Tree says, "Thủy-Tiên is not going to make it." My nephew does not turn around to address me. He stares at a photo of the Space Needle and Seattle skyline.

"We did not come all this way for her to die." I want to shove my nephew up against the wall and slap some sense into him. How dare he inflict his doubt on me? Of course, my daughter will make it through open-heart surgery. She's stubborn and resilient. I know Tree is still angry with me for bringing him here to America. I want to punch something.

"I have never seen her skin so blue. And her fingernails…They were black." Tree looks directly at me and challenges me to acknowledge the possible truth that my daughter may die. What if I never hear her laugh again? Never feel her soft, sticky hands holding my own? Never soak up her kisses or melt into her arms?

Sky looks at me questioningly. He does not understand Vietnamese. I give him an unnerving smile. He stands up and mutters, "I'll get us coffee," and strides off quickly. I want to shake him, too, but I remain calm.

How did I get here, to this space where I hate the world and resent those closest to me?

Five months ago I stood on a boat that was docked at Galang Island in Indonesia, saying goodbye to the refugee camp that was home to Tree, Thủy-Tiên, and me…and saying goodbye to my friend, Ommo. To him, I was the woman he loved and wanted to marry, but to me, Ommo was my ticket out of the refugee camp. That was, until Skyler successfully sponsored us to the United States.

The five-hour ferry trip from the Galang camp to Singapore went by quickly, and the two weeks we spent in the Sembawang camp were amazing. As a response to the humanitarian crisis following the end of the Việt Nam War, the British army barracks at 25 Hawkins Road were converted to a Vietnamese refugee camp by the United Nations High Commissioner for Refugees. It was a small transit camp that housed only 150 people; the revolving door of refugees that came through was high.

Everyone there had been accepted for resettlement and was waiting for the next leg of their bon voyage. It was paradise to me with its simple, but clean, accommodations. Each day food was brought to us, and I felt like royalty. The library that became my reading room was painted a happy yellow, and the schoolroom where I tried sewing again was always filled with laughter. Thủy-Tiên and I spent our days playing badminton while Tree explored the area. He often wandered off for hours but always stayed within the confines of our five-star prison.

The number of women and children combined equaled the number of men. I never felt afraid of rape, torture, or murder by the camp leaders, volunteers, or military officials. What a difference between 25 Hawkins Road and the Galang Refugee Camp.

Our sponsorship to America by the Presbyterian Church in Kent, Washington, was surreal. Before long, we flew from Singapore to Hong Kong, then to Japan, and finally to the United States on a Pan American transatlantic flight. I'll never forget my first Boeing 747 experience.

To say the plane was big was an understatement; it was nicknamed the "jumbo jet" for a reason with its gargantuan double-decker body, a spiral staircase leading to the upper seating section, ten doors of entry, wide aisles with a cabin that was eight feet high and twenty feet wide, and rows of nine seats across. It was like flying inside a blue whale, only it was two-and-a-half times bigger. We sat in the bubble of the jetliner and enjoyed Western cowboy movies. Seeing Clint Eastwood on the screen made my heart ache for Sam. It was the closest I had felt to him in a long time.

"Aunt Eight, America is so rich." Tree settled comfortably in the leather seat and admired the spacious airplane. "I cannot wait to see the streets paved in gold and the big houses."

"We are going to a place in King County, and I bet a place with the word 'king' in it has to be majestic." I was as excited as my nephew.

"Will there be a lot of food and sweets for me to eat?" my little dolly asked. I nodded.

"I hope they have all the bacon we can eat." Tree's eyes lit up.

I was reminded of the Christmas dinner we had so long ago with my family when I fell in love with Corporal Sam Hammond over bacon and hot dogs, items my niece, Tâm, stole from the air force base where she had worked.

We thought of America as grand, wealthy, and beautiful but quickly became disillusioned as we saw how dreary, underdeveloped, and sparse it was. We arrived at Seattle-Tacoma International Airport on a cold, rainy day. It was March 20, 1980, on the eve of spring, yet the chilling fifty-degree

3

temperature made us all shiver in our tropical clothes.

"It is colder here than Đà Lạt," Tree commented. He referred to the central highlands region of Việt Nam where the mild climate vastly differs from the rest of the tropical country.

The three of us deplaned and were ushered through a long walkway before spilling out into a room of pale, white faces, all crowded together with cheers and smiles. People held signs that read "Welcome to America!" and "We love you LE family!" A dull headache formed as my pulse quickened. It was quite overwhelming to see fifty strangers jumping up and down, eager to shake our hands, give us hugs, pat our backs, and thrust flowers or stuffed animals in our arms. Thủy-Tiên whimpered but did not cry. Tree basked in the love and energy of the welcoming committee and unabashedly accepted their gifts.

The first face I recognized was Joseph's, our VOLAG representative, there to assist with the settlement. He was shorter than I expected at 1.7 meters tall; when we met at the UNHCR office on Galang Island, he was sitting behind a desk. Still, five feet, ten inches tall is bigger than the average Vietnamese man.

Joseph pushed his way toward me, a big grin on his face. "Ms. Le, it is good to see you again. Welcome to Seattle." He extended his hand, and I warmly accepted it. "There are a lot of people anxious to meet you. Are you tired?"

"No, but very cold," I said, "but also so happy to be here finally to America."

A very tall, balding man with silver wisps of hair and a full white beard strode up to us. He was wide-chested and heavyset, in his late fifties and full of muscle. The sheer brown and cream striped polyester shirt he wore clung to his skin and accentuated his protruding nipples. His expression was full of mirth, revealing a big smile, two dimples, and shimmers of pure joy in his eyes. He held in his left hand a petite woman's hand. She stood a foot shorter than he did, her hair curly, peppered with blue and white highlights. Her glasses were askew as she fought to keep up and not get knocked down by others. Her crooked smile revealed crooked teeth, but there was no mistaking the merriment on her face. Right next to her was her replica, except she wore makeup, a string of pearls, high-heel shoes, and no glasses. Looking at the two sisters was like looking at Elizabeth Taylor and Joan Collins. I thought I was among movie stars.

Joseph piped up with the introductions. "Ms. Le, this is Mr. Theodore Vanzwol, his wife Catherine, and her sister, Katrina Cunningham. They are your primary sponsors. They were not only huge financial donors, but they fought tirelessly alongside Skyler Herrington and the church to bring

4

your family here as quickly as possible. Katrina is Skyler's mother, and as you can see, she and Catherine are twins. You will stay with Theodore and Catherine in Kent until we get you settled into your apartment."

Theodore could not contain his excitement. He ignored my hand and went in for a tight hug. "Toots and I couldn't be more thrilled." He shook Tree's hand and patted him hard on the shoulder. Tree fell forward but quickly regained his balance. He towered over us at six feet, four inches tall. "You can call me Teddy. Only I get to call the wife Toots, though." He jabbed Tree in the ribs with his elbow and expelled a hearty laugh. Teddy swung Thủy-Tiên up in his right arm and gave her a loud peck on the cheek. I was afraid he'd break all her bones. She squealed like a piglet. I was not sure if it was fear, pain, or delight she was expressing, but then she laughed when he poked her in the stomach.

We next said hello to Pastor George of the First Evangelical Presbyterian Church and his family. He was handsome, unusually tan with dark, feathered hair and a square face. Unlike Teddy, he was quite reserved and formal. He stood a couple of feet away, bowing his head before offering a handshake. His wife, Dawn, was equally matched in looks with her feathered blonde hair and flawless makeup. Their three girls were attractive as well in their Sunday dresses, with their porcelain white skin, sparkling hazel eyes, and silky hair.

"Snow!" A voice I hadn't heard since April of 1972 sang out loud. The crowd swayed left and right as Skyler emerged from the thicket of people.

"Sky!" I yelled. We embraced, and I did not want to let go. It felt for a moment like I was holding Sam in my arms again.

"You're a sight for sore eyes."

"What you mean?" I asked.

"It means I am happy to see you." Sky squeezed my hand. "I see you've met my mom, aunt, and uncle-in-law."

Katrina took hold of my hand and cupped it in her warm, soft ones. "Well, actually, I was waiting for my turn to welcome them to Seattle." Sky's mother was beautiful and glamorous. I did not see much of Sky's features in her and wondered why their last names were different, why Sky was so tall and she so small, and why they both looked sad despite their smiles. In time, I would understand.

Sky squeezes my hand and brings me back to the present. He smiles at me. "A penny for your thoughts." I hold out my hand, and Sky laughs. "It's an old English expression. You don't actually get a penny."

"I have much to learn with expressions," I say. "When we first land

5

in Seattle, meeting your mom, Teddy, and Catherine. I so happy."

"That was the first time I met Dolly. I'm sorry. I still have a hard time pronouncing your daughter's name. Twee Tin, is it?"

I laugh at Sky's attempt. "Yes, that good. I maybe give her American name. Easier to say."

Sky chuckles. "You always refer to her as your little dolly so, in my mind, she's Dolly…but Le, not Parton, without the big boobs. Shit, who knows, she might be the Asian version of Dolly Parton, with big knockers like yours—"

"Sky, I not understand what you saying."

"Never mind. I'm just gonna shut up now." Sky scratches his head and stands up. "Here, drink more of your coffee before it gets cold."

I take a sip of my lukewarm coffee and cringe. "This like water but dirty. I miss the Vietnamese coffee, so strong with condensed milk back home." I remember a time when I would have given anything for a cup of coffee. The war seems so long ago. "It been six hours. You think surgery go well?"

"Seattle Children's has the best cardiologists and surgeons. Don't worry," Sky says.

I nod and turn my attention to Tree, just in time to see him pick his nose and wipe his finger on the chair. He looks at his fingernails and inspects the dirt lodged underneath. He is a mess. He needs a haircut. I will have to see if I can borrow Catherine's scissors when we are back at home.

He will be eighteen in four months. The Vanzwols tell me I need to register him and Thủy-Tiên for school this summer; she will start first grade at Springbrook Elementary. As for Tree, he is too old for high school, but we will try enrolling him just the same.

"What took you all so long?" Sky asks.

Teddy, Catherine, and Katrina rush into the waiting room. Katrina looks beautiful and graceful as usual, but I notice the bags under her eyes. She hugs her son. "Sorry, sweets, traffic was bad, and your father was giving me lip again. I finally had to hang up."

I wonder what Katrina means by "giving me lip." Maybe they were too busy kissing and "hanging up" means a handjob. These Americans must have no discretion at all with their intimate side of life. Public displays of affection are inappropriate in Việt Nam.

"Parking was a bear." Catherine walks toward me and hugs me. "Sorry we are late. By the time we got off work, we had to rush home, feed Biscuit, and let him out to potty. How are you holding up?"

"I tired," I answer. "In my country, we eat dogs to stay alive."

I must have said something strange because everyone except Tree, who does not understand English, freezes, and stares at me. They are all mute, expressionless.

Sky is the first to break the awkward silence. "Dolly has been with the sawbones for six hours now."

"Well, we brought pizza and sodas." Teddy strides over to Tree and offers him the first slice. "I know how teenage boys can eat. You must be famished." Tree looks at the cardboard box and crinkles his nose. Teddy laughs. "Here, like this." He picks up a slice with his hand, folds it in half lengthwise, and takes a bite. "I love me a good anchovy and pineapple pizza. Extra pineapples, light on the parmesan."

The smell is unpleasant, but Tree takes a slice to be polite. Upon biting into the doughy pie, his frown dissipates. Tree bobs his head up and down and grins as he takes a larger bite before swallowing the first one.

"Atta boy." Teddy slaps Tree hard on the knee. "You'll be bulking up and taking girls away from their daddies in no time." He roars in jest. The two of them sit content, chewing their fishy cuisine.

I opt for the "volcano" pizza which has ham, pineapples, jalapeños, and extra mozzarella cheese.

"Why pizza call 'volcano'?" I ask, to no one in particular. "Because Mount Saint Helens blow up and lost the...oh, how you call red sauce from its mountain hole?"

"You mean when she erupted, and lava and ash spewed everywhere?" Katrina asks.

"I can't believe that was just three months ago," Catherine says.

"I can't get over the huge cloud and the destruction," Teddy says. "I doubt the forest will ever recover. You know, Snow, the day you arrived in Seattle, on March 20, there was a magnitude 4.2 earthquake. I think our cheering when your plane landed caused it." Teddy winks. "Then in May, a bigger earthquake, magnitude 5.1, I think, hit and that broke the camel's back. Helen popped her cherry." Teddy laughs and the sound rumbles down the hall. "Now, that's a knee slapper!" Teddy slaps Tree's knee.

Catherine shoots Teddy a look that makes him close his mouth. I understand only half of what they are saying. Poor Tree does not understand a word, so he sits and smiles when others smile.

"It's so sad how many lives were lost, properties destroyed, vegetation wiped out, and all the animals that died," Sky says.

"Hey, let's change the subject," Teddy says. "I got some Seahawks tickets this season. Want to go?"

"Duh," Sky replies. "Is the Kingdome indestructible? Does Largent pee standing up?"

"So that's a maybe?" Teddy says with a twinkle in his eye.

Sky throws a crumpled napkin at him. "Fuck, yeah I want to go…As sure as it rains in Seattle. The SuperSonics just won the NBA Championships. It'll be the Hawks' turn to clench the Lombardi trophy this season. I can feel it in my bones."

I listen to my hosts talk passionately and loudly about American football for thirty minutes. Their conversations stack over one another. As soon as one person barely finishes talking, someone else steamrolls over with an opinion. They never did answer my question of why the pizza was called the "volcano."

Dr. Hall enters the waiting room. His presence blankets the air like a cloud of smoke, and just like that, all talk comes to a halt as if a referee blew his whistle. I hold my breath. "I have an update on the surgery." His face is stolid.

2. EDUCATION LEADS TO SUCCESS (SEP–OCT 1980)

I walk into Thủy-Tiên's room at the hospital. The sun shines brightly through the window and the warm glow of the light wraps its rays around her face. She is my angel. My eyes mist up seeing her small body connected to all the monitors with tubes and wires. I sit beside her bed and caress her cheeks. Her eyelids spring open but quickly close again. She smiles.

I flip her upper and lower lip like a light switch and listen to the blip sounds as her lips smack into each other. She laughs.

"I know you are awake," I say. "I saw your eyes open. You cannot trick me."

"Mama," she says weakly.

"You are as tough as Aunt Six's callouses," I say. "Our family back home would be so proud of you for being a brave and strong girl."

"How do you know?"

"Because they love you," I say.

"Do I have a new heart?"

"Better than a new heart. You have the same one God gave you when you were born, but the doctors patched it up—"

"I want a new one," Thủy-Tiên says, and the tears threaten to jump, "because the one God gave me had a hole in it."

"Yes, but your old heart stores all the love that Aunt Six, Uncle Seven, and cousin Tâm gave to you."

"And Daddy's love too?"

The mention of Tý startles me. She cannot possibly remember him. She was nine months old when Sài Gòn fell. "Yes, your Daddy too."

"Then I will keep the same heart."

The door swings in, and an entourage of people walk in slowly and quietly. Behind them is Dr. Hall, the amazing surgeon who brought us this miracle. I leap up and scurry past Sky and the others.

9

"Dr. Hall," I say and take hold of his wrist, "thank you very much. You save my daughter. She awake, and she look not sick anymore."

"I couldn't have asked for a stronger patient or a smoother surgery." Dr. Hall pulls the hospital gown down to inspect his work. I am in awe of the six-inch cut down the center of her chest, from the base of her throat to a couple of inches above her belly button. The staples in her chest make her look vulnerable. "Looking good." He checks my daughter's temperature and listens to her heart. "We will remove the sutures in a few days, and soon, you can go home." Dr. Hall jots down some notes. "The incision should heal nicely, but it will be at least a month before she feels better."

Tree climbs into the bed with Thủy-Tiên and holds her hand. He whispers something in her ear and she giggles.

"She will start school in a few weeks," Catherine says.

"She is going to need her rest and to take it easy," Dr. Hall advises. "Delay her start until October. I'll give you a note to give to the school. It'll be six months before her heart can handle anything strenuous, so limit the exercise and play."

"We'll take good care of her, Doc," Teddy says, "and make sure she eats a lot of burgers and steaks to regain her strength."

"But no shrimp," I say. "Shrimp make her scar."

"You'll want to check the incision daily. If you notice any swelling, redness, or drainage, these can be signs of infection. You'll get a chart to take home to track her progress and check for signs of fatigue, chest pains, and such. The nurse will give you more instructions when you check out along with some dermal adhesive and dressings."

"Don't worry," Sky says.

"Yes, we'll take good care of Dolly," Katrina adds.

"Dinner should be here soon," Dr. Hall says. "I'll check back tomorrow."

Shortly after Dr. Hall leaves, a tray of food is brought in. Thủy-Tiên eyes the food suspiciously. There are noodles covered in red lumpy sauce, a green gelatinous cube, a bowl of mushy fruit, milk, and a green soda can.

Tree picks up her fork, a utensil he is familiar with after he was introduced to it on the Norwegian ship several months ago. He stabs the noodles, twirls it around the tines of the cutlery, and feeds it to her. Her eyes light up.

"She likes the spaghetti," Catherine says. "I'll make you some when you get home."

"Toots is a great cook," Teddy says. "Where do you think my year-round winter coat comes from?" He pats his belly and laughs. He playfully pats Catherine on the buttocks and leans down for a kiss.

10

"Oh, stop," Catherine gushes, "you burly beast. Underneath that sexy winter coat is a whole lot of iron."

Teddy flexes his muscles, and biceps emerge like mountains on his arms. He urges Tree to feel them. "You and me, we're gonna work out together. Put some iron on your bones, fatten you up."

We watch Thủy-Tiên eat and observe her facial expressions. She tries the bowl of fruit and spits it out.

"I guess she doesn't like the fruit cocktail," Catherine says. "I don't blame her. Fresh is best."

My daughter washes the taste out with the milk. She swallows it and puts it back down. "This milk is bad. It is not sweet."

I translate for the others. "In our country, milk is sweet with sugar."

"Not here in the States, although we Americans do have a sweet tooth," Sky says. "Maybe she'll like the Jell-O." He points to the gelatinous cube.

"We call that *thạch rau câu*," I say, "but ours is thick and many layers. My favorite with coffee and coconut." Sky, Teddy, Catherine, and Katrina try to pronounce the words, and I laugh at their accent, especially with the word *thạch*.

"Here, wash it down with some soda." Katrina pops the soda can and pours the fizzy, clear liquid into a glass. She hands it to Thủy-Tiên. "7-Up."

My daughter takes a small sip, then a bigger gulp. She chugs the whole glass and asks for more. "Seven up!"

"Hell, she just said her first English words," Sky says proudly.

December 16, 1965. That is the birthdate I put on Tree's high school enrollment application. I tell the school he is younger than he is to give him a chance for a free education. With no official paperwork to prove his birth date and legal name, all lost after the communist party took over in Việt Nam, my nephew is now known as Lê Minh Trí and is fourteen again.

"I do not want to go to school," Tree says. "I have not been in a classroom since I was thirteen, and I'll be eighteen in a few months."

"If anyone asks, you are fourteen, turning fifteen in December. The war robbed you of your schooling," I say. "This is your chance to start over and get an education…learn English."

"Being life-smart is better than school-smart."

"You need to balance. Education leads to success. Besides, here, you do not need to work the streets to sell drugs or catch fish to eat or climb trees to survive. America is rich and friendly."

"I cannot learn if I do not understand English." Tree turns his head

11

to look at me.

"Sit still," I command. I stop cutting his hair for a moment and put the scissors down on Catherine's spinning wheel. "At least try. We have the opportunity to succeed. It is what your parents want for you. Otherwise, they would not have made me take you to America."

I hear the floor squeak and see Catherine walk down the stairs to the furnished basement. She shuffles over to us in her furry slippers. Even in her frumpy, pale pink bathrobe and no makeup, she is a pretty woman. She hands me a cup of coffee. "How's it going?"

"Almost done," I say. "Tree ready for school tomorrow." I pick up the scissors and resume cutting my nephew's hair.

"Oh dear," Catherine gasps. "Snow, his hair is very...layered."

I step back to see. His hair is jagged and uneven. The look on my face is enough to send Tree flying into the bathroom to take a look.

A loud groan escapes Tree's throat. He stomps out of the bathroom and stands with his hands on his waist. I have a flashback to when he was three years old and his mother, Hiền, gave him a buzzed haircut.

"Aiyah, he is so cute, like a baby monk," Hiền had said. We had a good laugh about it then. I dare not laugh about his hair now.

"Let me try," Catherine says. She motions for Tree to sit back in the chair. She picks up the scissors and then puts it back down again. "The first lesson of the day. Different scissors have different purposes. There are specific scissors for food, for gardening, for paper...What you have here are pinking shears. You use this on fabric and the zig-zag edges keep the cloth from raveling."

"Raveling?" I ask.

"Yes, it means fraying or coming apart."

Catherine tries to fix Tree's hair. The more she tries to even it out, the more hair drops to the floor. In the end, she cannot fix the haircut. Tree will have to start school with a shaved head.

###

We have been staying with the Vanzwols for six months. While Teddy is at work at Boeing, Catherine occupies herself with spinning wool, knitting, gardening, and cooking. In these past few months, I have learned how to cook spaghetti, sew a pillowcase, and start a garden. On Fridays we clean the house together in case we have visitors but mainly so that Teddy can relax after a long week at work. We often bundle up and take walks to get fresh air and help Dolly get stronger. We have been teaching my daughter basic English so that she will be prepared on her first day of school. Tree has gone to school each day for nearly a month. When he gets off the school bus, Catherine always has a glass of milk and a sandwich waiting for him,

12

usually bologna and mayonnaise or peanut butter and jelly. The milk makes his stomach hurt. We both crave rice, but we do not complain. It is nice not to feel hungry. Sometimes, though, I feel like we are a novelty to Catherine and Teddy, like exotic pets that they do not know what to feed.

Tree is having a hard time adjusting at school with his limited knowledge of the American language, culture, and education system.

Most of the time when I ask him how his day was, he simply answers, "Fine," and heads to his room. When I ask him what he has learned, he answers, "Nothing," and slams the door. His only real joy is bonding with Teddy over food, exercise, or American football.

Occasionally, I get more than one-word answers if I press a little harder and ask the right questions. This morning over breakfast, I take the opportunity. "Tell me what your initial reaction was on the first day at Kent-Meridian."

Tree chomps on his cereal and swallows before answering. "I was shocked."

"How so?" I ask.

"Everyone is white. There are no Asians or Mexicans or Blacks. Back home I saw so many but not here."

"Well," I say, "back home there was a war, so you saw soldiers from all parts of the world."

"Do you know how stupid I feel being almost eighteen years old and pretending to be fourteen, in a classroom of immature kids?"

"What about your ESL class?" I ask. "There must be other students you can connect with who are learning English as their second language."

Tree shakes his head. "I sit in the ESL class for an hour with four other kids. There is one boy from India, two kids from Saudi Arabia, and a girl who I think is Vietnamese, but her accent is so thick, and she squeaks like a mouse. I cannot understand her, much less hear her. We all look like mute, dumb, rejected orphans."

"It will get better. Do not give up. You were thirteen when you dropped out of school. This is your chance to start over."

Tree sighs with exasperation. "I have to catch my bus." He shoves the last bit of cereal into his mouth, brings his bowl to the sink, and exits out the front door without saying goodbye. I turn my attention to Dolly, whom I can count on to talk to me.

"Are you excited about your first day at Springbrook Elementary?" I ask my daughter.

"Yes. I will have new friends," Thủy-Tiên says as she devours her Lucky Charms cereal. "Why do I have to tell everyone my name is Dolly Le?"

13

"It will be easier for them to say 'Dolly' than 'Thủy-Tiên.' It is a cute nickname, and before you know it, everyone will want to be your friend because you are so special, like a doll from an exotic land far away."

"If they make fun of me, I am going to smash them," Dolly says as she grinds her right fist into the palm of her left hand.

Catherine drives us to the school, and the three of us walk hand in hand into the school's administration office. The single-story brick building is deceptively large inside. The office is as big as my father's house back in our hometown of Vĩnh Bình. There are papers everywhere and children's artwork on the walls. A loud bell rings, and children scurry in different directions. It reminds me of the many times the sirens sounded back home, alerting us that the Việt Cộng was raiding the village or a missile strike was taking place nearby. My family would run and hide in our bunker.

A voice comes over the intercom. "Good morning, Dolphins. This is Principal Jenkins. Please stand for the Pledge of Allegiance."

I watch as the office staff rise to their feet and turn to the American flag hanging in the northeast corner. They all put their right hand over their heart and deliver the same words. It brings me back to when the North Vietnamese Army announced their victory over the Khmer Rouge army, and we were forced to cheer to show allegiance to the Northern military forces.

Catherine pledges her allegiance to the flag of the United States of America. When they are done with the recitation, the principal resumes with announcements while Catherine gets my daughter checked in.

I feel Thủy-Tiên's small hand tremble in mine. "I want to go home." She pouts and looks down.

"I know you are afraid," I say and squeeze her hand. "First grade is going to be fun. You are about to start a new adventure."

Her lips quiver, and her skin turns pink. Her eyes puff up, and she wails, "Do not make me go!"

The tear gates open. She wraps her arms around my thigh and squeezes hard. I bend down. She flings her arms around my neck, constricting me like a boa, and hisses at me for being mean, for making her go to school. I try to pry her off.

"No!" she screams.

"You have to go to school," Catherine says. Her words fall on deaf ears. My daughter does not understand. She cries torrential tears. Her voice cracks like thunder and pierces through the principal's voice over the intercom. I remember the last time she had a hysterical fit; it was at the Galang Refugee Camp right before she fainted from getting so worked up. I fear she might pass out again from the exhaustion. I imagine her chest bursting and her heart gushing blood like a geyser out of the hole Dr. Hall patched.

The front desk administrator tempts my daughter with a Tootsie Pop candy. Thủy-Tiên slaps the lollipop away. It drops to the ground and skids a foot away.

"It's best if you all leave now," the administrator says. "The longer you stay and prolong this, the harder it will be for Dolly to adjust."

"She afraid," I say.

"I know," the school administrator acknowledges. She looks at me sympathetically. "We will make sure she has a buddy to help her."

I try to soothe my child. "This nice lady is going to take you to your classroom so you can meet your teacher. You have a friend who is excited to meet you." She gives me a despairing look, but I give her a brave smile. "I cannot wait to hear about your day later."

Thủy-Tiên calms down enough for me to free myself from her bear-trap grip. The administrator quickly takes hold of my daughter's hand. She leads her out of the office and down the hall, dragging my daughter like a ball and chain. One last look to see my child's face—her eyes drill holes into my heart. They turn the corner, and I hear the cries start up again.

I leave the school with Catherine and feel a hundred pounds heavier.

###

The telephone rings. Catherine and Teddy's four-year-old Cairn Terrier, Biscuit, looks at me as if to ask, "Are you going to answer that?"

With Catherine out visiting a friend and Teddy at work, I am home alone. After three rings, I lift the receiver from the yellow phone on the wall. "Alô?"

"Hello. This is Abigail from Kent-Meridian High School. May I speak to Tree's guardian?"

"I am his aunt, Snow," I respond. "How I help you?"

"Your nephew has not been in school the past two days," Abigail says, "and as a matter of fact, he has missed a total of ten days since school started. His absences, excused or not, can result in suspension and failing his classes. I am calling to check if he is okay and when we can expect him at school. If he is ill, we need a note from his doctor." Abigail is speaking so rapidly I do not understand everything she says. I do not know how to respond. "Hello? Mrs. Le, are you still there?"

I am concerned he has not been in school. Every morning Catherine and I see him onto the school bus. There must be a mistake.

"Thank you," I say. "I make sure he go. Bye-bye." I hang up the phone even though Abigail is still talking.

###

15

Catherine has set a lovely table for dinner. Tonight she prepares a feast of roast beef, mashed potatoes, roasted beets, and corn on the cob. The kitchen is filled with aromas of garlic, butter, caramelized meat, and fresh herbs. My mouth waters.

"I made strawberry rhubarb pie for dessert," Catherine says. "And this is what we call charcuterie." She glides her hand over the platter filled with colorful, edible snacks. There is an assortment of meats, cheeses, crackers, and things I do not recognize. America truly is the land of rich abundance and gluttony.

"We have this in Việt Nam, from the French," I say. "We have pâté, fruits, baguettes, and ham."

"I bet you are an amazing cook. You will have to teach me your favorite dishes."

I shake my head. "No, Catherine, I terrible, but I maybe try make rice and eel for you and Teddy one day. My sister, she good cook. Anything she know how to make."

Mentioning Sister Six makes me sad. A knot forms in my throat, and my eyes glisten with wetness. I turn away so Teddy and Catherine do not see me. But nothing escapes Tree, always observing and taking in his surroundings, never forgetting where he is, constantly ingraining in his memory bank other people's actions, remembering what has to be done.

I scowl at him, partly for witnessing my secret tears, but mostly for skipping school. I know your secret, too, dear nephew. I have yet to punish him. Anger swells inside me, but I suppress the feeling. I turn my attention back to Catherine, who is still chattering on about the charcuterie.

"These are rosemary crackers. I like to put orange marmalade and brie cheese on mine. This is foie gras, along with salami, chocolate-covered almonds, grapes, bleu and gouda cheese, and osetra caviar…very special caviar for this special occasion."

Teddy throws a grape in the air and catches it in his mouth. "But you'll have to wait until dessert for your surprise. It's wonderful to have your family here. Toots and I are excited about this cultural exchange."

While we wait for the roast to cook, we nibble on the snacks. Tree contents himself with talking to Thủy-Tiên and eating the crackers and foie gras. He follows Catherine's lead and spreads marmalade and brie onto a cracker to give to Thủy-Tiên. He scoops a large heaping of caviar onto a piece of salami and shoves it in his mouth. My nephew smiles, nods, and gives two thumbs up.

"Oh dear," Catherine whispers.

Teddy laughs. "The boy has a fine palate!"

"And expensive taste buds," Catherine says. "That was a hundred-dollar morsel he just popped in his mouth."

I translate for Tree. His face quickly changes from pleasure to guilt.

Teddy spoons a big amount of fish roe onto a slice of salami and puts it in his mouth. He winks at Tree as he chews. "Enjoy, son. Tonight we dine like kings. But only I get to sleep with the queen." He laughs at his joke and pinches Catherine on her butt.

"Teddy, stop," Catherine protests. "You're embarrassing them."

"One hundred dollar," I say. "More than my family make in one month."

"Really? And what about during the French occupation of Vietnam?" Catherine leans in. I can tell she is intrigued. I think she is well-intentioned and genuinely wants to know about our life and our history. Still, at times, I wish in my heart I could be rude and not answer. These memories should sink to the bottom of the sea. These sad, tragic stories belong to the dead. They should not have a place in the hearts of the living.

"The French occupy Việt Nam for long time. Under their rule, they turn Sài Gòn into a dizzy city. They call Sài Gòn 'Pearl of the Orient.' My family do not like the French much."

"But the French influenced a lot of your culture," Catherine says.

"Yes, that true. My favorite is French coffee. Việt Nam have perfect climate for coffee. I enjoy mine with ice and condensed milk," I say.

"You know, Sky's father is half French, half British."

The timer on the oven beeps. Catherine sticks a thermometer in the meat. "Roast is done." She takes it out of the oven. "We'll let it rest for a bit."

Why should it rest when it is already dead? I wonder.

"You know, speaking of coffee, I like mine mixed with hot milk for a café au lait," Catherine says.

"And I like mine the color of Tree's hair," Teddy pipes in. "Black!" He ruffles Tree's hair and gives him a jab on the arm. Tree rubs his arm and grins. "Although," Teddy continues, "I do like a good affogato."

I do not know what an affogato is, so I continue sharing my thoughts on the occupation. "The French tax my people big, force us do hard labor on coffee plantations, and make us sick on opium. They make us fight their wars. In my village, my oldest brother die during revolution against French. And Dolly grandmother on her father side raped by French soldier. Dolly father watch it happen when he was little boy. We are peaceful people, but too many years of war make us bitter and no trust of outsiders. My country is small, but we have longest coast. Make it good for fishing and import or export. That why so many want to rule us. The Việt Nam War, which we call

American War, change my people. The country is together, but the people are divide and nobody trust anymore. I pray for peace."

"It is good that the country is unified. It will make it stronger in the long run," Teddy says. "War is a terrible thing, but good can come out of it too."

"In time, things will get better, and I should hope you will be able to go back to your country," Catherine says, "and see your family again."

"I hope you right," I say. "I miss my country."

Teddy pops a large crumble of moldy cheese in his mouth. "Dolly, do you like cheese?" He gives my daughter a piece.

She immediately spits it out and shows great disdain for the violation of her taste buds. "Stinky!" Her face turns red. "Like poop."

"We not digest well the cheese and milk," I explain.

Teddy roars with amusement. "I don't think it's a matter of being lactose intolerant. I think Dolly hasn't developed a taste for bleu cheese yet." Teddy turns to Tree. "Here, give it a try."

My nephew reluctantly takes a piece. "Very pungent and salty." We all laugh watching his face morph into an expression of disgust. He swallows the cheese anyway.

"Teddy, you like smelly foods," I say. "We have a lot in my country, like fish sauce, dried squid, and shrimp paste. My favorite is *sầu riêng*, a fruit. On outside the skin is sharp but inside, so creamy and sweet. Very stinky."

"Dinner is ready," Catherine says. She puts the roast on the table. "Shall we pray?"

We all gather around the table, bow our heads, and clasp our hands together.

Teddy speaks. "Dear Lord God and Heavenly Father, we thank you for this time of togetherness. We feel your blessing with this wonderful meal that Toots prepared for us, so lovingly, to feed our bodies and nurture our souls. Thank you for Snow, Tree, and Dolly, for bringing them to safety and enriching our lives with their presence. In thy holy name…Oh, wait. I pray I get a chance to try this stinky, creamy fruit called 'so run' that Snow talked about. The stinkier the better. In thy holy name we pray. Amen."

I laugh at Teddy's mention of the stinky durian fruit.

Teddy carves the roast while Catherine passes the plates of food around for us to serve. We spend the next hour engaging in lively conversation. Tree tries to learn some English words and phrases with Teddy's encouragement. My daughter repeatedly asks for refills on her 7-Up. The meal is so delicious; I cannot stop eating even after I am full. I wonder what my family is eating back home, if they are eating anything at all. I can hear my sister-in-law, Hiền, say, "Aiyah, you do not peel the mango that

18

way," and I can see Brother Seven roll his eyes. I think about my niece, Tâm. Oh, my heart, are you still alive? I imagine her eating her vomit in prison for that false sense of nourishment. I think about my brother-in-law, Hải, and whether he ever received the food we snuck into the reeducation camp. My thoughts turn to Mrs. Trần's son, Lopsided, and hope he is in eternal enlightenment with his parents, suffering no more. Waves of faces come crashing in as I remember the ones lost at sea, the tragedy that struck my boat mates on trawler 93752, and the pain of losing friends at the refugee camp. Angry thoughts rush back over my husband's betrayal. I yearn to speak to my mother and father once more. I want to feel Sister Six's stinging insults and squeeze her so hard she lets out a fart. I half laugh and half cry thinking of her facial expressions. My thoughts turn to Ommo, to Minh-Hoàng, to my beloved Sam.

I taste the salty moisture on my lips. It tastes like the South China Sea.

"Snow?" Catherine reaches for my hand. "Are you all right? Are you crying?"

"Yes," I whisper. "I so happy." I lie. I want to scream, pull at my hair, and curl up into a ball. Poor Biscuit is under the table begging for scraps of food, and for one fleeting moment, I want to kick the dog to leave me alone. Instead, I smile to contain my sadness and feelings of guilt.

"Well, we are happy too," Teddy says. "So, Tree, how was school?"

I swallow my pain and resume my role as a translator.

"Hard," Tree says. "I do not understand anything."

"Give it time," Teddy says. "We are here to help. Just ask."

"I like the music class and the sports class," Tree says. "My teachers are patient."

"That's wonderful," Catherine says. "Have you made any friends?"

"I have a girlfriend," Tree says.

I stare at him in disbelief and sit in silence. Catherine asks me to translate, but I ignore her. I cannot listen to his lies any longer. I bolt up out of my chair and grab him by the ear. He howls in pain. Catherine gasps and covers her mouth with her hand. Teddy stands up. Thủy-Tiên whimpers.

"What girlfriend? The squeaky mouse? You have missed ten days of school," I shout. "What have you been doing? Where have you been going? How can you sit here and lie to us?"

"You do not understand, Aunt Eight," Tree yells back. "I am stupid. I cannot learn."

"You have not tried," I scream back.

"I am not you. I will never learn English. I have no friends. People laugh at me and point. I tell them 'đụ má mày,' but they do not even

19

understand when I swear at them. I hate it here! You should have never brought me. You should have let me go back." Tree briskly walks out of the dining room. He stomps his feet as he exits.

I follow him to the staircase. "I cannot help you if you do not tell me. By keeping my eyes blindfolded, you only serve to tie my hands."

"How can you help? Will you go to every class with me? Follow me around like a damn Việt Cộng? I am sure I will make many friends with my aunt as my shadow," Tree remarks sarcastically.

I want to slap my nephew for his disrespect and sarcasm. It hurts me knowing he is in pain, and I do not know what to do.

"Go to your room," I say with exasperation. "We will talk later."

Tree storms to his room and slams the door shut. From the dining room, I hear Thủy-Tiên cry.

I return to the table. "I sorry, Catherine, Teddy. Tree no go to school for ten days. I mad at him. He lying to us."

"Oh dear," Catherine says. "This must be so hard for him being in a foreign country and starting over."

"I'm afraid to ask how Dolly's first day of school was," Teddy says between mouthfuls of beets.

We finish our dinner quickly and quietly. I help Catherine clear the table and wash the dishes while Teddy reads Dolly a book about a flying boy in green tights who never grows up.

"Do you want dessert?" Catherine asks.

"No, thank you," I say. "I have no room in stomach."

"Do you want to know your surprise?"

"Maybe tomorrow. Tonight, I too sad to be happy."

Catherine rubs my shoulder. "Get some rest."

I nod and walk into the family room. My daughter is curled up on the recliner with Teddy. She fights to keep her eyes open.

Teddy closes the book and sings. "You are my sunshine, my only sunshine. You make me happy when skies are gray. You'll never know dear, how much I love you. Please don't take my sunshine away."

20

3. THE SURPRISE (NOVEMBER 1980)

Teddy and Catherine rise particularly early on this Sunday morning. I hear their movements downstairs. The smell of coffee brewing in the kitchen beckons me to roll out of bed. Outside the skies are overcast, and the dew of the autumn morning makes me hesitant to face another disillusioned day. The entire landscape is blanketed in a blue-gray haze. A row of pyramidalis trees line the property and are perfectly hedged to give the Vanzwol property privacy. Their backyard oasis is a swirl of blues, oranges, reds, and yellows as if an artist used his fingers to create his oil painting masterpiece. The bouquets of hydrangeas are mesmerizing, and the fall harvest leaves on the trees glow like fire. In the distance, a wisp of light makes the water fountain coruscate. The only sign of life outside is a ladybug clinging to the vastness of my window.

"I feel the same as you, lady beetle. So small in this big world," I say. "At least you can fly away with no worries. You do not suffocate from loss like me."

"Snow, are you awake?" Catherine calls from the bottom of the staircase.

"Yes, I awake," I respond.

"Good. We are going to the nine o'clock service this morning. Pastor George is making an announcement to the congregation, and you will want to be there."

I nudge my daughter awake. "Time to get your church dress on."

I lift her onto her knees and slip the pink, ruffled dress over her head. She slumps side to side like an intoxicated invalid. Her eyes remain closed as she slips her small arms through the puffy sleeves. Her curls tickle my arm. I work to pull her cotton tights up her legs.

Thủy-Tiên straightens her legs and stiffens her body. She makes me work hard to dress her. "Pretend I am a big rock, Mama." She giggles.

21

I play along with her game. "Dear Lord, help me move this heavy rock off the bed so I can get it to church." I pretend I cannot lift her. "Oh, what is that you say? If I tickle her, the rock will be easier to move?"

My daughter squirms to the other side of her bed and springs out from the covers. "Try to catch me." She laughs and protects her body from my wriggly fingers. She shrieks hysterically when I lunge at her.

I give her half a dozen kisses. "Brush your teeth and meet me downstairs."

I check Tree's bedroom. He is not in bed. I clutch my chest. My heart jolts into action. I run downstairs. My thoughts jump to memories of the refugee camp. Why did you run away? I find Catherine in the kitchen. "Catherine!"

She takes a small step backward and leans against the stove. Her mouth agape, she quickly puts the coffee pot down. "What is the matter? Is Dolly all right?"

Teddy and Tree appear from the dining room. I exhale with relief. "Dolly okay." My nephew's smile reassures me I have not lost him. "I…Do you have pantyhose I borrow?"

"Your nylons run off with my socks again?" Teddy winks and laughs.

"Oh, Teddy," Catherine says. She rises to her tippy-toes and kisses him. "Snow, what do you think of Tree's suit? Doesn't he look handsome?"

I nod. "It so perfect." My nephew looks very grown-up in his cobalt blue pants and matching jacket. I beam with pride and wish Brother Seven and Hiền could see their son now.

Pastor George greets us at the entrance of his First Evangelical Presbyterian Church. "Welcome. Good morning." His dark, feathered hair is shorter since I last saw him, making his face look more square and chiseled. He shakes my hand. "Cold hands but warm heart. Glad you can join us, Snow."

Pastor George's wife, Dawn, wraps her arms around me and squeezes. She is deceptively strong despite her thin frame and bony arms. Her blonde hair looks darker today, like it had been soaked in molasses. Perhaps it is the November dampness that has turned her golden streaks to ashy caramel. She appears prettier and younger each time I see her.

"Your hair so pretty," I say. "It darker."

"Yes, well, the summer sun gave me highlights, but now autumn has set in," Dawn says. "Your hair is getting long. It is lovely."

I smile and thank her. Dawn's three daughters walk over to us. The oldest, Olivia, takes hold of my daughter's hand. She is twelve years old and a replica of her father. Although pretty, the squareness of her features makes

22

her look oddly masculine. She is my favorite of the three with her sweet and calm demeanor, her love and respect for all beings, and her mature sensibility in handling distracted children. "Dolly, are you ready for Sunday school?"

Thủy-Tiên looks at me. "What did she say?"

I nod my approval. "Go with Olivia. She is going to take you to school."

"School again?" Thủy-Tiên shakes her head. "No."

Pastor George's middle child, Opal, leans down. Her hazel eyes look straight into my daughter's umber ones. "There'll be cookies and milk after worship." Her bribery does not work.

Thủy-Tiên scrunches her face and sticks out her tongue. "No milk."

Opal folds her arms. "Well, I tried." She turns and strides into the church. It is difficult to get close to Opal. She is a willful child who can be controlling and demanding when anyone disagrees with her or challenges her authority. In some ways, Opal reminds me of a ten-year-old version of Sister Six.

"She always looks mad. If she smiles, her face will crack," Thủy-Tiên says. My daughter believes Opal's face is broken and is dialed into the "grumpy" setting one-hundred percent of the time.

The pastor's youngest daughter, Ocean, is the prettiest, with tight flaxen curls, pearly skin, and inquisitive eyes. At age seven, she already knows how to turn on her charm. She takes hold of my daughter's hand and simply says, "7-Up."

The two of them walk off together toward Sunday school. Although Ocean is only a year older than Thủy-Tiên, she is almost a head taller. These Americans are so tall. What do they eat?

"Skyler, Katrina," Dawn says. "We're so glad to have you both today."

I turn to see Sky and his mom hugging Dawn. The mother and son duo look like they walked straight out of a glamorous movie set and into the foyer of God's house. Katrina is stylish in her houndstooth dress and trench coat. Poor Catherine looks so plain and homely next to her twin.

Sky walks over to Tree. "You sure clean up nice." He shakes my nephew's hand and comments on his hair. "Buzzcut, huh? It suits you."

"Well, apparently there was a mishap with pinking shears," Teddy says. The two of them laugh.

Catherine links her arm with mine and leads me to the front pew. Katrina walks with us. The men follow. How strange.

"In Việt Nam," I say, "the man is number one. Woman follow man."

"Oh, honey," Katrina says, "you'll soon learn that in the States, women come first."

23

"Hallelujah," Catherine says. "We let them think they are first, but we women are really in charge."

"Amen," Katrina says. "They are all big babies who need mothering. They couldn't find their ass unless we handed it to them."

The three of us laugh at our little secret. I feel a kindred spirit with these sisters.

The organ music plays, and Pastor George walks to the pulpit. My chest swells, and I am overcome with peace and grace. The choir sings, and the energy in the chapel is electric.

Following a scripture reading, Pastor George gives a powerful, emotionally charged homily about giving our anxieties to God. He is so passionate about addressing the assembly, his body shakes, and tears stream down his face. "Proverbs 12:25. What do you think he means when he says that an anxious heart weighs a man down, but a loving word lifts him up? Friends, many of our soldiers came back from the Vietnam War with a heavy heart and a burdened soul. We didn't see what their eyes saw. We don't know what it's like to fire an M-16 and instantly extinguish a life. Nor have we piloted a helicopter over the jungles of a foreign land, searching for our prisoners of war. We didn't breathe in the toxic gas, step on landmines, carry our fallen friends to safety, or watch helplessly as civilians died before our eyes. Our veterans have. And they came home to a seditious country, plagued with civil unrest and shame. They came home with missing limbs, with anxieties and fears and nightmares. Friends, they carry this deep in their hearts, and it is our job, yours, and yours, and yours…" Pastor George points at members of the congregation, including Katrina. "And mine…each and every one of us has a responsibility to help alleviate the anxiety in their hearts, to lessen the burden, to help wipe the tears. And all it takes, my friends, is kindness. But to help others, we need to also help ourselves. I want you to unload your anxieties on God. I want you to love and be loved. Only when we are free can we begin to free others. Brothers and sisters, we have many veterans here in our house this morning who are hurting. Let us show them kindness and help them give their anxieties to God."

I glance over at Sky. His sorrow, unharnessed, bursts through his eyes, and the tears flow unabashed. His wails resonate within the church walls and crash between the ceiling and floor. Katrina stands sobbing quietly next to her son. My tears escape, too, thinking how hard it must be for Sky to carry the burden of witnessing Sam die before his eyes and feeling powerless to save him. My hardened heart relinquishes the blame I hold over Sky. I reach over and squeeze his hand.

Pastor George continues. "First book of Peter, chapter five, verse seven. 'Cast all your anxiety on him because he cares for you.' Philippians

24

chapter four, verses six and seven. 'Do not be anxious about anything, but in everything by prayer and petition, with thanksgiving, present your requests to God. And the peace of God, which transcends all understanding, will guard your hearts and your minds in Christ Jesus.' Friends, turn to one another, and give thanks for one another."

"Peace be with you," Catherine says to me.

"And also with you," I reply. I turn to each person around me and say, "Peace be with you." I take hold of Sky's hand, and he pulls me in for a hug. "Peace be with you, Sky. There nothing we can do to save Sam. I forgive you, and I sorry."

As I hold Sky, I feel the tension in his body release. "I am sorry too. I let you down." He hugs me tighter, and together we exhale.

The choir sings "Praise the Lord," and we join in as the collection plate is passed.

Pastor George closes the service with some blessings and an announcement. The children are brought in from Sunday school, and all line up in front. Tree taps my shoulder and points to Thủy-Tiên, who stands next to Ocean and Olivia. My daughter tugs at her dress and scratches her thigh. The tights must be itchy on her. She fidgets and looks for me. It does not take long before she spots me in the front row. I wave to her. She waves back and gives me a "thumbs up" sign. She is catching on fast with the American culture.

Pastor George blesses the children and says a prayer. Each child sits down cross-legged and waits to be dismissed.

"Before we end service today, I have a special announcement," Pastor George says. "Snow, Tree, and Dolly…Can you please stand and come up here?"

Katrina and Catherine urge me to stand up. I hear Teddy say, "Stand up, son."

We both walk to the front. Pastor George and Dawn receive us on stage while Olivia, Opal, and Ocean escort Thủy-Tiên up to join us. I look out at the congregants, to the field of white faces. All eyes are on us. Most are smiling as if they are in on the secret surprise. A few are scowling and look away when our eyes lock. I feel uneasy being in the spotlight. I believe in their good intentions but feel like a charity case. I know it is because of their tithing and fundraising that my family is here, and it is by their generous grace that we have the necessities of food, shelter, and clothing. Yet I cannot help but feel guilty for being here while many other refugees have perished or suffered. I look at the warm, encouraging smiles from Teddy, Sky, Katrina, and Catherine and wish they were Vietnamese. I do not see one person with the same skin color as mine or anyone remotely Asian-looking. I

25

feel small, alone, and sad. Right now, more than anything, I yearn to be with my family as we were many ocean waves ago, eating Vietnamese cuisine, sharing stories, and teasing one another mercilessly.

"Last year you all answered God's call," Pastor George says, "and together we raised enough money to sponsor this family to the United States. In March we were there to greet them at the airport and welcome them to Seattle. Now, as you know, the Vanzwols, Ms. Katrina Cunningham, and Sky Herrington have been shepherding them in their day-to-day living, and they've been doing a splendid job helping Snow, Tree, and Dolly get acclimated. Today we reach another milestone as we give them wings to establish a new life here on their own."

The assembly claps. At the end of the long, carpeted aisle, I see Joseph, our VOLAG representative, walk toward me. His face lights up, and he quickens his pace to the front of the church.

Pastor George turns to us. "Snow, it is with great joy that your family here at First Evangelical Presbyterian Church presents you and your family with this gift."

Joseph extends his arm and sets a pair of brass keys into my hand. "Welcome home, Snow. We found your family an apartment of your own."

I look at Joseph, confused.

Joseph laughs. "These are the keys to your home. Just in time for Thanksgiving. How about that?"

My legs tremble. It hits me what he is saying, what the keys represent. I cover my mouth as the tears surge down my face. "Gia đình của mình có một ngôi nhà!" I scream in Vietnamese. Tree and Thủy-Tiên jump at the news. Arms fly all around me as they hug and rejoice. I realize the congregation looks confused. "Our family have house!" I yell in English. Cheers erupt, and congratulatory handshakes are exchanged.

"Do you want to go see it?" Joseph asks.

I nod and beam with happiness.

Katrina, Sky, and I follow behind Joseph's car, a beautiful glacier blue 1975 Buick LeSabre convertible with white interior, wood trim, and chrome accents. Tree rides shotgun in the front with Joseph, and although it is the start of November, they have the top down and the heat blasting high.

We cruise down to the East Hill-Meridian side of Kent and pull into an apartment complex along 108th Avenue Southeast. The sign out front reads Homestead Apartments. Teddy and Catherine pull into the parking spot next to us.

Thủy-Tiên is the first to jump out of the car. "Hurry. I want to see our new home."

26

There are three brown two-story apartment buildings in the complex, each separated by sidewalks that lead to a backyard area. The buildings look new, and each section has a letter of the alphabet nailed to the cedar boards.

Joseph points to the building marked H. "That one is yours, on top. The corner units are usually a little bigger, so I think you'll like it. These apartments were built in 1977, just three years ago. In the back is a grass area for the neighborhood kids to play, and in the center is a courtyard for basketball and hopscotch or four-square. There is a community clubhouse, too, that you can reserve for parties. Are you ready to see the inside?"

I am already ahead of him, bounding up the stairs, anxious to insert the key and turn the lock.

Thủy-Tiên counts the steps to the top. "Thirteen."

I cross the threshold and breathe in the fresh scent of pine and lemon. There are two doors to the right of the hallway and one door on the left. As if reading my mind, Joseph says, "There are two bedrooms and one bathroom. And over this way, there are two hallway closets."

Tree goes into the first bedroom closest to the entrance door. "This one's mine."

Thủy-Tiên runs into the other room. "And this one is mine, but you can share with me, Mama."

"Take off your shoes," I command. "Where are your manners?"

They both shuffle out of their shoes and run to the living room. I am still in disbelief. The light from the windows warm my skin, and I dig my nyloned feet into the soft, shag carpet. In the living room, a sliding glass door opens out to a deck with a storage closet to the left. Down below, I see the sloping grass area for the children to play, and on the far side of the fence, there is another apartment complex.

"The adjacent apartments are the Cascade Apartments," Joseph notes. "You can cut through those apartments to get to Dolly's school. Springbrook is a mile away and an easy walk through Cascade. You'll love the walk. There's a property next to the school that has horses, and they love to graze next to the fence where the children walk."

"There are a few community colleges nearby if you want to take classes," Catherine adds. "I think some vocational training for you and English language training for Tree would be a good start."

"Back home, I was math teacher and also bank teller," I say. "Maybe I get job like that here."

"That's splendid," Catherine says. "I don't see why not."

"You are very close to Safeway when you need groceries," Katrina says. "It's just at the corner. There will also be a new convenience store down

27

the road on the same side of the street as your apartment. Otherwise, you can cross the street to the 7-Eleven."

A loud whistle skewers my ear, and outside I hear a man yell in a deep, growly voice, "Melissa."

We all scramble out to the deck to see what is happening. The sharp, shrill whistle sounds again, and the same rough, masculine voice yells, this time with more authority. "Get your butt in here now!" The voice comes from the building to my right, around the corner.

I catch a glimpse of a man with long black hair that hangs down to the middle of his back. It looks coarse. He wears black shorts and a dirty, white tank top. His legs are thick and so are his arms. A large black and gray suncatcher tattoo covers his neck. His skin tone is dark, almost red-brown. He walks inside his apartment from the deck before I can see his face.

A moment later, two girls appear from behind the community building and run toward us. They both have long blonde hair that sticks to their faces from sweat. The smaller of the two children look up at us long enough for me to see her green eyes and freckles. My guess is she is six or seven years old. The other child is older, perhaps nine or ten. The freckled blonde waves to Thủy-Tiên.

"Come on, Jen," she says to the older girl. Both girls run off and disappear between the two buildings.

"Well, I hope that doesn't become a regular occurrence," Sky remarks. "That's kind of annoying."

"Are they going to be safe here?" Teddy asks. "Maybe you all should just live with us forever."

The thought of living with Teddy and Catherine forever does not appeal to me at all. "Thank you, Teddy, but we cannot trouble you more. Joseph, please, how we can pay for this?"

"Your first year of rent will be taken care of. Homestead Apartments is low-income housing that the government subsidizes. With your permanent-resident alien status, you are eligible for public assistance to help you transition to independence and citizenship. You are very fortunate. Katrina and Sky are covering the difference in rent, and the Vanzwols have hosted you for eight months, which is seven more than what was initially planned. Even the church has gone above and beyond. Members of the community are stopping by shortly to deliver some furniture and food for your fridge and pantry."

I am speechless and ashamed of my thoughts earlier of feeling like a charity case. Once again, my eyes mist up. "Oh, thank you. Thank you all. Thank you so much!" I hug everyone and tell Tree and Thủy-Tiên to show their gratitude.

"I get to teach you and Tree how to drive," Sky declares.

"Yeah, he picked the short straw," Teddy exclaims. He playfully punches Sky in the arm.

"Short straw?" I ask.

"It's a thing we do to decide who has to do an unwanted task," Catherine says. "We didn't actually draw straws though."

We all chat a little bit more about logistics, such as how I receive my welfare benefits, how often I have to check in with the Department of Social and Health Services, and how the food bank operates. I also learn about dialing 9-1-1 for emergency help and a book called the *Yellow Pages* that lists every telephone number to all the businesses nearby.

"It looks like the pastor and his entourage are here," Katrina says. "I'm going to bid you farewell and stay out of their hair. See you all in a few days for Thanksgiving. Joseph, you are welcome to join us."

"I came with Mom," Sky says, "so she's my ride. I'll check in on you later, Snow, and we'll have our first driving lesson after Thanksgiving."

"Smart idea," Teddy says. "You'll want some of that turkey and cranberry relish in case it's your last meal."

Catherine elbows Teddy in the ribs. "Always the jokester."

They say their goodbyes to us and greet Pastor George and his crew of three men on the way out the door. I send Tree down to help unload the truck and bring up furniture and supplies. After an hour of going up and down a flight of thirteen steps, we finally bring in the last box.

Pastor George stands before me, panting and sweating. "I'm not as young as I used to be."

We both share a chuckle. He helps himself to a glass of water from the kitchen faucet. It still amazes me how easy it is to get access to clean, drinkable water here in America. And Western toilets are my favorite invention. Where our waste goes after flushing is a mystery to me. It beats squatting over rickety bamboo boards over a pond of fish, hoping you do not fall in and that no one disturbs you while you're in the outhouse. This truly is the land of technology and riches.

"Pastor, the sermon today very good," I say. "Make me cry."

"I'm glad you received the message," Pastor George replies. "What are your anxieties?"

I sit down on my previously-owned sofa donated to us by a church member. I pat the fuzzy velour cushion and invite the pastor to sit down. I am undecided on whether I love it or find it hideous. The design is a bit busy. The fabric has repeating images of a rustic barn with red and gold daisies around it and pheasants peering at the barn from between the flowers. The dark wood accents on the arms and legs have rust-orange markings on them like it has been scratched and dented one too many times from being moved. I do like the smell of it, with its hints of peppermint and sticky-sweet mothballs.

"I have many anxieties," I start, "but today, I let go of the one I hold in my heart for Sky. Many years I hold anger and cannot forgive him. I forgive him now."

"That is good. Love and forgiveness are what he needs, but it is what you need as well. It is important to love and forgive yourself."

"Yes. When my Sam die, my heart die too. It freeze and turn to stone. Sky with me when Sam die, and I think he freeze too. I did not know I was mad all this time. I too busy running from the Việt Cộng and keep us alive. Now, no more running, and I realize many emotions. I feel bad I hate Sergeant Skyler for so long."

"My dear Snow, such is life. When you stop, everything comes crashing. God gave you the grit and tenacity to make it this far. He will give you the strength to get to the finish line. Giving your anxieties to Him is the first step. Learning to love and forgive, not only yourself but others are the next step."

"Thank you for everything."

"You're welcome. Come talk to me at any time. Dawn and I are here for you and your family. You're stuck with us like this barn is stuck to this couch."

4. THANKSGIVING 1980

Today is Tuesday, November 25. Tree, Thủy-Tiên, and I spend the day getting settled into our new apartment. Outside the rain comes down steadily but not pounding hard like in Việt Nam, where the streets boil from the pummeling water droplets. My daughter is in charge of sorting all the clothes into piles for each of us, then folding or hanging them in their respective bedrooms. I empty the boxes filled with kitchen items and put them where they belong, while Tree hangs our framed art pieces and decorates the home.

"Where do you want to hang the cross and this picture of Jesus?" Tree asks as he takes a voracious bite of an apple.

"Above the television," I respond.

He walks over to our previously-owned RCA color TV in its wooden box and powers up the console. "I wish there were more than six channels…four, five, seven, nine, eleven, and thirteen. That is it." He turns the dial a full rotation.

"We are lucky to have a television," I remind him.

He goes through all the channels again and stops at channel four. A familiar, funky tune catches my attention.

"Oh, yes," I say excitedly.

Thủy-Tiên runs out of the bedroom into the living room. She recognizes the tune as we have watched the show many times with Teddy and Catherine.

"Come knock the door," she sings.

Tree echoes the same verse. We all hold our hands out like we are holding a microphone.

"We wait on you," she sings.

Tree and I chime in. "We wait on you…Where kisses hers and his and hers, three company too."

31

"It is eight o'clock," I say. "We will watch this show and then get ready for bed. School tomorrow, then Thanksgiving the next day."

The three of us huddle around the television set and watch the Downhill Chaser episode of *Three's Company*. It is the happiest period we have had together in a long time as we laugh at the slapstick comedy.

We carpool with Catherine and Teddy to Katrina's house. As we pull off the main road, we are welcomed by umbrageous pink dogwood trees that line both sides of the six-hundred-feet driveway. Teddy slows the car as we approach the immaculately landscaped circular drive. An asymmetrical, mid-century home sprawling across the high-noon sky comes into view. Unlike Teddy and Catherine's multi-level home, Katrina's is a custom ranch with a low-pitched gable roof that extends out to give the front entryway shelter. Bright hanging baskets with blooms of fiery orange and crimson red adorn the wide hanging eaves. The home is nestled six hundred fifteen feet from the road, surrounded by twenty acres of lush woods, blackberry thickets, a greenhouse, a barn, stable, and a large, fenced, round pen, about one-hundred feet in diameter—big enough to train two horses in the bullring at the same time.

Katrina opens the door before we have a chance to knock. "Come in! Happy Thanksgiving!" She is dressed in classic black slacks, a cream-colored V-neck sweater, and black Mary Jane pumps. How polished and regal she looks.

"For you," I say and hand her a floral bouquet.

Sky is a couple of steps behind her. He wears an apron with an image of a big turkey on it. He looks funny since the entire apron is brown with ruffles around the trim in alternate colors of red, yellow, and orange. In the center of his chest is the face of a turkey. He holds a drink and greets us. "What would you like to drink? We have eggnog, virgin or spiked, your choice…and wine, regular or mulled. There's also hot buttered rum, champagne, and of course, 7-Up."

Inside, the smell of cinnamon and chocolate tantalizes my senses. Catherine and Teddy hand over their homemade honey rolls, cranberry-orange relish, and pumpkin pie. They head straight into the living room. I kick off my shoes, eager to see the house.

"Keep them on," Katrina says. "We keep our shoes on here."

"In my country, it bad to wear shoes inside. We do everything on the floor. Eat, sleep, prepare our food, play…"

Sky takes our coats. "Is that why? All this time, I never knew. That makes sense though. It's as if you're walking on someone's bed or dining table with your dirty street shoes." He disappears down the hallway for a couple of minutes and reappears with a wrapped gift. He hands it to Thủy-Tiên. "I hear you've been a good girl, Dolly."

My daughter nods and accepts the gift with both hands.

"Say 'thank you,'" I remind her.

She tears open the present, and a big smile spreads across her face. "Thank you!" The box contains a pink Barbie wardrobe closet, one Barbie doll, and a few accessories, such as tiny pink shoes, sunglasses, a purse, and a suitcase. The closet has three outfits including an evening gown. "Pretty." My daughter strokes the long blonde hair.

"Good heavens," Catherine says. "That should entertain Dolly for a while."

"A dolly for Dolly," Teddy says.

My daughter sits down on the floor and looks at Teddy. "Mr. Van, you play."

Teddy sits down in a procession of three steps: first kneeling on both knees while his hand uses the coffee table for support, then leaning sideways onto his hip before finally swinging his legs around to sit cross-legged. "Sky, get your dear old uncle a drink, will ya?"

Sky comes into the living room. "Here you go."

With his eyes still on my daughter and his arm outstretched to receive his drink, Teddy grabs what Sky hands him—only it isn't a cocktail. "What the—?" He looks at his hand to find a Ken doll. We all laugh. In Sky's other hand is the cup of hot buttered rum for Teddy. "That's more like it!"

Tree sits down and plays with them. Katrina hands him four plastic horses. "You can play with these. I've had these since I was a kid. This one," Katrina points to the gold horse with a flaxen mane and tail, "is my favorite. My first horse was a palomino named Butterscotch."

"Pal-oh-mee-no?" Tree asks.

"Yes, that's right. And this one here is a Cleveland Bay."

"Clee-lun-bay."

Katrina smiles. "A great uncle of mine gave me this one on my fourteenth birthday. This one here is an Arabian."

"Uh-rab-un."

"See how its tail is up? That's partly because of their breeding but also because they have fewer vertebrae than most horses. And because of their compact bodies, it's more comfortable for them to hold their tail up, especially when they canter." Katrina points to the fourth horse, a spotted white and brown one. "This is a paint. Tree, I think your first English words will be equine ones!"

Sky takes my elbow and leads me to the sliding glass door. "Want a nickel tour of the place?" I do not understand what he means. He must have sensed this or read the confused expression on my face as he explains. "It's another idiom of ours…an expression meaning a quick look. Back in the old days, people paid five cents for a guided exhibit."

We walk into the open kitchen, and the aroma of a roasting turkey invites us to peek in the oven. Sky turns on the oven light. "Another half-hour and the turkey will be done. It'll have to rest for a bit before I carve it."

"Sky, you cook?" I ask, impressed to know a man is not afraid of the kitchen.

"I'm no cook like Aunt Catherine, but I'm not bad. I had a lot of practice growing up." The corners of Sky's mouth lift into a smile, but he looks sad. Perhaps I am imagining it, but I sense a memory has emerged that he would rather forget.

"The kitchen so big," I exclaim, "and bright." The big windows let in a lot of natural light while the white walls give the room an airy feel. On the walls are three art pieces from the 1950s, replicas of Pablo Picasso's *Women of Algiers* series.

We walk into the dining room next. There is an accent wall painted in teal with a graphic wall hanging in geometrically opposed shapes of squares and circles in colors of orange, brown, green, and bright blue. It is very eclectic.

"I made that in art school," Sky says. "I hate it, but Mom loves it."

"I think it wonderful, like splashes of life," I say. "You see?"

"What do you mean?"

"The blue for sky, the brown for earth, green for life, and orange for sun. See? You have talent too."

"I never looked at it that way. My dad is the one with artistic talent." That sad expression appears again on Sky's face. He is quiet for a moment, and in the few seconds of awkward silence, I study his eyes. They look at me but do not truly see me. He looks distant and lost. I want to ask him what is wrong but dare not intrude. I touch his arm, worried that the wetness on his lower lashes will develop into thick tears. Sky clears his throat. "Anyways, my grandfather was also very talented. He built this teak table for my parents as a wedding gift. It seats six but expands to accommodate ten people. Maybe Grandpapa hoped there'd be more grandkids."

"The table lovely," I say.

The centerpiece on the table is a gorgeous floral arrangement dominated by orange gerbera daisies. In front of every chair, resting on red placemats, are crystal wine glasses, fine china plates, silver flatware, cloth napkins, and hand-blown water tumblers in swirls of tangerine and avocado. The table is set for eight tonight. How odd as there are only seven of us.

Maybe it is a place setting to honor a dead relative. The memory of my niece, Tâm, surfaces. Now it is my turn to feel sad.

"We have more guest coming?" I ask.

"There is a chance my dad might show up," Sky answers dryly. "Let me show you the rest of the house."

Sky leads me into the bedrooms and bathrooms. Each of the three bedrooms proudly displays some kind of abstract art on the textured wallpaper, and every bathroom has a sunburst mirror in either a rustic mahogany finish or brushed silver lines. My favorite room in the house is the reading nook. Books huddle cozily together from floor to ceiling; their spines beckon me to touch them; the pages vie for my readership. The plant-based motifs of floral slate wallpaper and block-print ferns on the throw pillows give the room a private, treasured sanctuary feel. One day I hope to have a nook such as this.

Back in the living room, everyone is drinking, chatting, and munching on appetizers. Teddy has given up on the Ken doll and is now fiddling with a glass of wine. Tree sits soaking in his surroundings and straining to catch a word he understands.

Katrina holds court and tells us about her new horse. "I just got him this past Saturday. He's a quarter horse, four years old, and just a hair over fifteen hands. Isn't he beautiful?"

Sky points to the window, and my gaze follows his finger. I catch a glimpse of the magnificent animal standing in his pen. He is a tincture of black, like sable, with a small strip of white between his eyes.

"What his name?" I ask.

"Blazing Six Guns," Katrina answers. Her face lights up, and she shifts back and forth in her blue velvet egg chair. "He's named after a western comic anthology." She speaks of her horse with wildfire energy, and I find her enthusiasm so infectious that it almost makes me want to own a horse of my own. The memory of my pet chicken, however, tugs at my heart and reminds me that the joy of owning an animal is too fleeting. "There I was at the Enumclaw auction. Mind you, I had no business being there if it weren't for that handsome Judd. He's the auctioneer. There's just something about a cowboy in ripped jeans. Oh, Lord, have mercy." Katrina fans her heart with her hand. "I tell you what, whatever he's selling, I'm buying. Next thing I knew, I was raising my paddle willy-nilly and lo and behold, Judd looked me dead in the eyes and said, 'yours,' and I nearly fell off my rocker."

I have never seen Katrina so animated. I want to hear more about cowboy Judd, but the oven timer rings.

"Oh good. I'm starving." Catherine makes her way to the kitchen before we all can stand up. "That turkey's been resting for four hours in the oven. I say we carve her up and let her rest in our bellies."

Sky tends to the turkey while we women bring food to the table. Tree fills everyone's tumbler with water and helps Thủy-Tiên pour her soda. Teddy follows with a decanter of wine and opens another bottle to let it breathe.

"Snow," Catherine says, as she lowers the oven temperature to 140 degrees, "why don't you put the pies in the oven to keep them warm?"

I look at the four pies on the counter. Catherine made the pumpkin pie, but I wonder about the other three. "Sky, you make pies?"

"Yes," he answers, as he carves the turkey and puts it on a large blue and gold platter. "There's chocolate bourbon pecan pie, apple cinnamon pie, and pear and almond cream tart."

"I think I will like all," I say. "This platter so pretty."

"Augarten porcelain from Vienna. This platter has been handed down in my family from generation to generation to the first-born. My dad gave this to me right before I joined the army. He told me I had to come back alive if I wanted to claim this heirloom."

"And you hand to your child one day," I comment. "What if you have twins?"

Sky pauses to think for a second. He shrugs. "Ask me again when I have twins. I first have to find a woman who'll want to marry me. You want to marry me, Snow?" He smiles, and I realize he is being playful.

"When you learn Vietnamese, maybe I marry you," I tease.

"Well, when you can drive a stick shift and your feet touch the pedals, maybe I'll marry *you*."

We laugh and join the family in the dining room, already salivating over the feast. Teddy takes hold of my hand and bows his head. I reach for Thủy-Tiên's hand on the other side of me and close my eyes.

Teddy's rich baritone voice soothes me as he says a prayer. "Oh gracious God, thank you for the blessings of this feast, so lovingly prepared by Skyler and Catherine. Even Katrina's salad is a blessing, but Lord, you know me. I'm a meat and potatoes kind of guy." A few chuckles overlap the prayer. "Gracious Father, please kindly withhold pie from whoever just kicked me. We thank you for our health, our home, our family and friends, especially those present today and gathered around this table. In your name we pray. Amen."

And just like that, we go from holding hands to grabbing plates of food and everyone asking to pass the gravy. What took two days to prepare only takes us thirty minutes to consume.

"Round two," Teddy declares. "Pass me the stuffing, won't you?"

Amid our chatter, we do not notice the looming figure in the foyer until a loud *pop* ricochets off our ears and into our chests.

Sky jumps up, startled and programmed to fight. His fists clench, knuckles white. His eyes are wild with rage. Like a caged animal whose iron gates spring open, he lunges toward the man in the hallway. I wrap my arms around Thủy-Tiên and duck in fear. My heart pumps fast. For a millisecond I think about running to my bunker for safety.

A throaty laugh and then a gasp. "Sorry I'm late, but I brought some Perrier-Jouët!" The man stands with a bottle of champagne in the air.

"Damn it, Dad!" Sky screams. "You're always one for piss-poor timing."

Katrina walks over to her husband and son. She looks calm on the surface, but her pursed lips betray her cool exterior. "Let's not ruin Thanksgiving."

Skyler's father sits down at the table. A wisp of sweet musk and menthol flirts with my senses. He interrogates me with his intense gaze. I cringe as the joyous mood of the room evaporates. I imagine lurking behind those dark pupils is a communist countryman eager to drag me home to the jungles of Việt Nam. He says nothing but nods politely. Bald and clean-shaven, the only things on his head are the pair of dark caterpillar eyebrows clinging to his face. There is arrogance in the way he sits and places the dinner napkin on his lap. His movements are fluidic, even poetic, but the graceful way in which he moves makes the hair on my arms rise. The devil himself has floated in for dinner and is now sitting across from me. He is dressed from top to bottom in black, from his turtleneck sweater and blazer to his pants and loafers. Hard. Strong. Beautiful…just like the black opal that is nestled in the tungsten carbide band he wears on his pinky finger.

He pours himself a glass of the Cuvee. "Jean-Adrien. And you are?"

"Snow," I half-whisper.

The presence of Jean-Adrien rattles my core yet kindles warmth between my legs. I dare not make eye contact for the rest of the evening.

5. THE OOPSIES (NOVEMBER 1980)

Sky opens the door to his old Lincoln Town Car. "Ready? Thought I'd teach you in my old college car first. After you get your driver's license, we'll advance to a stick shift. Everyone should know how to drive a manual."

Tree, Dolly, and I slide into the vehicle. The smell of the leather seats combined with the pine air freshener hanging from the rearview mirror washes over my anxiety and restores my excitement.

Sky drives us to Hazen High School. "They have a large parking lot. Plenty of room for oopsies."

"Oopsies?" I ask.

"You know, accidents and mistakes." Sky grins. "You and Tree can give it a go without worrying about hitting anything…or anyone."

Tree leans forward from the backseat of the old Lincoln sedan. "Can I go first?" He has a big smile on his face.

I volunteer my nephew, as he is eager to drive. It is nice to see his face light up with such enthusiasm. "Tree go first. I never drive car before, only my scooter back in Việt Nam. My brother, Seven, he truck driver, but he never teach me."

"It's never too late to learn." Sky puts the car in park and turns off the engine. I slide out of the passenger seat and sit in the back with Dolly. "Okay, Tree, before you turn on the ignition, you need to adjust your seat and all your mirrors." I translate every step of the way. Sky goes over which pedal is the brake and which one is the accelerator. We learn the basic anatomy of the car, its quirks, and what every knob, lever, handle, and letter mean. Finally, Sky permits Tree to put the car in reverse. "Seatbelt on. Then, nice and easy, take your foot off the brake and push down on the gas."

Tree drives us around the parking lot and around to the back of the school. He practices stopping and starting, going forward and reverse, using his turn signal to go left or right. Sky even encourages Tree to accelerate and stop the car using the emergency brake. Dolly and I slosh around in the back seat at every turn as Tree negotiates each corner, going around and around the building. My daughter's eyes and mouth are wide open, but she claps her approval whenever Tree makes a sharp turn. I hold tightly to the grab handle and breathe out an "oh Jesus" while Sky growls a "yee-haw."

"This is so fun," Tree declares. He steps on the accelerator again, pumping the brakes only for the speed bumps. Nausea is permeating out of my stomach and making its way up my esophagus.

Sky punches the roof of his car a couple of times and sticks his head out the window. "Waa hoo!"

After thirty minutes of driving around the parking lot, Tree takes the car to a hard stop. Our heads jerk forward. "Can I take it out on the road?"

I take a hard swallow of my saliva.

"Yes, let's go," Dolly squeals.

Sky lets Tree drive around the neighborhood a few blocks, careful to stay within the residential speed limit. The last lesson is parallel parking.

"Okay, Tree, pull alongside this parked car. Good. Now, put it in reverse and slowly back up until the front of our car is by the driver's side door of that car." My nephew handles the car with confidence. "Turn your wheel softly to the right and let the car roll back nice and slow. Good. Now turn it to the left, nice and easy, and slide straight back."

It takes Tree three tries to park the car five inches from the curb of the sidewalk.

"Well done!" Sky whips his head around and winks at me. "Snow, you ready?"

Tree tosses the keys back to me.

"No," I say but get out of the car anyway. I manage to suppress the gopher knot bubbling up my throat.

"Mama's turn," Dolly says. "You can do it. And then it will be my turn."

I laugh. "When you can reach the pedals and see over the dash, we will teach you." I get in the driver's seat and start the engine.

"Adjust your seat, and check your mirrors," Sky says. "Seatbelt."

I turn on the blinker and slowly pull out to the street. I cruise at fifteen miles per hour and keep alert. My eyes dart left and right. I rotate my gaze to the front and rear. Before long, I relax my grip on the steering wheel and enjoy the drive.

"The speed limit is twenty-five miles per hour," Sky says. I step on the gas and take the car to thirty. "Slow down, Snow. You'll get a ticket."

The road unexpectedly curves to the left. I take the sharp turn, oversteering enough to drift a little bit. I glance at the speedometer. It reads thirty-five. I self-correct and jerk the wheel to the right to straighten out.

My daughter claps her hands. "This is fun!"

"Stop!" Sky points to the red, octagonal sign. His sudden scream and jerky movements cause panic. I step down on the gas for a half-second, then slam my foot onto the brakes. We all lunge forward. The screech of the tires beckons pedestrians to stop and stare.

"Oopsies," I say.

Sky pulls the e-brake. "Let's have you practice in the parking lot."

Back at Homestead Apartments, Sky promises to take us out again for another driving lesson. "We'll keep practicing until you're ready to take the test."

"Sky, you stay for dinner?" I ask.

"Sure," he answers. "You've never cooked for me before."

We head up the stairs together, and on the last step, a high-pitched whistle wedges itself between the damp air and the caws of the crows.

"Melissa! Dinner!" The same jagged, macho voice yells from the other side of my corner unit.

The blonde girl with freckles runs past us. She stops and waves at Dolly. "Want to play?"

Two more children appear below. I recognize the other blonde girl, Jen, but to my surprise, they are with an Asian boy around the same age. I am guessing seven or eight years old.

My daughter waves to them and gives me a pleading look.

I nod. "But play in the back where I can see you."

Dolly bounds down the stairs. "Hi."

Melissa lifts her head, closes her eyes, and yells at the sky. "I'm not hungry, Tony! One more hour? Please?"

A woman's voice responds. "Fine."

I address the boy in my native tongue. "Are you Vietnamese?" He nods. "And do you live here?" He points to the apartment unit across from mine. "So we are neighbors. Do you live with your parents? Do you have any brothers or sisters?"

"It is just my mom and me," the boy answers.

"C'mon," Jen commands. "I have to be home before dark."

The four of them walk off and disappear around the corner.

"If only I could make friends that easy." Tree opens the apartment door, saunters straight to his bedroom, and closes the door.

From the sliding glass door of my deck, I see Dolly and her new friends playing foursquare. Sky is in my kitchen rifling through the cupboards and taking inventory of what is in the refrigerator. "I should have brought leftovers from Thanksgiving."

40

"You cooking for us?" I ask.

"Sure." He pulls out the chicken drumsticks. "You can keep an eye on Dolly while I make us some fried chicken. Do you have any stock?"

"What you need sock for?" I ask.

Sky laughs. "Stock, not sock." He opens the last drawer. "Oh good, you have chicken broth. I'm thinking some dirty rice and greens on the side should do it."

"You wash rice," I say, "so not dirty." I glance down at the courtyard. The children jump rope now. The Vietnamese boy and Dolly laugh hysterically over something funny. I smile to see pure joy in her face. This was the dream for us in America.

"Sky, tell me about your life. Tell me what happen after you come back from Việt Nam." I sit down at the table and notice a small cockroach crawling out from behind the refrigerator. Not long ago I was so hungry I would have dived for the insect.

Sky stops and turns to me. "I just want to forget. Can't we talk about something else? Anything, just not that." Sky clenches his teeth.

"I want to know. You not want to know about me after war? After Sam?"

Sky blinks rapidly to will the tears away. He lowers his head and is silent. I hold my breath. His voice is a half octave lower when he speaks again. "I've spent the past eight years trying to forget, to move on."

"That something we never can forget." I pull on Sky's hand. "Sit."

"Damn it, I said I don't want to talk about it." He pulls his hand away but sits down next to me. He slumps forward. "Do we have to do this now?"

"I talk. You listen." I hope that by sharing my story, Sky will open up and share too. "One year after Sam die, I meet Dolly father, Tý. He was teacher from Sài Gòn. He transfer to my village to teach. My father was head of school. He arrange my marriage."

"Was he good to you?" Sky places his hand on mine. His face softens. "Please tell me he gave you and Dolly a good life."

"He good in beginning, but he tell many lies. He already have first wife. American. Her name Annette. And they have son. When Sài Gòn fall, he leave with Annette and son to America."

"What? That bastard." Sky's face is hard again. He scowls and exhales a heavy sigh. "Do you know where he is now?"

"Yes, but it not matter now. He have his life. I have my life."

"But, Snow, he needs to be a man and take care of his family."

41

"No." I shake my head vigorously. "I take care myself. I do not need him. After communists take over, my family starve. My father die. We lose everything. The Việt Cộng arrest Tâm—"

"Your niece? But why didn't you tell me all this in your letters when you were at Galang?"

"I no trust military at refugee camp. I afraid they read letters. I afraid they not mail to you."

"What about Ommo?" Sky asks. "Weren't you going to marry him?" Just hearing his name makes me more sad. I crushed his heart. I owe him a letter. I owe Sister Six and Brother Seven a letter as well.

"Yes, Ommo is good, but he in past. I not in love with him. I make decision come here. Cannot go back." I look out the window to check on my daughter. The children stand in a circle with two kids and bounce an orange ball to one another. "I want to live in present. I want to look to future."

"I am tired of living within my memories," Sky says. "It's torture. I feel suffocated. The screams of the dying play over and over like a damn broken record."

"Who we can trust if we cannot trust ourself?" I ask.

"Exactly," Sky says.

"The only man I trust is Tý brother, Hải. The Việt Cộng take him away too. I not know if Tâm or Hải still alive in prison camps. So many time, I try escape my country. So many time, Dolly, Tree, and me could die." My voice trembles and cracks. I am fired up now with emotions. I push through the tears and swallow the knot in my throat. "I almost lose Dolly at refugee camp. You save her. You sponsor us to Seattle. You are good man."

"I had to find a way to bring you here. Sam would have wanted that. He was a brother to me. I failed him. I failed my country. I wasn't going to fail you too. I just couldn't." Sam stands up and walks to the window. I cannot see his face, but I suspect he is holding back the tears. His voice shakes to a whisper. "I am not a good man."

"The war not your fault," I say.

"My life has been a failure. You don't know about all the things I have done."

"The war feel a lifetime away. In a place ocean apart. War make all people criminal, even children. Good people turn bad to survive. Like me."

"What could you have possibly done?" Sky questions tersely. "You are as pure as your name implies. Who did you kill? Who did you have to fuck to forget?" He pounds his fist on the window. It rattles loudly. His body shakes. "You have no idea what it was like to come back here, not as a hero, but as the foul heathen who should have died in Nam." Sky is yelling now. "This damn country…this goddamn country. I fought for this country, and it

42

turned its back on me when I got home. Instead of peace signs, I got the middle finger. This ungrateful society that we live in. I was so confused and fucked up in the head. I still am. Not once did I get a thank you. Not once did I hear 'glad you made it home safely.' 'Baby-killer.' That's what I heard. 'Rapist.' I've been spat on, kicked, harassed, fired at, cursed. Yeah, I'm a loser. Thirty-four years old and still living with my mom because I can't hold down a job. People I grew up with turned away like they didn't know me." Sky cranks his head and looks over his shoulder. "We lost the war. You don't get the red carpet and fireworks when you come home. You don't get a welcome reception. No. You get the devil's asshole. Piss and vinegar. Fire and ice. I wasn't returning home. I returned to an institution where a death penalty would have been more humane than a life sentence."

"Sky—"

"You wanted to know what happened after I got back. Well, I'm telling you. I got back to Seattle and developed symptoms of malaria. Did the VA take care of me? No. They denied me health care because I didn't have symptoms in Nam. They pushed me out faster than Charlie taking a shit. I tried to cash in my education benefits and go to college. My GI benefits were worthless! My entire payout was a hundred-fifty dollars when the cost was three hundred dollars per credit. *Per credit*, Snow! Yeah, as soon as I applied for jobs and they found out I was a Vietnam veteran, they treated me like a ticking time bomb."

"But Katrina and Jean-Adrien—"

"What about them? My dad is a son of a bitch. Don't let his money and looks and charms fool you. My mom fell for it, and we're all paying the price. Time and time again my dad has failed me, for as long as I can remember. And my mom is the bigger fool for staying married to him."

"Why?" I ask. "What happen?"

"Hell if I know why she stays. He's a cheat and a womanizer. He travels around the globe, flexes his big shot architect muscles, smiles, and people just fall at his feet. Take our house, for example. He built it to buy our love, but he was never around. Where the hell was he when I was six years old? When I fell off my bike and scraped my knee? He was MIA. When I needed a man to talk to, he was screwing his coworker. Where was he when I was…when I needed…" Sky's words trail off. I wait for him to continue, but he does not.

"Need what?"

"His protection," Sky whispers. I barely hear him. "I needed him to protect me." The tears burst from Sky's eyes. Wetness covers his mouth and nose. He wipes them away with the back of his hand like a toddler drying his tears.

"Protect from what, Sky?"

"My uncle." The anguish in his cries sounds like cats mating. He crumples to the floor with a haggard howl. The wailing gets louder, more jagged. He is reduced to a vulnerable, scared child, not the sarcastic, confident soldier I once knew.

I am shocked. "You mean Teddy?"

Sky shakes his head and wails louder.

Tree flings his bedroom door open and appears in the hallway, a grim expression on his face. I shake my head as if to say *not now*. He retraces his steps back to his room and quietly closes the door.

If not Teddy, then who?

I did not see Sky at church. He did not come to give Tree and me another driving lesson. When I call, Katrina says he is not home. For days, I wonder who had hurt Sky. Whatever accident or mistake took place, it is clear the incident still haunts him.

Christmas is not far away. Teddy and Catherine have been busy with their families. While Tree and Dolly are at school, I occupy myself by watching television and spying on my neighbor. The Vietnamese woman next door has been elusive. I have caught a few glimpses of her from my bedroom window, but we have not met. I know her name, though, having overheard voices two nights ago. Someone had knocked on their door, and when it opened, I heard a woman say, "Hi, Yip." I wonder if her name is Diệp. In Vietnamese, if the letter D does not have a straight line across it, the letter sounds like the English letter Y. Hearing her name makes me sad for old Mrs. Trần, who is probably haunting all of Hồ Chí Minh City. Tomorrow I will visit Diệp and introduce myself. It will be nice to have another female to banter with in Vietnamese like the old days back home.

I turn on the television and flip the channels. Every channel is the news. I turn past channel two but something catches my eyes. I turn the knob back. Although the channel does not come in clear and the sound is distorted, there is no mistaking the face reporting the news is that of an Asian woman. I cannot see her full name but can make out the word "Chung." To my surprise, she is Chinese. I am more fascinated by the features of her face than what she is saying. Her teeth are perfect and her lipstick a vibrant shade of red. Her sultry voice and how she moves her head are graceful. Her skin is smooth and flawless, her nose high and regal, her bone structure immaculate. She is on screen for only a minute before the camera switches to footage of another Asian woman.

44

I gasp. Yoko Ono! The news is talking about Yoko Ono and John Lennon. I strain to listen, but the report is unclear. Words of *dead* and *age forty* assault my ears. I change the channel to find better reception.

"We interrupt this program to bring you a special report from NBC news. Late last night, former Beatles member, John Lennon, died at St. Luke's-Roosevelt Hospital from gunshot wounds to the chest. One police officer says they are treating this case as seriously as the assassination of John F. Kennedy. New York City's Chief of Detectives, James T. Sullivan, surveyed the scene and interviewed the witnesses, as well as the officers who responded to the call. The gunman has been identified as Mark David Chapman from Hawaii, whom one witness said had been lurking outside Lennon's New York City apartment. Another witness said she saw Chapman approach Lennon for an autograph yesterday morning. Lennon and his wife, Yoko Ono, were on their way back from the studio late last night, where they were recording a track for their new album 'Double Fantasy.' When their limo pulled up to the Dakotas building on the Upper West Side, a gunman came from the shadows and fired several shots at close range. Four bullets entered Lennon's chest, of which three exited through the back. Police confirmed the weapon was a thirty-eight caliber Charter Arms pistol. Lennon was still alive and conscious when they arrived on the scene but was pronounced dead around eleven-thirty eastern time. At one-fifteen this morning, a mortuary division vehicle left the Roosevelt Hospital with Lennon's body. Yoko returned to the residence where a crowd of about four hundred people had already gathered around Seventy-Second Street and Central Park West to hold a vigil and mourn the singer. We will bring you more news as it breaks."

My heart cracks in two. I clutch my heart and cover my mouth to muffle my cries. I imagine being in Yoko's spirit. I understand the irreparable pain her entire being is suffering right now. That despairing feeling of being alone and lost, that horrible feeling of guilt and helplessness because someone took your lover's life, robbing you both of happiness. I cry for her. I cry for John Lennon. And I cry for my Sam.

6. FULL CIRCLE (DECEMBER 1980)

Dolly sings as she soaks in the bubble bath and plays with her Barbie doll. "Jesus loves me, this I know, for the Bible tells me so. Little ones to him belong. They are weak but he is strong."

I kneel on the floor beside her and gently massage the shampoo into her hair. Her hair is fine like mine, but much shorter. "Did you learn that in Sunday school?" She nods, then coughs. I feel her forehead. It is a little warm. "Do you feel sick?"

"Sometimes it is hard to breathe," she says.

"Dr. Hall said it would be six months after surgery before you felt better." I look at the long scar down the center of her chest. "Does it hurt anywhere?"

"Sometimes my stomach hurts. After I go poop, it feels better. My poop is runny."

"Mama will ask our neighbor next door if she has any tiger balm we can borrow."

"Hùng's mom?" Dolly asks.

"Oh, is that your friend's name? Hùng?"

"Yes. He says it means hero. What does my name mean?"

"Thủy-Tiên means water angel. It is also the name of a flower."

"Hùng's mom is Mrs. Diệp."

"And their last name?"

"Trần."

I sit back on my haunches. I find it strange that my neighbor next door has the same name as the she-Jekyll who lived next to us in Sài Gòn. Even in Seattle, I cannot escape Mrs. Trần. Full circle.

"What a coincidence," I say, more to myself than to Thủy-Tiên. "What about Mrs. Diệp's husband?"

"Dead."

46

Interesting…so was Mrs. Trần's husband back home. Now, if Mrs. Diệp also has two sons, of which one is a communist, then it can only mean one thing—Mrs. Trần is here to haunt me.

"I think you should grow your hair out long," I suggest, changing the subject.

"No. I like it short."

"But you look like a boy."

"Boys do not wear dresses," she says. "I do. And I look dangerous with short hair."

I make the mistake of laughing. My daughter glares at me.

"All right, keep your short hair. Before you were born, I had a short pixie haircut like Elizabeth Taylor."

"Who?" My daughter dismisses her question and tells me about other lessons she is learning in Bible classes. "I learned about the Trinity. God, Jesus, and the Holy Ghost. I think Olivia is like God and Ocean is like Jesus. But Opal, she is the ghost for sure. She is scary."

I chuckle. "Pastor George and Mrs. Dawn might have something to say about that. What makes you think Olivia and Ocean are like God and Jesus?" I am curious to know how her little mind works.

"In the beginning, there was God," she says, "and he is wise and knows everything. Olivia is the oldest and smart. She knows everything. She is a good reader and loves all animals. Ocean is my best friend. She is like Jesus because she loves me."

"And you think Opal is scary like a ghost?"

"She is mean and bossy. I do not like her, even when she smiles or laughs."

"When the Bible talks about the trinity, it is referring to God being the Father, the Son, and the Holy Spirit. The word 'holy' means good or divine. A holy ghost is a good ghost."

My daughter puts her doll down and takes my face between her wet, wrinkly hands. She looks at me squarely in the eyes. "Then Opal is the devil."

"Stop this nonsense." I am taken aback that she should feel this way. "Opal is ten years old and the middle child. She has to work twice as hard to outshine her older and younger sisters. You should be happy you are the only child and get all the love."

"Do you like Opal?" Dolly asks.

Indeed, she is not my favorite out of the three girls, but in many ways, Opal is like my sister; she speaks her mind, calls things as she sees them without sugar-coating anything, and does not care what others think.

I reach under the water to pull the plug and drain the bathwater. "I like Opal. She reminds me of your Aunt Six. People like Opal make the best

47

kind of friends because they will always tell the truth and not lie to you. You will see. I am going to set you and Opal up for a playdate."

"No!" Dolly slams the palm of her hands down on the water. "Only Ocean. I want to play with Ocean." Her outburst takes me by surprise.

Thick, round tears make their appearance behind Dolly's curtain of lashes. They race down her cheeks and pause at her chin before leaping into the water. I hoist Dolly out of the tub. She arches her back and kicks the tub. We both fall back onto the linoleum floor. She runs out of the bathroom, naked and dripping wet, into the bedroom. She slams the door shut. I hear pounding on the wall and drawers slamming shut. A loud thud assaults the floor. I am guessing she has thrown a book or toy. She wails louder. I peek into the room to make sure she is all right and am greeted with an angry stare. My daughter is acting like a spoiled, entitled child.

I do not give in to her tantrum. "I am giving you a warning. Behave or get a spanking." I close the door and walk into the kitchen to make some tea.

###

Another cold morning. The drizzle outside dampens my mood. I yearn for sunshine and tropical heat. Dolly appears in the kitchen wearing a long periwinkle dress with tiny white dots. She has done a wonderful job dressing herself this morning with white tights and white, polyurethane, double strap Mary Jane shoes. Her expressive face, however, does not match her beautiful dress. She scowls at me, no doubt still upset about the playdate.

"You know the rules," I say. "No shoes in the house."

"We are not in Vietnam anymore," Dolly reminds me. "We are in America. I hate your stupid rules."

"Listen, child—" I say.

"And I want a different name. I hate Dolly. The kids call me names."

"What do they call you?" I ask.

"Dolly Parton and Dolly Pop-Up." My daughter crosses her arms across her chest. "And Dolly Hand Truck! I hate it here. Why can't we go back and live with Ommo or back to Vietnam and stay with Uncle Seven?"

Tree puts down his Cap'n Crunch cereal. He lifts Thủy-Tiên onto his lap. Her beady eyes cast suspicion. Her claws are ready to pinch him.

"You look like a princess to me," Tree says. "Do you know how many princesses there were in Vietnam?" Dolly shakes her head. "A lot. And do you know how many princesses there are here?" Again she shakes her head. "None. Here, you are special. They do not know it yet, but they will. Why not go with your real name? Thủy-Tiên is a beautiful name and it means 'water angel'."

48

"I want to be called Nancy. I told a girl at school my real name and she laughed and called me 'Tiny Tim'. Stupid girl."

Tree and I look at each other, speechless. I hear a horn honk outside.

"They're here," I say. "We will talk about this after church."

The three of us gather outside, and as I turn the key to lock the apartment, I hear a gasp from Tree and a scream from Dolly. My gaze shifts in time to see my little girl tumble down the last ten steps and lie crumpled on the cold, wet cement. We all rush to her.

"Tiên!" I yell. There is a tinge of blood on her lips.

Teddy kneels next to her. "We don't want to lift her in case she broke something."

"Oh dear," Catherine exclaims. "Did she trip on her dress? What happened?"

"Can you sit up?" Tree asks. "Where does it hurt?"

My daughter sits up and points to her abdomen. She yelps.

"We go to hospital," I say.

Teddy gently lifts Dolly into his arms. "Toots, open the car door." He eases my daughter into the back seat of his Nova. She winces and sobs. The drive to Seattle Children's Hospital is thwarted by road closures, detours, and traffic.

"Faster, Teddy," I urge.

"There is construction everywhere," Catherine notes. "I-5 is gridlocked. Do you think there is an accident ahead?"

"Let's get on the viaduct and cut over." Teddy exits the freeway. We head north on the SR-99 corridor and travel on the elevated freeway above downtown Seattle. Despite our present situation, the drive along the waterfront is still breathtaking as we pass the piers, cruise terminal, and port marina.

"If the clouds burn off," Tree says, "I bet we can see Mount Rainier looming over the lake." I nod in agreement. "It would be wonderful to see the snow."

I rub my daughter's arm for reassurance. "We are almost there."

We cannot get there fast enough. The surface streets are riddled with one-way roads and plagued with red traffic lights.

"We should have called the ambulance," Catherine mumbles.

We arrive at the emergency entrance. The doors open, and a rush of odors attack my nose. The smell of disinfectants wafts through the air and dances with the scent of diapers. I can taste the baby powder and antiseptic.

Teddy and Catherine do all the talking. Tree and I stand helpless but vigilant. An orderly wheels Thủy-Tiên down the hallway for X-rays. We follow and are instructed to wait in a different room. I cannot lose you.

A Bangladeshi woman with an olive green hijab walks into the waiting room. Her silk headdress accentuates the brightness of her green eyes, and the gold caduceus dangling from her necklace rivals for attention with her nose piercing. "I am Dr. Khan. Are you Dolly's mother?"

"Yes," I say. "I am Snow."

"The good news is she did not break anything from the fall," Dr. Khan states. "However, we did find something concerning."

"What is it?" Catherine asks. "What's wrong? Is it her heart?"

Teddy rubs his weary eyes. "Dr. Hall was the surgeon who operated on her. Four months ago. Here, at Children's."

"It is not her heart," Dr. Khan continues. "You are from Vietnam?" I nod. "And you are new immigrants? War refugees?" Again, I nod affirmatively. "That explains it."

"Oh, for Pete's sake, what is it already?" Teddy rubs his bald head and narrows his eyes. I wonder who this Pete person is.

Dr. Khan looks at the documents in her folder. A frown settles on her face. "There is a parasite living inside your daughter...intestinal worms."

The mention of worms brings me back to when my nephew, Tuấn, had pinworms in his rectum. I shudder at the memory of having to clean the house thoroughly, of washing all the sheets and clothes, and my nephew screaming in pain as Brother Seven scrubbed his son's body raw.

"Who knows how long she's had them," Catherine says. The blood drains from her face, turning her flushed cheeks white.

I translate to Tree what is going on. A strange sound escapes his lips. He half laughs and half groans. "We made a full circle, Aunt Eight."

Dr. Khan speaks again. "Roundworms can live inside the small intestine for a couple of years and grow to a foot long. It is a vicious cycle. Health conditions worsen once you're infected. It wreaks havoc on your immune system, which can be fatal. This is my fifth case of helminths since Washington started resettling refugees five years ago."

"Did she show any symptoms, Snow?" Catherine asks. "Actually, what are the symptoms?"

"Fever, coughing, rash—"

"Dolly have all them, but she alway sick since she born," I say.

Dr. Khan looks at me sympathetically. "Because of the micro-nutrient deficiency caused by the worms, the infected person can lose concentration, suffer abdominal pain, and be anemic. In children, it can stunt their growth because nourishment is siphoned from the host. There are a lot of adverse effects if left untreated, causing liver and bladder failure, lung disease—"

"Okay, but you can treat it, right?" Teddy asks.

"We are going to do some more scans to make sure the parasite hasn't gotten into her brain or spine, and take a stool sample to test for the presence of eggs…but yes, it can be treated with anthelmintic such as mebendazole."

All these years, I believed my daughter was frail, small, and sick because of her heart, but in truth, she was battling more than a heart murmur…she was sharing what little food she had with damn worms. I want nothing more than to hold her, comfort her, and protect her. My poor baby.

The phone rings.

"Alô?" I answer.

"You were not at church." It is Sky. "Everything okay?"

"You not talk to Teddy or Catherine?" I ask.

"No, I've been out of town," Sky says, "and came back Saturday night. I didn't see you at church. Mom hasn't heard from anyone either."

"We at hospital—"

"Oh my God. Which one? I'll come now."

"No, we home now." I give Sky an account of what happened and how Dolly is on medication so her body can expel the parasite and kill any eggs that may be in her system.

"That poor girl has been through so much," Sky says. "How are you holding up?"

"I good, I think."

"Listen, Snow, I owe you an apology." I wait for Sky to continue, but there is only silence, then a sigh. "I need to explain some things about my past. Are you coming to Christmas Eve dinner?"

"Yes."

"Good. We'll talk then. See you Wednesday."

We say our goodbyes, and I resume my chores. I gather up the dirty clothes in the hall closet, grab the laundry detergent and money, and check on my nephew.

"Tree?" I call from the other side of his closed bedroom door. No answer. I open the door. My nephew sleeps. My daughter is curled next to him. His room smells like damp, sweaty socks. It is dark with the curtains closed. Black fluorescent lights illuminate the large, velvet posters of menacing cobras and evil dragons on his walls, pinned on either side of his bed. Teddy had taken us to an outdoor flea market a couple of weeks ago on Aurora Avenue, and Tree had to have them. I gather up his dirty clothes and put them in the large trash bag.

It is partly sunny outside, but the chill nips at my nose. I walk down the steps and around the corner to building F. Hauling my garbage bag of soiled socks, stained shirts, and thricely worn pants, I make the short trek to the community laundry room. Thoughts of Cường carrying his bags of loot out of the US Embassy the morning Sài Gòn fell makes me smile and ache for home. I dream of the day I am reunited with my family.

Inside the laundry room, it is nice and warm. A man transfers wet clothes into a dryer. He looks familiar. Two boys help him, one dark-skinned teenager, about Tree's age, and a young boy of elementary age with a milky-white complexion. I cannot help but stare. The man reminds me of someone.

"Can I help you?" The gentleman starts the dryer, and all three of them approach me.

"I...sorry. How I wash?" I ask.

He lifts the lid to one of the machines. "You'll probably need to do two loads." I dump my bag into the machine, but he stops me. "Whoa. Maybe you should separate them into dark and light." I stare at him blankly. "Let me help you. Do you mind?"

I shake my head. I watch as the stranger sorts my clothes and loads two machines, separating the white clothes from the black ones. I blush each time he touches my delicates.

"The colored items go with the blacks," the man says.

After sorting the items, I see that the white pile is very small and only fills the machine a third of the way. It seems wasteful to have the washer so empty.

"Fifty cents to wash and a dollar to dry," the stranger says.

I put the quarters in the machines. It pains me to spend four quarters for both machines when I can shove all the clothes in one load.

The man fills the tray with laundry soap. He closes the lids and presses the different buttons. "It takes thirty minutes to wash and an hour to dry."

"Thank you," I say. "My name Snow. You movie star?"

"Me?" He laughs. "No, but people tell me I look like the younger version of Philip Drummond from *Diff'rent Strokes*."

"Oh, yes. I watch show. You look like rich man on television."

"Pretty much, down to the adopted kids too. These are my boys, Jason and Ricky. And I'm Donald." I smile at the boys. Jason is the younger child, pale and knock-kneed. His shaggy blond hair could use a good washing. His face is dirty and his eyes dull. He lowers his eyes. "Jason's my shy one."

Ricky is a big boy, both tall and burly. His dark complexion is coated with pubescent acne and stubble on his face. "Hi...Hi, I'm...I'm Rick...Ricky...Hi."

"Ricky stutters, as you can see, but he is not shy," Donald says. "He wants to be an entertainer one day."

Donald and I get acquainted while I wait for my clothes to wash. I learn he moved into Homestead Apartments three weeks ago. His wife passed from Parkinson's disease. He and his boys left Oregon to get a fresh start and away from the painful memories. I share bits of my story and we agree to get our families together after Christmas.

After the laundry is done, I stuff everything back into the garbage bag and walk home. My neighbor is walking up the stairs, carrying a plastic bag. She wears rainbow-colored suspenders to hold up her pants which are two inches too short above her ankles. Her polka-dot turtleneck sweater has a hole on the right shoulder. I imagine a gecko poking its head through and making an escape.

"Chị Diệp?" I call out to her.

She stops and adjusts her glasses. "Chị Tuyết?"

"Yes," I say. "I think your son and my daughter—"

"Yes, they are friends. Nancy is cute."

"Her name is—"

"She is much darker than you. You know, I thought she was a boy at first."

"She looks like her fath—"

"Our kids play well together. I see them play with the other children here. Your daughter is good at basketball and throwing the football."

"Really?" I ask.

"That is why I thought she was a boy...and her short hair...and her dark skin. She does not look Vietnamese."

"She is one hundred percent—"

"So I am just getting home from Safeway."

"Did you—"

"Walk?" Diệp nods. "Yes. Would you like to join us for dinner tonight?"

"I would love—"

"Splendid. Come over at seven." Diệp pats me on the arm. "I look forward to getting to know you, Sister Tuyết."

"Me too," I say. "What can I bring to—"

"Nonsense, just you and Nancy and your nephew." Diệp bounds up the stairs. I follow behind her. She smiles and enters her apartment, closing the door as I nod farewell to her. What an odd woman. Her appearance is youthful, perhaps in her late twenties, but the eyes behind her glasses reflect the eyes of a grandmother who has experienced much. Perhaps she has secrets like me. I wonder if my forty-year-old eyes look old.

My exchange with Diệp was brief, but I feel devoid of energy. She did most of the talking, and yet I feel exhausted. Small doses…I can only handle Diệp in small fractions of time and space.

Diệp's apartment has the same floorplan as mine, only flipped. The pungent smells of fish sauce and Chinese herbal medicine greet me. It smells like Việt Nam. Incense burns in the corner, and I detect a faint hint of menthol. It makes me homesick.

In one corner of the kitchen are bags of dog food and canned cat food. There are pictures of the Virgin Mary and Jesus on the wall, a cross above the sliding glass door, and statues of Happy Buddha, female Buddha, and serenity Buddha on a bookcase.

Thủy-Tiên and Hùng sit on the floor and play together. They both pretend the green GI Joe action figures are waging war against each other, using the matchbox cars as shields.

I pause a moment to take in the scene before me. Diệp's apartment does not have the luxuries of a sofa or TV. She has one hammock, a few folding chairs, and a glass table. While the décor is of muted colors, mostly gray and burnt sienna, Diệp's outfit is rather eclectic. The décolletage of her vibrant rainbow-colored bathing suit leaves little to the imagination, while her bright turquoise spandex pants accentuate every lumpy, subcutaneous fat deposit on her thighs and butt. A green sweatband hugs her head while neon orange leg warmers cover her calves.

"Do you like my hot socks?" Diệp asks. "I noticed you looking at them. I got them at the Goodwill store for ninety-nine cents."

"Yes," I say. "You are very colorful. Do you need help?"

"No. Sit. Where is your nephew?" she asks.

"He is coming," I say. "He is cutting up apples and—"

"I told you not to bring anything."

"Do you have a dog or a cat?" I ask.

"No. Why do you ask?"

"I noticed your bags of dog food and the cans of cat food."

Diệp grins. She wipes her hands on the kitchen towel and saunters over to the corner. She picks up the canned cat food and hands it to me. "I got these on sale. Nineteen cents. There is an aisle at Safeway that has all flavors of cat and dog food."

"Yes, but if you do not have any pets—" It then dawns on me.

"No, silly woman. This is food made of cats and dogs, like back home, but ready-to-eat."

I swallow hard. I recognize the pet food only because Teddy and Catherine feed their Cairn Terrier, Biscuit, this stuff. I mull over how to tell her delicately. Luckily, I do not have to.

Tree lets himself into the apartment. He places the plate of apples and grapes onto the table and grabs the can of cat food from my hand. "You have a cat."

"No," Diệp says, "I was just telling your aunt it is made of cat."

"No, Cô Diệp. This is food *for* cats." Tree points to the bags of dog food. "And those are food *for* dogs. Not for people."

"That is right," I say and point to the ingredients. "See here? The ingredients say chicken, meat by-products, guar gum…no mention of cat."

Diệp's eyes open wide. "What am I going to do with all this food?"

"Tell me we are not having this for dinner," Tree says.

I give him a disapproving look to remind him of manners.

"Mama!" Thủy-Tiên abandons her play and runs to me. She fans her mouth. "Hot." She sticks out her tongue. I see nothing. Tears bead up and make her eyes sparkle. "It burns!"

"What happened?" I ask. Neither she nor Hùng confesses.

"Do we need to go to the hospital again?" Tree asks.

Timidly, Hùng hands me a small bottle with green liquid in it. The label is printed in Chinese, but I recognize what it is. "She swallowed a drop of this menthol." It is a medicated oil, an external analgesic manufactured in Singapore by Eagle Brand. It's a cure-all for muscle aches, itchiness from mosquito bites, headaches, stomach pains, and congestion.

"Why would you drink this?" I ask.

Diệp hands Thủy-Tiên a glass of tap water. "Drink up. You will be fine."

My daughter drinks the whole glass. "He dared me." She points at Hùng. "So I did."

"That was a stupid thing to do," I yell at my daughter, who is holding her throat like she is going to die. She gags and stifles her tears.

Diệp stomps off to the bedroom and returns with a paddle. Her son darts behind me for protection.

"Chị Diệp, that is not necessary." I urge her to put the paddle away. "This is not a spanking offense. They are just being children."

"I think we need to try dinner another time," Diệp says. "I am sorry, Chị Tuyết. Have a good night."

Tree, Dolly, and I leave the apartment, and as we close the door, we hear Hùng cry for mercy and forgiveness as the paddle thuds against his body. "Mother, I will not do that again!"

"At least we are not eating dog food for dinner," Tree says.

"Or cat food," I say.

"I wanted to prove to him I was tough," Dolly says.

7. CHRISTMAS EVE 1980

Katrina's house is a magical adventure park, inviting us in with Christmas lights and garlands strung throughout the property, both inside and out. Smells of pine and caramelized sugar beckon me to take off my coat and stay. A Christmas vinyl spins on the turntable with The Jackson 5 group harmonizing to "I Saw Mommy Kissing Santa Claus." Potted poinsettias in colors of red, white, and pink adorn every room in the house. Hanging on the fireplace mantle are large, furry socks in alternating colors of red and green. In the corner is a twelve-foot, frosted tree, decorated with ornaments, tinsel, and lights. On top of the tree is a beautiful angel, and below are piles of boxes wrapped in shiny paper and hugged with ribbons or bows.

Dolly's eyes are wide with wonder and excitement. Katrina takes my daughter's hand and leads her into the family room. "Dolly, honey, I thought you could help string some popcorn and cranberries for the birds."

"Ocean!" my daughter calls out.

"Dolly! Come sit with me," Ocean says. "Opal, move over." My daughter and Ocean hug. Ocean shows Dolly how to thread the puffy kernels. They alternate the popcorn with raw cranberries, making an edible garland. Olivia puts together a gingerbread house, and Opal cuts paper snowflakes. All four girls are in festive spirits, chatting animatedly about Disney princesses and the gifts they asked for from Santa.

A merry-go-round of "Merry Christmases" passes from everyone's lips to receptive ears. I give Pastor George and Dawn hugs. Tree joins them on the sofa to watch TV and help himself to the bowl of popcorn. I follow Katrina, Teddy, and Catherine into the kitchen.

Perching on the counter stool, I watch Katrina navigate through the kitchen and hope to learn the art of cooking through osmosis. Like a lost tourist, she fumbles her way around, opening cupboards, rifling through the spice rack, opening the fridge, and finally throwing her hands up in defeat.

"Where in the world is the balsamic glaze? Maybe there's some in the garage. Be right back."

Meanwhile, Teddy and Catherine maneuver around each other in the kitchen like two birds during a mating ritual. "Santa Claus Is Comin' To Town" blasts from the record player. Teddy wiggles his hips and swivels his legs like he is crushing a bug underneath his shoes.

"Motown with me, Toots." He swings her around, and she laughs.

"Why, Mr. Vanzwol, I do declare. I knew there was a lot of gospel and soul in you, but you might be too R&B for me."

"I'm channeling my inner Stevie Wonder," Teddy says. "You like my groove?"

"Oh yes," Catherine says in between breaths. "It's a heatwave." The two of them laugh as one lovebird. "Come on, Snow!"

With a little pressing, I agree and hop off the stool to synchronize my dance moves with theirs.

"What's this?" Katrina asks. "A dance party without me?" She stands behind the counter with a bottle of balsamic in her hand.

The four of us dance and giggle, embracing the magic of the holidays. Seeing Teddy and Catherine in love after thirty years of marriage gives me hope that it is possible for me too. Teddy surprises me by swinging me around and dipping me. I am filled with love for these people who, nine months ago, were strangers but have now become family.

"Where Sky?" I ask.

"He'll be here shortly," Katrina answers. "He's picking his dad up from the airport."

"Oh, Jean-Adrien coming tonight?" I ask. The thought of sharing Christmas Eve with him makes me nervous. I remember his steely eyes were cold at Thanksgiving, yet his gaze made me flush with desire. He exudes strength, power, money, and charm. I can understand how Katrina got swept away by his current and why other women threw themselves into his arms. His good looks and pocketbook are abyssal.

"Yes," Katrina breathes, "it's going to be a full house tonight."

"Our daughters are coming," Catherine says.

"You'll get to meet Frances and Penny," Teddy says. "Plus their husbands."

"Penny and Todd are expecting their first child," Catherine says. "They live in Oregon. Frances and Frank have two little boys, Jacob and John. They're driving in from Wenatchee."

Over the next thirty minutes, guests trickle in. I meet the family and feel overwhelmed with the buzzing conversations crisscrossing from room to room. I cannot keep up with their talk, so I seek out the children, but they have their own game of hide and seek. I sit with Tree.

"How are you feeling?" I ask my nephew. "Hungry?"

Tree nods. "I am always hungry, but I eat a lot, too, so I do not have to talk much."

"He who eats a lot talks the least," I say. "I wonder how our family back home is doing."

"I think they are fifteen hours ahead, so it is already Christmas there," Tree says. "I miss them. Have you written to them?"

"Yes," I say, "but have not mailed it yet."

"Good, I want to add my letter before you send it."

"I need to find a job and make money to send home," I say. "I keep praying every day for a job."

"How are you looking for work?" Tree asks.

"Our apartment building has a board in the laundry room that has announcements," I say. "I saw a 'help wanted' post for a babysitter."

Tree grimaces. "Aunt Eight, you can do better. You have a university degree, and you worked at a bank. You also taught math, and your English is good. You need to talk to everyone here, and maybe they can give you a job."

"You are right," I say, "but I feel we already ask so much of them."

"What does Katrina do?" Tree asks. "She is rich. Maybe she can give you a job."

"I do not know what she does. Sky is in between jobs right now, and Catherine is a housewife. Teddy is a big engineer boss at Boeing. The company makes airplanes, like the one we flew in on. Pastor George and Dawn have the church."

"What about Katrina's husband?"

"Jean-Adrien is an architect," I say, "and a very successful one. He travels a lot and built this house. He is coming tonight."

"Ho, ho, ho!" comes a voice from behind me.

"Sky!" I am startled to have him so close to me all of a sudden.

He sits down with Tree and me. "I need a drink. Twenty minutes in the car with my dad is more than I can take."

"It good to see you," I say. I reach over and pat his hand. "Merry Christmas."

"Merry Christmas, Snow. Merry Christmas, Tree."

The three of us stand up and join the family in the kitchen and dining room. I see Jean-Adrien standing with Katrina, his arm around her waist. The two of them laugh and look happy.

Sky hands me a wine glass. "Look at her, still looking at him with puppy-love eyes." He pours me some merlot from the decanter. "After dinner, let's talk privately in the reading nook. I owe you an explanation…and an apology."

The pace of the evening picks up with Sky's presence at the dinner party. He does not leave my side and is attentive to me, making sure I am comfortable until it is time for us to sit down and eat. I allow myself to enjoy the occasion despite the guilt gnawing at my conscience thinking of my family in Việt Nam.

With Teddy and Catherine's children and grandchildren present, nineteen of us are gathered tonight. Pastor George says grace before we all swarm around the food. I learn the menu tonight consists of prime rib, bone-in ham, butternut squash, smashed garlic and thyme potatoes, bacon-wrapped dates, buttery rolls, sweet potato fries, Portobello mushrooms, creamed spinach, and balsamic roasted vegetables.

Sky leans in and whispers into my ear. "Do you know the seven deadly sins?" I shake my head. "There's envy, gluttony, greed, pride, lust, sloth, and wrath." Sky explains what each means.

"What sin belong to you?" I ask.

"All of them," he answers and winks. "Let's play a game. Let's guess who here has committed these sins."

"Okay, how about lust?" I ask.

Sky rolls his eyes. "Easy. My dad. How about gluttony?"

I imitate Sky and roll my eyes. "Easy. Me."

Sky laughs. "And greed?"

I scan the room and point to Dolly, who is trading her roasted vegetables for Tree's bacon-wrapped dates and sweet potato fries. We laugh.

"Envy?" I ask and keep the game going. "I think Catherine. She envy your mom."

Sky disagrees. "I think it's the other way around. My mom envies Aunt Catherine. She wants the kind of marriage that Catherine and Teddy have."

"But maybe Catherine wish she have fortune with nice clothes, big house—" I argue.

"If anything, I think Catherine has pride. There is nothing my aunt cannot do that she does not do well. She's managed to raise her children, learned to spin wool, knit, sew, and crochet. She has her garden, cooks like a master chef, keeps Teddy happy…"

"Maybe you right," I acknowledge. "Sloth?"

Sky drums his fingers on his thigh. "Hmmm. Teddy for sure. He may be big and manly, but he looks like Santa Claus. He can stand to shed some pounds."

"Teddy work hard. He not lazy. I think Tree is sloth. He sleep all day."

"Okay, I agree. What about wrath?"

We say "Opal" in unison and burst out laughing. Opal must have heard her name because she looks straight at us and narrows her eyes. We both smile at her but she does not relent.

Sky and I grab a slice of warm apple pie and some Asbach brandy before heading to the reading nook. I sink into the green upholstered chair and feel the billowy softness of the cushions. I admire the floor-to-ceiling bookshelves, full of literary wonder and richness of adventure.

Sky pulls out a gift-wrapped book from the top shelf and hands it to me. "For you."

I tear open the shiny foil and am speechless. As I run my fingers delicately over the words, I can think of only one person: Sam. I hug the book and inhale the faint smell of vanilla coming from the pages. "How you know?" I ask as one tear escapes the corner of my eye. "I lost book. This Sam give to me. It burn with shrimp boat when I go Indonesia."

Sky flips open the cover of Carlos Castaneda's book *A Separate Reality* and points to the photograph lying loosely between the first two pages. It is a picture of Sam and Sky in their army fatigues, posing with their M-16s on the beach. A tear falls down my cheek and blazes a trail for more to follow. I finally have a picture of my Sam.

"That Christmas he spent with you and your family when he was on R and R was the happiest he had ever been," Sky says. "He told me he gave you this book. Told me he was going to marry you and that he'd read it to you each night."

"Yes," I say, "and he say this book about different visions of life. What look real may not be real."

Sky nods. "Nam was terrible for us all. It was a quicksand war. Sam and I used to daydream all the time. We'd be on our cots in the barrack and think about our favorite foods or in the foxhole talking about what we'd do once we got back home. Hell, even when we were sitting on the crapper, we'd talk about girls, and I'd say, in a separate reality, I'd be married to both Heather Locklear and Ann Margret." A sad smile graces his lips. He takes a swallow of his German cuvee, aged twenty-one years, and pours a second helping. "Sam would always say his reality was you."

"We can still have the reality we want," I say. "We can still have love and freedom, but different vision of it."

"Different version?" Sky asks. "Yes, I suppose. I'm sorry, Snow, for my outcry at your home. I hope I didn't scare you. I'm just so angry all the time. It's like, what's the point of living. You know?"

"You not scare me," I say. "I have many worry. For you, for my family, for finding job. You can talk to me and tell me everything. We help each other."

"I need help, Snow. I was already a broken man before I went into the military. My uncle…" Sky trails off and purses his lips. He takes another gulp of the brandy and stands up. His head lowers, his shoulders slump, and his body trembles. I sit patiently waiting for him to continue, fearing if I say anything, he will dismiss his pain and leave the room. Sky turns his back to me and leans against the back of the chair. "I was sexually abused by my dad's brother, Uncle Dawson, when I was eight years old. I kept that secret for years." When I say nothing, Sky turns around to check and see if I am still here. "My dad was never around. Too busy building his career, whoring his way across the globe, while my mom sat at home pining for a husband who made up for lost time with expensive gifts and cheap promises. She knows of his affairs and still, she loves him, or the idea of him. Uncle Dawson was around when Dad wasn't. He was the only man in our life at the time. Thank God Aunt Catherine married Uncle Teddy. I stayed with them every chance I got. Aunt Catherine is like a mom to me. You know, after I was drafted and before I left for Nam, I told my parents what happened with Uncle Dawson. Mom slapped me, and Dad laughed."

Sky's story claws at my heart and kicks me in the throat. "I sorry this happen to you. You not tell Teddy or Catherine?"

"I was too scared," Sky says. "Uncle Dawson said I had to keep it a secret, that no one would believe me if I told them. He said he'd just deny it and claim I was making up stories for attention. He made me think my parents would divorce if they knew what a bad boy I had been. At the time, that scared me tremendously."

"Where Uncle Dawson now?" I ask.

"Rotting in hell, I hope." Sky curls and uncurls his fingers. His tight fist presses down on the table until his knuckles turn red. "He died in a car accident. Drove drunk and bowled down a family of four."

I am unsure what to say but keep talking, trusting the right words will drip out. "Remember Pastor George? He say we must give anxiety to God. You keep big secret. It too much. That why you broken. Your secret like a monster, a tumor. It grow too big for you and rip you apart."

"But how do I let it go?" Sky asks. "I thought joining the military and being a world away from here was going to bury my problems, not add to them."

"You tell your story," I say. "You forgive yourself, and you forgive your parents…your uncle too. Then," I place my palm on Sky's chest, "you make room in your heart for what make you happy."

"But how? Don't you think I've tried to forget?"

"Not forget, Skyler…forgive." I take hold of Sky's hand and give it a hard squeeze. "It what we both must do."

"You know, after our driving lesson, I went to Massachusetts for a meditation retreat. My mom suggested I go clear my head."

"Maybe I meditate too," I say. "I try yoga. It nice."

"There's a meditation retreat in California I wouldn't mind trying. You can come with me."

"Maybe. I need job and I have Dolly," I say. "I watch yoga on TV. I learn down dog to cobra and child pose."

"I have no idea what that means, but okay." Sky gives me a soft hug. "Let's get our shit together for Sam. He'd want us to be happy."

I hand Sky his brandy, and we lift our glasses. "For Sam."

The church is bursting with members this morning. Outside the air is wet, and the clouds are ombre shades of gray. A loud rumble of thunder ripples across the evergreens, and with one crack of God's whip, a bolt of lightning pierces the sky, signaling the start of the race. Everyone runs into the house of our Lord like there is a free television inside and takes shelter from the rain. Teddy drops us off at the entrance and circles the grounds for a parking space.

Pastor George and Dawn greet each one of us with cheer as we rush in like good Christians on Christmas morning. Dolly runs off to Sunday school. She knows the routine now. Frances and Frank, together with their two little boys, Jacob and John, are already seated in the church. They will drive back to Wenatchee following the service.

A very pregnant Penny waddles toward Catherine. "Hi, Mom." She points to her husband, who stands and waves at us from the fourth row. "Todd and I saved everyone a seat."

I follow them to the front and sit next to Tree and Catherine. We wait for Teddy. The room is filled with radiant energy. A choir of large poinsettias, dressed in delicate robes of crimson and white, stand in front of the podium with their green foliage outstretched, welcoming us to service. White lights are strung around the pew; they glow and give off God's love. On either side of the room is an artificial tree, adorned with shiny ornaments and more lights. The fragrance of citrus fruits seduces me to sniff the air around me. I pinpoint it to the wood benches. I imagine this is what heaven is like—bright, warm, peaceful, and lemon-scented.

The time is 9:05 a.m. Teddy taps Tree's shoulder. We stand up and let him slide in beside Catherine. He is drenched from the rain, and beads of water trickle down from his shiny head into the thick forest that is his beard.

The children file into the room. There are whispers of confusion among the congregation. My eyes instinctually search for my daughter. She is the second to last in the line. Dolly looks so out of place being the only brown child in the group, but she certainly does not look like she feels out of place. My daughter smiles and fidgets with her dress. She looks for me, and we lock eyes. I wink. Her smile gets bigger.

The children sing, "He's got the whole world in his hands," as they sway back and forth and do hand gestures to the lyrics, raising their arms above their heads and forming an O to symbolize the world. I watch with delight as Dolly cradles her arms and rocks side to side while singing, "He's got the little bitty babies in his hands." They sing two more songs and then settle on the floor in the front. I beam with happiness and pride.

Pastor George addresses the congregation. "Merry Christmas." We all echo "Merry Christmas" back. "We started this morning off a little unorthodox, didn't we?" The audience chuckles. Tree and I do not understand, so we look at each other and shrug. "Well, today is not a typical day. It's not every day our Savior is born. Today we celebrate the Son of God."

I look around the church to see if I can spot Katrina and Sky but do not see them. Pastor George continues his message, opening with Hebrews 4:16. I partially listen, too distracted by Sky and Katrina's absence at church. I keep looking for them and wonder if Jean-Adrien's visit has anything to do with them not being here today.

"When we seek his grace and mercy," Pastor George cries out, "we must do so with confidence. In times of need, that is when we must approach God's throne boldly and ask our Father to help us. What happens if we keep quiet? If we absorb all the pain and hardship ourselves? If we internalize the fear, the guilt, the sadness…when we bear our burden alone, it becomes a poison. It eats away our joy. It robs us of our mental, spiritual, and physical health. It devours our soul and paralyzes us so that we are held hostage in our solitude."

"Amen," the congregation responds.

"When we show our vulnerability and confide in him our woes," Pastor George continues, "our God can take away our paralysis. Be it financial or health, be it cultural or spiritual…whatever is holding you back from living your life in his glory, turn it over to him, and trust that he will lift your burden. Join me in reading a passage from Mark, chapter two, verses one through twelve."

I follow Teddy's lead and open the Bible to page 1074. The house reads in unison about Jesus not only healing a paralytic man but also washing away his sins.

Pastor George closes his Bible. He takes off his reading glasses and looks straight at me. His gaze is intentional. "Your sins are forgiven."

Through Pastor George, God speaks to me. The angels and Sam and all my friends and family…they speak to me. They forgive me.

Without warning, I burst into uncontrollable tears. I am saved. Pages and pages of images fly through my thoughts. I see Sam's eyes roll back as I cradle him in my arms, his blood drenching the sleeves of my tunic. I see my father, cold and still, dead from the trauma he suffered. Sister Six's face flashes in front of me. I imagine a look of terror in her sunken eyes as her daughter is taken from her. I see Hồng-Mai's face, gaunt and painted with tear tracks, as she was raped…as she took her own life. I could not save any of them. I only saved myself. I left them all behind. So many lives lost or ruined. This burden has been with me for too long.

I can hear the screams of the women at sea as the Thai pirates violated them. Even more deafening are the silent cries of those who gave up and slipped away, letting earth and sea claim them. Maybe if I were a better wife, I could have held on to my husband. Maybe if I had fought harder, I could have saved Hải from torture and starvation. I should have tried. I could have tried. Why did I not do better?

The sadness and guilt are too much to bear. I climb over Tree and run out of the church. The doors feel heavier than usual, but I manage to push one open. I repeat to myself: I am forgiven. I am forgiven.

Outside, rain hammers the pavement. The roar of thunder urges me to stay indoors, but I see the outline of a man emerging from the parked cars. I run to him. The sting of every raindrop pricks my skin, needle and threading every memory into my body, telling me I can never forget, but that I can forgive. I am forgiven.

"Snow," Sky breathes. He takes me into his arms and holds me. I cling to him tighter and tighter, wanting to dissolve into him so that I no longer exist. I sob uncontrollably. I have been an imposter this whole time, pretending I am strong. The paper-thin veil drops. I am exposed, vulnerable, and fragile.

Sky picks me up and carries me to his car. Inside the safety of his 280ZX, I let it all go.

8. EAST IS NOT WEST (JANUARY 1981)

Some days, it is easier to pretend I do not speak or understand English than to engage in meaningless conversations with children who only value their point of view.

Dolly's friends, Melissa and Jen, sit at my table and help themselves to a bowl of rice. While my daughter dribbles soy sauce over her steamed jasmine rice, Melissa pours cold, bland milk into her bowl, and Jen sprinkles three spoons of sugar on top of hers. I cringe watching the kids shovel the white kernels into their mouths. What is it with Americans and their dairy and sugar?

Jen, the oldest of the three girls, has no problem taking charge. "We should have a slumber party at my house this weekend." Dolly and Melissa nod in agreement. She mother hens the other two, and they eagerly lap up her praise and opinions.

"What slumber party?" I ask.

"It's when everyone sleeps over at someone's house," Jen says, "and we stay up late playing and talking."

"And play dress up," Melissa chimes in, "and we can do each other's hair and paint our nails and put on makeup."

"And eat junk food and watch scary movies," Jen adds.

"Dolly cannot slumber party," I say. "She sleep at home. She only six year old. When she in college or marry, she sleep away from home."

Jen frowns at me. "She goes by Nancy now. And I am eight. My mom let me have slumber parties since I was four."

I am not going to let this child intimidate me or challenge my authority. "You call her Dolly or Thủy-Tiên, or Tiên, but never Nancy." I cross my arms and narrow my eyes. "And no slumber party. We not do that in Việt Nam."

"We are not in Vietnam," Dolly says defiantly, "and my name is Nancy."

66

I do not appreciate her tone. If I dared to disrespect my parents and talk back to them, I would have gotten spankings or kneeling time on the tile floors and would have been staring at the corner of a wall for an hour.

I scowl at my daughter. "Why Nancy?"

Dolly rolls her eyes at me. "Nancy is our new president."

"What?" I ask.

Jen sprinkles more sugar on her rice and says, with her mouth full, "Actually, she is the first lady. Ronald Reagan is our president. It's all over TV."

"Don't you know anything, Mama?" Dolly asks.

I do not know if it is the American culture or the influence of Melissa and Jen, but I will not tolerate the insolence. "Girls, time go home."

"But we are still eating," Melissa states.

"Home, now." I point to the door.

Both girls put on their shoes, wave, and say, "Bye, Nancy."

Thủy-Tiên stands on top of her chair and screams "why?" at me in Vietnamese. "Tại sao? Tại sao?" She stomps her foot and throws her spoon across the kitchen.

This temper of hers can only be from her father, I conclude.

I walk to the hall closet and pick up Tree's size ten sneakers. Thủy-Tiên sees the shoe and runs, but in our small apartment, there is nowhere to hide. I have her cornered.

In my calmest voice, I speak to her in Vietnamese. "East is not West. Do you understand what that means?"

She shakes her head no. The tears stream down her face.

"How we lived our life in Việt Nam is not how we will live our lives in America. Everything on the outside is different—how we dress, what we eat, where we live…even the name we are called, but everything on the inside, under the surface, must never change. That means our values, our beliefs, and our identity. You will respect your elders. You will respect our traditions. You will never roll your eyes or scream at me. Do you understand?"

"Okay," she mumbles.

"Not 'okay.' 'Yes, Mama.'"

"Yes, Mama," she whispers.

"Ask for forgiveness, and I will not spank you," I say.

"Con xin lỗi Mẹ."

The apartment smells like home as I add curry, lemongrass, and coconut milk to the chicken. I let the food simmer and join Tree and Dolly on the velour couch. On the television screen, a man welcomes everyone to

67

the historic first inauguration, under the west front terrace of our nation's capitol. A decorated marine by the name of Michael Ryan steps to the podium and operatically sings.

"We are supposed to stand," Tree says.

I take hold of Tree and Dolly's hands and together we stand.

"Is he the president?" Dolly asks.

"Of course not," Tree says. "Presidents do not sing and presidents are supposed to be old."

The soldier finishes his song, a short verse of "America the Beautiful."

"Please be seated," the man on television says. So we sit.

A reverend of a Presbyterian church is introduced, and we are asked to stand again. Before long, Governor Ronald Reagan and his wife, Nancy, dressed meticulously in red, step up to the podium. We watch as he takes his oath and is sworn in as the fortieth President of the United States. I am mesmerized with the lovely couple and can feel the love Nancy has for her husband as well as the adoration he has for her. That is the kind of marriage I hope for Tree and Thủy-Tiên as well as for me one day.

"Is he our president?" Dolly asks. "I like his hair."

I am so engrossed in his speech and his mention of Arlington National Cemetery, I forget there is curry on the stove. His mention of rice paddies and jungles of Việt Nam catch my attention, and the tears flow seeing the white grave markers. I dismiss the aroma of burnt meat, and instead, hug my daughter and nephew. President Reagan tears up as he concludes his speech. "We are Americans. God bless you and thank you."

A sudden, jarring succession of beeps pierces our ear canals. Startled, I curse out, "Má mày!" The sound of the alarm and the smell of smoke wafting past my nostrils triggers a flashback to the sirens in my province of Vĩnh Bình. I beg for mercy. "Mother Mary, please do not let us die!"

Dolly squats down and covers her ears. "Make it stop!"

I squat down and wrap one protective arm around her. Tree jumps up from the couch, but I pull him down onto the floor. "Lay down! We are under attack! The Việt Cộng are here!"

Tree pulls away from me despite my plea. He runs into the kitchen and turns off the stove. My nephew removes the pot of curry from the electric burner, but the alarm continues to wail. He runs from room to room, cursing, "Đụ má mày."

"Stop!" I order. "What are you looking for? Get down!"

"Aunt Eight, it is a stupid smoke detector or something. It is not an air raid. Help me find it so we can turn it off!"

68

I ease back into reality and run to the deck. I open the sliding glass door and look outside. All is calm. There are no pulsating chuk-chuk sounds of helicopter rotors, no pops of M-16s or rat-tat-tats of AK-47s. The air is still and moist but not humid like the streets of Việt Nam.

The three of us look for the source of the beeps.

Dolly points to the ceiling. "Is that it?"

Tree drags a chair to the smoke detector and steps up. He searches for a switch. He pulls on the cover and rips out the batteries. The beeps stop. It is quiet once again. I let out a sigh of relief and look at Tree. He smiles at me.

Dolly hops onto my lap and takes my face in her small hands. "Can I have a dollar?"

I smile at her. "What for?"

"I found the alarm."

"Fine." I stroke her hair. "Thank you."

"Mama, you have some gray hair. Can I pluck them for twenty-five cents? Each?"

I laugh. "Each? I will pay you fifty cents for an hour of head scratches, massages, and gray hair plucking…but if you pull any black ones out, you pay me."

She gives two seconds of serious thought. "I charge five cents for every gray. I have fast fingers." She wriggles them as proof.

It amuses me that at age six, she is already hustling to make money. I agree to her terms. "You are just like your father."

"No," Tree says. "She is just like you."

A loud knock at the door disrupts our moment and kick-starts my heart. "Who can that be?" The knock comes again, urgent and louder.

"Are you there?" It is my neighbor, Diệp. "Chị Tuyết, ơi!"

"Ơi," I call back.

Tree lets her into the apartment. "Alô, Cô Diệp."

"Are you all right? I heard the alarm." Diệp and her son, Hùng, barge in. Both of them wear sweatbands on their foreheads, shorts that go to their knees, white socks pulled over their calves, and brown, oversized rain boots. I think of Sister Six's definition of *ragamuffin chic*. "Ơi, you found the smoke detector. It is so sensitive. Next time, open the doors and windows and wave a towel below it." She demonstrates by vigorously waving an invisible towel overhead and thrusting her whole body back and forth. "The 'eeeek, eeeek' will stop. The first time it happened to me, I wet my underwear and smashed the smoke alarm with a frying pan."

Tree stands behind our neighbors and tries to suppress his laughter. I force my composure as well.

69

"I burned the curry," I say. "What are you wearing?"

Diệp lifts her leg and curls her back like she is a dog about to mark his territory. She points to her man-boots. "You like them? I got these boots from the dumpster. Somebody threw these perfectly good shoes away! If you want, you can have his." She points to her son. "Hùng, give Cô Tuyết your boots."

"No, I have a pair of rain boots the church gave me." I lie. "But maybe Tree wants them?"

My poor nephew is put on the spot. Tree furrows his eyebrows and shakes his head vehemently but quickly smiles when Diệp insists he takes the hideous boots. He enthusiastically accepts. She is pleased.

"If your curry cannot be saved, come over for dinner. We have plenty." Seeing Tree and me look at each other hesitantly, she adds, "It is not dog food."

We all burst out laughing, and I heartily accept her invitation.

Inside her apartment, the pungent smell of fish sauce assaults my nose, but it is balanced with the aroma of pan-fried garlic, green onions, and scallions. Despite it being forty-three degrees outside, she has all the windows open to air out the smell. I watch as she lifts the lid of the clay pot with one hand and dips a pair of chopsticks into the sauce with the other.

Diệp licks the chopstick and nods. "Perfect."

"You need to teach me how to make the braised catfish," I say.

She waves me over. "Come have a taste."

I must admit, Diệp is a good cook. "Your *cá kho tộ* is delicious! My Sister Six is the best cook. This tastes exactly like her recipe." I admire the caramelized, golden color of the fish steaks and the vibrant hue of the green onions. My stomach rumbles.

"There is a small grocery store in Seattle east of I-5 in Little Saigon. It's the Mekong store." Diệp sprinkles ground black pepper on the catfish and turns off the stove. "I hear that later this year there is going to be another market opening called Việt Wah. I spoke to the owner, Đức. He came here in 1976."

I call Tree and Thủy-Tiên into the kitchen to help set the table and bring food out. My neighbor hands them sets of chopsticks, soup spoons, and bowls. There are only four chairs but five of us.

Diệp and her son, Hùng, bring out the catfish and winter melon soup. I grab the pot of rice and a plate of fried eggplant.

"Do you want me to feed you, or do you want to eat at the table and stand?" I ask my daughter.

"I want to eat with you," Dolly replies. Standing at the table between Hùng and me, Dolly is the same height as I am seated.

Tree searches for an extra plate in the kitchen. "We need something for the bones." He finds a small saucer in the dish rack.

Diệp invites me to eat. "Mời ăn, Chị Tuyết."

I give her my thanks. "Cám ơn."

I remind Dolly she needs to invite her elders to eat, as is customary in our culture.

She lets out an exaggerated sigh. "Why do I have to do that? We do not do that at Mr. and Mrs. Van's house or Aunt Katrina's house."

"They are not Vietnamese. We all are," I remind her. "We may be living among Westerners, but we must never give up our roots."

Dolly rolls her eyes. She starts with the hostess, then me. "Mời Cô Diệp. Mời Mẹ."

"Do not roll your eyes. I have told you this before. If you disrespect me again, you will eat pea vines for the rest of the week," I say.

My daughter apologizes and extends the invitation to Tree and Hùng. Diệp's son picks up his chopsticks and shovels rice into his mouth.

Diệp slaps her son behind the head. "Your turn."

After the formality of the kids inviting elders to eat, we dive in family style with our spoons and chopsticks; no one cares to use separate serving utensils for the food.

"Cô Diệp," Tree says with his mouth full of rice, "thank you for dinner. You must have owned a restaurant back home."

"No, we did not have a restaurant," she says, "but my mother was a good cook. I learned from her." Diệp's eyes mist up with the mention of her mother.

A small lump forms in my throat as I briefly recall my mother's face and the lovely smile she wore. I shove the memory aside. "What province are you from? Did you come here by boat like us?"

Diệp adds more catfish to Tree's bowl. She licks her lips and opens her mouth to speak, but nothing comes out. She shakes her head and stops chewing. She does not look at me. A lonesome teardrop splatters on the table. Diệp wipes her left eye but another droplet of water escapes. "Mỹ Lai."

She whispers the words so quietly I am not sure I hear her correctly. "Mỹ Lai?" I ask. "In the Quảng Ngãi province?"

She nods. Her shoulders shake. The massacre that took place there in 1968 was unspeakable.

I place my hand on her shoulder. "I am sorry."

Diệp looks at me. Her lips quiver. Her hand trembles as she puts her chopsticks down.

"Why are you sad, Auntie?" Dolly asks. "I thought 'mỹ lai' means half Vietnamese and half American."

"No, that is the name of the village my mom is from," Hùng says.

"Tree, take the children to our apartment," I say. "I want to talk to Cô Diệp alone."

My daughter protests. "I am not done eating."

"Take your bowl of rice and go," I order. "Both of you, go with brother Tree."

Tree loads up their bowls of rice with fish, eggplant, and soup and ushers the kids out the door. My daughter complains her rice is now soggy from the soup. Once the door closes, I turn my attention back to Diệp.

Tears run freely down her face. I sit in silence with my hand on hers. Patiently, I wait as her emotions run their course, from quiet mist to flowing sobs, onto jagged, thunderous cries and wails of anger. Diệp leans into me, and I soothe her until she is quiet once more.

She sits up and takes a deep breath. Diệp closes her eyes and exhales. "The helicopters flew in early that morning. It was March 16, 1968…a date I will never forget. I was around Tree's age, just seventeen. When the shooting started, everyone ran. I was on my way to the market but had turned back to fetch more money. When the helicopters landed, all these men in fatigues and M-16s spilled out. I ran as fast as I could to my house, but then a heavy body fell on me. He had been shot from a distance and was dead before he fell, his eyes wide open in terror. I heard the people screaming, their pleading voices screeching like wild cats. I wanted to run to my family, but I was frozen in fear, so I stayed down in the field and pretended I was dead. Another corpse fell on me. I could see between their bodies the soldiers rounding up people and shooting their rifles indiscriminately. It was horrible, all the shooting and stabbing…raping. Hours went by before it was over, and I lay there for a long time after they left. I felt like a coward. I saw one man with his scalp removed and a boy with his hand cut off. There was blood everywhere. I went crazy trying to make sense of it. Why? We were not armed. We were not Việt Cộng or sympathizers. What did we do? We were just trying to live day by day. I hated the Americans. That hate consumed me for years. It was like a meat cleaver chopping my heart into pieces. I lost my mother and father, my brothers and little sisters. I should not be alive, but I am because I was a coward, pretending to be dead while my village was getting burned down and my family and friends killed."

I pat her knee. "You did what you had to. You were smart to play dead. I do not think you acted cowardly. I believe the heavens have a plan for you."

"Do you know what it is like to live while the people you love die? It is like a ratchet around your entire body that tightens every time you let joy into your life. The guilt brings you back so you cannot let go."

I nod in agreement. "For me, guilt is the giant boulder at the end of a noose around my neck. Learning to love and forgive ourselves is hard. My mom told me a woman's fate is to suffer. I hope we were spared so that we can end that cycle of suffering."

"I am glad I have a boy." Diệp smiles. "The misery will skip a generation, but you have a daughter. Her fate will bring her sorrow too."

"We all suffer to some degree. It is part of the journey to self-love and self-worth. Do you still hate the Americans?"

Diệp shakes her head. "I came to realize that it was not hate I felt for those soldiers. I think the heart can learn to love again. I love Americans now. Life is defined by the heart. If the heart dies, you die. Do you agree?" My neighbor does not give me a chance to answer. "I think fear is more poisonous than hate. I feared the Americans more than I hated them. Fear lives in the mind, and the mind does not know how to be strong. The mind is weak, unlike the heart."

"You need both a strong mind and heart to have a healthy life," I say. "Thủy-Tiên's mind is stronger than her heart, but I think it is more balanced now. She had a hole in her heart when she was born and had open-heart surgery last August."

"Look at us, single women raising our children alone in a foreign country. I do not recognize my life. I always envisioned marrying a handsome man from my village, and we would have ten children, a field of water buffalos, and all the mangos and rice we could eat!" Diệp cracks a smile. "And I would grow old to raise a few dozen grandchildren."

"You can still have a version of that dream, minus the buffalos." I chuckle. "It is ironic that you feared the Americans and yet ended up here. I think fate brought us together. You could have gone to Australia or somewhere else, but you ended up in Seattle."

"This was not fate, Sister. This was by design. Tell me, if a pack of street dogs attacked you, would you not be afraid of all dogs?"

"Yes, I think that is to be expected," I say.

"Exactly, but I was not going to live the next sixty years of my life mottled by fear. We live and struggle and fight for our children, do we not? I chose America so that I could face my fears and not let them steal more of my life."

"See? That kind of thought is an emblem of bravery not an insignia of cowardice."

Diệp rubs her eyes and grinds the salty tears into her crow's feet. She licks her dry, cracked lips, and looks out the window. "I know not all Americans are bad. I am learning to forgive what happened so I can move on with my life and learn to be happy with the family that I have. My son has been a blessing."

"Hùng is a good boy," I assure her. "I feel the same about Thủy-Tiên or Dolly…or Nancy. I do not even know what to call her! She is all I have. Each time I think I am going to lose her, her heart beats on. Tree is a teenager, and he has a wandering spirit. He will leave me soon. That is what boys do."

Diệp drapes a few rogue strands of hair behind her ear and looks at me. "I am too hard on my son sometimes. It is because I love him so much. Our children will have a good life. They will have the freedom to choose who they love and marry and get a good education and job."

"I think it is our motherly duty to suffer so that our children do not. We are paying the price to lessen their debt."

"Where is Thủy-Tiên's father?" Diệp asks.

The memory of Tý disappearing into the Mercedes sprinter van and leaving us behind haunts me more than I care to admit. "He left Việt Nam in 1975 right before we lost Sài Gòn. He lives in Texas now. We did not make it out until 1979. It feels like a lifetime ago. What about Hùng's father?"

"I met Duy in 1972. We loved each other right away and had a small wedding. It happened so fast. A year later, Hùng was born. We left in July 1979 and drifted in the ocean for seven days before a German ship found us and dumped us on Kuku Island in Indonesia. I was seven months pregnant with our fourth child. I lost her a month after she was born. Hùng is my only child who survived. A month later, my husband fell ill and died. One day, I want to have my ashes brought to Kuku."

"I am sorry. I cannot imagine how devastating that was for you. What was it like on Kuku?" I ask. "We were on Galang, and it was terrible at first."

"Kuku was a small, remote island. There were fifty-three people on our boat. Our engine died, so we drifted aimlessly. We lived like savages, fighting over morsels of food that we scavenged and climbing trees to get bananas. That first week, it rained so hard. We had no shelter, so we took the beating. The jungle was thick with flies and mosquitos everywhere. There was no toilet, so we just pooped wherever, which made problems worse with the flies. We made huts from bamboo and plastic, whatever we could find, and lived on the beach until one day a helicopter flew over us and dropped parcels of canned food and supplies. It had a big red cross on it and the letters U and N."

"You must have been so relieved," I comment.

"Yes, we thought we were saved. A week later, a ship called *World Vision* came and brought us dried foods, fish, and potatoes. I boiled the fish in seawater. It was sandy and salty with a lot of bones, but Hùng and I devoured it."

"What did the Indonesian government do?" I ask.

"They were so overwhelmed. They erected a camp for us refugees, but before long, more and more boat people were tossed onto camp Kuku's shores...hundreds of them, two or three times a week. It soon was very crowded. I would wait until nightfall to go to the toilet. Eventually, we got organized and dug holes a couple of kilometers away from camp. The women would go in groups, and we all shared this one poncho for modesty. Some of the men just did their business in the ocean. More and more boats came, from Save the Children or UNHCR, and delivered food and supplies. We ate a lot of cabbage and canned tuna or sardines, but we were always hungry. One time, a group of us caught a stray cat and ate it. You know the saying, '*ăn thịt mèo nghèo ba năm*'?"

"Yes, eat cat meat and you will be poor for three years. My mother used to say, '*tránh xui xẻo, không ăn thịt mèo.*'"

"Yes, avoid bad luck, do not eat cat meat. Well, we were too hungry to care."

"Now I understand why you purchased dog food and canned cat food," I tease.

My neighbor laughs. "You will never let me forget, will you?"

"We are sisters now, and as your big sister, I have the duty of chastising you."

"You know, despite the hardships, there were a few fond memories on camp Kuku. One time, another refugee boat washed on the shore, and Hùng rushed to me, so excited to show me what he had found on the boat. His little hands flowered open, and there were tiny kernels of rice that he had picked off the floorboards. Time went by so slowly then. We swam a lot to exhaust the daylight. The coral reef was pretty, and there were so many colorful fish. It was a magical dream world beneath the water."

"We spent a lot of time in the water as well," I say. "Above the water lived weariness and disease...diarrhea...malaria...It was better to spend our days in the water catching crabs."

"Look at us, talking like old women. I am not even thirty years old yet," Diệp says.

"I will be forty one years old this April," I say dryly.

"What?" Diệp slaps my thigh playfully. "You look my age. We need to find you a husband. I will be your matchmaker. I know this doctor…"

9. ONE CHANCE (AUGUST 1981)

Dear Sister Six, Brother Seven, and Family,

I have been in America for over a year now. So much to tell you all, I do not know where to begin. More and more Vietnamese refugees are coming here. We are like an army of ants storming to take over the American picnic tables. Tree dropped out of high school and found a temporary job as a school janitor. He spends his time removing gum from under the classroom tables and restores the rooms each night for summer classes. It pains me to see his mind and talent go to waste. He turned eighteen in December but looks fifteen like his documents state. Here in America, you are entitled to do whatever you want after you turn eighteen and are treated like an adult. He has been hanging out with other refugees. He does not have a car or scooter, not even a bicycle, so he walks everywhere. I see buses here, but we do not know how to ride them or how much it costs. He has been staying at other people's homes, moving from one couch to another like a homeless vagabond. I have no way to contact him. He calls home and checks in every once in a while. Most of the time he plays soccer with other refugee kids and loiters with new friends. I do not understand why their parents allow him to stay with them.

Thủy-Tiên is doing well in school and making friends. We speak two languages at home. I speak in Vietnamese, and she answers in English. I am afraid she will forget her native tongue. I think she is having an identity issue. A couple of months ago, she wanted to be called Nancy, but now she wants to be Kristine or Christie…She has not decided yet. I have one chance to raise her right, and I worry I will ruin her doing it alone. There are moments when I do not recognize her. Her body is frail but her spirit is strong and defiant. She questions me, challenges my patience, and talks back to me. Many of the children here are not afraid to be disobedient. They are not dutiful and accepting of authority. Thủy-Tiên is like a sword. Only time will tell if she will save me or kill me.

I hope to find a job soon so I can send money home to you. The government welfare system here is good. Every month I get food coupons from an organization called DSHS. They give us cash and medical assistance and my apartment is subsidized. It is nice, but we now share our home with cockroaches. Some are as big as my toenail. When I turn on the kitchen light, they scatter as fast as we all used to every time you, Sister Six, farted. I miss those funny days. I do not miss eating cockroaches to stay alive though.

My neighbor, Diệp, has been teaching me how to cook a few simple meals, and I am learning to make a variety of sandwiches at Green River Community College. They have classes for everything. I took some English and computer drafting classes at ITT Technical Institute. Thủy-Tiên wants to eat only American food, like cereal, peanut butter and jelly sandwiches, and pancakes with syrup. Her favorite is macaroni and cheese. We do not have these foods back home so I cannot explain what they are. Basically, anything with sugar, starch, and no vegetables is edible to Thủy-Tiên. I miss your cooking and I am desperately in need of a good bánh mì. The baguettes here have too much dough filling.

My sponsors continue to be a big part of our lives. We go to church every Sunday. I have a driver's license now and can drive but no car. I rely on Mr. and Mrs. Van. Sometimes Katrina or Sky takes us. After I get a job, I will save some money to buy a car. People do not ride scooters here. The streets are wide and organized with lines, signs, and lights. It is not crowded at all like back home. Animals here are spoiled pets not to be eaten. The Vanzwol family has a dog named Biscuit. He is smart. They talk to him like he is a child and give him human food. Such waste! They let Biscuit sleep on the bed with them and he has domain over the house and furniture. It amazes me how much the people here kiss their animals and take them to places! It makes me miss Dirty Butt, that poor chicken.

Please write and give me news about our family. Any word from Hải or Tâm? Has Tý written? Hiền, I hope you will achieve your dream of opening a fabric and tailoring shop one day. I am getting better at sewing, and my stitching is straight. You would be proud of me. Tell Tuấn and Trinh Auntie Eight misses them.

All my love,
Snow

While my daughter plays outside with Melissa, Jen, and Hùng, I cut up the sweet potatoes, lemongrass, and chicken to make curry for dinner. It is the one meal I have perfected and have been cooking at least once every couple of weeks.

It is quiet in the apartment without Tree to talk to. I turn on the television and listen to KING-5 News.

"In April 1975, with the collapse of the South Vietnamese and Cambodian governments, over one hundred forty thousand refugees were evacuated and resettled in the US under the Indo-Chinese refugee program. Now, six years later, the exodus from Vietnam hasn't let up. Many state and local organizations, voluntary agencies like IRC, the International Rescue Committee, wonder if the waves of boat people will ever cease. Even private citizens like Nathaniel Knobb are scratching their heads and pushing back."

I turn down the stove to let the curry simmer and pay close attention to the news. A local reporter interviews a Seattle resident.

"These gooks are leaching off the system. We spend hundreds of millions of dollars helping them with education and public assistance. Our hard-earned tax dollars support them while our citizens struggle," Nathaniel says. "We need to shut our doors and not let any more of them in. Hell, we should send some of them back."

The reporter turns to the camera and says, "Refugee task forces have undertaken massive humanitarian efforts to get refugees resettled and integrated into society as quickly as possible. There are those like Seattle native, Jean Dragseth, who welcome the Vietnamese and appreciate the cultural richness of their presence."

"They are here to stay, and we need to embrace them," Jean says. "They have to overcome so many obstacles to be self-sufficient again. I cannot imagine losing my home and having to start over, adjusting to new customs, dealing with language barriers and employment issues. The American thing to do is to help them."

The reporter continues. "Earlier today I sat down with sisters, Phuong and Van Nguyen, who were among the first wave of refugees to arrive in the United States in April 1975. They were brought to Travis Air Force Base in California because refugee reception centers had not yet been established. In June of that year, they were resettled in Washington State through the efforts of the VOLAGs."

"When we arrived," Phương says in Vietnamese, "we were provided one month of financial assistance to help transition into the community. We were so happy to receive five hundred dollars, but we discovered that five hundred does not stretch far in the United States."

Phương's older sister, Vân, agrees. "Our VOLAG representative directed us to apply for state welfare. In Việt Nam, I was a pharmacist, but now, I clean rooms at a motel. My sister cleans tables at a diner. Our English skills are not very good. I want to practice pharmaceuticals again, but there are different requirements here to practice."

"In 1975," the reporter says, "Washington State received three percent of the total refugees who resettled in the US. The unemployment rate back then was nine percent. Today, with the Iran-Iraq War raging on, Americans are once again up in arms as the unemployment rate rises to an all-time high of ten percent. People are worried."

I am worried also. I must find a job. I turn the TV off and walk back to the kitchen to check on the curry. I hear sounds of laughter and look out the window. My daughter jumps rope with her friends. Donald, the man I met at the laundromat, is also outside playing basketball with his adopted sons, Jason and Ricky.

"Alô, Donald," I call out.

Donald dribbles the orange ball and launches it into the basket. He stops to wave. "We never did get together after Christmas, did we? And here we are the middle of summer already."

"You join us for dinner tonight?" I ask.

"Another time," Donald says. "The boys and I need to finish packing. We're taking a road trip and doing some camping before school starts up. Ricky has been accepted into WSU."

The words "camping" and "WSU" are foreign to me, but I smile and nod anyway. "Have safe trip. I see you next time."

Ricky waves to me. "Hi...hi. Hi, Snow. I'm...going...to Wazzu."

"Washington State University, also known as Wazzu," Donald explains, "for the sheer reputation of being a party zoo."

"Oh, Ricky become animal doctor," I say. "Very good."

"No, actually, well...nevermind." Donald pats Ricky's head. "Who knows, maybe he will become an entertaining animal doctor one—"

"Mama, can Melissa and Jen sleep over?" My daughter cuts Donald off and yells to me in English.

"No," I respond in Vietnamese. "Time to come in and take a bath. Dinner will be ready soon."

"What is for dinner?" Dolly asks.

"Chicken curry."

"Again?" She pouts. "Can we eat at Hùng's house? They are having egg rolls."

"No," I say. "Come in now."

My daughter thrusts the jump rope on the ground and says goodbye to her friends. She stomps her feet as she walks to our apartment. Moments later, I hear the door open and slam shut. She emphatically kicks her shoes off and drags her feet to the bathtub. I pretend not to notice her dramatic entry.

She turns on the water and screams. "I hate curry!" She stands before me in her underwear, arms crossed, and lips quivering. "I am going to live with Brother Tree in California."

"Really?" I call her bluff. "After your bath, we can call him. If he says yes, I will pack your clothes and put you on an airplane."

Forty minutes later, Dolly emerges from the bathroom, wrinkled and wet. She hastily dresses and slumps in front of the bowl of curry. My daughter slowly draws the spoon to her lips. She takes a bite and gags. My patience wears thin. I do not find her defiance amusing. She takes another bite and coughs, heaving and spraying yellow sauce all over the table. I stare at her, secretly wanting to shove the food in her mouth.

"Not too long ago, we were starving and living in a jungle," I remind her. "And you almost died. You had a hole in your heart, you had worms in your gut, and you were bony thin. Now, eat your dinner and be thankful you have food."

"It looks like poop," she says. "And it tastes like vomit. And it stinks like farts."

"If you do not want to eat it tonight, you do not have to," I say.

Her eyes light up, and instantly, the tears that threatened to drop vanish behind her lids. "Can I have cereal?"

"No. Go to bed."

Dolly bangs the spoon down and storms into the bedroom. She shuts the door but opens it to shut it again with a loud thud.

In the morning for breakfast, a cold bowl of curry awaits her.

Sky darts around the car with an athletic gait. He opens my door, bows, and takes my hand. He leads me into the seafood restaurant.

The beautiful hostess greets us. "Welcome to Ray's Boathouse. Reservation for two?"

"Three, actually," Sky says. "It's under Bill Cushing."

"Yes, your other party just arrived. Follow me."

I follow the hostess but lag behind Sky as I take in the breathtaking waterfront view. The ripple of the Puget Sound glistens like diamonds under the rose-colored hue of the evening sky. Boats drift lazily by, cutting the glassy water on their rendezvous with the Olympic Mountains. A dark outline of a bird catches my eye, and I watch the eagle dart in front of the carrot-ginger sun. It swoops down to bathe in the inlet of the Pacific Ocean and rises like a phoenix with a prize in its beak.

The sizzle of steaks seduces my ears while traces of garlic, onions, and sea salt perfume the air. I am aware of how underdressed I am seeing the diners in suits and cocktail attire. We approach a table by the window, and a man with curly gray hair stands up. His round glasses and the dark gray suit make him look polished, esteemed, and very professional. He smiles with the warmth of a cozy fire.

The gentleman shakes Sky's hand, and the two of them hug. "You're too thin." He reaches for my hand and gives it a gentle squeeze. "You must be Snow."

Sky pulls out my chair and introduces his friend. "Snow, this is Bill Cushing, a long-time friend of the family. He is with the *Seattle Times* newspaper."

81

"Let's enjoy some food and get to know each other a little before we talk business." Bill winks, and I immediately feel at ease with him. "I ordered a seafood platter to start. I hope you like oysters, scallops, king crab, and shrimp cocktail." He pours me champagne from a bottle of Dom Perignon, but I stop him.

"She's a lightweight," Sky explains. "A couple of sips and she'll be the same shade as the sunset."

Bill pours a generous amount of the light-amber liquid into Sky's flute. "You will find, Snow, that Ray's serves the best cuisines, offering flavors exclusive to the Pacific Northwest. They were the first local restaurant to purchase their own wholesale fish buyer's license, so they can buy directly from the fishermen. There is nothing better than fresh, wild-caught seafood. They also have an impressive beer and wine list."

Sky laughs. "Bill is a sales and marketing guy. He can sell you wool socks in the summer. She's not in the market to buy a restaurant."

"Maybe not now, but in the future when she is ready, she will remember me and know who to come to. You not only sell to the now but to the future. Have I taught you nothing, boy?"

It is heartwarming to see the two of them engage in an easygoing manner as if they are father and son who genuinely love and respect one another. I am curious about their relationship. "Bill, how you and Sky meet?"

Bill looks at Sky mischievously. "Well, he peed on me, you see."

Sky rolls his eyes and leans back in his chair. "Okay, here we go."

Bill takes a sip of his champagne. He rolls his neck and pretends to crack his fingers as if he is about to settle in for a night of storytelling. "Before Skyler was a twitch in his daddy's pants, Katrina and I were high school and college sweethearts. We were young, in love, and had the whole future ahead of us."

"But Bill was not ready for marriage," Sky says.

"I was stupid, but let's paint the picture in black and white," Bill says. "Katrina was in no hurry either. There were things we both wanted to do before we settled down and started a family."

"He wanted to be a journalist," Sky says, "and was very career-driven. He wanted to travel and see the world first."

"Yes," Bill says, "I wanted to move to the UK and work for the *London Star*. Katrina romanticized about moving to Paris and becoming a model. We were both twenty years old and had been together for almost five years. Our love was strong, and we thought it would last forever, but we were naïve."

Our waiter interrupts us by bringing out the appetizers. I have never seen prawns and scallops so large in my life and the oysters so small…and raw! The crab legs look intimidating, but it is the one I find most inviting.

"Ladies first," Bill says.

"I not used to ladies first," I say and place one of each, except the oyster, on my plate. "In my country, men always first."

"You will get used to it." Sky spoons a dollop of red sauce on my plate. "This is cocktail sauce for your shrimp. It's tangy. In the States, women have more rights and yield more power than they do in Vietnam. We, men, are smarter than we look. We know who truly holds the power." He laughs. I love it when Sky laughs. I know that at this moment, he is happy and not haunted by memories of the past.

Bill nods. "Women have a spell on us."

I watch with revulsion as Bill squeezes lemon juice on his oyster and slurps it down. I look away, unable to stop imagining the slimy mollusk slithering down his throat. He offers me one, and I politely decline. "Oysters are rich in zinc, which helps with testosterone production. They also boost dopamine, which is good for the libido, if you catch my drift." Bill winks at Sky. "I need all the help I can get."

In my attempt to distract myself from the gray, raw shellfish, I reel the conversation back to Katrina and Bill. "Bill, you and Katrina separate after college?"

"They parted ways right after ringing in the new year together," Sky says. "It was January 1945."

"I had these big dreams," Bill reflects. "I wanted to cover World War II from overseas and be in the middle of the action before it was over. The action was short-lived because months later, Germany surrendered, and Hitler killed himself. We bombed Japan and they, too, surrendered. I came back home for Christmas only to find Katrina married to Jean-Adrien. So tragic."

I sit dumbfounded and speechless. I sip my champagne and decide it is delicious. Bill is perceptive. He pours me more.

Sky finishes off his glass and refills. "I was a month old when he met me, and yes, I peed on him."

"Katrina had met Jean-Adrien at a museum. He seduced her with his Frenchy-French charms, his talks of travel, and his lifestyle of luxury and adventure!" Bill speaks sarcastically and twirls his pointer finger. "I was furious at him for moving in on my territory and heartbroken that Katrina allowed herself to be so vulnerable, but I soon realized I was the fool to have left. I chased my career when I should have chosen love. I felt I had this one chance to report for *The Star*. I didn't realize I also had only one chance with

Katrina, and I blew it. She is a beautiful woman who had needs. Jean-Adrien gave her security and affection. He made her feel desirable and safe."

Our waiter comes back to check on us and takes our dinner order. Bill orders a bottle of Quilceda Creek Cabernet Sauvignon to go with our steaks. "Did you know, almost all wine grapes grown in Washington are grown on their own roots? This is special, you see, because most of the world's wine regions grow their grapes on grafted rootstock. A century ago, a louse ravaged vineyards, and the only solution was to graft new vines onto rootstocks that were resistant to the pest. There are a few vintners who still plant vines on their roots, but that's a gamble because they are susceptible to disease, especially if the soil is not resistant to the louse. For some reason, Washington has not had any problems. Own-rooted vines are old and deeply rooted, so they do not need as much fertilization and water, which makes them better equipped to survive harsh weather and resist diseases."

"That's Bill for you," Sky says affectionately. "The walking, talking, live encyclopedia."

"That's right, my boy," Bill jokes. "I've got the brains and the good looks."

I have no interest in wine and louse but every interest in the love triangle. "Tell me more about you and Katrina."

"Well, I went back to London and poured my heart into my work," Bill says. "I interviewed some of the world's greats like Bob Hope and Bing Crosby. I met the Glamour Girls, fashion models at the time. I was there to cover the royal wedding of Queen Elizabeth II and Prince Philip. I had my share of trysts to forget Katrina, but no one captured my heart. If you're lucky, you get one chance to find the great love of your life. You have a better chance of getting kicked to death by a horse while serving in the cavalry than finding your soulmate."

"You and Katrina remain friends?" I ask, already knowing the answer. I finish my champagne, and Bill pours me a little bit of the cabernet sauvignon in a fresh goblet.

"It was easy at first to harden my heart toward her," Bill says, "but then one day, Katrina and Jean-Adrien had a fight, and she called me. I wanted to be there for her as a friend, and since I still held a flame for her, I hoped she'd leave him and come back to me."

"But she stayed with him because of me," Sky says. "Although it's not like I'm still a child. She doesn't need to be tethered to him anymore. Don't get me wrong. I love my father, but he's a pompous, arrogant, narcissistic horse's ass who has no clue how to be a husband or father."

"You both deserved better," Bill says. "Anyway, leave the past where it belongs. It is the present we can control, and the future we can plan."

"Let's talk about you," Sky says. "You are much more interesting."

"Me?" I ask. "You know everything."

"Let's pretend you are on an interview," Bill says, "and Skyler and I are meeting you for the first time."

"Yes, Ms. Le, tell us about yourself." Sky grins and straightens his posture. He clears his throat and tries to look serious.

I play along, mostly for Bill's sake, and hope to impress him. "I from Vĩnh Bình in the Bạc Liêu Province of Việt Nam. I youngest of seven children. I was math teacher and bank teller, but after war, I sell medicine."

Bill clasps his hands and leans forward, resting his elbows on the table. He nods. "So you were in sales, and you are good with numbers. I like it. Go on."

"I have daughter. She seven year old, and her name Dolly."

"Tell me, Ms. Le," Sky says, "what is your dream job and why?"

I try not to laugh and mirror Sky's professionalism. "Mr. Herrington, my dream be like you and Mr. Cushing. I wish to be important and shaping our future's history. I believe in truth, and my dream job to story-tell the truth so people make right choice for themselves."

"How would you do this?" Bill asks. "Give me an example of when you were able to shape someone's future and help them make the right choice."

"I give two example." I hold up two fingers for a visual. "First, when I was in Sài Gòn, I shape my own future. I get communist soldier help me with license to sell dry foods. I able to go from my village to the city freely. I was friends with his mother, and after she die, I tell him she haunt him if he not help me. So I help him make right choice. I get license, and he sleep peaceful at night."

Bill roars with laughter. "That worked, huh?"

"Oh yes, the Vietnamese believe in ghosts," I say. "So many wars, so many deaths. Our country have many ghosts."

Bill frowns. "What is your second example?"

I smile and bring levity back to our conversation. "Every day, I help my daughter make right choice. For example, I make curry for dinner, but she no want to eat. She say yucky. I tell her people go hungry and die every day so she lucky, but I tell her she no have to eat the curry if she not want. So she go to bed with no dinner. In the morning, instead of Lucky Charms cereal for breakfast, I give her cold curry from yesterday. Oh, Mr. Bill, she cry, but she eat it all. Now, she eat anything I give her."

Sky and Bill burst out laughing. Bill claps his hands and wipes a tear from his eye. People in the restaurant look our way. Some smile, others look confused.

Sky raises his wine glass. "What did I tell you? Let's celebrate."

I raise my wine glass. "I get job?"

"You got the job, Snow." Bill clinks my glass with his. "Congratulations. You not only won our hearts but our respect."

"That fun," I say. "What else?"

"Bill," Sky says, "I don't think she understands what just happened. You better tell her."

"Snow," Bill says, "I am pleased to offer you a real job with the *Seattle Times*. We have a media coordinator position open that reports up to me, and it is yours if you want it."

"What?" I yell loudly. More heads turn, and one man gives me a demeaning stare, but I do not care. I lower my voice to a whisper. "Really?" They both nod. "What I have to do?"

We discuss the details of my job over dessert, and I agree to start the following week at $4.25 an hour. Sky insists on taking me car shopping and does not take no for an answer. I promise to pay back the loan from the Bank of Skyler.

10. THE THIRD WHEEL (OCTOBER 1981)

School is back in session, and Dolly is in second grade. In the morning, she walks one mile to Springbrook Elementary with Melissa, Jen, Jason, and Hùng. Because Jason is knock-kneed and because they always make a point to stop and pet the horses nearby on the way to school, the group leaves the apartment an hour before the first school bell rings.

Every day at eight in the morning, Hùng and Dolly meet outside and walk to pick up Melissa, then Jen, and finally, Jason. The five of them disperse once they are on school grounds and play with other classmates until it is time to line up, walk to class, and say the pledge of allegiance. By a quarter after four, the kids arrive back home.

It is a battle each morning to get my daughter ready for school. It can be raining, and she will refuse to carry an umbrella. It can be cold and forty degrees Fahrenheit outside, and she insists on not wearing a jacket. I tell her if she gets sick, the American tooth fairy will not visit for fear of germs. When Dolly disobeys me, I take a piece of paper out and write Santa Claus a letter. I never have to write more than "Dear Santa" before she consents to my requests. My child is not an accepting child and challenges my authority most of the time. Currently, she sports a short pixie haircut with a train of hair in the back that looks like a thick shoehorn. The Americans call this style a mullet. I want to cut the tail off, but she will not let me touch it.

This morning is like any other morning. I help Dolly with her backpack and give her a weather report. "I put an umbrella in your backpack. It is supposed to rain later. After school, I want you to come straight home. Do not open the door to anyone. You can watch cartoons for an hour, then cook two cups of rice like I showed you. Do your homework, and when I get home, I can help you."

"I know," Dolly says. "Can you buy more cereal after work?"

"Yes," I say. "I will be home a little after six o'clock. No playing outside, and no friends over. And no going to a friend's house."

"I know," she says.

I kiss her on the cheek. "Have a good day at school. I love you."

"I love you too."

My car is my confidante. I can talk to her or sing with her, and she does not judge. She is my partner in crime, always reliable when getting me to work, keeping me warm in traffic jams, and ensuring I get to the grocery store and home. What freedom and power to have at my fingertips! I slide into the seat of my silver, two-door, 1980 Honda Civic hatchback. As I wait for the engine to warm up and the windows to defrost, my thoughts drift to Tree. We used to be close. We used to rely on each other because life depended on it. And while I knew in my mind that he'd detach from me like Velcro one day, my heart is not ready. I miss him and look forward to talking to him later today.

It is foggy this morning. I push the cassette tape into the stereo and listen to Lionel Richie and Diana Ross proclaim their endless love. The drive to downtown Seattle is relaxing. There is little traffic since it is Friday. I pull up to the corner of John Street and Fairview Avenue to admire the three-story art deco building. I cannot believe I work here and wonder if Jean-Adrien would approve of the reinforced concrete and Indiana limestone office building. It was renovated two years ago and takes up the whole city block in the South Lake Union neighborhood.

I walk to the ornate aluminum gate, decorated with patterns of spirals, florals, and octagons. Above the main entrance, the newspaper's name is etched into the stone. I walk inside to the lobby, where the walls are made of tan Botticino marble and the floors are in a terrazzo pattern. I breathe in the scent of rubber, ink, and vanilla-scented paper. I am at home.

Bill sits in his office animatedly talking on the phone. He looks up and waves. I smile and wave back. I sit down at my desk, clean and clear except for a personal computer and phone. I stare at my new machine, an IBM PC with its sixteen-bit processor, sixteen kilobytes of memory, two floppy drives, an attached dot matrix printer, and a 720x350 pixel green screen monitor. I turn it on. It beeps good morning to me. I am pleased to have fancy technology at my fingertips. While the machine boots up, I walk to the kitchen to get a cup of coffee.

Bill's assistant, Magdaleine, sits at one of the four-top tables, flipping through *The National Enquirer* newspaper. Her long auburn hair is swept up into a messy bun. She is twenty-four years old with a figure of a model and the emotional intelligence of a dolphin. She is extremely self-aware, knowing her strengths and limitations. As intelligent and perceptive as she is, I question her choice of reading material. Magdaleine is naturally beautiful without makeup but I cannot decide if her fashion sense is outdated or in vogue. Today she sports a chic, button-up, silk gray shirt, untucked over her mustard yellow capris, a tartan plaid print ascot, and burnt-orange loafers.

"Do Bill agree you read that newspaper?" I ask. "We work for *Seattle Times*."

Magdaleine rolls her eyes. "Oh, please. Snow, they are not even in the same league as us. I read for pure entertainment. Hey, do you watch *Dallas*?" I shake my head. "It's a soap opera. You'd like it. Do they have soap shows in Vietnam? Well, Victoria Principle is an actress in the show, and she's dating this singer, Andy Gibbs. Do you know who that is? He's a younger brother of the Bee Gees, only he's not one of the Bee Gees. Anyway, they just released a duet song...Victoria and Andy that is...called 'All I Have to Do Is Dream.' Well, they are going to get married! Imagine that. They are going to have beautiful babies. Andy is so dreamy. Why can't I meet someone like that, with perfect teeth, a sexy accent, and thick hair worthy of running my fingers through? And talent. Where are the men who have talent? I just want to run away to Los Angeles or New York City. Do you ever want to just run away?" I nod. "Me too. I want champagne and caviar, not a Mad Dog 20/20 and ramen life. You know what I mean? I need a raise—"

"Magdaleine," I interrupt her, "take a breath." I laugh. "You talk so fast. I understand half what you say."

She closes the magazine and sips her coffee. "Sorry. You're so easy to talk to. You're a great listener. I'm really glad you're here. We need some diversity around here. Your presence just makes the newspaper more cosmopolitan. How do you like the Pacific Northwest? How's your job going? Everyone treating you all right? You let me know if they're not. That's what I am here for, to straighten everyone out and run this operation like the little general that I am. Is Bill being good to you? I know he can be a hard man to work for, but it's only because he is so damn smart...sometimes too smart for his own good. His mind works faster than his mouth. When he is in meetings with big wigs, he trips over his words, only he's not a stutterer. Anyway, he needs strong women like us to tug at his ego strings and pull him down to earth."

Magdaleine takes another sip of her coffee, and I take the opportunity to speak while she swallows. "I need to find Jerry—"

"In accounting?" she asks. "He's on vaca—"

"No," I interrupt. "Jerry in advertising. He have new advertisements for Sunday's layout."

"Go see the creative team, and then find Allison's desk. I bet you'll find him there. He's been drooling over her. I swear he's going to find his heart in a blender. She is way out of his league. He's such a nice guy, but you know what they say. Nice guys come in last, but I swear, if I find out she's double-dipping here with both Jerry and Ted, I'm gonna—"

"Okay, thank you," I say and briskly walk away.

"Let's do lunch today," she calls out behind me.

"No can do," I call over my shoulder. "My nephew call me over lunch break." I wave over my head without looking back and leave her to the tabloid newspaper. I round the corner and bump into Bill.

"Good morning, Snow," Bill says. "Have you seen my secretary?"

"Magdaleine in kitchen," I respond. I walk slowly to my desk and hear Bill ask his assistant if she has purchased his ex-wife a birthday gift yet.

"I thought you were going to do it," Magdaleine says.

"If you've made that assumption," Bill says, "then you've already failed me. Please get her something nice."

"There's a new designer that just launched his women's label—"

"Fine. And get yourself something too…my birthday present to you."

The morning goes by quickly as I work on the promotional ads Jerry gave me. At three minutes to noon, my desk phone rings.

"*Seattle Times*," I answer. "Snow speaking."

"It is me." Tree's voice sounds breathy over the receiver.

"Are you well?" I ask. "Where are you?"

"You do not have to worry about me. I am not a child anymore."

"I do not think you were ever a child."

Tree laughs. "I just finished playing soccer with my friends in Renton. I have a job now, but I called in sick today to move into Chú Bình's house near Southcenter Mall. He is one of the people who comes and plays soccer with us. Poor man. His wife left him, and he is all alone."

"What is the job?" I ask.

"A mattress production company. I work in a warehouse and operate the machines that press the foam to make it firm, and then I stuff it by hand to make mattresses. It is nice. No more scraping bubble gum from school desks and walls for me. I make $3.35 an hour now and work only weekdays. I get the weekends to play. There is this Spectrum Nightclub in Kent that is nice. There are a lot of kids my age, all under twenty-one. You would not believe how many Blacks there are. They leave us alone though. It is funny because they are all so big, and my friends and I are small next to them. At school they bully us, but here we dance and play pool together like friendly cats and mice. Everyone has a good time. The club plays rap music and popular songs from Michael Jackson."

"Are you dating anyone?" I ask.

"Not really," he says. "There are always two or three girls who hang around and flirt with me, but I am not interested."

"Be careful," I say. "Your parents are not ready to be grandparents. You're the oldest, and they will expect you to choose wisely and marry properly."

"I know. How is Thủy-Tiên?"

I twirl the telephone cord around my finger and glance at the clock. Plenty of time. "She is very stubborn and independent, like you. She does not want to learn how to read Vietnamese and speaks to me in English. She has new friends at school. One of them is Jackie Osario. I am told she has black hair with bangs, lots of freckles, crooked buck teeth, and walks funny. Then there is Nadirah Ahmad from Saudi Arabia, who is tall and has a birthmark on her face. I tell you, Thủy-Tiên is becoming Americanized so fast, especially with this terrible hairstyle she has now. It is short like a boy's haircut but long in the back. I am going to cut it when she is asleep. It is not becoming of a proper girl."

Tree chuckles. "Aunt Eight, you are brave. She was born the year of the wood tiger. If you cut it, prepare to get scratched or bitten."

"Yes, I know. She wanted her hair to look like the mom on the *Brady Bunch* show. Did you know that July is the Leo zodiac? Not only was Thủy-Tiên born a wood Tiger but also a lion. The other day, I witnessed her taking a piece of Ex-Lax and selling it as chocolate for twenty-five cents to her friend Melissa. Imagine, selling a laxative as candy. She is ruthless taking advantage of her friends."

Tree laughs. "Auntie, she hustles like you. What is she doing with the money?"

"I do not know," I say.

"What name is she calling herself now?"

"Chris with a C-H."

"How funny," Tree says. "I better go now. I will call you after I get settled in at Chú Bình's."

We hang up, and I finish my work for the day. Bill has been in meetings all day. I rarely see him, but Magdaleine is good about letting me know when he has a little bit of free time. Before leaving work, she shows me the Saffiano leather wristlet she bought for herself with Bill's credit card. It is cute with its monogram MK design and gold emblem that says *MICHAEL KORS – EST. 1981*.

On my drive home, I stop at Safeway to buy cereal for Dolly. I still cannot get over how big the indoor grocery stores are and how wide the aisles. I pay with my food coupon and drive the two blocks home. As I pull into Homestead Apartments, I see my daughter wave to Jen and scramble up the stairs to our apartment. My face flushes red from the warm heat of anger brimming to the surface. She knows I do not want her playing outside after school when I am not home. I need to teach her a lesson and not be so lenient with disciplining her.

I get out of the Honda and step over the parking curb. The rain from this afternoon has left the sidewalk slick. I slip and fall to the ground, scrape my knee, and rip a hole in my pantyhose. There is a small scratch on my new black boots I purchased from Payless ShoeSource.

"Are you hurt, Mama?"

I look up to see Dolly looking down at me from the bedroom window. "I am not hurt."

Inside the apartment, I smell the aroma of white rice. Dolly runs to me and wraps her thin arms around me. She tells me to take off my shoes. I unzip my boots and kick them off. Dolly takes the plastic grocery bag and checks to see which cereal I brought home. "Oh, Cap'n Crunch. And there is a toy inside." She opens the box before I can stop her and drills her fist to the bottom of the bag to find the toy.

"Thank you for making the rice," I say. "What did you do today after school?"

Dolly crunches on her cereal and examines the tattoo sticker she dug out of the box. "I watched Scooby-Doo and cooked rice. I did my math and reading homework. I played with my Barbie doll and sewed her a new skirt."

"You did not go outside?" I ask. I narrow my eyes keenly and observe her face closely.

She looks at me and shakes her head with a smile. "No, you told me not to. Melissa and Jen wanted to play but I said I could not."

"Are you telling the truth?" I ask.

"Yes."

"I saw you run inside right before I came home. You were with Jen. You disobeyed me, and now you are lying to me." My daughter's lips quiver, but I hold firm. "What if you got hurt? Or kidnapped?" She shrugs her little shoulders. "Go get the yardstick."

Salty droplets bubble up in her eyes and shimmy down her cheeks. Her sobs get louder as she walks to the hallway closet to get the wooden stick. Dolly lies down on the floor on her stomach with her arms by her side. This is not the first time she has been spanked for being defiant or naughty. She clenches her butt cheeks. It pains me to discipline her this way, but this is what my parents and grandparents did when we were insolent kids. They believed a spoiled child would dishonor the family and become a menace to society. Perhaps that generation believed it was their job to rule by fear.

92

My father used to inflict pain on my brothers with a long, dried bull's penis, which was both sturdy and flexible. Brother Seven used to say the rod smelled like stale jungle water and stung like a colony of giant honeybees. The Việt Cộng used these Asian bees as weapons during the conflict, relocating hives to enemy trails and attaching firecrackers to the honeycombs.

I raise the yardstick above my head and give Dolly's bottom a hard whack. She shrieks in pain. The stick comes down a second time, and she yelps. I raise it a third time but cannot bear to inflict more pain on my child. She has been through so much already since the day she was born. Do American parents spank their children? I wonder. Why am I hurting my child? Am I crushing her spirit and hardening her heart by striking her? I make a vow to discipline her in other ways, to be fair, and to counter her rebelliousness with love.

I put the yardstick down and scoop her into my arms. "I think that is enough spanking. Did you learn your lesson?"

"Yes," she whispers. "I am sorry."

"Sorry for what?" I ask.

"For lying and not obeying you," she says. "I will be good. Please do not write to Santa."

I hug her tight and kiss her forehead. "I will not tell Santa. I am sorry for hurting you, and I think we both learned a lesson today."

I rock her in my arms until her sobs subside, and she exhales deeply.

My eyes are dry and itchy. I flutter my lids to alleviate the burning. I have not been sleeping well lately. Most nights I think about all the tasks waiting for me at work, and during the day I worry about how Tree and Dolly are adjusting to American life. I lie down on the couch and drape my forearm across my face, letting the push and pull of my hypnagogic thoughts battle between insomnia and slumber.

An image of Dolly walking down the aisle on her wedding day lures my conscious mind to enter the dream state. I lean in and fall weightlessly until I see the Galang Refugee Camp transformed into a botanical garden in the middle of an evergreen forest. A dusting of snow cascades softly to the ground. I am in Đà Lạt, but it is not the same city I remember when I was a math teacher there. This Đà Lạt is more like heaven because all my family and friends are there, smiling and happy. Thủy-Tiên is beautiful in her traditional red áo dài dress and gold lace robe. My American and Vietnamese families are all there as well as my family from trawler 93752 and the camp. I strain to see the face of Thủy-Tiên's groom. It eludes me at first but soon comes into focus. Minh-Hoàng! His smile is sinister. *"No!"* The reflection in his eyes is a self-portrait, and I stumble back, realizing it is me getting married. I look around the room. Minh-Hoàng's brother, Lopsided, and their she-Jekyll mother laugh at me. All the men who have loved me are there— Ommo, Tý, and Sam. They look sad, disappointed, and in pain. I run and trip on the train of my garment, only it is now a white wedding gown. Hands, hundreds of hands, grab, pull, and scratch me. Hải and Tâm wrap their arms around me. I cannot breathe. Cường, Dr. Nguyễn Văn Đức, his wife, and my neighbors in Vĩnh Bình are chasing after me. They want something from me. I cannot escape! I see my chicken and follow her, but I cannot catch her. I call out to her. "Mông Dơ!" Her little legs pick up speed, and she runs faster until her head falls off. It rolls to my feet. Her black beady eyes condemn me to hell.

I wake from the nightmare with a jolt; a residual tingle of electric currents sends shockwaves down my spine to my toes. I abandoned and betrayed them all. I failed them. I am here…free, alive, safe, and without hunger. How do I expiate this guilt?

Sleep comes in crumbs these past few days. My dreams intertwine like pretzels and I cannot make sense of them. I decide it is best to forget. I have an unhappy child at the moment who demands my sympathy.

The people here in America have a strange holiday custom on October 31. Children and adults dress in costume and demand candy from their neighbors, chanting, "Trick or treat. Smell my feet. Give me something good to eat." Last year, Dolly was too frail and scared to go out at night and knock on strangers' doors. It was cold, and I would not allow it. Instead, we stayed at home and handed out candy with Teddy and Catherine. This year, however, she has no fears about knocking on doors and asking for chocolates. No doubt, she will turn around and sell those to her friends at black market prices.

My daughter steps out of the bedroom in full costume, looking like a melting wax figure from a horror museum. "This mask is hot and sticky, and it smells bad."

"You chose it," I say. "It is plastic, so you will be hot, but it will feel better in the cold air outside." Her cheap, store-bought costume crinkles when she walks, and the Wonder Woman mask is grotesquely large over her small frame. "I offered to sew you something this year. I am getting better at it."

Dolly tugs at her mask. "But Melissa is going as Batgirl and Jen is going to be Supergirl."

We exit the warm apartment into the chill of October, crossing the threshold into another dimension where little princesses, superheroes, and goblins roam the streets. We knock on our neighbor's door.

Diệp opens the door. "Ah, alô Chị Tuyết."

My jaw drops. She is wearing a wiry orange wig, a big yellow pajama suit with sleeves, and knee-high socks in stripes of red and white. Her face is painted white and where her eyebrows should be, there are two thin black arches drawn in. Her nose is red and she has smeared bright red lipstick all over her mouth up to her cheeks.

I burst out laughing. "Diệp, why are you in costume?"

Dolly hums the McDonald's tune. "Baba bum bum bum."

"It is Halloween. Where is your costume?" Diệp asks. "I am the clown from McDonald's."

"I see that. Halloween is for children," I say.

"If you want to stay young, Sister, you need to do as the children do. Play, dress up, and use your imagination," she says. "I made this myself. Do you like it?"

"I love it," Dolly exclaims. "What is Hùng dressed as?"

Hearing his name, he jumps out from behind the door. He looks incredibly adorable. His costume complements his mother's.

"I am a Big Mac," Hùng says.

Dolly and he say in unison, "Two all-beef patties, special sauce, lettuce, cheese, pickles, onions, on a sesame seed bun." They giggle.

It dawns on me that McDonald's is my daughter's second brand recognition with 7-Up being the first. The four of us walk down the steps and pause to take in the scene. Under the bright moon, children and their parents jabber about which home to hit and who gives out the best candy.

We spot Donald and his son. I wave to them, and we walk toward one another. Donald looks handsome in his black suit and cape. I conclude he is a butler superhero. Little Jason is dressed in a shaggy carpet thing with a plastic mask that looks like an angry dog. His costume confuses me.

"Wow, that's a great costume," Donald says to my neighbor. He smiles and shows his fangs. Ah, you are Dracula!

I introduce Donald to Diệp, who gives him a big smile and sheepishly looks down, clearly shy and enamored by his vampire good looks. I giggle silently, thinking how ridiculous and hideous Diệp looks with her clown costume. The two of them stand awkwardly looking at each other, smiling and trying to communicate with one another in two different languages. Diệp just smiles and nods. I have seen this look before when there is a mutual attraction between two people.

"What is your costume, Jason?" Dolly asks.

"Chewbacca," he says. "You know, a Wookiee from *Star Wars.*" He lifts his head as if to howl at the moon but instead lets out a low-pitched, moaning gurgle and tongue trill that sound like a wounded monster in distress. We all have a good laugh at his strange noises.

We head out together, going door to door, building to building. Every once in a while, Jason grunts and gurgles, and we are amused at how he stays in character.

I eavesdrop on Donald's and Diệp's conversation. I was going to offer to translate for them, but they seem to be doing fine on their own.

"So, Yip," Donald says, "Do you like America?"

Diệp smiles and nods. She answers in Vietnamese. "Amer-rica đẹp quá nhưng không đẹp như bạn." *America is beautiful but not as beautiful as you.*

"Diệp," I say, "you are speaking so boldly."

She laughs at me. "He does not understand me, so what does it matter?"

"Do you understand what he is saying?" I ask.

"Only a little," she says. "Let me have my fun."

"Now I feel like the third wheel," Donald says. I give him a curious look. "Third wheel... it means I don't belong, like a bicycle that does not need an extra wheel."

"But three wheel safer. You here with us, make us safer."

Donald laughs. "Like a tricycle, which is a bicycle with three wheels."

We continue our trick-or-treating and along the way meet up with Melissa and Jen by the Cascade Apartments complex. The girls are chaperoned by Melissa's parents. Tony, Melissa's stepfather, has his thick, black hair tied back in a loose ponytail. His mustache is thick with a touch of gray. He wears jeans and a black leather jacket. A portion of his suncatcher tattoo peeks above his white crew neck cotton shirt. His smile lights up his eyes and twinkles under the street lamp.

Melissa's mother, Stephanie, is a slender woman with green eyes and the perfect cleavage, her firm bosom pushed together showing only an inch of smooth flesh above the V-neck sweater. She is fair. Her skin creamy vanilla and her hair strawberry blonde. We walk behind them, and I take the opportunity to study them from behind. They walk with ease alongside one another. The two lovers hold hands and talk like best friends. They laugh and tease as if they are young teenagers in love.

Melissa holds her stepdad's hand. "Tony, once you adopt me, will that make me Cherokee too?"

"If you can master the Iroquoian language of the Tsalagi people, you will be more Cherokee than me, little Lissa."

"What's important," Stephanie adds, "is that we are a family, no matter what blood runs through our veins."

By eight-thirty a few droplets of water sprinkle from the sky, and we rush back to Homestead Apartments. Stephanie and Tony invite us to their apartment for hot chocolate. I decline, but the children beg to go, and even Diệp agrees wholeheartedly.

"If I did not know better," I say to Diệp, "I would think you are prolonging the evening to spend time with Donald."

Donald's ears perk up at the mention of his name. "Are you talking about me? That's not fair. Good things I hope."

Tony and Stephanie's apartment is spotless; everything is neatly arranged and color-coordinated in shades of teal and copper. The walls are adorned by both minimalistic artwork and avant-garde paintings, two styles that clash and yet work together to complement the décor, similar to how Stephanie and Tony seem to clash from outward appearances but work so symbiotically well together.

"Anyone want my peanut butter cups?" Dolly asks. "It is full size."

Hùng snatches her Reese's candy. "Me."

My daughter slaps his hand. "What will you trade?"

"My Gobstopper."

"What else?" she asks.

"What do you mean, 'what else'?" Hùng asks. "Gobstoppers last longer than chocolate and peanut butter cups."

My daughter ignores him. "Jen, do you want my peanut butter cups?"

Jen tosses her a Kit Kat, Whoppers, and Tootsie Pop. She takes Dolly's full-size candy. The two of them are satisfied with the trade, and poor Hùng is left wondering what just happened.

While the children sort and trade their sweet treasures, Donald and Diệp sit on the couch and duct tape words together to formulate a conversation. Tony and Stephanie are in the kitchen making hot chocolate and flirting. I feel like the third wheel now. My thoughts drift to Skyler and Tree, wondering how they are spending their night. I am in a room full of people yet feel lonely. Somewhere in Texas, Tý is probably enjoying Halloween festivities with his American wife and son. I wonder if he and Annette have more children and if he thinks of Thủy-Tiên and me.

"You're a million miles away." Stephanie hands me a cup of hot chocolate. "What were you thinking about?" She sits down on the carpet with me while Tony lies down on his side and props his head on his hand.

"Maybe the question is 'who are you thinking about'?" Tony says. "Where is Chris's father?"

"Chris?" I ask, temporarily forgetting that my daughter is going by that name at the moment. "Oh, you mean Dolly. Her father live in Texas. We separate in 1975. Long story."

We spend the next hour getting acquainted. I give everyone a synopsis of what brought us to Seattle and how we got here. By the end of the night, I did not feel like the third wheel anymore nor did I feel lonely. A new community is forming tonight in Tony's and Stephanie's living room.

11. PINKY PROMISE (NOVEMBER 1981)

Dear Eight,

It was good to receive your letter. I have to start by saying that Tâm is home! Little Sister, my poor Tâm has been through so much! She has been starved, beaten, humiliated, and shuffled around from one prison to another, but she crawled her way home. I did not even recognize her. Five years! It is as if she came back from the dead, frail, ghostly thin, with lesions, scars, and open wounds. She is missing teeth, fingernails, and hair, but worst of all, she has lost the light in her! My heart is at the bottom of the ocean floor.

It is bad here. People are still flocking to new lands and risking their lives to leave the country. I dare not think about their fate. The family is getting by. We do our best to oblige under the new regime and stay under the radar. Thắng and I are doing the best we can. Send money when you have a job. Maybe you can find a way to sponsor the children in America. I do not want them to grow up here. Brother Seven and Hiền were right to send Tree with you.

We started a money pool, and your brother-in-law and I are in charge of the hui. There are seven of us in the lending circle, including Thủy and Doctor Đức and our neighbors Tú and Vân. We each put in fifty-thousand đồng each month. Hiền was able to start her fabric shop with the 350,000đ hui money, and Brother Seven still drives his truck every morning. I wish you could see the dresses Hiền makes. They are almost as good as Thủy's!

The children are back at school, but I am not sure how much they learn. It is all propaganda. I know this because Trinh comes home singing praise to Hồ Chí Minh, and Tuấn believes Tâm and Hải were traitors because they spoke ill about the government and supported "the enemy." And no, I have not heard any news about Hải. It is best to forget him and move on. He would want you to. If he is not dead already, then he is nothing more than a worthless man begging to die. I know that sounds harsh, but a man who survives the re-education camp and loses everything will not feel like a man again.

Thủy and Doctor Đức are doing well and are pregnant! Can you believe it? They are going to have a baby, after all these years! What a miracle. Thủy's tailoring business has picked up. I hope to afford one of her tunics or áo dài one day, although Hiền is becoming quite the seamstress too. Doctor Đức's practice is also good, but his patients pay him with fruits and vegetables. He is still peddling his bananas on his cyclo and now peddles the other fruits he receives from his patients.

I am happy to hear Thủy-Tiên is doing well in school and making friends. I do not know how I feel about her speaking only English…maybe it is a good thing to immerse herself wholly into the new society so she can thrive. Do not be too harsh with her. America, not Việt Nam, is her home and the only one she will truly remember. You need to make America your home too. The Việt Nam we knew no longer exists. Do not give up on Tree. He is a good boy who is learning how to be a man without his father or his uncle to teach him. He is far from home, but give him time to figure things out, and he will come back to what matters most—family.

So you are learning how to cook? That must be a disaster, but sandwiches are a good start. Remember when Tâm brought home hot dogs and bacon for Christmas dinner? If that is American food, then you should have no problem learning to cook. Their food is not as delicious and delicate as ours. I heard a saying once from the Americans…You are what you eat. That makes us delicate and delicious and them greasy and stuffed with leftover, mashed up meat. Maybe that is the secret why Westerners are so big.

I hope your neighbor, Diệp, is a good friend and sister to you. Is she a good cook? In my mind, I imagine she has replaced me as your sister, but remember, I am still your favorite. It is good she and I are separated by land and water because I would sink her in a cooking competition. I hope this letter gets to you. I do not know how much the government regulates our mail, whether they check everyone or randomly. I will take my chances. I am testing a new recipe for egg noodle soup with char siu pork. Ingredients are hard to find and expensive when I am lucky enough to find them. When it is my turn to receive the hui money—I am last because I own the hui and since there are seven of us in it, I have to wait until the seventh month—I will open a small restaurant and serve egg noodle soup with pork or duck. It will be the only thing on the menu, but it will be the best.

One last thing. Tý has written. He sent us money. I gave him your address. Do not be mad. It is too late to be mad. What has happened, happened, and we cannot undo the past. I cannot glue the chicken's head back on after it has been chopped off any more than you can go back in time to save your soldier, Sam. Tý wants to take care of you and his daughter. Let him carry this burden for you.

Until better times, do not burn anything and stay safe. Promise with your pinky to me. Remember that I love you, little Eight. There, I said it.

Your favorite sister,
Six

###

The thought of Dolly's father having my address worries me. Will he try to combine our families? I am curious about his life with Annette. What would Dolly think if she knew she had a brother and stepmother? Will she want to live with them? I cannot let them into her life. I will wait to receive Tý's letter and tell him this.

I dial Sky and Katrina's number, waiting patiently for the rotary wheel to return to zero after each digit.

"Hello?" the voice on the other end says. I do not recognize the voice.

"Alô," I answer. "I speak to Skyler please."

"Bonjour, this is Jean-Adrien. Is this Snow?"

"Oui," I answer affirmatively in French, surprised it rolled off my tongue so effortlessly. I have not spoken French in over twenty years. I remember what Sky and Bill told me about Jean-Adrien, and his voice grates my patience into slivers.

"Vous parlez français," Jean-Adrien says. "How wonderful. Your French is perfect."

I frown. I said one word and he thinks my French is perfect. "I prefer English. I speak to Sky now?"

"Bien sûr." I hear the rustle of the phone being placed down and Jean-Adrien calling for Sky. While I wait, I think how rude of him to answer in French even after I tell him I prefer English. I hardly know the man, but his presence makes me feel like my shoes are on backward and I have shown up to a fancy dinner party in my pajamas.

The phone crackles, and Sky's familiar voice caresses my ear. "Hi."

"I receive letter from my sister," I say, not bothering to greet him first. "Dolly father write her. He know where I live. She give him my address. I not want him to come. I worry he and Annette take Dolly or claim me. I not want to be second wife and live with them. I—"

"Slow down," Sky says. "Listen, this is America. He does not own you and can't force you to live with him. Do you want me to come over and we can talk? I can use a friend to talk to right now too. You-know-who is driving me mad."

"Yes," I agree. "I see you soon."

I pour Sky a cup of green tea. He swirls the loose leaves in his cup and watches the tea settle to the bottom of the mug. He looks tired.

"Sky, you not sleep well?" I ask. I sit across from him and touch his hand.

"Where is Dolly?" he asks.

"She play with her friends next door," I answer. "Tell me, you okay?"

Sky sidesteps my question and volleys with his own. "How is your job? Bill treating you good?"

I sigh and give in to his questions. "I not see Bill much, but job and everything good. Bill assistant, Magdaleine, very nice. She help me a lot, and for young person, she very patient. Together, we manage database and make reports for managers and creative team, people in newsroom. They do advertising and circ…circu—"

"Circulation?" Sky asks. I nod. "Any interesting news the reporters are working on?"

"Sky, you not come here to talk about my job," I say. "If Dolly father write and he want to visit, what I do?"

Sky gulps his tea and helps himself to a vanilla wafer. I wait patiently for him to collect his thoughts and offer me advice. "Well, I think you need to face him. You cannot continue to run from him, and he is Dolly's father. He has the right to see her."

I shake my head vigorously. "No. He left us. He give away his rights."

"You let him go, Snow. He tried to take you both out of the country. It was your choice not to go with him." Sky squeezes my hand and lets his fingers linger on mine. "Was it wrong that he didn't tell you about his other wife? Yes. Should he have kept his secrets from you about his mob affiliations? Probably. Look, I know you feel betrayed, and you still harbor anger for him. But maybe this is a good time to start over and forgive him. Your resentment will weigh you down. Imagine how free you will feel if you let go. If he comes, I can be here with you to give you support."

"Words easy to swallow but not easy to digest," I say bitterly. "Maybe you should take advice and forgive Jean-Adrien." I remove my hand from underneath his and cross my arms over my chest. "He trying to be in your life. I see he has regrets."

Sky leans back into his chair. "That's different." His expression is cold and threatening. He purses his lips.

"How it different?" I ask. "You still angry with him. You feel he betray you. He not there for you when you grow up. He not protect you when you need him. He cheat on Katrina. How, Sky? How it different? He throw money at you both, like Dolly father throw money at us, but he still lie to us as Jean-Adrien lie to you."

"At least Ty wants to be in your life and is trying to make amends. He loves you."

"How you know, Sky? You talk to him? You know his heart and believe his stories?" I am angry now. Sky knows nothing.

"My dad is garbage. He's fake. Your husband at least fought for you and used his connections to get you exit visas."

I laugh. "Look at us. We fight for burn rice at bottom of pot. We so hungry for love, for attention. We throw away pride and take leftover of what Tý and Jean-Adrien give us."

"You're right. For a long time, we have accepted their crumbs because we didn't know better."

We sit in silence, each marinating in our own thoughts. Minutes tick by, and Sky is the first to break the silence. "Sometimes I feel like I'm walking between two planes of existence. Not quite dead but not alive either. My feelings get jumbled up like wet jeans spinning endlessly in a wad of bedsheets, trying to get dry but forever damp and rotten. Do you ever feel that way?" I nod. "When I want to laugh, it comes out as cries. When I want to cry, it comes out as laughter. I'm so fucked up. Where's the reset button when you need one? I want to be surrounded by people I love but withdraw because it is easier to be alone. Self-loathing becomes an addiction."

"But when you alone," I say, "the ghosts come to haunt you."

"Yes. And that is when I want more than anything to have someone there to get me through it all. I'm afraid the moment I find happiness, I'll sabotage myself. I shouldn't be alive and happy while Sam and others died a senseless death. You know?"

"What we do now?" I ask.

"I think you need to receive Ty when he writes and wants to visit. You can throw the burnt rice in his face and show him how strong you are, no thanks to him."

"You do same," I say. "You promise with pinky." I offer Sky my small pinky finger and wrap it around his.

"I pinky promise," he says.

"Good, you first. Before Thanksgiving. You make peace with Jean-Adrien. I be there for you if you want."

"I want," Sky says.

12. RETURNING VET'S SAGA (NOVEMBER 1981)

I drive up the familiar stretch of road to Katrina's house, admiring the Pacific dogwood trees that have dropped their leaves but still look regal with the last of their fall foliage. I round the circular driveway and notice the hanging flower baskets have lost their luster. Beneath them, rows of winter heathers catch the fallen petals and welcome the softness of purple pansies.

I turn off the engine and take a deep breath. I am here to support Sky today. It will be a difficult morning for all of us, but I expect it will be emotionally volatile for Sky. I feel drained and taxed already thinking about the conversation ahead. I check myself in the visor mirror to make sure I am presentable. My lips are dry, and my lipstick is cracked at the corners of my mouth. After reapplying a fresh coat of mauve moisturizing gloss, I step out onto the crunchy dirt. The biting Pacific Northwest air forces me to pull my scarf up over my ears and nose.

One more deep breath and I ring the doorbell. I wait, but no one answers the door. I knock hard on the door and wait again.

"Alô?" I open the door and step inside. "Sky? Katrina?" No answer. I feel strange intruding despite being invited. Sky said to come Saturday at ten for brunch. I glance at my watch. I am three minutes early. I hear a voice from the kitchen and follow the sound.

Sky looks up, startled. He is on the phone. "Wait for me in the reading nook," he whispers and points toward the hallway.

Inside my favorite room, I admire the books on the shelves and look to see if there are any new titles. I remind myself to read the book Sky gave me last year. A book catches my eye, and I take it down. *Black Beauty* by Anna Sewell. I thumb through the pages and discover folded sheets of paper tucked inside. Curiosity gets the best of me, and I unfold it carefully. It is a long poem written in cursive. At times the penmanship is artfully and legibly written, but more often than not, the letters trail off. Some of the words slant forward and the ink is smeared as if the poet was angry and crying. I read it.

"Returning Vet's Saga"

On top of the world, I was and a once kind, gentle person was I.
Goals I had and dreams I had, of better things ahead.
No cares did I have and no problems were around,
I was enjoying a life of delight,
With destiny under my control, and me controlling my destiny.
Life was good and it was great to be alive.

Then, one day, a letter I received,
From the President of the U.S. of A. it was sent.
I did not want to go, you know.
In fact I once said, "I would never go!"
But what would I do, what could I do?
I could not say, "Hell, no, I won't go!" as many my age had already made known.

Torn away from the life I had and the life I was building, all on my own.
I went as I was asked, to serve for God, country, and apple pie back home.
My president and government had asked me to go, and I could not say, "No."
It was to protect my family, friends, and to defend my country that I called home.
I was informed I would be fighting against a woeful aggressor
So his deeds would not come to haunt my home!

So I departed and went where I was ordered to go.
Lifelong goals and dreams now shattered they had become.
New ones I would be granted, but simple they would now become.
Exactly what would I be, where would I go, what would I do?
How long would I live and would I ever return?
Questions I had and no answers were there to be found,
I would have to wait to see what the future was for me!

Off to war I went, like so many before and after me.
Leaving family, friends, wives and lovers far behind me.
Young and innocent I was, returning I hoped, but dying I might.
Forgotten I became, unwanted I thought.

Off I went, young and innocent and hardened I became.
That kind, soft, gentle person that once was I,
Now became hard and abrasive and disillusioned was I.

105

A shell I built up, hard as a rock it became, for protection and sanity it was made.

Before, life and dreams had surrounded me,
Now death, hurt, and sorrow are all around me.
If I sleep, would I live to wake? If I woke would I live to sleep?
Alone and helpless I felt, with destiny now dominating and controlling me!

Fear, it became my constant companion and was always with me.
Will relief ever come to me?
Loneliness, so close we became.
Death, I stared it eye to eye, on many occasions, I thought I would say bye!
Only I know how close I really came,
To this day I wonder why I survived, and others did not!
And now I wonder what significance my survival has really meant.

While serving in those foreign waters, a saying was heard over and over:
"Mine was not to reason why, mine was just to do or die!"

While serving family, friends, God, and country in that war-torn land,
Letters I desired, but few I received.
Then one day a letter I received, and it was written to me,
"Dear John, another I have found."
And I thought, "Oh, if only I had stayed, that wouldn't have happened to me."
And I wondered, "Does no one longer care to stick by my side?"

New friends I now gained and buddies we were called and mostly nicknames we had.
Moose, Tiny, Slim, Shorty, Sweet-Pea, Ski, Chicago, Oly, Texas, Buzzard, Doc, and much more.
But how close can I get to someone who is here today, but tomorrow is gone.
How much loss can my mind endure?
How much sorrow can my heart now endure?

Up and awake for a day, two, three, or more, without sleep I went.
I had to stay awake and alert because others depended on me.
And then came their turn, awake and alert they had to be, and now I depended on them.

At times the intenseness was great.
No noise dared I make, and no sound could I utter.

106

Quiet and still I had to remain, all to stay undetected and hidden from those who were around.
This I had to do so another day I could return for more of the same!

A country that loved me I once departed. To countries that hated me I arrived.
Un-liked I was, but never mistreated was I over there.
Then that day arrived, to return to a country that abhorred me back here.
Un-liked, unwanted, and mistreated I now became over here.

Returned, I did and then left alone to recover from the death, hurt, grief, and sorrow.
My stories of woe you did not want to hear.
When I returned, where was the handshake to welcome me back?
Where was the thank you for the job I had done?
Where was the encouragement to move on ahead?
Where was the hug to make me feel loved?

Where were the words, "You're okay and everything will be fine"?
Where were my friends, so many I once had?
Where was the thank you I needed to hear?
Where were the words, the kind words that would do so much good?
Where was the love I so desperately needed?

Where was the job I now needed even more than before?
Why was there no one that to me could say, "I am proud of you for serving!"
And why did no one dare say, "I am glad you survived!"
And why did no one care to say, "I am glad you came back!"
And why was no one so kind to say, "Welcome back home, and we're glad you're back alive!"

Hard it became because work there was none.
"Hire a vet" was the saying heard loud and clear throughout all the land.
But country and men wanted those that had stayed,
But not those who had served in that war-torn land!

It caused me to wonder, "Where would I be, if only I had stayed?"
It made me think, "Where would I be, if served I had not?"
And then I began to ponder, "Who would I be, if only I had stayed?"
And the ringing in my mind became, "What would I be, if served I had not?"

On returning back here, it was angry faces and voices that I found in front of me.

"Baby killer, mother raper" words they scolded and screamed at me.
But such things I had never considered because that really wasn't me.
I only did as I was asked, so why are you scolding me?
Why all the anger that was directed at me?
Didn't they know that if they would have gone, they would be just like me?
Didn't they know "I defended them, so they didn't have to go?"

The war was over for everyone but those that had gone and had fought where they had been.
Give me a chance to forget where I've been.
But country and men would blame us for where we had been.
They blamed us for the problems they were in.

Where was the home I left so long ago? This is not the same as I remember from before.
This was not the home I remember leaving when I went off to war.
Away from home I was taken, and never allowed to return to the home I once knew.
I returned, but it was not to the gentle life I had known before.
Rather, I returned to be scorned and hated by those I had defended.

Then there were the cold sweats and nightmares, almost nightly for many a year.
How do I explain what's happening to me? How do I forget what happened to me?
The tears, will they ever stop, and they start for no reason at all?
Will anyone ever bother to gently wipe a tear from my eye?
Why is it so easy for them to bring tears to my eyes, and they don't even notice?

Oh, if someone would just listen, oh, if someone would try to understand
The hurt I feel, the losses I have endured.
If I talk, who will dare to listen?
If you hear my story of woe, will you kindly listen?
Or will you say, "We've heard that story before?"
And will you add, "You crybabies are all the same. You need to forget and get on with your life."

Now, I need help.
Where is my government when I need them most of all?
I helped them when they needed it!
Who will defend me now, those I once defended?

The medals I wore over my heart while serving,
Have now become a burden my heart is bearing!

The frustration of war was bad,
The frustration of life after war is overwhelming!
Will I ever be taken off the battlefield?

In an instant, immediately I am back to where the danger was!
Reliving those life-threatening situations I once endured.
Again, so close to death I am,
Why am I here? What am I doing? Who cares about me?
No time to think. I must react.
Then the tears come,
And finally, I once again return to the present.

That war-torn, hardened shell, born for protection over there,
Now becomes harder and more battle scarred back here
Because of the war I now fight back over here.

On occasion, I now drift to the place in my mind, where solitude and peace are all around!
A place I have made of what I would like it to be.
A place to retreat when I need comfort and rest!
Only to regretfully return to this place I am now in.

Will I ever recover, fully recover?
Will my hard, outer shell ever soften?
To let that kind, gentle person out,
That is hidden so well?

Will I ever again control my destiny?
Will I ever enjoy that life of bliss I once knew?
Will I ever recover, fully recover?

Will you remember me for what I once was? Or will you remember what I have become?
Will you remember me for what I want to be? Or will you remember what I have become?
Will you remember me for what I could have become? Or will you remember what I have become?
Will you remember me for what I wanted to become?

Or will you remember me for what I really became?

"Snow, what are you doing?" Sky touches my shoulder and turns me around to face him. "You're crying."

My hand trembles as I give Sky the poem. "I sorry. You write poem?"

Sky shakes his head and sighs. "My friend Charlie Peters did." He sits down and stares at Charlie's handwriting. Sky smiles. "I never met anyone who talked as much as he did. His spelling and grammar are shit but man could he tell a story. And his jokes…" Sky chuckles. "So here's a joke he used to tell over and over." Sky puts the letter down. "So an American soldier and a Vietnamese soldier are in the trench together. Neither of them understands the other, so the Vietnamese soldier tries sign language." Sky laughs as he uses his arms to demonstrate. He holds his left forearm parallel to the floor across his chest. "The Vietnamese soldier asks, 'Are you a paratrooper?'" and with his right arm, Sky imitates a tree falling. "'Are you a field runner?'" He uses two fingers from his right hand to demonstrate legs running across the left forearm. "'A gun loader?'" Sky pokes his right pointer finger into a hole formed by his left hand. "'Or a lookout?'" Sky circles his fingers around both eyes like he's looking through binoculars. He slaps his knees. "The American soldier was so freaked out! He jumped out of the trench screaming, 'Help, help, there's a crazy Vietnamese soldier who said, *When the sun goes down and all the people start running, he's going to fuck me until my eyes blow out!*'"

Sky roars with laughter. He leans back and lets out a loud howl. His breathing becomes shallow, and I worry he will choke on his spit. Sky bends forward and clutches my hips. He pulls me hard to him and buries his head into my stomach. He is no longer laughing but weeping uncontrollably. His cries of angst and pain leave me speechless. I wrap my arms around his head and hold him tight.

13. UNTETHERED (NOVEMBER 1981)

We wait for Katrina and Jean-Adrien to come home. Sky pours a glass of bourbon and offers me the drink. I decline. He swallows the shot in one gulp and switches over to scotch. I patiently wait for him to speak. In the past ten minutes, he has aged ten years in my eyes. The character lines on his face are simply wrinkles now. The tear tracks are remnants of the anguish he displayed earlier. His hair is tussled in different directions and is the only visible evidence of distress to the untrained eye. Will Jean-Adrien understand his son's sadness and offer to carry the weight of Skyler's burdens? Will he seek forgiveness for the pain he has caused? Will Katrina recognize her son's cry for help?

"I don't know what I'm going to say to him." Sky puts his scotch down after one sip. "Where do I even start?"

"Ask God be your voice," I say. "He be your eyes…your ears. You only need to ask."

The sound of tires rolling on dry leaves and pebbles signals they are home. The door opens. Katrina and Jean-Adrien laugh. A thud echoes from the hallway, and the sound of only one high-heel shoe clops on the hard flooring. We peek around the corner in time to see Katrina and Jean-Adrien fall to the floor. Their bodies squirm like snakes in heat. Katrina sinks her teeth into her husband's neck while he moans and lifts her skirt and fondles her behind.

Sky slaps his palm against the reading nook doorframe a couple of times. I catch a glimpse of his Adam's apple bobbing up and down. "Bloody hell you two!" He storms toward them and reaches them in four big strides. Katrina and Jean-Adrien scramble up and compose themselves. Sky takes a swing at his father and connects with Jean-Adrien's face.

Jean-Adrien rubs his jaw. "You son-of-a—"

"Careful, Dad," Sky warns him.

The two men lunge at each other like unwieldy dancers vying to lead. Katrina shrieks and tries to break up the fight. She pulls at Sky's arms to hold him back, but she might as well be a gnat pulling on shoelaces. She takes one of her plastic horses—the palomino one—and hits them both on the neck and shoulders.

"What is your problem?" Jean-Adrien yells.

"What is my problem?" Sky asks. "Seriously? You're my problem!" Sky takes another swing and misses. "You spread your butter over every goddamn muffin in town and you think Mom's just another piece of ass. You're a cheating, good for nothing—"

Jean-Adrien tackles Sky to the floor.

"Enough!" Katrina screams. "Both of you!"

The men ignore her plea. Katrina looks at me with helpless, pleading eyes.

I swing open the front door and scream, "Fire! Everyone, fire outside!"

I run outside and halt in front of my Honda Civic. Skyler runs outside with Jean-Adrien right behind him. The two of them look frantically for the smoke and flames. Katrina appears at the stoop, hands on her hips, looking satisfied.

"Where's the fire?" Sky asks. "Are the stables—"

"No fire," I say. "You both cool down outside."

"She's right," Jean-Adrien says. "Why don't we talk like mature men?"

"Yes," Katrina calls from the doorway, "like civilized adults, shall we?"

I take hold of Sky's hand and search for calmness in his eyes. "When I say you make peace with Jean-Adrien, I not mean like this. You pinky promise, remember?"

The muscles in Sky's jaw twitch. His face softens. "All right." He looks past me and points at his father. "You were never around for Mom and me. Instead, you left us with Uncle Dawson, that bastard."

"I was trying to build my career to support—"

"Cut the bullshit. I've had enough of your rotten excuses."

"Son, what my brother did to you—"

"—was my imagination…Yeah, that's what you said, and then you laughed at me for being foolish, as if I misinterpreted his intentions. He fucking had his hands on me for over a year. I was eight! And you…" Sky faces his mother and rolls his eyes. "You slapped me. I kept that secret for ten years, and when I finally told you both, you didn't believe me. That was

112

the send-off I got before my tour. That was the care package I took with me overseas."

Katrina whimpers and covers her face with her hands. Jean-Adrien says nothing. He simply casts his eyes downward. Sky looks at his parents, but neither returns his gaze.

The November chill nips at my skin, and I shiver. Sky notices. He wraps his arm around me. "Let's go."

"No," I say. "You stay. Make peace with them. 'Remember that grit and tenacity will take you far in life, but love and forgiveness will carry you to the finish line.'"

"That's nice," Sky says. "Did you read that somewhere?"

I shrug. "Pastor George tell me. He say have strength."

"Did you have to look in the dictionary to see what 'grit' and 'tenacity' meant?" Sky asks. I nod. He gives me that wonderful smile that only he can radiate. "I'll call you later. Thanks for being here with me."

I leave Sky to tend to his family affairs. In the rearview mirror, I witness Katrina hugging her son.

Sky rings me two days later, but I miss his phone call. His message on my answering machine is brief. He will be gone for another meditation retreat. "You were right, Snow, about love and forgiveness. I need to learn how to love myself again before I have the strength to forgive my parents." I am not to expect him back until Christmas.

I dial Katrina a few times but always receive the same recording. "You've reached the Herrington's. Please leave a message."

I call Catherine and Teddy. After three rings, Teddy answers.

"Alô, Teddy," I say. "How everything?"

"We are having a great time. Toots and I are about to make some chocolate chip cookies with Dolly. Do you want to talk to her?"

Two blinks later, my daughter's voice greets me. We speak for a few minutes with her telling me how much fun she is having this weekend. They baked a pumpkin pie yesterday. She tells me about seeing rabbits in the backyard and how she wants a pet for Christmas.

Eventually, she hands the phone back to Teddy. "What are your plans for Thanksgiving?"

"Teddy?" I ask. "We not do Thanksgiving at Katrina house?"

"Oh." Silence. "I'm sorry. I thought Katrina or Catherine told you. Katrina canceled Thanksgiving. We would host, but Penny and Todd invited us down to Oregon. They had their baby, you know, so we're going to go meet our new grandson." Pause. More silence. "Want anything in Oregon? There's no retail tax there."

"No, thank you," I answer. "And Frances and Frank? They go to Oregon too?

"Nah. They and the boys are staying in Wenatchee. Frank's family is traveling there for the holidays."

"Well," I say, feeling alone, "you and Catherine enjoy. I see you tomorrow. Please kiss Dolly for me and tell her I see her at church."

I collect my coat and knock on Diệp's door. "Diệp ơi, it is Tuyết." Hùng opens the door. "Hello, Auntie."

I hear Diệp's laughter inside and a man's voice saying, "Open wide."

"You have guests?" I ask.

"Yes, Donald is here, and so is Jason. Mom invited them over for dinner."

"Are you their translator?" I ask. Hùng nods. "Have your mom come see me tomorrow."

It is a rare occasion for me to be alone without responsibilities. I do not know what to do with myself. It is too cold to take a walk as nightfall approaches. I can drive somewhere, but where would I go? I return to my apartment and cook a bowl of ramen noodles with poached eggs. Only the slapstick comedy of Lucille Ball and Desi Arnaz keep me from feeling lonely.

I think of Tree and wonder how he will spend the holidays. My mind meanders to Sam, and I remember I have a book to read. I crawl into bed and leaf through the first few pages of *A Separate Reality*. The photo of Sam and Sky bookmarks the Introduction page. On the back of the photo is a handwritten note: *Tuy Hoa, Vietnam 1971. Sergeant Skyler Herrington and Corporal Sam Hammond. US Army, 180th Assault Support Helicopter Company.*

I blink back the tears and read the first page of the book. I reread it two more times and take out a highlighter to mark the words I do not understand. *Yaqui, appellative, denote, fortuitous…* The list goes on and on.

This morning I wake to a November sky that promises sunshine instead of rain. Dressed in my favorite blue skirt with white polka dots and a cream-colored blouse, I float into the church feeling rested and untethered. I arrive in time to see my daughter head off to Bible study with Olivia, Opal, and Ocean. They all wave to me before disappearing behind a curtain.

"Good morning, Snow." Katrina's voice is easily recognizable, but the scent of her perfume is unforgettable—Chanel No. 5.

Katrina hugs me and hesitates to say more. She looks at the door as if expecting someone.

"You see Teddy and Catherine?" I ask.

"Not yet."

I scan the room in search of the Vanzwols but stop when I notice Jean-Adrien approaching us. His eyes lock onto mine. His startling good looks turn me into a mute.

"Good morning," he says. "You look lovely, Snow." I mumble a thank you. "After the service, will you join us for lunch? Kat and I want to clear the air."

"I have Dolly with me," I say.

Katrina waves her hand as if to swat an imaginary fly. "Of course Dolly is invited. Come, let's take our seats. I see Teddy and Catherine in the second row, and it looks like Pastor George is ready."

I sit between Teddy and Jean-Adrien, feeling like a pocketbook nestled between two great volumes of the *Encyclopedia Britannica*. Ten minutes ago I felt optimistic about the day. Now, I fear it will take just one raindrop from the heavens for me to unhinge.

I drift in and out between Pastor George's words, vaguely hearing something about a crushed spirit. "So as we let those words from Psalm 34:18 rest on our lips, let us savor the meaning, for the Lord is nigh unto them that are brokenhearted and saveth those whose spirit is contrite. Let us pray."

I say goodbye to Teddy and Catherine who are driving to Oregon after Pastor George's sermon. I follow behind Katrina and Jean-Adrien in my car, with Dolly begging from the back seat to sit in the front.

"When can I?" she asks.

"Maybe when you are ten years old," I say. "You have some growing to do."

"Can I have this car when I am old enough to drive?"

"Yes."

"Promise you will not sell it?"

"I promise."

I pull into a parking spot in front of a French bakery and take Dolly's hand. We follow Katrina and Jean-Adrien inside. The bakery is small and seats about a dozen patrons. The décor is in colors of blue, white, and red—colors of the French flag. Hanging on the walls are paintings from local artists. The smell of coffee and pastries seduces me to the display case where macarons, beignets, chou à la crèmes, and viennoiseries tempt me.

"I want the cream puffs, Mama." Dolly cannot contain her excitement. "And that." She points to the crème brûlée. "We can share."

"The maître pâtissier here is a friend of mine," Jean-Adrien says. "You both are in for a treat."

We sit down and order from the simple menu. I choose the crab bisque, Katrina orders a quiche, and Jean-Adrien opts for their charcuterie board. Dolly wants French fries, or steak frites, as they are called.

I dive into the heart of the conversation and skip the formalities. "Teddy tell me no Thanksgiving together this year. You cancel. Why?"

"After last week's incident, Sky took off to California for another silent retreat," Katrina answers. "He gave us a lot to think about and we've decided to do a couples retreat. We want to work on our marriage and be a family again."

Jean-Adrien looks at Katrina with genuine love and admiration. "It is going to take time to strip away all those years of grime...layers upon layers of selfishness and disillusionment."

"Snow," Katrina says, "we have you to thank for helping us realize we've been in a fog all these years, but we are starting to see now. After you left, Sky broke it down for us."

"And we listened," Jean-Adrien says. "He opened our eyes to his pain, his suicidal thoughts—"

Katrina wipes a tear from her eyes. "What kind of mother doesn't protect her son? He was always a loving child, wanting to help and please others. Even after the molestation incident, and even though he built this wall around him so others couldn't get in, he still offered himself to others. He has this innate desire to serve and give."

"He was the kid who helped carry in the groceries and said 'please' and 'thank you,'" Jean-Adrien says. "In some ways, the draft was a good thing for him. As Skyler got older, he engaged in self-destructive behavior, always angry and drinking to blackout mode. He'd get pissed off at the littlest things, punching holes in doors and walls. The army provided discipline and structure. The war though...it messed him up bad."

I take a sip of my coffee and am pleasantly surprised at how delicious and strong it is. "That good," I say.

Jean-Adrien and Katrina look offended. "The coffee so good, not the war." They nod and smile. "When I meet Sky first time in Tuy Hòa, he scare me. He so mad. A boy steal his gas can and windshield wipers from his truck. And he yell so much at the boy sleeping in his truck. He supposed to watch the truck so no one steal it."

Katrina smiles. "He told us that story. That's how we learned about you and your niece...and Sam."

A lump forms in my throat, and I swallow hard. I refuse to let the mention of Sam's name continue to affect me so deeply. It is the past. I steal a steak frite from Dolly's plate. She is content eating her fries and cream puff while coloring in her book.

"Sam's death was very hard on Sky," Jean-Adrien says. "What little joy Skyler had in his life died that day. And when he came back, he was worse than when he left. It didn't help that people spat on him and threw eggs at him. He took up LSD and heroine for a while but managed to quit cold turkey."

"That was rough." Katrina shudders at the memory. "Anyway, we all agreed to work on our dysfunctional selves so we can be a family again. We're going to get some counseling."

"And maybe Miss Cunningham here will shed her maiden name and be a Mrs. Herrington again," Jean-Adrien says. He winks at his wife and squeezes her hand.

"I believe," Katrina says, "that if Mr. Herrington can be faithful and true, I will let him be a Mr. Cunningham." She winks back.

The next hour goes by quickly as we share our opinions about food and culture. Dolly tells us that 7-Up is still her favorite soda but she likes hot chocolate too. This Christmas she is asking Santa for a pet, but she is not sure yet what she wants. She has to think about it.

14. LIFE CHOICES (SUMMER 1982)

Dolly plays with her friends in the living room while I fix them peanut butter and jam sandwiches. We have the television on in the background so that we can learn English.

Tree is here visiting with his new girlfriend, Ngọc. She is a sweet girl who grew up on the island of Phú Quốc. She spent her youth working to survive the war, helping her mother sell fruits, vegetables, and herbs at the market. The family was so poor that they sold her younger sister, Ann, to a husband and wife in a nearby hamlet. The husband and wife were childless, and the wife was disabled; she needed help cooking and cleaning around the house. The husband became a trader, like me, who sold items on the black market.

"After we lost our country, I ran to fetch my sister and steal her back," Ngọc says. "My mom did not want to leave without her. Ann had become attached to her new parents and I had to drag her home. It was traumatizing for both of us. She kicked and scratched and bit me most of the way. She cried and cried, would not speak to me for days except to scream how much she hated me."

"And now?" I ask.

"As long as we do not talk about it, we are fine," Ngọc says. "She lives in Everett now with her boyfriend."

Something on the television catches my attention. I hear the reporter say something about Green River. Can they be talking about my college where I take classes? Tree turns up the volume.

"The body of a young woman floating in the Green River was discovered on August 12 by Frank Linard. The remains of twenty-three-year-old Debra Lynn Bonner, a prostitute who disappeared on July 25, were found yards from a Kent slaughterhouse where Frank works. Further investigation links the Bonner killing to two other cases, that of Wendy Coffield and Leann Wilcox, both known prostitutes. Police believe they have

118

a serial killer on the loose targeting young women who are soliciting sex along the Pacific Highway. We will continue our coverage on the Green River Killer as new evidence arises."

"What is it?" Tree asks. I tell him about the murders. Tree and Ngọc urge me to quit my sewing and cooking classes at the college.

"The killer is targeting teenagers who are sex workers," I say.

"Aunt Eight, promise me you will drop your classes."

"He is right," Ngọc says. "Anything can happen. I heard there was another serial killer from here. His name is Ted Bundy, and he was arrested four years ago for raping and killing women. They were college students, not prostitutes."

"All right," I agree. "I will withdraw from Green River College. My newspaper is going to be busy covering this killer."

My response satisfies Tree and his girlfriend. We pack up the sandwiches and grab the sodas, potato chips, and fruits and head outside for a picnic. Behind our apartment is the community room where the neighborhood summer potluck takes place. Donald sets up a sprinkler system while his son Ricky, home from college for the summer, lays down a sixteen-foot Slip 'N Slide for the children to play. It is a glorious summer day—not a cloud in sight and nothing but blue sky above.

Ngọc spreads our blanket next to Donald's under a young cherry blossom tree. Jason runs over to join Dolly, Melissa, and Jen.

"Jason, sit next to me," my daughter commands.

I listen to Dolly boss her friends around and rip them off with the candy exchange. I do not know whether to be proud or concerned.

"Melissa, you owe me five cents," Dolly says.

"I do not."

"Yah hah, you do," Dolly says. "Remember? I gave you my Haw Flakes."

"But I gave you a turn on my big wheel," Melissa argues. "And I shared my popsicle with you."

I interrupt their childish argument. "It looks like Donald and Ricky are done setting up. Go play in the water."

Tree, Ngọc, and I content ourselves with watching the kids jump through the sprinklers and slide down the wet, plastic sheet. Donald and Ricky offer us some watermelon, and I offer them pears. Diệp is not with Donald and I wonder if their romance ended. I open my mouth to ask, but who should appear fifty yards away?

Diệp walks toward our group, her hips swaying back and forth to accentuate her figure. She wears a yellow one-piece bathing suit with green stars, looking like a moldy banana. Where does she buy her clothes? The

119

large straw hat and brown sunglasses give her a Hollywood vibe if one can look past her neon green flip-flops and long tropical palm tree and flamingo-print shirt. She waves. Donald and I wave back. Hùng runs ahead and joins the children at the sprinklers. Diệp sits down and wedges herself between Donald and Ngọc.

"Why are you wearing a swimsuit?" I ask Diệp. "You are not joining the children, are you?"

She shrugs. "It looks fun." She dismisses me and analyzes Ngọc. "Who are you?"

"This is Ngọc," Tree says. "She—"

"Girlfriend?" Diệp asks.

Tree nods. "She lives in West Sea—"

"Where are your parents?" Diệp dismisses my nephew. "Any siblings?"

"Yes," Ngọc answers. "My sister lives in Everett and my parent—"

"Where are you from?"

"Phú Quốc."

"Island girl, I see," Diệp says. She squeezes Tree's cheeks as if he were a toddler. "And where have you been?"

Tree explains that he has been living with a man named Bình, whom he met on a soccer field, and whose wife left him.

"My mom and Mr. Bình are friends," Ngọc explains. "He came over to our house one day, and Tree was with him. It was fate for us to be together."

"Actually," Tree says. "it is your mom's egg rolls that draws me."

Ngọc playfully punches him and pouts, pretending to be offended.

While Diệp interrogates Tree and Ngọc, Donald strikes up a conversation with me. He scratches his head and asks, "How do you pronounce Tree's girlfriend's name?"

We have a good laugh over his attempt. He puffs his cheeks out to form the proper sound but the closest he comes is "nop."

Ngọc interjects. "You call me Kelly."

Donald looks relieved. "Good, because this old dog can't learn new tricks. I thought I'd have to avoid saying your name forever."

Tree tells us the two of them go to Spectrum Nightclub often. Apparently, according to Kelly, my nephew has a trail of admirers there.

"We plan on moving in together after he gets a job," Kelly says. "I can keep an eye on him every day."

"What happened to your mattress job?" I ask.

"The company moved, then work was slow, so they laid me off," Tree says. "If my English were better, maybe they would have kept me."

"You were fired?" I ask. "And your parents? Ngọc, are they fine with you two moving in together?"

Tree shifts his weight and takes a bite of his sandwich. He sits up straight and gazes at the children. Neither of them answers my question. Kelly takes a sip of her cola and jabs Tree in the arm.

"Well?" I ask.

Tree takes a deep breath. I have never seen him this nervous. "I asked her parents for her hand in marriage."

I stop chewing and stiffen my posture. Donald and Diệp make their escape and spring up to join the children in the sprinklers. I toss my pear down. "You are too young—" I stop myself and try not to lecture them. "What did your parents say?"

"My father does not agree to the marriage," Kelly says, "but my mother said it was up to me to choose my husband. She said I am to make my own life choices, and if I am either lucky or miserable, then it is my choice."

The rest of our afternoon is pleasant but a little awkward. I make a conscious effort not to impose my opinions and to be supportive. The last thing I want is to drive Tree away. Kelly's mom is right; they have to make their own life choices and handle the outcome of those choices. I cannot wait to write Brother Seven.

This summer has gone by slowly. Tree still checks in every once in awhile, but he and Kelly have not visited. Dolly spends most of her days playing outside and has a social network of friends. They spend a lot of time in the brush between the parking lot and the elementary school on the other side of the intersection, building forts and playing chase or cops and robbers. The blackberry thickets do not bother her. Bumps, scratches, and bruises are standard badges in her repertoire. Strangers who meet her mistake her for a boy. Her dark, dirt-smudged face and rigid way of walking make me feel like I have a son. Teddy says she is a tomboy and not to worry. I miss the sweet little daughter who liked cuddling with me and playing with my hair. She now has her own bedroom, having taken over Tree's old room, and spends a lot of time on the phone with Jen, gossiping about Melissa and Hùng being boyfriend and girlfriend.

Dolly sports a rat tail now, a hair trend worse than the mullet she had ten months ago. Gone are the frilly dresses and here to stay are T-shirts and shorts or jeans. Her dolls are put away in the closet and have been replaced by a skateboard. Tree's velvet posters of cobras and dragons remain on the walls. She says it makes her room feel like she's in the *Secret of NIMH* movie. Lately, the kids rotate houses to play in, deciding which house based on who is serving the best dinner that evening. Tony and Stephanie usually win. Dolly argues that Donald cannot cook, Diệp's food is stinky, and my cooking is weird. Oddly, she never says anything about Jen's parents, and I still have not met them. Jen is usually with my daughter and rarely home.

A new convenience store is being built across from the Safeway store. The children are happy they will be able to buy junk food at Circle K without crossing the street, but they are upset to lose the wooded area past the parking lot. Bulldozers are coming next weekend.

I take out my book, *A Separate Reality*, and pick up where I left off. Half the book is highlighted in yellow. There are too many words beyond my comprehension. I glance at the framed photo of Sam and Sky and wish I were in Sam's arms, listening to his voice. He had promised to read this to me.

After two pages of reading, highlighting, and referencing the dictionary, I give up. "Thủy-Tiên ơi?" I call out to Dolly, but she does not answer. I remember she is outside playing, but it is getting dark. The street lamps are lit. I open the window and call out to her. I hear a scream. My stomach somersaults to my throat. I recognize that scream.

Dolly runs out from behind the bushes. Hùng chases her. He is holding a stick with a snake draped around it. He flicks his wrist and sends the snake hurling at my daughter. It lands on her shoulder. She shrieks and brushes the serpent off her arm. She flails her arms and jerks her body like she has fire ants crawling up her legs. The snake falls to the ground but does not slither off. It is not alive. She kicks it for good measure.

"I hate you!" Dolly charges at Hùng. "I hate both of you!"

Hùng and Melissa laugh and run off together while holding hands. I call out to my daughter. She halts and looks at me, then runs to our apartment. I hear her bound up the stairs; urgent, heavy footsteps quickly spill into the hallway.

Dolly leaps onto my bed and into my arms. She buries her head into my breasts and sobs. "They are so mean to me."

I comfort my daughter and offer her ice cream to lift her spirits. We sit on the couch, and between spoonfuls of mint chocolate chip, she divulges what happened.

"I was chasing a grasshopper," she says and hiccups. "I saw them in the fort and saw them kiss." She hiccups again but declines my offer to get her water. "If I hold my breath, it will go away." She plugs her nose for five seconds and exhales. "They told me to leave and not tell anyone. And then

Melissa threw dirt at me and stupid Hùng found that snake." She weeps. "I hate them, and I hate snakes!"

I rub her back and hold her. "Kids can be mean, even your friends. All your life, you will meet mean people or people who do stupid things. What is important is how you face them and handle the situation. Will your actions make you stronger and better? Will your decisions make that person or the situation better?"

"What if they are just mean and I cannot change them?" she asks.

I look at my daughter's face, still innocent and cute, despite the mullet-rat tail disaster that is on her head. "If they are just mean, then you have a choice to make. You can cut them out of your life until they change, or you show them love and compassion so that they learn how to be loving and compassionate. Do you understand what I am saying?"

"I think so," she says. "I love Hùng but he loves Melissa, so if I show him love, he will love me back."

That was not the answer I expected. My eyes open wide but she does not see my reaction. "You have a crush on Hùng?" My daughter nods. "Why do you think he likes her and not you?"

"Because she has pretty long blonde hair and green eyes," she says. "And she wears nice clothes and has a bike with a banana seat and a bell and a basket. She gives him candy and brings him presents."

I sympathize with her rationale. "She may have all those things, but let me tell you a secret about boys." Dolly sits up and locks her eyes with mine. She leans in to listen. I laugh. "Most boys are stupid and blind. They do not have the power like us girls do. They cannot see beyond the surface. Sometimes, they cannot even see what is right in front of them. And sometimes, they do not know what they want, so you have to tell them."

"I am going to grow my hair out," Dolly says. "You can cut my tail off when I am sleeping. He will see. I can be pretty."

My heart bobs with joy that she wants to cut the rat tail. Hallelujah. "Honey, grow your hair out if you want to, not because you think Hùng will like you more."

"I know," she says. "Melissa can have him. Who wants a dumb and blind boyfriend?"

I laugh and make a funny face. "That's my girl. Remember that you are worth a million times more than what you think you are. There is a better boy out there for you who will have the same powers as you and be your equal. He will appreciate your natural beauty and see how smart and funny you are. He is going to be so lucky because you're not like the other girls. You like sports, you are amazing at making money, and you have a good heart that has survived so much."

Dolly hugs me tight and kisses my cheek. "I love you."

"I love you too."

I stare at the envelope in my hand. The return address is from Humble, Texas. I do not have to look at the sender's name to know the handwriting is distinctly Tý's. My husband writes to me after all.

I suppress the urge to rip it open and devour his words. I remind myself I am not a young naïve girl hungry for love. Surviving the South China Sea and the refugee camp hardened me and made me wiser. I have a choice to make...open the letter or toss it in the garbage.

How many more slashes to my heart can I withstand before I run out of thread to mend it? What good would it do to have him in Thủy-Tiên's life when she already has a good life without him? I play several scenarios in my mind and decide there are too many unknowns and variables to risk tempting fate. I tear up the envelope and toss it in the trash.

The phone rings. I stare at it, fearing it is Tý on the other end, but the likelihood of him having my phone number is slim. I pick up the phone with trepidation. "Alô?"

"Hot damn, it's good to hear your voice." Sky's greeting drains the stress from my neck. He sounds happy and full of energy.

"Sky!" I exclaim. "How the retreat?"

"It was incredible," Sky says. "The longer I sat in silence and focused on my breathing, the more aware and alive I felt. All the pent-up feelings of despair and disgust eroded. I had no one to answer to but myself, and the alone time forced me to be truthful, to come to terms with the past. It was like with every inhale I sipped in healing powers and every exhale expunged the poison that has tormented me. I still have a ways to go but I experienced an epiphany—"

"What 'epiphany'?" I ask.

"It's like a realization," Sky says, "an 'ah-ha' moment where things become clear. What I learned was that my fears paralyzed me. My fears are not based on truth or reality. They are conjured by my wild imagination. The past few months...these sojourns...they have awakened in me a will to live and be happy."

"You deserve happiness," I say, thinking of Diệp's fear of the Americans after the massacre. "The core of you is survivor. Dark days of war and childhood over now."

He rambles on about his past three retreats since missing Thanksgiving last November. He has been to California, Tibet, and England and has sat in meditation and silence from fourteen days to as long as ninety days at each retreat. He went on reflective hikes and watched in awe how

124

nature and nurture symbiotically work together, and how relationships unfold. He woke up early to catch the sunrise and witness the birds catch their breakfast. At night, he fasted and prayed with only the sounds of crickets to keep him company. Each time he finished a retreat, he came out on the other side feeling more buoyant than before. He became more in tune with nature, with the universe, and with his body.

I listen eagerly to his excitement, and although he speaks rapidly, I understand his enthusiasm and the successes of his experiences. "A tree that does not bend in the wind will break and die."

"Yes," Sky says, "an old proverb. We humans can be adaptable and thrive if we have the strength and willpower to do so."

The conversation swirling around his healing journey tapers off, and I take the opportunity to change topics. "How Katrina and Jean-Adrien?"

A waterfall of praise tumbles out of Sky's mouth. He is full of optimism about how his parents have stuck with counseling, taking trips to reconnect and fall in love again, and Sky feels he now lives with June and Ward Cleaver—references of people I have not yet met but hope to one day. They sound lovely.

In between breaths, Sky asks me about Dolly or Tree and how I am doing with work and my classes. I gossip about Donald courting Diệp, to which Sky declares we need to dine together soon so that he can finally meet my infamous neighbor.

"Anything else?" Sky asks. "Any news to catch me up on? What about your family?"

"I receive letter from my husband today," I say. "I throw away and not read it."

"Why?" Sky asks.

"I not want him in Dolly life or my life," I say. "Why, Sky? Why I let him back when he make choice already with first wife? Dolly and I do fine and do not need him."

"I think you are still very angry with him and need to make your peace with him. Mark Twain once said that anger is like acid that will do more harm to the vessel that holds it. And besides, you helped me make peace with my dad and to let go of the anger and pain…and guilt. You should do the same. It is liberating."

I give more thought to Sky's advice and before hanging up the phone, I tell Sky I will read the letter and make a choice about what to do next.

"Don't let anyone or anything have power over you." Sky's last words toss my thoughts around like a cyclone and for two weeks, I cannot think of anything but Tý. Dreams of him coming to claim Dolly and take her back to Texas drown me in night sweats. I have to face him.

15. TYPHOON SEASON (SEPTEMBER 1982)

My husband's letter, taped together like a macabre jigsaw puzzle, lies between two scarves in the top drawer of my dresser. I take it out and read it again for the one-hundredth time, searching for secret messages within his words. An infestation of paranoia creeps in. When I think about the truths he omitted and the danger he put us in, I shudder with disgust.

I remember back at the refugee camp when we had bed bugs. Tree and I noticed the tiny bloodstains on our sheets but did not question them. We simply accepted the condition of our squalor because at least we had a place to sleep. The darks spots on our pillows that were bug excrements were thought to be dirt stains, not fecal matter. The foul, musty odor of the bugs' glands blended in with the scent of tropical sewage. It was simply the stench of impending death.

Funny how thinking of Tý brings back memories of the bed bugs. Maybe he was the dark spot on my pillow, the shit on my life while I lived day to day not knowing any better. Old feelings of betrayal brew inside like a storm, and I say out loud, "You are less than a tick's dung to me now."

Tuyết,

Sister Six has been kind to write and give me your address. I want to see you and Thủy-Tiên. I cannot continue life while the guilt stacks higher and heavier. It will crush me to death unless you forgive me and I can atone for my mistakes.

I want you both to be a part of my life. I want us to be a family again. It has been seven years, my beloved wife. Your face haunts me every day, and at night your beauty haunts me in my dreams. I am not the same man you remember. Older, yes, but in this old heart there still burns a bright flame for you, and I am as young and alive in my dreams, in your embrace, as I was on our wedding day.

Whether you read and answer my letter or not, I will be coming to Seattle. I purchased my airplane ticket already. I understand now why Annette only bought a one-way ticket to Việt Nam to find me. I thought she was crazy, but look at me, doing the same thing now. I have many questions. I am sure you do too. I want to get to know Thủy-Tiên and she needs to know her father.

I land in Seattle from the Houston airport at 10:10 a.m. on Saturday, September 25, on a United Airlines flight. I hope you will pick me up but if I do not see you, I will take a taxicab.

Please welcome me with a forgiving heart, and in case you do not recognize me, I will be the beggar on my hands and knees, kissing your feet with a forlorn heart.

Always yours,

Tý

I collect my coat from the closet and Dolly's pink jacket with the fake fur lining around the hood. She hates the coat and thinks she looks like a big cotton candy with two sticks protruding at the bottom. It is the only coat she has and it will have to do. Outside, the rain falls sideways while the wind howls.

I place our coats on her bed and gently rouse her. "Time to get ready. Your daddy is coming to see you today."

The past few days, all she could talk about was seeing Tý and showing him her scar. She bragged to Melissa, Jen, Jason, and Hùng that her father was traveling from far away and that he had finally found us.

I had asked Tree if he wanted to come to the airport, but he had said, "The reunion should be between Uncle and you only."

I asked Sky, also, to come with us, and reminded him that he pinky promised, but he only parroted Tree's sentiments. "I'll be there for you but not at the airport when you pick him up."

Dolly and I sit in the Honda Civic and let the car warm up. The defroster blasts on high. It rains marbles; the pounding on the car roof makes me nostalgic for Việt Nam. Sometimes it pummeled so hard there that the raindrops were cacti needles on my face. I cannot believe that in less than an hour, I will be face to face with the man I once vowed to obey and love until the day I die.

I turn on the radio and scroll through all the stations. No good songs are playing. I stop on KUBE 93 FM hoping to catch a Lionel Richie song or a top forty hit I recognize. Nothing. Instead, I hear a brief news update on Typhoon Ken, a tropical storm that has been punishing Japan the past week. I forgot it was typhoon season. I wonder how my family is faring with the tropical storms. The rainfall reminds me of the time Tree and I caught frogs for dinner. It was also the day Father died.

Before long, Dolly and I drive in circles up the spiral ramps to level four of the airport parking lot. I do not even remember getting on the interstate and taking the exit to the airport. I park, and we make our way through the sky bridge to the terminal. We find the gate and wait.

My stomach is in knots. Despite the cool air, my hands are clammy. I sit down for a couple of seconds only to spring back up again. I want to make sure I see him the moment he steps out of the gate. I check my reflection in the window. My hair is damp and flat. I run my fingers through them to give them volume. Will Tý still find me attractive? Have I changed in his eyes? I gained ten pounds since arriving in Seattle.

"Will Daddy know who I am?" Dolly asks. "I was a baby when he last saw me."

"You were only nine months old," I say, "but of course, he will recognize you."

"I am eight now," she says. "I have a scar on my chest now."

"Yes, but you are still his daughter," I say. "A daddy never forgets his daughter."

I look around and notice my reflection in the window. I comb my hair with my fingers and check my face for any smudges.

"You look pretty," Dolly says.

I smile warmly at my daughter. How far she has come, traveling through mosquito-infested jungles, sailing over ripples of a never-ending sea, and flying above freedom clouds made of hopes and dreams. She is alive, and I kept her alive, no thanks to my husband.

"He is here!" Dolly jumps out of her chair and runs to the window. She points at the Boeing 767 aircraft. I grimace, thinking Typhoon Tý has landed in the Pacific Northwest. What stories will he spin up this time? What lies will he use to shield himself from my prying lips?

The terminal gate opens. Passengers disembark and exit the jetway. It is a circus of clowns tumbling out of the narrow bridge. They wear expressions of delight, skepticism, or weariness on their faces. A young man in a naval uniform rushes to kiss his wife and hug his twin girls.

And then there is my husband.

He has not changed. It is as if he walked through a time machine from Sài Gòn 1975 to Seattle 1982. Still handsome and fit. Except for the ASICS running shoes on his feet, everything remains the same, from the lean muscles that show off his athletic build to the slight bow in his legs accentuated by tight blue jeans. His skin is tan and his teeth bright. I was expecting to hate him, but seeing the familiar face of the man I once loved, however briefly, makes my heart flutter. The happiness that descends on me catches me off guard. I let my defenses down; the curtain of insecurities pulls back. Tý swoops me into his arms and kisses my lips. I respond and cling to him.

"Hello, sweetheart," he says. The corners of his eyes brim with wetness. He drops his duffle bag and swings his daughter into his arms. Father and daughter hug. They both cry.

For our first dinner together since April 1975, I put out some stir-fried anchovies, barbecued chicken, pork chitlins, sautéed water spinach, pickled leeks, steamed rice, and winter melon soup.

Tý's eyes open wide. He cracks a smile and grunts. "Vietnamese soul food! Do you have any beer?" I pop the tab of a Rainier beer and place it on the table. I can hear Sam saying it was the only beer he drank because it was brewed here in Washington. "Where is yours? You have to *nhậu* with me and celebrate."

"You know I get drunk after a few sips," I say. It feels traitorous serving Sam's beer to my husband.

"Still a light-weight, I see, but now you can cook." Tý pinches a few anchovies with his chopsticks and pops them in his mouth.

"I have learned a few things since we separated," I say drily, finding how he chews his food annoying, lips parted and tongue slapping against the roof of his mouth. He does not even wait for his daughter and me to sit down. Typical man.

"Thủy-Tiên, honey, grab daddy some chili sauce," Tý says in English. "I like it spicy." He winks at her.

My daughter's ears perk up hearing her father speak perfect English. I see the look of pride and adoration in her face for him. It irritates me that he commands her to do his bidding and pulls her strings like a puppet. He has been absent from her life for seven years. He does not have the right to parent her. He should be groveling at my feet, begging for forgiveness, and selling his soul to the devil for a sliver of a chance to be in our lives.

I pull out my chair and sit down. I say a quick prayer and bless myself with the sign of the cross. "How long are you staying?"

"I just arrived, and you are already quick to send me away," he says. I do not know if the inflections in his voice are in jest and he is teasing me, or if he is being sarcastic and condescending. His words course through my veins like a thousand volts of electricity. I bite down and lock my jaw.

Dolly hands him two types of chili sauce and fresh red chili pepper. "Daddy, do you believe in Jesus?"

My husband slurps his soup before answering. "No, I'm an atheist or maybe agnostic. I don't believe in God, but there may, or may not, be a higher power out there. I don't know."

"Are you going to live with us?" Dolly asks.

I stop chewing and look at Tý. I hold my breath for his reply. He shrugs. "Depends on your mother."

I have no answer for them. My face feels flushed and my neck warm. My patience for Tý is a mudslide away from destroying our family reunion. He sits there at my table, in my home, uninvited, talking to my daughter, and resumes this pretend life as if time, war, and a failed marriage had never separated us.

"Mama says I was found in a garbage can," Dolly says. "Is that true?"

"All naughty children in Vietnam come from the dumpsters, honey. Are you a bad girl?"

"Not anymore."

"Make sure you stay a good girl. Otherwise, your mommy might throw you out with the trash, back in the dumpster, and the next person who fishes you out might be a mean mommy who will not feed you or buy you toys. Instead of candy, she will give you chores from sunrise to sunset."

"You need to speak to her in Vietnamese." It was all I could say without losing my temper.

"We are in America now," he says. "This is her home. There is no returning. Adapt or die."

His last three words are rusty nails impaled into the core of my beliefs. I do not want my daughter to forget her heritage. She must always remember where she came from and be proud of her roots. I bite my tongue. I do not want to argue in front of Dolly.

"Yeah, Mom," Dolly says. "It's stupid to talk in Vietnamese."

I glare at my daughter. She scowls back and challenges me. She straightens her posture and sets her fork down. If Tý were not here, I would claw at her false sense of security. Surely, she does not think that her father is her ally and his presence will protect her from punishment?

Tý defends me. "Do not disrespect your mother. Apologize, or back in the dumpster you go."

Dolly offers an apology and asks for forgiveness for talking back to me. I excuse her from the table and make her watch a documentary about birds.

Long after I have finished eating, Tý still picks at his morsels of food. Right when I think he is full and done eating, he picks up his chopsticks again to taste another anchovy or shovel more rice into his bowl. I try clearing the plate of water spinach, but he takes the dish from me and scrapes the last bits of garlic and leafy greens into his bowl. He finishes off the winter melons and reaches for the last drumstick. The only things left are three pickled leeks and fragments of chitterlings.

"Does Annette not feed you?" I ask. I am picking a fight tonight. All these years of pent-up disappointment and unfinished business are about to burst out of my mouth.

Tý ignores me. "You know what these chitlins remind me of? The L&M back in Sài Gòn." He pushes the fried pork chitterlings around like he's sifting through river sand for gold. "The restaurant was always full of black soldiers. They would sit and nhậu all day and order plates of chitlins at two-hundred *piastres* a dish. It was a brotherhood. They had this way of greeting each other, called the dap, and it was like a secret handshake. I later learned that 'dap' was an acronym for dignity and pride."

"How many children do you have other than Timothy?" I ask. My body temperature skyrockets. I am a tea kettle about to blow my steam.

"While we are on the topic of brotherhood," Tý continues, "how is my brother?" He pushes the chair away from the table and stands up. He clears the table and tells Dolly it is bedtime.

I help her get into her pajamas and watch her brush her teeth. She kisses us both and runs off to bed. In the kitchen, Tý lathers up a sponge and scrubs the dishes. I grab the sponge from him and throw it into the sink; a couple of soap suds splash onto his golden arm.

"Why are you here?" I scream. "All these years...why now? Are you dying? Do you need money? Did Annette leave you?"

He picks up the sponge and resumes washing the dishes. It infuriates me that I cannot get a rise out of him. If he does not engage, then I am only fighting with myself. I stare at my husband. I want to scratch his eyes out and tell him to go home to his precious American wife and children.

"I will answer your questions if you can calm yourself down and talk to me like a dutiful wife."

"You mean a sedated and mindless wife," I say. "What I would not give to have a bottle of Maotai right now. This time, I would not miss."

"Is that what you want? To split my skull open with a bottle of baijiu? Go ahead. You already trampled my heart when you did not get in that van. You could have spared yourself and our daughter a lot of suffering, but you let your pride get in the way."

He will never understand my position. How can he? He is a man. What did he have to lose? He will never feel the humiliation of being the second wife. He never had to worry about his next meal. He did not live his life perpetually tense, praying that the next man he sees is not the one who will rape him today. He will never understand the crippling fear a mother has of losing her only child.

"It is not like I can make more babies whenever I want," I say.

"What?" Tý asks. "You are not making any sense."

"Do not bother unpacking. You can sleep on the couch."

I sleep through my alarm. Feeling like a beached seal, I am too distressed to move. It is Sunday. Church service has already begun, and I am sure Sky will be anxious to know what happened. I hear sounds in the kitchen and decide I should be a good hostess and make coffee.

I drag my feet off the bed and shuffle out of the bedroom. Dolly stands in the hallway with a tray. Two bowls of cereal, two glasses of orange juice, and two spoons. "I made breakfast for you and Daddy."

"Where is Daddy?" I ask. Confused, she looks at my bedroom door. I rush past her into the living room. The couch had been slept on but is empty now. I walk into the kitchen, but Tý is not there. His duffle bag is gone and so are his shoes. I look for a note, but there is none. I take the tray from Dolly's hands and set it on the table. "Daddy is gone. He went back to Texas."

I hold my daughter and console her the best I can. This is my fault, but I convince myself it has to be this way.

It is better this way. Is it not?

16. THE CRUSH (DECEMBER 1982)

My daughter has been simmering in her thoughts the past month. I know her father's sudden appearance and disappearance crushed her. She has not been her usual hustling self, selling sticks of Juicy Fruit gum for five cents a stick or begging for sleepovers with friends. She has lost interest in Melissa and Hùng's relationship and declines invitations to play football or basketball with Jason and Jen. She spends her afternoons drawing, playing quietly by herself, reading, or watching cartoons. She assures me she is not sad and looks forward to another Christmas. She has not given up on a pet and has reminded Santa that she has been an extra good girl this year.

Teddy and Catherine have invited us over for a holiday party. "It's an ugly sweater party," Teddy announces, "and we are going to do a white elephant gift exchange." Teddy explains the concept of the white elephant game to me and the rules. "Be sure you each bring a wrapped gift of something you do not want."

If Tý were here, I would take him to the party as my white elephant, wrapped in paper with a bow on top. Someone else can have him. I giggle at my private joke.

Katrina, Jean-Adrien, and Skyler will be there. Pastor George and his family have RSVP'd as well. I am excited for them to meet Tree's girlfriend. The last time we were all under one roof was Christmas Eve two years ago. It is impolite to come empty-handed, so I make shrimp and pork fried rice to bring to the party.

I rummage through my closet and dirty clothes pile looking for the ugliest sweater I own. I have never been to an ugly sweater party and do not understand the purpose. Desperate, I tug at the orange and green crocheted cardigan. I found it at a thrift shop for fifty cents and have worn it twice. I hope it is ugly enough.

Then an idea strikes me. I dart out of the apartment and knock on Diệp's door. No answer. I rap louder and call out to her. "Diệp's ơi."

She opens the door. "What is the urgency?"

"I need to borrow a sweater for a party. Can I come in?" I push the door, but she stops it from swinging in. "Is something wrong?"

"It is not a good time," she says. "When do you need it?"

A man's voice calls from within. "Come back here, Yip."

"I need it now," I say. "Is that Donald?" My neighbor does not have to answer; it is written all over her flushed face. "Can I borrow one of your colorful sweaters...that one with the puffy sleeves and doily collar?" She returns in a flash and hands me her sweater. It is gaudy, loud, and ugly, with the cast of *Diff'rent Strokes* centered on the front. There are a few holes from moth bites and strands of yarn poking out by the armpit area. A pink stain runs down the center of it and dribbles over Philip Drummond's eyes, the dad from the sitcom. He resembles Donald, so of course, she had to have it. My audacious neighbor found it at a yard sale and negotiated with the seller down to ten cents; she would have paid a dollar for it. She wore the sweater proudly, even after she spilled juice on it.

"Perfect. Thank you," I say. "Tell Donald I say 'hello.'"

Two hours later we arrive at the Vanzwol house. It is a beautiful night despite the harsh winter air. It gnaws the warmth off my bones and sands down the traction on my shoes. One day I hope to acclimate to the Seattle weather and maybe then the cold, damp air will be inviting.

Dolly and I park thirty feet from the house. Cars fill the driveway and line the street. I wonder who else is here. As we approach the house, with its white lights clinging from the roofline, giving it a magical, winter wonderland touch, I slip and skate to my knees from the slick black ice on the sidewalk. I shiver in the night and exhale frost as the bowl of fried rice slips from my hands. Luckily it is salvageable. Dolly helps me right as the door opens. Holiday music spills out to the lawn and Sky stands in the doorway.

He looks me up and down. "Wow." He invites us in. "That sweater is..."

"Perfect?" I ask. "I borrow from neighbor."

"I was going to say ugly." Sky laughs. "It is obnoxious and hideous. Am I going to have to stare at his face all night?" He points to Philip Drummond's stained face.

"Do you like my sweater?" Dolly asks.

She wears an oversized purple sweater with a shiny, patent pink belt around her waist. It would swallow her whole if it was not cinched tightly.

"Very nice," Sky says. He stands before us in a V-neck sweater. Tinsel and a string of popcorn adorn his green pullover. Tiny ornaments cling to parts of the cloth, and a large gift-wrapped box covers his crotch. It is attached to his belt and hangs like a fanny pack.

I point at the box. "Present under tree?"

Sky grins. "For the naughty and not so nice."

Dolly runs inside and leaps into Teddy's arms. She kisses him on the cheek and strokes his beard. "Are you Santa's brother?"

Teddy puts his finger to his lips. "Shhhhhh." Dolly slides down and hugs Catherine before running off into the family room. Teddy whistles at me. "Snow, that sweater…"

My jaw drops. Teddy and Catherine are wearing similar sweaters, but his shirt has an image of a woman's breasts covered in a bikini top and Catherine has a fat man's hairy chest on hers. I laugh uncontrollably.

I offer Teddy the fried rice and go into the kitchen to help Catherine. The house smells of melted butter and sugary pies. Catherine hands me a glass of champagne. "Now, get!" She shoos me out of the kitchen and insists I enjoy myself in the family room.

I hear chatter and childish giggles in the next room, so I follow the sounds. To my astonishment, my boss is here and so is his assistant, Magdaleine. They are talking animatedly with Sky and laughing. I scan the room and see Jean-Adrien with Katrina, engaging in serious conversation with Pastor George and Dawn. Meanwhile, Opal, Ocean, Olivia, and Dolly sit on the floor by the fire. They play the Milton Bradley game of Operation. Opal picks up the tweezers and concentrates as she slowly removes the wishbone from Cavity Sam. The game buzzes and flashes red. The children giggle.

I walk toward Sky, preferring to join their lively conversation over Katrina's boring one, but I hear Dawn call my name. The women wave me over.

"Snow, perhaps you can settle a debate for us," Dawn says. "Nice sweater by the way."

Katrina pats the couch cushion and invites me to sit next to her. "Now, let me ask you this…If you got a vacuum cleaner as a present for Christmas from your husband, would you be excited?"

"But you complained about the old one and—" Jean-Adrien stops mid-sentence. Katrina covers his mouth with her hands.

Pastor George leans in. "It's the lastest, top-of-the-line, high-end, most expensive vacuum on the market, and it's on sale at Sears. Not to mention, it's compact and will save you a lot of time as it picks up everything."

"But giving your wife a vacuum is unromantic and sends the wrong message," Dawn argues. "Wouldn't you agree?"

"It's a thoughtful, functional, pragmatic gift," Pastor George says.

I glance at my watch and wonder when Tree and Kelly will arrive. Thank heavens Sky rescues me. He saunters over to our group and takes my hand. "I need your help in the kitchen."

I smile thinking I would never have heard those words back in Vĩnh Bình. Sister Six and Sister Seven protested sharply if I tried to help them cook. Sky and I join Teddy and Catherine around the kitchen bar.

Sky refills my champagne flute. "Your tolerance for alcohol is improving."

The three of us catch up on what has been happening in our world. Sky kicks it off. "The VA is phenomenal…at treating people terribly. Every time I see a doctor, there's someone new, and I have to tell my story over and over again." He recalls how he had major drug addictions after the war because he did not know how to be normal at home. "Normal was hunting for Charlie Company, watching your back so you didn't get killed, and protecting the locals. It was rushing into an ambushed area to save people and being in the crossfire, not knowing if the plastic bag on the side of the road was a bomb or simply trash."

My boss, Bill, joins our conversation. He pats Sky on the back. "Son, no country has ever historically taken care of their soldiers once the empire is at peacetime because no one wants to be reminded of how they got there. Soldiers become collateral damage."

"At the VA, you see guys sitting there, and they'll tell you they're waiting to die because no one talks to them or gives a flip about them. Some are missing limbs, some are homeless or jobless, others are hooked on crack." He tells us about a new treatment for people suffering from post-traumatic stress called stellate ganglion block injection. He had to write that down for me to comprehend what he was saying. It is a numbing medication for the nerves at the neck. The injection is used to treat chronic pain and has been shown to relieve the symptoms of PTS in as little as thirty minutes and can last for years. It essentially reboots the sympathetic nervous system to its pre-trauma state. The nerve bundles in the neck help regulate the body's fight or flight mechanism. Sky says the treatment is expensive.

"It sounds promising and too good to be true," Catherine says.

Sky scratches his head. "I'll try anything. The meditation is working. My friend Charlie deals with it by writing poems. Man, the stories you hear in therapy sessions. There was one girl in her twenties whose husband came back from Nam and stabbed her repeatedly. She was left on the ground bleeding to death and was able to call 9-1-1. There was another guy who served on a navy ship in Vietnam. They'd go through harbors and crush fishing boats and watch kids get eaten by sharks." Sky pauses and catches his breath. He blinks back tears.

137

Bill puts his arm around Sky's shoulders. "I sent him a letter almost every week while he was overseas."

"And I'd lie and tell him everything was fine so he wouldn't worry," Sky says. "The VA has well-intentioned angels who want to help veterans, but they're handcuffed by the government red tape. Restrictions, policies, funding, slow progression…it all lead to frustration and they quit. It's a revolving door of new faces, new names. I don't want to be the vet who tells the same story over and over, and all I have is that story." Sky looks at me with tenderness and squeezes my hand. "You and Sam were my story that I lived repeatedly in my mind."

"I have trauma stress like you," I say. "I have nightmare of Sam dying and worry Dolly father come back, make me live with him as husband and wife. In my dream, I sometime see my enemy want to kill me, and I see friends who die trying to escape communist. But Dolly and Tree…because of them, I keep going."

"That's because you have a purpose," Bill says. "We all need to find a purpose in life to keep us from giving up. We also have to recognize that we have the willpower to get through the adversities."

Sky snickers. "Like basic training. Everyone who went through basic training was quitting something, whether it be sugar, foods, cigarettes. Man, I was so miserable, but I made it, even the tear gas chamber training. You go in there, take off your helmet, and breathe in tear gas. Your eyes sting and so do your lungs and throat. Guys were coughing, drooling, and vomiting afterward…snot dripping everywhere, and because we had to shave every day, our skin was raw. We were all flapping our arms trying to escape it like a bunch of dumb, flightless birds. Anyway, sponsoring Snow here was my purpose, and now that we have Snow in Seattle, ensuring she thrives here is my purpose."

The layers of brick and historical rubble that have been crushing me these past few years suddenly lift. One look at Sky and I realize how much I love my friend. My angelic, handsome, and kind Skyler, who, despite suffering so much, can still be giving and selfless. Tears gush from both of us, and we do not hold back. I wrap my arms around Sky's waist and rest my cheek on his chest. He holds me tighter, and I hear the crunch of his fanny-pack box that covers his crotch.

We have a good laugh.

Tree and Kelly show up in time for dinner. Kelly apologizes profusely for being late, claiming they got lost, but Tree says she took too long getting ready. The two of them show up dressed like they are going to a wedding reception. Tree wears the same cobalt blue pants and matching jacket that Teddy and Catherine gave him two years ago. Kelly has a new perm and is wearing a burgundy *sườn xám*, a traditional Chinese cheongsam. The mandarin gown is made of velvet and has delicate white cherry blossoms running the length of her dress, from the high-collar neck down to her hemline at her ankle. The S-shaped design of the floral print forces admiring eyes to follow the curve of the female body. She looks magnificent.

She whispers in my ear, "I want to make a good first impression."

"You look stunning," I whisper back, feeling like a jungle monkey in my ugly sweater that has Philip Drummond's face on it.

Tonight's dinner party is perfect. Love and laughter fill the room, and peace fills my heart. Our conversation revolves around the new Vietnam Veterans Memorial Wall in Washington D.C. The black granite walls were brought in from India. The 144 panels list nearly 58,000 names of service members in the U.S. armed forces who fought and perished or are missing. I wonder if Sam Hammond's name is engraved on one of those slabs.

Jean-Adrien and Katrina present themselves as a new couple, smitten with one another once again. I wonder if Tý and I will ever feel that way about one another again. I catch Bill glancing in their direction every so often. If he feels jealous or forlorn, he hides it well. He is cordial to Jean-Adrien, and the two men keep the topic of their conversation light-hearted and high-level. Jean-Adrien shares with Bill that he used to work for John Graham & Company, the Seattle-based firm that designed Northgate, the Space Needle, and Southcenter Mall.

"What is mall?" I ask.

"What is a mall?" Magdaleine asks, flabbergasted. "It's a place to go shopping for clothes, shoes, and cosmetics. There are toys and gifts…just about everything you can imagine. I'll take you."

I ask Magdaleine to pass the salad dressing. While I have her brief attention, I inquire about the latest scandal on her favorite soap opera, *Dallas*.

Magdaleine's eyes light up. She shifts in her seat so that she can face me. "Okay, so they just aired episode ten. JR is getting married to Sue Ellen, again, and JR goes and does a mean-spirited thing. He invited Cliff to the wedding. Awkward! Sue Ellen and Cliff used to be a couple. Well, on the wedding day, Sue Ellen is walking down the aisle and sees Cliff, which is jarring, but what has my panties all in a bunch is the episode ends right in the middle of the wedding as Cliff stands up to protest the wedding. Oh, it is getting so good. You have to watch it."

"I will watch it," I say. "I watching *Dynasty* now and *Days of our Lives*."

"It's nice to see you outside of work," Magdaleine says. "We never get a chance to do lunch because Bill keeps us all so busy, and you always scurry home after work. I understand why. Your daughter is quite a character. She's a rebel, that one. Do you know she tried to sell me fried rice? She said you were a good cook and that I could have a free sample tonight, and if I like it, I can buy more."

I laugh. "Me? A good cook?" To think my daughter is proud of me and boasts about my culinary skills makes me happy.

"She's endearing and hard to say no to," Magdaleine says. "Anyway, I'm so glad I'm here. I prefer the company of older, more mature people. My generation is boring, and they have nothing substantive to talk about."

"You and Bill dating?" I ask. It is an innocent question. Despite the big age difference, it is not out of the ordinary in my country for women to marry young, especially to older men who are established in their career and can provide for the family. My assumption, however, causes quite a reaction.

Magdaleine is quiet. Her face puckers like she just drank sour milk or ate a bug. She closes her eyes, bends forward, and covers her mouth. Her body shakes. She laughs hysterically and puts her hand on my knee. "Good God, Snow! You are a riot! No!"

"What's so funny?" Bill asks.

All conversation comes to a halt, and ten pairs of eyes turn to us. Magdaleine laughs so hard she chokes on her food and coughs.

Catherine clutches her pearl necklace. "Oh, dear."

Sky rises from his chair and rushes to Magdaleine. "Can you breathe?"

Magdaleine shakes her head. Sky steps behind her, bends her forward slightly, and wraps his arms around her waist. He makes a fist with one of his hands, grabs hold of it with his other hand, and repeatedly pushes into her abdomen inward and upward, thrusting her up and down, crushing her back against his chest. A crouton shoots out of her mouth. Biscuit quickly runs to claim his prize and licks up the cubed piece of dried bread.

Magdaleine gasps for air and seizes the back of her chair. She faces Skyler and thanks him. "Your Heimlich maneuver saved me."

"That's my son, the hero," Katrina says, "coming to the rescue." She applauds him, and we all join in clapping our hands.

Sky grins. "I feel like I need to give a speech now."

Jean-Adrien and Katrina chant, "Speech, speech!"

Sky takes his seat. "Instead of a speech, I've got a joke for you that my old buddy, Charlie Peters, used to tell. You're going to love this malapropism." He clears his throat, takes a sip of his wine, and begins. "Two rednecks are sitting at a bar. They see a woman choking at a nearby table. One of the rednecks springs to his feet. He spins the woman around, bends her forward, lifts up her skirt, pulls down her panties, and licks her bottom. The woman, shocked, spits out her food, slaps him, and storms off,

140

humiliated. The other redneck says to his friend, 'Wow, that hind lick thing really works.'"

Teddy is the first to roar with laughter. I join in after Magdaleine explains the difference between hind-lick and Heimlich.

After dinner, we take our blueberry pie and ice cream downstairs to the second living room. Catherine explains the rules of the white elephant gift exchange. I tell them that in the Buddhist belief, white elephants are revered as good luck. The game becomes very competitive as we steal one another's prizes. Tree opens his wrapped gift from the center pile and shows his Fisher-Price Little People figures. Dolly steals them from Tree, Ocean steals them from Dolly, and I do the final steal from Ocean. Dolly bounces up and down with glee and hugs me so tightly I pretend to faint. Poor Tree ends up with a toilet seat as his take-home white elephant gift. There are great prizes tonight, and the most fought-over items are the Mickey Mouse and Pluto lunch box, a Lite-Brite game, and acid-washed button fly jeans. Dolly and I make a great team. She steals for me a Lionel Richie record, and although I do not own a turntable, I am determined to take the LP home with me. After all, it is Lionel on vinyl!

17. MY DATE (FEBRUARY 1983)

Christmas was a blur. Dolly and I were spoiled. We received a record player and two albums: Michael Jackson's *Thriller* and Lionel Richie's self-titled debut solo album. "You Are" is my favorite song on the album and Dolly teases me when I try to sing along. Teddy and Catherine got Dolly a beautiful Holy Bible, the New International Version. It is a children's edition, engraved with her name, Dolly Le, on the cover. The pages are filled with wonderful pictures that bring the stories to life, and in the back are maps of the exodus, world of the patriarchs, the empire of David and Solomon, and travels of the apostles.

Her favorite, however, is the bicycle, blue with a banana seat, training wheels, and a kickstand. She calls it the "mean machine." It is a generous gift from Katrina and Jean-Adrien but takes up a lot of space in her bedroom. It is also a burden to carry the bike up and down the thirteen steps of our stairway.

Dolly also received roller skates that strap on to her running shoes. She has been practicing all week rolling on the carpet and using the walls to keep herself steady. Perhaps the most surprising and most cherished gift, however, is the present from her father.

The package from Tý is wrapped in a brown paper bag, like the one from the supermarket to hold our groceries. Dolly tears the packaging tape away and rips open the brown paper. She can barely contain her excitement since the package is addressed to her.

There is no letter from him. Oddly, it disappoints me that he did not care to write or send me anything. I tell myself I do not care and do not need anything from him.

"It's Connect Four and an Etch-A-Sketch!" she exclaims. "And a picture of Daddy when he was a baby." She hands me the photograph.

The picture is grainy and bent, warped from moisture. The baby is sitting on a red chair with a doll dressed in a yellow onesie. The black eyes in the photo staring back at me look like Tý, but it is not.

"This is you," I say, "when you were around nine months old at Ông Ngoại's house." Memories of Dolly's grandfather surface to the top of my memory bank. A fresh coat of sadness washes over me. I miss my parents deeply. Tý sent me a gift after all, a most priceless gift that I will take care to never lose. I wonder if he has any old photos of our life together. Did this photo stay close to his heart all these years? Does he have one of me?

I forgive my husband and commit to making peace with the past. We were young and thrown together during desperate times. Our arranged marriage was not unique, and our life together was brief. However, we had love between us for a time, and from our union came Thủy-Tiên. A new devotion and purpose blooms within me. To love again, I need to let compassion for him reside in my heart and allow forgiveness to dwell in my bones. I sit at the kitchen table and compose a letter to Tý.

Anh Tý,

Thủy-Tiên and I received your package. Your daughter loves her gifts. It warmed my heart seeing the photo of our daughter when she was a baby. She thought it was a picture of you. The resemblance is remarkable. You should be proud of how far our daughter has come and how brave she has been all these years. I do not know what I would have done if I had lost her...if we had lost her. I know she is your daughter too and of course, you should be in her life. We have already lost so much precious time. Forgive me. I have held onto this anger against you for so long but I am ready to let it go. In some ways, the wall I built around me has helped me survive and stay focused. I recognize now that the danger is over, that we are living a life of freedom, and the past is the past.

I stop to read my letter. My penmanship looks rushed, almost as if it is written in anger. My words slant forward, sometimes backward, and all the while, the letters are either round or jagged. He is going to think I wrote this letter while jostled on a tiny boat in the middle of an ocean storm. I am not sure how to sign the letter but decide on "your friend" in case his wife Annette sees the letter. I also do not want him to think there is a future for us.

If you would still like to be a part of our lives and want to visit again, you are welcome to come.

Your friend,
Tuyết

143

###

Dolly has been playful and endearing for the past few months. The holiday season was joyful, and now that it is February, we have the Lunar New Year to look forward to. This year is the year of the Water Pig and falls on Sunday, the thirteenth of February. I call Sky and ask if he is free this weekend to have dinner with Dolly and me to ring in the new year.

"Can I take a rain check?" he asks. "I have a date this weekend."

I cannot believe it. I am dying with curiosity to know who the woman is, how he met her, and where they are going. I tell him to give me all the details afterward. I ring my neighbor to see if she has plans for the new year, but Donald is taking Hùng and her to the San Juan Islands for the weekend. I sigh and summon my daughter into my bedroom. She runs out of the bathroom and jumps into my room. She startles me. Her face is painted with lipstick, blush, and eye shadow. Her fingernails have pink nail polish smeared on more than just her nails. From ten feet away, I can smell my new Gloria Vanderbilt perfume. She must have rolled in it because she is caked with the strong aromas of jasmine, pineapple, and cinnamon. My third grader is growing up.

"You look and smell delicious," I laugh. "Do you want to be my date this weekend? We can celebrate the lucky year of the pig, which represents good fortune and wealth."

Dolly agrees and asks if we can invite Bill from work and Mark Hartman, the new boy at school. "We can have a double date."

"No," I exclaim. "Bill is my boss, and you are too young to have a boyfriend."

She frowns and argues that she has a crush on Mark, but so does everyone else, and she wants to be his first friend. I learn he has blue eyes, thick brown hair, tan skin, and pretty teeth. Her friends at school, Nadirah and Jackie, have a bet to see who he will notice first, and Melissa recently dumped Hùng because she has her eyes on him as well. I fear my little girl is growing up too fast, already noticing boys.

The workweek goes by quickly. To my surprise, Bill asks me over for a casual dinner, but I decline. "Sorry, Bill. I have date with my daughter. We go see *The Dark Crystal* and *Tootsie* movie at theater."

"Well, I don't suppose I can join you?" Bill asks.

It is hard to say no twice, so I agree. This upsets Dolly. She feels I betrayed her. I plead my case, saying it is not a date and bribe her with cotton candy, popcorn, and 7-Up. She agrees to the terms.

Dolly and I pull into the parking lot of the Cinerama in Seattle. It is raining cotton balls so light I mistake it for snow. Bill waves to us. He wears a black trench coat and fedora, making him look mysterious and dangerous but also dapper.

The Cinerama is a flurry of activity tonight. Teenagers huddle in groups, animatedly talking about school, sports, or the latest gossip. Their attention span is short, and they are easily distracted with people-watching. They googly-eye every person walking through the door as if they are expecting someone they know.

Bill is vigilant and leads us to the shortest line. "This one is moving fast." We fight over who is paying, but Bill's English is more succinct and authoritative than mine. The girl behind the register accepts Bill's cash. I thank him and insist on treating him next time. Dolly suggests I treat us to ice cream next time.

The movie is not what I expect it to be. While it is a children's movie, I find it dark and eerie. At times, it is scary with creepy characters. However, Dolly is engrossed and seems to enjoy it.

"I love scary movies," Dolly whispers. "I want to watch more."

When the credits roll and the lights come on, the three of us make our way to the lobby. Dolly yawns but insists she is not tired and is ready for the next movie. She is excited to do a doubleheader and stay up late.

After sitting for nearly two hours, we go outside for a breath of fresh air and stretch our legs. Once outside, however, the howling wind scares us back inside. It is a chilly forty-three degrees, too cold to stand outside. Instantly, I am awake and feel more alert than after having six cups of coffee.

While we wait for *Tootsie* to start, Bill opens up about life after Katrina. He had trysts with many women and two serious relationships that lasted three years each. He married one of them but admits it was a mistake. He never had children with any of his past relationships. He poured his devotion and energy into his work, and when he got the job at the *Seattle Times* as their executive director of marketing, he let his foot off the accelerator and has been coasting through life since.

"Even if Katrina and I had worked out and we had gotten married," Bill wonders, "would our marriage have lasted?"

"Why not?" I ask. "I think you find way."

"I was a workhorse, driven to climb the career ladder, and if Katrina and I married, my aspirations would eventually drive a wedge between us. I guess we will never really know." Bill rests his hand gently on mine. He looks at me tenderly like a loving father might on his daughter's wedding day. "The next time love comes, seize it, and make it work. Life is too short to be alone."

I rolodex through my past relationships, remembering how Sam, Hải, and Tý made me feel. I am indeed alone now, but am I lonely? Dolly keeps me busy. My community keeps me entertained. I have been broken-hearted enough times to believe I will be fine without another man in my life. Learning to cook and sew keeps me fulfilled, and my job is wonderful. I believe the year of the pig will bring me good fortune, and if a life partner is part of that, then I will be ready to receive it.

Soon after the second movie starts, Dolly falls asleep in her chair. Bill and I enjoy our movie, and before long, it is time to say goodbye. We hug and go our separate ways. While driving home, I think about Bill and wonder what his lips feel like and if he has chest hair. I quickly dismiss my thoughts. One thing at a time. I need to resolve my feelings for Dolly's father first and determine if there can be a future for Tý and me.

The following Sunday after church, Dolly enjoys a playdate with Ocean, Olivia, and Opal while I make my way to Southcenter Mall in Tukwila to meet Magdaleine. I park in one of the 7,200 stalls and hope I can find my little silver Civic later.

The 1.1-million-square-feet shopping center, with its 110 retail spaces, is the largest in the state and second biggest in the country, trailing second to Ala Moana Center in Honolulu, Hawaii. Inside the mall, the shiny terrazzo flooring gives the building a castle presence. A large chandelier, twenty-four feet in circumference, emits a warm amber light that reflects off six hundred bent and polished brass reflectors hanging from brass strings. I feel I have stepped into the house of nobility.

It is a bustle of activity with shoppers moseying in and out of stores. I stop briefly to admire the jewels at Ben Bridge Jewelers before making my way to Nordstrom. Magdaleine waves me to the perfume counter. She exposes her wrist so I can smell it.

"It smell funny," I say, "like spicy dirt."

Magdaleine laughs. "It's a men's cologne. Wait." She flags down a man in his late thirties or early forties and asks if he'd be her guinea pig. She spritzes a sample of the cologne on his neck and leans in for a whiff. "Now, you smell it, Snow."

"Oh, I cannot," I say. "That okay." Putting my nose next to the stranger's neck is rather bold and taboo. I would feel like I fondled him in public. However, the man gives me his permission and Magdaleine goads me to be wild and free. The salesman behind the counter winks and joins in on the coercion. I cave in and take a quick sniff. Lavender. Berries. Sandalwood. Citrus. I smile and give a thumbs up.

Magdaleine claps her hands. "Ding, ding, ding. We have a winner. I'll take it." The salesman rings up the bottle of Drakkar Noir. "I had the most wonderful date last weekend." She leads me to a bench outside the store entrance. "I know we're moving fast, but I feel I know him so well. He's thirteen years older than me, but that's what I like. He's mature and kind and, well, he's my hero." She pauses from boasting about her new love interest and looks at me playfully. "Any guesses?"

"Sky?" I ask.

She grins and nods. A strange sensation overcomes me. My stomach churns like it is in the spin cycle. I shake that brooding feeling that I have lost my friend Sky forever. I remind myself this is Magdaleine, my beautiful, smart, and kind friend. Of course, Sky and she deserve happiness together. She retells how after the holiday party, Sky called to check on her, even though he knew full well she was free and clear from the choking catastrophe. It was sweet, she says, and the two of them met up for coffee, which later turned to dinner, and finally led to buying a dog.

"You buy dog together?" I ask, surprised, and thinking they truly are progressing quickly.

Magdaleine clarifies that he helped her pick one at the pound. Her apartment was broken into last month, and Sky suggested a dog could keep her company and make her feel safer. The animal shelter was waiving adoption fees for the holidays through the end of January. It did not take long before she fell in love with Tank, a four-year-old, blue-nose Staffordshire Bull Terrier. The dog was jumping up and down when they approached his cell and tried to climb the chain-link gate. His eyes and smile hooked her, and his alert, perky ears won Sky over.

"I think maybe I go to shelter too for Dolly pet, but she have to wait ten months before Christmas come again," I say.

"You will have to come over," Magdaleine says. "We can watch *Dallas*, eat take-out, and you can meet Tank. He's a lovey and such a goofy dog!"

Feeling like kindred spirits, I keep our rapport dancing along by sharing with Magdaleine my story of going to the movies with Bill. I am quick to let her know it was a friendly outing between two business associates and that Dolly was present.

I enjoy my time with Magdaleine. Although I am twenty years older than she is, my youthful outlook on American life and her mature perspective on everything American helps us meet in the middle. We spend a couple of hours shopping—I mostly window shop—and then carpool to downtown Seattle to the Pike Place Market.

Magdaleine finds a lucky parking spot on First Avenue and Stewart Street. It is sunny today and comfortably fifty-one degrees. I have my scarf, gloves, and a knit cap to keep me warm, and with the sunshine on my face, I feel alive and in good spirits. I have never been to this open-air market before in downtown Seattle. What an amazing spectacle; it reminds me of the outdoor markets back in Việt Nam with people darting in and out of shops, selecting fresh fish, fruits, or vegetables to take home. A mix of ethnicities—Italians, Russians, Asians, Latinos—roam about all speaking their native tongues. I am delighted to see such diversity among the populace in this tiny corner of Seattle. Most of them are tourists, but even the locals appear lively and happy. Like me, they admire the fresh flowers for sale or the tantalizing bakery items on display. I decide that one day, I will live near Pike Place Market so I can be down here every day.

Beyond the market is the waterfront and view of Elliott Bay. There is a park nearby where families and lovers picnic; they enjoy the distant views of the Olympic National Forest, ferries, and Mount Rainier. A musician stands at a corner playing his guitar while a passerby drops money into his case. Magdaleine and I linger to listen to him sing and admire his talent. We each drop a dollar into his case before stepping into Starbucks Coffee to buy a pound of ground French pressed coffee.

"You are great tour guide," I say to Magdaleine, who is beaming with joy. "I love it here."

She whisks me to the Pike Place Fish Market. "You're going to love this, Snow." At the fish market, I watch fishmongers yell and throw fish to one another, quickly wrapping it before ringing up the purchase for the customer. I notice a sign that reads "Caution: Low Flying Fish" behind one of the fishmongers. Just then, a fish comes flying at me and hits me in the shoulder. Startled, I jump back.

Magdaleine laughs. "Not to worry. It's a foam fish." She whispers something in the salesman's ear and points to an albacore tuna resting on ice. She grabs my hand and pulls me toward Eric, our fishmonger. With a mischievous twinkle in his eyes, he drapes an apron around my neck and hands me a pair of latex gloves. Magdaleine shimmies a shower cap over my head, but it slips down over my eyes. They both have a good laugh at the folly. My protests and state of confusion go unnoticed and unanswered.

Eric grabs the tuna and yells, "Flying albacore tuna to the lady in purple." The two other fishermen repeat in unison. Eric launches the torpedo-looking fish at me. I have no time to think, just react, and to my surprise, it slips through my fingers. I catch it a foot from the ground. Everyone cheers. A rush of pride washes over me. Magdaleine buys the fish and has it divided in half for us both to take home.

"Eric," Magdaleine says, "please be a doll and keep this chilled for us. We are going to grab some food and drinks and be back to get our prize before you close." She gives him her name, phone number, and a flirtatious smile. "C'mon," she says to me.

We walk through Post Alley and stop in front of a pink door with no name, number, or address posted—no signage whatsoever to indicate if it is a residence or a business. She turns the knob, pushes the door in, and steps onto a small landing. I follow her down the stairs to a slightly musty restaurant, where the aromas of wine-soaked corks and cheeses tickle the senses.

"This is a small hidden gem," Magdaleine says. "You will find that Seattle has many of them. The restaurant is run by word of mouth. They do not run advertisements. A lot of Europeans dine here. I hope you like Italian food. I went on a date here once with a gorgeous Italian soccer player. The sex was yummy, but he was so shallow. Anyway, it's an intimate space, as you can see. I think the maximum capacity is like thirty or something."

The dining section is dimly lit, romantic if you are with someone you are enamored with...and I am quite enamored with Magdaleine. She is an enigma to me. Her femininity makes men fall at her feet and women clamor to learn from her. She is intelligent, kind, funny, and savvy, without the pretentiousness of most young adults trying to prove themselves to the world. I enjoy her company and stories very much and laugh at how she fawns over the show *Dallas*. In two hours, I learn a little about Seattle's history, about the Great Seattle Fire, and how the city was built on top of itself. I learn about the ghost tours and underground tours where we can see the old city below. Most mind-boggling are the stories of prohibition and how speakeasies came to fruition. She shares the secrets of Tavern Law, a small saloon in the Pioneer Inn, where behind a bank vault door is a private bar that seats twelve people. A phone will ring by the vault door, and if you know the password of the hour, you are admitted inside.

"You're escorted up a narrow staircase in the dark," Magdaleine says. "There is just enough light at the top for you to see the black and white portraits of nude models hanging on the wall. All tasteful pictures. There's soft lounge seating in one section and a few tables and chairs in another section. There's no drink menu. You tell the bartender what flavors and notes you like, and he'll design a drink for you."

"Magdaleine," I say, "this best date I be on!"

We leave the Pink Door in time to catch the sunset and retrieve our tuna from Eric as he packs up for the night. It has been a perfect day.

I pull into Pastor George's driveway to pick up Dolly and sense something is wrong. The lights are out, including the porch light. The windows are open. How strange, on a chilly February night, to have the windows ajar. I hear the girls scream and Pastor George laughing.

I do not think to knock or ring the doorbell. I burst into Pastor George's house and follow the sound of sinister laughter and a deep gurgling voice. Pastor George stands in front of the four girls, all huddled together with Dawn on the sofa, baring his teeth and curling his fingers above his head. He growls and lunges at them. I find the light switch and flick it on. All eyes turn to me. Dawn inhales deeply and clutches the children closer to her bosom. Pastor George gasps. I step forward, ready to charge at him over the couch and beat him with my purse.

"Snow!" Pastor George exclaims. "You scared the nutsack right off my—" He stops abruptly and laughs.

Dawn looks embarrassed. "You gave us a good fright."

Dolly jumps out of Dawn's arms and runs to me. "Mama, I had so much fun. Can I sleepover? Please?"

"Another day," I say and watch the enthusiasm wax and wane from her face. "It is Sunday."

I have Dolly collect her belongings while Dawn gives me a recap of their day. They had fellowship and lunch at the church, then went to the video store down the street to rent a movie. The girls picked *Poltergeist*. They played at the house, baked cookies, and ate dinner before settling down for the movie. I had walked in as the movie ended to witness Pastor George capitalizing on their fear and relishing the moment.

18. A WEDDING TO PLAN (AUGUST 1983)

I put my cup of coffee down and snatch Dolly's spoon to use as a microphone. Lionel Richie is singing to me on the radio, and I serenade him back.

"You are you so," I sing, "you need not know, I love you so."

Dolly giggles.

My neighbor barges into my apartment and calls out my name. "Chị Tuyết ơi." She finds us at the table enjoying our brunch of canned sardines and rice, our staple diet back at the refugee camp.

Diệp crinkles her nose. "How can you eat that?"

"It is cheap and familiar," I say. "At least it is not dog food."

"Not that again," she says and laughs. Diệp sits down. "I have a dilemma…oh, oh…" She points to the radio. "Turn it up."

Dolly rushes to the stereo and cranks up the volume. The song "Puttin' on the Ritz" by Taco is airing on KUBE 93 FM. Diệp jumps to her feet and thrusts her hips side to side to the beat, looking like a broken robot short-circuiting. She reminds me of the robot Twiki from the show *Buck Rogers*. Diệp takes the spoon and sings into it. "If yoo is bloo, dunt no waa to go to, wai dunt yoo go, fa shoon seets… Pooty on da Rex." I sneak a peek at Dolly. She glances back at me. We exchange a smile and try to contain our laughter. "Diff'rent tips gorillas go pantz—"

I burst at the seams and cackle like an evil witch. I beg her to stop singing and dancing before she breaks something. She feigns sadness but perks up when I compliment her on learning English. "Has Donald been teaching you?"

She nods. "Donald's son, Ricky, is transferring from Washingon State to the University of Washington this September. His son is coming home for the summer, and Donald wants me to spend time with them so I can get to know Ricky. He wants me to go with them, too, when Ricky moves into his dormitory. Our relationship is getting serious."

151

"What is the dilemma then?" I ask.

"What if Ricky does not like me?" Diệp asks. "What if I cannot relate to him? What if he does not want me to help him settle into his new college?"

"Talk to Jason," Dolly says. "Ricky and Jason are best friends."

"That is a great idea," I say. "They are so close. Little Jason can tell you all about Ricky and offer suggestions. Honestly, though, Ricky seems like a sweet boy."

"If I pass this test," Diệp mutters, "maybe he will ask me to marry him."

"Is that what you want?" I ask.

"Yes, I am sure of it. He is the kindest man."

"Then he is not testing you," I say, "so stop thinking it is something you have to pass. Be yourself. Donald and Jason love you. Ricky will too. And if Hùng can accept Donald as a father and his kids as brothers, then you will be a family."

###

A week goes by. I have not spoken to Diệp but have seen her from afar getting in or out of Donald's car with both Ricky and Jason two steps behind. I suspect it will not be long before they marry. They are an odd couple but complement each other nicely, with her so quirky and him so patient, and she so animated while he subdued and conservative.

The phone rings. It is Tree on the line. "Aunt Eight...Ngọc is pregnant."

I panic. They are too young to start a family. "I hoped you would have a longer engagement. How do her parents feel about it?" I ask.

"Upset. Nervous. Excited."

Tree and I are at a loss for words and do not know what to say next. An asteroid of silence separates us. I am not sure what he expects or hopes to hear from me. Does he want advice or my blessing? Is he expecting me to get angry and yell at him? Perhaps he hopes I will help with the wedding and the baby expenses.

"I need to speak to her parents," I say. "Arrange for me to come. You make the introduction."

The next day, I drive with Dolly across the West Seattle Bridge and follow Tree's directions to the house. Dolly is my navigator and reads the directions from the notes I jotted down. At the end of the bridge, turn left onto Thirty-Fifth Avenue Southwest, then right at Southwest Graham Street.

Dolly points to the yellow house on the right. "That one."

The house is painted in a muted yellow with white trim. Two old chairs, pots filled with lush green weeds, and brown, dried-up flowers clutter the small porch. The front is partially fenced with white picket posts, stained green from moss and mildew. A big pile of fresh dog dung greets us at the threshold between the sidewalk and the lawn, overgrown with yellow foxtail grass and bright dandelions.

"Gross," Dolly says and steps around the pile of poop.

I look at the windows, half expecting to see a face staring out, spying on me. Instead, I see only two single-paned windows, one with a crack in it, and the other covered by bent and skewed blinds. The front yard is littered with car parts, a deflated basketball, one soiled sock, and a mess of glass and aluminum cans. I shudder and wonder what kind of people Kelly's parents are, but remind myself they raised a sweet daughter. After all, they were farmers on Phú Quốc and worked hard to survive, even if it meant they had to sell their youngest daughter to a childless couple. I respect honest people, hard-working people…survivors. At least they have a house, unlike me, sharing an apartment with hundreds of roaches.

I raise my hand to knock on the door when suddenly it swings open and a small woman with a round face and high-pitched, nasally voice greets me. She wears an *áo bà ba*, a traditional short shirt with long sleeves and buttons from the neck down to the stomach. The olive shirt is paired with black silk trousers. At once I am transported back to the countryside of Việt Nam, to the rice paddies and farmland of Vĩnh Bình.

"Sister Tuyết," Kelly's mother, Lan, says, ten decibels too loudly. "Come in." She ushers me inside and pats Dolly's head. "What a pretty girl you are." I realize this is her normal indoor voice. She is not shouting. If she and the laundromat had a humming competition, she would win. Perhaps she is hard of hearing.

"Thank you for having me over on short notice," I say softly.

"It is ridiculous that the kids have been dating for a year and we are only now meeting," she says. No, not hard of hearing—just a loud talker. Lan scurries down the hallway like a mouse on a mission to find cheese. "Ngọc's father will be home soon. I sent him to get coconut water for us." She steps over a shirt lying on the floor like it is a speck of dirt not worth noticing. I look around the room. They are Buddhist. There is a veneration table with eight pictures on the wall and a large handful of burnt, ashy incense sticks jammed into a tiny container of gray rice kernels. I assume they are pictures of parents and grandparents on both sides of the family. A large statue of Buddha and Lady Buddha sits prominently above the ancestral altar.

"Where are Ngọc and Tree?" I ask, admiring the pickled jalapenos, leeks, mustard greens, daikon, and carrots on her kitchen counter.

The front door creaks open. I hear six distinct voices down the hallway…four men and two women. Dolly runs out to the backyard and hops onto a rusty swing. It is fully fenced in the back, so I am not too worried she is out there by herself. A little Pomeranian trots out to greet Dolly but stops to eat a dry nugget of poop. I look away.

A parade of bodies filters into the room led by Tree. The only person I recognize is Kelly. Tree introduces me to Kelly's father, Toàn. He bows respectfully deep to me, bending at the waist and almost parallel to the floor. "Welcome to our home. Please sit and relax. Let me pour some coconut water for you."

Kelly's younger sister, Ann, greets me with the honorific title of Aunt Eight. "Cháo Cô Tám." She is a prettier, younger version of her sister but is not blessed with a straight and high-bridged nose; it rounds out wide at the bottom and reminds me of a pig's snout, albeit a cute one. Her boyfriend, Quang, does not greet me. He merely acknowledges my presence by looking at me and nodding, not in a respectful way but in an arrogant fashion. Ann walks into the kitchen to help her father, Toàn, bring out the iced coconut waters while Quang makes himself comfortable on a chair. He lights a cigarette and inhales deeply the Marlboro Reds. I can tell Ann is demurring and subservient in how she casts her eyes down, moves quietly, and looks for praise upon serving our drinks. Ann is like her father whereas Kelly is like her mother in terms of confidence, ease, and social skills.

I turn to the stranger behind Tree. He is the last to be introduced. Tree pulls a chair out, and the stranger sits down. He smiles at me. I smile back. He is attractive, although his top lip is thin and I have a superstition about people with thin lips—they are terrible kissers and not to be trusted. I quickly dismiss this delusional notion because I find him to be a good-looking Vietnamese man. His hair is thick and slicked back. He sits with a straight posture and clasps his hands comfortably on the table. Still, he says nothing, as if he is taking me in, bit by bit, just as I am dissecting him with my gaze, piece by piece. His polo shirt is clean and his pants wrinkle-free. He smells masculine, clean, and made of money. Who are you?

"Aunt Eight," Tree says, "this is Uncle Bình, the one I have been living with." Yes, of course, the man whose wife left him. I remember now. The man who plays soccer on the fields with men half his age. The man who lives in a house near Southcenter Mall and is friends with Lan.

Lan sits across from me and blurts out, "My daughter is pregnant." She states what we already know and the reason why we are together today for the first time. "Of course, we need to move up the wedding date. It needs to be this month."

Out of the corner of my eye, I see Quang roll his eyes and exhale with exaggeration. What is his problem? No one in the room speaks up. The men are unusually quiet. I gather this will be a conversation between Lan and

154

me. That is a first—women doing all the talking and decision-making. Back home, I was used to the men making arrangements and managing everything.

"I am sure Pastor George can marry them in the church," I say.

"No, we are Buddhists, not Christians," Lan says. She is adamant that there not be a church wedding and we need a traditional Vietnamese wedding. I understand her point of view, but with short notice and limited resources, not to mention we do not know many people here, it would not be feasible to have a traditional one. Whomever we invite will likely gift the couple household items instead of money in red envelopes, and what good would that do them when they do not even have a house of their own? I argue there is no time, no temple, and no seamstress who can make an *áo nhật bình*, the elaborate and intricate wedding gown of our people.

Lan takes my argument under advisement. "We will have to do a hybrid wedding then, but we must seek counsel from a monk to determine the best date to marry based on their horoscope."

"Or a fortuneteller," I say. "Do you know any?"

Tree interrupts us and questions which birth date we plan to use when we seek advice from the fortuneteller. That is a good question as it is important to be accurate.

"Your real birthday, of course," I say. "December 16, 1962, not '65."

At this juncture, Bình speaks up. "I know a fortuneteller and a seamstress, and if the kids do not get married in a church or a temple, why not a botanical garden?"

A man with ideas, connections, and solutions…My interest in this stranger and my curiosity over him spike. Lan and I fold him into our conversation and listen to what he has to say, giving him stock in our wedding planning venture but making it clear we have the final decision-making power.

Bình advises we must move quickly and be willing to pay extra to motivate the seamstress. We agree that he will arrange a meeting with the fortuneteller as soon as possible so that a wedding date can be pinpointed. I ask him to schedule a reading for me and Thủy-Tiên as well. We will get Kelly and Tree in with the seamstress as soon as possible to get measurements and pick out fabric. Lan and Toàn will plan the menu, Ann and Quang will find a venue, namely a park, and I will ask Pastor George to perform the ceremony. Tree and Kelly will manage flowers and the remaining details. Dolly, of course, will be the flower girl, as is customary in a Western wedding.

I leave the house excited for the wedding, where East meets West and the union of two souls will soon be witnessed. In eight months, Tree and Kelly's baby will be born and we will welcome the second generation of

Vietnamese boat people. We will have a footprint in American civilization. It makes me happy knowing a legacy will be left from my generation's sacrifices. So begins the fusion of two souls, two families, and two cultures.

19. THE FORTUNETELLER (AUGUST 1983)

Tree, Kelly, and Bình are the first to arrive at the fortuneteller's home, immediately followed by Toàn and Lan. Dolly and I arrive twenty minutes late as I took a wrong turn, having never been to Federal Way before. I underestimated the time it would take to get here from Kent with I-5 traffic.

I pull into the government-subsidized trailer park for low-income immigrants and locate the mobile home that is rented out to Hồng Nhung, our fortuneteller. Many residents are outside tending to their tiny plots of land, pulling weeds, watering plants, putting down gravel, or lounging on the front porch. Everyone's face is brown, goldenrod, or cocoa…a rainbow of refugees. They all take great pride in their homes as the roads are clear from litter and junk and the homes immaculately landscaped and gardened. It must be nice not to have neighbors right next to you, sharing the same wall. I hope to upgrade to a mobile home of my own one day and start a flower and vegetable or herb garden.

Inside the single-wide home, the blinds are closed. Hồng Nhung limps to the big window with her walking stick and draws the extra curtains to block out sunlight. "We do not need any distractions or voyeurs."

She shares with us that she is sixty years old and that her cane was a gift of war. An explosion in her village left stubborn shrapnel in her thigh and she has learned to coexist with it the past ten years. Like most fortunetellers I have met, she is calm and patient, an oracle of wisdom and truth to those who believe.

"Spring arrived unexpectedly this year," Hồng Nhung says matter-of-factly. "My tulips noticed, but my daffodils are still hibernating." She invites Tree and Kelly to sit down at a small table with her. She takes Tree's hand and looks at his palm. "You were born on Sunday, December 16, 1962. A water tiger. Were you born at night or in the morning?"

"Morning," Tree says, "although I do not know what time." Tree looks to me, hoping I can provide the answer, but I do not recall the exact time.

Hồng Nhung studies the lines of his palm. "Your tiger sign shows that you are brave and take risks. You are smart, too, but street smart, not business smart. You are also the black sheep and will have many challenges ahead of you. Music will center you so you can make good decisions." She continues to tell him he is a born leader, a competitor, and not afraid to fight or overcome obstacles. He must be careful because he lives dangerously.

Our sage next reviews Kelly's hand but then takes out a deck of cards. She confesses to being self-taught but was a highly sought after practitioner of cartomancy back in Việt Nam because of her accuracy. Many who contemplated escaping the country by boat sought her advice, and if she predicted they'd make it, then they would go. If she said they'd get caught, sure as war and famine, they got caught. Even after the communist government banned readings, she had many Việt Cộng men come to her because they could not resist in times of uncertainty. After all, it is part of our heritage and custom. It is in our DNA and will forever be a part of our culture. They never arrested her because she dove deep into their fears and superstitions.

She asks Kelly to shuffle the cards and think about what she wants to know. She then lays out four columns of cards, each column with seven cards from the deck. She consults the cards quietly to herself before saying, "You two are quite compatible." This declaration makes Tree and Kelly look at each other lovingly and smile. "I see a lasting marriage and two, maybe three children. One of your children, the second one, may not live. Her life will be up to you."

"What do you mean?" Kelly asks.

Our spiritual counselor raises her hand to dismiss the question and continues. "You two will have many homes in different states. I suggest you see a geomancer when buying a house to ensure the chi flows positively. Any miscalculations will result in a life of suffering for you and the next three generations."

Kelly's eye twitches, and she shifts in her chair. "Suffering how?"

Again, our prophesier ignores her. Ultimately, our advisor tells them Thursday, August 25, is the best date for the wedding according to their astrological charts and zodiac signs.

We take a break following the readings with tea and coconut butter biscuits. To my surprise, Bình takes the lead and orchestrates who does what, by when, and how. He appoints himself as the wedding coordinator. Depending on which lens I have on, he can either be a charismatic, confident man who is marriage material or an attractive gay man who has done a great job hiding his true identity. Either way, I want to know him better and figure out how he identifies himself. At least he is beautiful to look at.

When it is my and Dolly's turn to have our fortunes read, I send everyone out and encourage them to go home. "This is a private matter, and whatever I learn, it will be my burden to bear."

They all protest except for Toàn, who is the ultimate introvert and happy to excuse himself from this nonsense. I bid them farewell and promise to give them a status update on Pastor George's availability on August 25.

After everyone leaves, my foreseer asks, "Who do you want me to read first?"

I decide on Dolly. I give Hồng Nhung Dolly's birth name, Lê Ngọc Thủy-Tiên, her birth date, and the time she was born. "Tuesday, July 30, 1974, at 11:53 p.m."

"Wood tiger," she says. "They like to be in charge. They are courageous and popular. Because she was born close to midnight, this makes her cunning. She will be successful, perhaps even famous and rich. Your daughter is charming and impulsive. She will have many admirers. She will need to lead a pious life or be thwarted into a life of instability. If she marries after age thirty-two, she will have a stable marriage. Her husband will love her very much, but if she marries before that, she will suffer greatly." Hồng Nhung pauses and frowns. "Your daughter was very sick." She points to the line of life on Dolly's hand. "See here how her lifeline starts out jagged, not deep and straight? But she grows stronger every day, so do not worry. She will live a long life and be lucky and prosperous." She frowns again. This is disconcerting. "I see Thủy-Tiên may have two husbands, three pregnancies, but only one birth." My look of alarm makes her quickly foretell the next thing she sees. "Tiger girls have strong personalities, but as mothers, they are very protective. You will have an important role as grandmother to provide a solid foundation for your grandchild."

The idea of being a grandma one day makes me happy. I hope Dolly will have a son to break the cycle of suffering women in my family inherited. Boys are more revered, more respected, and tend to have more freedom. I wish that for my grandson. Hồng Nhung finishes the reading and says to come back in a few years so she can read my daughter's chart again. I take a deep breath and give her my hand as it is now my turn, but she does not take it. Instead, I am asked to shuffle the deck of cards and think about what questions I want her to answer. I think about my family and whether they will be all right. I wonder about Tý and Hải and whether they will be in my life again. Finally, I wonder if I will find love again.

Hồng Nhung turns over the cards and arranges them in four columns. She hovers her hand over them and touches a few of them. She nods, umm-hmms and ahh-hahs several times before looking at me. "You said you were born on a Thursday?"

"Yes," I answer, "on April 13, 1939."

"The Earth Rabbit then," she says, "or Earth Cat depending on if you prefer the Vietnamese zodiac over the Chinese one."

I recall a conversation I had once with Dolly's father, who was born the year of the rat. Tý teased that it was me who chased him and was smitten with him first. "You are a cat," he had said, "and I am a mouse. Of course, you chased after me."

I told him if that were the case, I would have killed my mouse, not married it. I also clarified that he was a rotten street rat, not a cute mouse. He feigned being hurt and coaxed me into kissing him until he felt better. We made love that day and a part of him stayed with me. Eight months later, our daughter was born, prematurely with one hand clinging to life and the other to death.

I ask Hồng Nhung if identifying with a cat or a rabbit makes a difference in my reading. She says, "Not really," so I let her read my fortune at her discretion. She tells me my traits, for example, my thirst for knowledge and how I enjoy school more than work. She says I am an accepting person and do not like to argue. These are characteristics, perhaps flaws, I am acutely aware of.

"Because you are easy-going and do not quarrel or challenge others, many see you as timid. However, you have strong desires, and when you latch onto something, you will prove others wrong and contradict their beliefs." I ask her if I will love again. "You have many admirers and many lives. You have escaped death multiple times. I see two husbands in this lifetime, but as beautiful and kind as you are, you are very unlucky in love." She continues to tell me that my daughter and I will not live together, and we will not only be divided with our life choices but separated by state lines. She tells me to avoid a lot of travel as there will be complications. Additionally, while I will live to be an old woman, heaven will claim me shortly after I return from a trip.

I ask her if I will return to Việt Nam one day and if my family will be all right. She says yes to both. "Will I see Tý and Hải again?"

"Your husband will be in your life again," she says, "but his brother will not. You must forget him."

Hearing that saddens me. It can only mean Hải did not survive the re-education camps and will never come home. I did not tell her Hải and I became lovers after the war, but I did not need to. Hồng Nhung already knows and is legitimately the best fortuneteller I have ever met.

At the end of our session, I pay her and leave, feeling lighter and optimistic about the future, yet sad for Hải.

20. I DO (AUGUST 1983)

Chagrined by Ann and Quang's failure to find an affordable venue or a public park that could host a small wedding on short notice and specifically, on Thursday, August 25, I ask Sky if his parents would mind hosting the wedding on their property. Fortunately, the Herringtons come to the rescue and are delighted. As a matter of fact, Katrina and Jean-Adrien insist on it, which is a good thing, because I question whether Ann and Quang even tried to find a suitable locale. Both of them have been in foul moods leading up to the wedding day, see-sawing between hot-tempered arguments that flare up out of the blue to cold, uncomfortable silent treatments with stares that could turn Medusa and her Gorgon sisters into stone.

"I haven't been this excited since the Enumclaw auction when that stud of a cowboy, Judd, sold me Blazing Six Guns!" Katrina exclaims. She immediately takes action and prepares the property for the big day, making endless phone calls to a vast network of friends and associates. She takes the liberty of renting tents, tables, and chairs, purchasing party favors, and securing a live band. No detail is overlooked. She even orders fans and water misting stations to keep guests cool. I tell her it is too much and a simple ceremony will do. We plan to do a potluck reception afterward to keep things casual, but Katrina would not hear of it.

"This is our gift to Tree and Nop...er, Kelly," Katrina proclaims. "We are family."

The day finally arrives, and it is a clear day with nothing but powder blue skies. All morning, the house buzzes as Katrina, the caterers, Lan, Binh, and I finalize the little details. An hour before the guests arrive, we stand in the backyard to admire our work.

Folding chairs stand firm near the barn, split equally with twenty-five chairs on either side of the fifty-foot red-carpeted aisle. White clusters of gardenias from Katrina's greenhouse adorn the first chair of each aisle on either side of the red carpet. At the front, a hedge of purple hydrangeas grows naturally and forms the perfect backdrop.

Between the stables and riding pen, a five-member band tunes their instruments to rehearse the first set in front of five empty banquet tables. Each table seats ten and is dressed in white linen with lavender centerpieces. The fenced, round pen has been transformed into a dance floor, and all around are white lights strung along poles to illuminate the area. Hitched in front of the stable are Katrina's two horses, Blazing Six Guns, the quarter horse she impulsively bought at the auction from Cowboy Judd, and a beautiful palomino named J'adore Champagne. Both beauties are hooked up to a carriage where guests can get their photos taken under the romantic sunset haze of summer sky. After the reception, J'adore Champagne and Blazing Six Guns will take the bride and groom around the nearby trails to a private yurt on the Herrington property. All these years, I never knew there was a small cabin, and Sky promises to show me sometime.

What was supposed to be an intimate affair with twenty people has now ballooned to fifty guests. It is still considered a small wedding, but I realize I do not know half the people coming.

Teddy and Catherine's daughters traveled in with their families yesterday from Oregon and Wenatchee. Tree invited our VOLAG representative, Joseph, who RSVP'd for two people and is bringing his wife. Sky and Magdaleine invited Bill, who surprised us all by saying he was bringing a date…a woman he met in May when the *Post-Intelligencer* and the *Times* entered into a joint operating agreement.

When I told Diệp about the pending nuptials two weeks ago, she invited herself, saying of course she will come and bring Donald and the boys. "I love weddings. Maybe Donald will get the hint."

All in all, between our guests and those on Kelly's side, there will be plenty of witnesses to celebrate the union of two people in love.

At last, we take our seats and wait for the bride entrance song to play. In front, Tree stands with Pastor George. Both men look handsome, Tree in his tuxedo and Pastor George in this linen suit. Tree gives a confident smile for the photographer but reverts to a nervous groom the moment the shutter closes. The band cues up the melody for "Here Comes the Sun" by the Beatles. All eyes turn to the back.

The back door of the house opens, and Dolly presents herself in a yellow A-line dress that Catherine worked tirelessly to sew, using the satin and tulle fabric she had on hand. My daughter walks hurriedly toward the front, tossing handfuls of white petals onto the red-carpeted aisle, no doubt nervous with all the faces focusing on her. A few people giggle, but I beam with pride.

I turn back and hold my breath for Kelly. I know what her red *áo nhật bình* looks like but have not seen the entire ensemble on her. She steps out, and we all stand. The wedding dress is made of red satin with intricately embroidered phoenix designs on the front. A gold robe drapes around her hourglass figure; the hems of her sleeves have five bands of colors, each representing the five elements of our culture: earth, metal, water, wood, and fire. Completing the outfit is a royal purple turban that frames her oval face. She is breathtaking.

Before Kelly reaches the front of the aisle to stand with Tree, Diệp bawls loudly and blows her nose into a handkerchief. Her cries become the catalyst for more tears as Lan wails with her. I stifle my outbreak and wipe the wetness from my eyes. Oh, Brother Seven, Sister Hiền, if you could see your son now.

Kelly hands her bouquet of hydrangeas to Dolly and takes her place next to Tree. The two join hands.

Pastor George invites everyone to sit. "Friends and family, today is a blessing that has been bestowed upon us. When two people find each other, as Tree and Kelly have, and love one another, we must commit to support this union and help them with their journey. When two become one…when the halves become whole…we all become family."

The ceremony goes by quickly. Pastor George finishes officiating the wedding and the lovebirds kiss after their "I Do's." Cheers and clapping erupt to send the newlyweds, walking hand in hand, back to the house. The band plays a lively Fleetwood Mac song, and the guests disperse. Some head to the banquet table to find their seat; others visit with the horses and get their picture taken in the carriage. Dolly and the other children run over to Penny and Todd to meet the baby, Andrew, who is now two years old.

Bình takes my elbow and asks if I would like something refreshing to drink. He leads me through a honeycomb of talking people, and we find the punch bowl with floating fruit. I take a sip and realize there is alcohol in it. I look at the sign. Sangria. I throw caution to the wind and fill my glass to the top. While we wait for Tree and Kelly to emerge, Bình and I take our seats at the reserved table where the bride and groom will join us shortly. Already at our table are Kelly's parents, her sister, Quang, Donald, and Diệp.

Quang and Ann are enjoying themselves and seem to have resolved their lovers' quarrel. They engage in boisterous conversation with the others, but it is Diệp and Quang who do most of the jibber-jabbering.

"You look like a sun goddess," Bình says to me. "Yellow looks radiant on you."

I blush and grasp for a compliment in return. "Thank you. You did a good job coordinating the wedding."

164

"All I did was get them to a fortuneteller and find a seamstress," he says. "Katrina relieved me of my other duties."

I laugh. "She did an amazing job. She should be a wedding planner."

Bình nods and asks casually whether I have given much thought to letting Dolly's father back into my life…and be a family again. His abrupt change in course puts a sour taste in my mouth. He does not know me well enough to ask about such intimate details of my life. I give him a stark look of annoyance and stiffen my body. "Why are you asking about him? It is a personal matter." I am not sure why, but Bình's inquiry about Tý strikes a nerve. The audacity!

"It is merely a question," Bình says. "Tree shared with me a little bit about your history and mentioned you two recently reconnected after all these years."

"You do not see me asking why your wife left you, do you?" I turn away and sip my sangria.

I can tell my comment stings more than my body language by the way he brusquely puts his drink down. "Are you still in love with him?"

I tell myself I have forgiven Tý. So what is the problem? Now, I am upset with myself for not knowing the reason behind my attitude. I dismiss Bình by turning my attention to Quang and Diệp, who are having a sprightly debate about the role of husband and wife after the wedding.

Bình deflects my standoffish behavior by pounding his drink and storming off to join Tree and Kelly, who have reemerged to greet their guests. Both bride and groom have shed the outer layer of their wedding attire; gone are the robe to Kelly's áo nhật bình and Tree's tuxedo jacket. The guests cheer as the two of them join hands and kiss.

"What do you think, Chị Tuyết?" Diệp taps my wrist. "You are kilometers away. Did you hear any of what I said?"

Something about the way my neighbor dresses and carries herself always makes me chuckle. She is an effervescent woman, and despite having gone through so much tragedy with the annihilation at Mỹ Lai, she chooses to live a life in color and optimism. I must learn to do the same. Today, Diệp is wearing a sleeveless, chartreuse green V-neck jumpsuit cinched at the waist with a gold braided curtain rope. The ensemble is couture-looking despite costing only three dollars at the local thrift store. Now that is the next level of refugee chic. I smile with endearment. "I heard you, Sister Diệp. And I agree with both of you. Quang makes a valid argument that after marriage, a wife must serve her husband and make him happy. She should nourish him with good food, keep the household orderly, raise the children to be well-mannered and productive. She should give her husband power."

165

Diệp's jaw drops, and Quang smirks smugly. I continue. "However, a husband, at least a smart one, knows that his powers come from his wife, and she can easily reduce him to a worthless man if he cannot make her proud and happy." I repeat this for Donald who has been left out of this conversation for the past twenty minutes.

"Aw, yes, happy wife, happy life," Donald replies. "The sooner he learns that the better off he'll be."

Quang stands firm with his masculine pride. "Women serve men. It has always been that way. We are stronger, faster, smarter, and have always been in charge. That is why boys are more valued than girls. We are providers and protectors."

The argument continues. Quang holds strong to his traditional beliefs and leans into the backlash from Ann, Donald, Diệp, and me. I admire Quang for not backing down and staking his claim on his convictions; however, the more we dig our heels into this topic, the more intense it becomes. By the time Tree and Kelly arrive at our table, we are shouting. The debate has turned into a sparring match. I have no doubt it would have escalated to a street brawl if the bride and groom had not shown up.

Quang stands and kicks the chair. "We are leaving." His eyes cast knives at Kelly before pulling Ann roughly out of her seat and dragging her to the front of the house. Ann looks apologetically at her sister and embarrassingly at us. She leaves with him and does not resist.

Lan and I chase after them. We yell at them to stop and not ruin the day for Tree and Kelly. Moments later, Kelly appears at my side.

"If you want to, leave," Kelly says, "but my sister is not going with you." She takes Ann's hand and pulls her to her side. Quang pulls her back. Lan grabs her daughter's arm, and poor Ann is jostled like a rag doll by grown children.

I try to remain calm and diffuse the situation with reasoning. I make a plea to Quang to be a better man and not make a scene. It is a stinging mistake. The piece of shit slaps me!

I am stunned by what just happened and slap him back. Quang advances one step forward, but before he can lay another hand on me, Sky grabs Quang by the neck, sweeps his leg, and pins him to the ground. I watch in horror as Quang's face goes from bright pink, flush with fury, to pale and cowering in fear. Sky's fist drills into Quang's face repeatedly and pulverizes his face to a bloody pulp. His skin shreds like it came out of a meat grinder. Sky towers over Quang and continues to beat him mercilessly as one by one, he flicks us off like annoying earwigs.

"Die, you commie bastard!" Sky screams.

166

Ann shrieks in terror and wails for Sky to stop. Teddy, Jean-Adrien, Bill, and Donald rush to Quang's aid. It takes the four of them to pull Sky off. This whole evening has turned into a debacle. Sky falls onto the grass and cries. I feel horrible for Quang, who despite being an egotistical and chauvinistic boar, did not deserve to have his face smashed in by a blender of fists and blades of revenge.

"Violence is not the answer," Bill says. "Don't let hatred be the virus that destroys us all."

Sky weeps and apologizes. "I don't know what came over me. Forgive me." Katrina holds her son and rocks him like a baby. She tells him he needs help and that his fight with war demons is not over. The resurgence of flashbacks and stress is hurting him still. Perhaps it is a quixotic notion to think we can control our demons before they completely control us.

I pity Ann and see myself in her…at least the old me. I used to be so accepting of everything that I was blind to what lay beneath the surface of things…the surface of people. It was old Mrs. Trần back in Sài Gòn who taught me to be strong. She reminded me that my greatest artillery lies in the strength of my voice. Having a voice means having a choice. I tell myself that I can be Mrs. Trần for Ann.

Bình hoists Quang up to take him home. Ann follows them, but I hold her back. "Let him cool off. Your place right now is with your family. It is your sister's big day."

Ann frees herself from my grip and nips at me with her angry words. "My place is with him. This family," she points at her parents and sister, "sold me when I was a child." She sidesteps past me and yells at Toàn and Lan. "I had a new family, and you took me from them." Ann whips around to face Kelly. "And you, big sister, always have to steal whatever piece of happiness I have. First, you drag me to be sold like one of your fruit baskets at the market, and after I adopted a new life with my host parents, you drag me back and force me to come to this country. You should have left without me, forgotten me. Maybe my parents would still be alive if I were there to protect them! And now, look at you. You cannot be happy with one man. No, you have to steal mine too? His heart belongs to me. I will not share him." Ann's body shakes with rage.

"What are you talking about?" Kelly asks.

Ann impales her sister with a look of disgust. "Like you did not know. Quang loves you, but since he cannot have you, he settled for me. In time, he will love me, but not while you are around." She storms off and chases after Bình and Quang. The three of them disappear onto the main road in Bình's old Cadillac. I sigh in defeat and let the boulders roll off my shoulders.

167

It is Pastor George who breaks the spell and ropes us back to why we are gathered here today. Despite the heavy interruption and the shocking news of a twisted love triangle, we manage to get the celebration back on course. Even Sky manages to shake it off, perhaps for Magdaleine's sake. He puts on a brave face and mouths an "I'm sorry" to me before sitting with Magdaleine at the farthest table. The band rocks a high-tempo song, and the guests sit to devour their dinner. I admit we all drink more than our share of sangrias and whiskeys tonight. Alcohol is our bandage and the elixir to forgetfulness. As the night rolls on, the moon shines, and the music gets louder. Soon, I forget about the scuffle from earlier and enjoy the present moment.

I barely take two bites of my slice of lemon chiffon wedding cake when Bill asks me to dance. I look around for his date, confused.

"She left," Bill says. "Well, I sort of kicked her out. Seeing Skyler beat the crap out of that guy made her thirsty for a story. She wanted an article in the paper by tomorrow, 'Vietnam Vet Loses Control.'" He waves his hand in a semi-circle above him like it is a headlining title on a marquee sign.

We dance until my feet ache, and the stars drip into the pine trees. At midnight, Tree and Kelly ride off in the carriage pulled by Blazing Six Guns and J'adore Champagne. The remaining guests watch and wave as the couple disappears down the trail toward their yurt. As people leave I hear whispers of how the fusion wedding was the most exciting one they have been to and how the blending of cultures in today's matrimonial ceremony was a treat. People pay compliments to the hosts for the food, the wedding gown, the music, and the decorations, and when they run out of things to say, they marvel at the night sky and applaud the beautiful weather. No one dares bring up the sour discord that happened earlier in the day.

I offer to help Katrina and Jean-Adrien clean up, but they demand I take Dolly home. My daughter can barely keep her eyes open. I say my goodbyes; I hug the Herringtons and kiss the Vanzwols. Bill escorts me to my car and carries a sleepy Dolly in his arms. He slides her in the back seat of my small Honda Civic and buckles her seatbelt.

"What an interesting day," Bill says.

I nod. He removes a wisp of hair from my forehead and tucks it behind my earlobe. I blush at his touch. Bill strokes my cheek and follows the contour of my face until he reaches my parted lips. My heart is beating fast. Can he hear it? I dare not look into his eyes.

"You look beautiful." He bends down to kiss me, and I stand on my tiptoes, stretching my calves as long as they can go, to meet his mouth. Perhaps I am a little lightheaded from the alcohol. Perhaps it is the moonlight that has me bewitched. It does not matter. My body tingles. I melt into his arms and hungrily press my lips into his. I breathe in his scent of musk and whiskey and taste his lemon-tinged mouth. A million goosebumps ripple from my head to my toes and back up again, stopping at my womanhood. The curls and folds between my legs drip with desire. I cling to him, hungry for love, hungry for tenderness.

It has been a long time since the heat of desire has been awakened within me. I wrap my arms around Bill's waist and press my body into his hardness. I let out a moan and guide his hand to my breasts. We stand in each other's embrace, hungrily devouring each other's scent and taste. He offers one last lover's kiss before he abruptly pushes me away.

"You better take Dolly home," he says huskily.

I gaze into his eyes and search for clues to how he feels. My tongue is heavy and anchored down. I am too embarrassed to say anything.

His eyes are soft, yet I feel rejected. Does he pity me? Is he playing games with me? How can he turn his emotions on and off so easily? Maybe he will never love anyone because he still loves Katrina. Perhaps he feels guilty because he is my boss.

I take a step back, annoyed now. "Goodnight, Bill." I get in my car and drive down the driveway. I force myself not to look in the rearview mirror.

21. MOVE ON (JANUARY 1984)

Dolly is in fourth grade now, and Cabbage Patch Kids are all the craze with every child I know. I cannot change channels on TV without seeing a commercial about these dolls that come with a birth certificate and adoption papers. The retail stores have been selling them for thirty to fifty dollars, and the demand continues to skyrocket. I do not understand how a sixteen-inch doll with wool hair and a vinyl face can cost so much.

My daughter makes a plea and promises to get straight A's in all her classes if I buy her a doll. "Please, Mama, all my friends have one."

I give in to her nagging and sad face by pinky promising a doll in exchange for perfect attendance and perfect grades. In the pit of my stomach, I know I cannot afford to spend this frivolously on a toy. By June, if she accomplishes her side of the deal, I will have to take her to Sears or Toys "R" Us and buy a doll. Katrina says people have been fighting over these toys in the stores. It seems so long ago that my people fought over food, water, country, and home. They worried about how to live, not what presents to buy.

I will be lucky to find any "CPKs" as Dolly calls them. Both Katrina and Catherine vow to keep an eye out for me. If they find one, they will snatch one up. In the meantime, I have five months to budget and save a little from each paycheck. For once, I am hoping Dolly does not do well in school.

Ever since Tree and Kelly's wedding five months ago, I have been sorting through the cobwebs of that day and compartmentalizing the events. Kelly and her parents still pick apart that day like a scab. They cannot believe Quang was in love with Kelly and that he felt jilted by her. He had been harboring resentment and using Ann to get Kelly jealous. It backfired. Kelly only has eyes for Tree. Poor Ann fell for Quang's games and believes there is love between them to salvage. Perhaps in time, she can fuel that ember of love. Kelly and Tree are moving nine hundred miles away to San Jose,

California, to start a new, independent life together. For the past four years, Tree has been in my care, and I watched him grow from a cuddly baby to a cunning teenager and now a resourceful and resilient young man. I could not be prouder of him than if I were his mother.

Kelly's parents have a family friend in San Jose and can give Tree a job in the sheet metal machinery industry. Kelly hopes that her distance from her sister will make Quang's love for Ann grow stronger. Her decision to leave Seattle opens my eyes to the great love she has for her little sister and the sacrifices she will make to give Ann a chance at happiness. This makes me miss Sister Six and the sacrifices she made for me. However, if I were in Ann's shoes and Sister Six were in Kelly's, my sister would chase Quang out of the village and punch me until the only bruise of love I had was hers. Yes, my Sister Six is a bully, but I mean that in the most cherished and loving way.

I have been thinking a lot about Bình as well. I owe him an apology for snapping at him. With Tree moving out and down to California, he will once again be alone. Had I chosen to receive his question at the wedding in a different light, I could have seen that he was merely making conversation. I could have opened up to him about my relationship with Dolly's father, and perhaps he would have shared what had happened with his wife. There are several sides to every story, and for all I know, maybe his wife did not leave him. Tree tells me he thinks Bình is infatuated with me. Since our first meeting, Bình asks a lot about me, and even after the episode at the wedding, he still inquires about my well-being.

I have been trying to reach Sky the past few days, but Jean-Adrien says Sky and Magdaleine are on a couples retreat. He describes the program as akin to oxygen and sunlight for relationships…therapy for couples to enhance their communication, build empathy for one another, strengthen their romance, and open doors to resolving conflicts.

"Sky is trying to be the best he can be for Magdaleine," Jean-Adrien says. "He's tired of self-sabotaging and he thinks this seminar will help."

"That good," I say. "You and Katrina prove it possible."

I mentally applaud my friend Sky for grinding at his fears like a mortar and pestle until those fears become fine specks of dust. Magdaleine will be the breeze that comes along to blow those "fear dusts" away. This makes me happy and hopeful for them both. I am one-hundred percent Team Skyler and Magdaleine and pray for them to make it together.

Sky has been through so much. He once told me about his addiction to opiates after he got back from the war. It was his way of forgetting, but he knew his self-destructive behavior was hurting those who cared about him, especially his mom, Bill, and Teddy.

"I decided to quit cold turkey," Sky had said. "Do you know what it's like? Your body goes through withdrawals, and it's like ripping your skin off. You're on fire, but you feel you deserve the pain because of what you've put others through." Sky lived recklessly and had a death wish, but he found purpose when he had the chance to sponsor Dolly, Tree, and me to the US. After we arrived, his purpose was to make sure we acclimated and thrived here. Now, it appears he has found another purpose, and that is to love Magdaleine the way she deserves to be loved. In doing so, he is learning to love himself again.

Will I find love again? I touch my lips and remember Bill's kiss. I know he is a kind and intelligent man—a living encyclopedia as Sky once called him. Bill is also financially established, achieving the pinnacle of success that he has wanted to achieve with his career...He says it is too late for him to have children and start a family but not too late to find love. I romanticize what life could be like with Bill, for us to grow old together and have his help raising Dolly. However, with our vast age difference, we may have only ten good years together before his mind and body deteriorates. I can see myself living another twenty years as a widow. One day when Dolly marries and has children of her own, will Bill have the energy to keep up with his grandchildren? I am getting ahead of myself. I mentally flush these ideas down the toilet, and at the same time, marvel how easy these Westerners have it with sanitation and plumbing. My days of squatting behind trees are long gone.

I bounce down the stairs, feeling jovial and free, to check yesterday's mail before heading into work. The elation quickly ends. My heart trips over itself. In my mailbox is a letter with a return address from Humble, Texas. It is not from Tý. The curlicue handwriting is round and flows poetically across the envelope. I say the name out loud just so I can hear it and know its truth. "Annette." I tear open the envelope.

Dear Tuyet,

I am not sure where to start except to say I am happy to know you and Thuy Tien are safely in Seattle. I wish you would have come with us all those years ago, but I understand why you did not. I suppose if I were in your situation, I would have taken my chances and made the same decision.

Life with Ty has been challenging. I love him with all my heart, but it is hard to know him. He has a lot of nightmares. His guilty conscience prevents him from being fully present with me and his children. He shuts us out and does not share with me his thoughts or feelings. During the holidays like Christmas or the children's birthdays, he never celebrates or buys presents for them...nor for me, for that matter.

I pause. How strange we know the same man, and yet he is not the same man to both of us. In Việt Nam, he always brought home gifts. Even now, he sent Dolly toys and me the photograph of our daughter as a baby. I continue reading the letter.

Ty and I have four children: Timothy, Theodore, Tessa, and Tina. Our youngest is two-and-a-half years old. Timothy is now thirteen. He was just five years old when Saigon fell and we left Vietnam. If I remember correctly, Thuy Tien is now nine years old? I am sure she is adjusting to life nicely. Children are so resilient, aren't they?

We have a good life together, nonetheless. Ty is studying to be a nutritionist or dietician and dreams of opening a wellness and supplements shop. I am a linguistics professor and author. I am sure you have certain notions about me, but I assure you, I am a devout Christian woman, educated, and devoted to my family. I am a good person.

I am aware that my husband's visit to Seattle did not go well. I was surprised to see him home so soon. I begged him not to go, but he is a man who sees only black and white and walks a linear path. I often think about what it would be like if we met. Do you? Sometimes I wonder if my children would like to know their half-sister, but then I play the scenarios in my mind, and it never works out. I believe in another time and place, you and I could have been great friends. I admire your strength and beauty and your devotion as a mother. Ty told me you have a university education and follow God. Yes, I should think we could have been the best of friends, but we should remain strangers. Wouldn't you agree?

Please respect my wishes as a mother, a wife, and a woman who wants to protect her family—do not contact my husband again. You should move on with your life and enjoy the freedoms this country has given you.

I wish you well.
Annette

I reread the letter two more times. *Four children? Best of friends? Enjoy my freedoms?* I hate to admit it, but Annette is right. I must move on and live my life. Enjoy the freedoms I have which include the liberty to choose my life partner and the best father for Dolly. I deserve to be loved, to be the sun and moon…and stars…in someone else's sky.

I crumple up the letter and throw it in the dumpster to dissuade myself from digging it out. Why reread it and torment myself? I try to remember what I wrote in my letter to Tý. Did Annette intercept the letter? Or did he hand it over so she could read it? I imagine her face flushing through the spectrums of red with doubt, fear, and fury before washing to a pale white, replacing the anger with cold composure.

###

As I pass the I-405 and I-5 interchange, I think of Tý and am not convinced he is out of my life for good. He has always been a strong-willed man who does what he wants. When he was a child, he intentionally left his home to live on the streets so that his mother would have one less mouth to feed. As he got older and the testosterone kicked in, he got stronger and learned how to fight. At first, it was to rebuff the store owners he stole food from, and then it was to protect those same vendors from street kids in exchange for daily meals and a percentage of their sales. Ultimately, he was recruited to fight with the Việt Minh against the French oppressors. He was fourteen. Somehow, he managed to continue his education. He attended classes during the day and did his lessons under the street lamps at night. He never shared with me what he did for the Việt Minh, but I imagine some wicked and gruesome things. How he loathed the French because they raped his mother and ruled Indochina for so long.

Despite his torrential life, he loved school and learning. He was the only student to have won fairly through hard work a scholarship to study abroad. The other five students were awarded that opportunity because of their family's station in life or their father's rank in the corrupt system. Tý took classes at the Milwaukee Institute of Technology, now called Milwaukee Technical College. No, my husband is a determined man, and if he wants to see us again, he will. Annette cannot stop him.

Stuck in traffic, my thoughts now drift to Bình. What do I know about him? Is he worth getting to know? I do not have many Vietnamese friends here in Seattle. I have Diệp of course, with her eclectic fashion choices and fast-talking wit, but the tides of American life are taking her adrift, away from me and onto Donald's shores. Maybe Bình can be my shore, my safe harbor? He is only a few years older than I am, and he is Vietnamese. Therefore, he has the advantage of sharing a similar footing, history, and common ground with me. He is a good-looking man, with eyes that curve down, giving him that babyface charm. When he smiles, he looks like a cute boy who is both happy and sad at the same time. Tree admires him for his kindness and soccer athletics, and I trust my nephew. After all, Bình did offer my nephew room and board and treats him like a son. I admire his connections and networking abilities. He knew of a fortuneteller and a seamstress when we needed one, and he took charge of coordinating Tree's wedding. He also gracefully let Katrina take over the details and played the supporting role flawlessly. No Vietnamese man in my life has ever been as comfortable with gender-bending roles as Bình. He is not the typical Asian man I am accustomed to. In my village, to know one man was to know all men. They all thought the same way, disciplined their wives and children the same way, and stuck to the patriarchal ideals of society. When I think about how diplomatic Bình was in escorting Quang home after the fight with Sky, I wonder what he could have done to drive his wife away. I must learn more about this anomalous man.

KUBE FM is now playing a Michael Jackson song. The media refers to him as the "King of Pop," but I have yet to figure out why. Tree says pop is another word for soda. I saw him in a Pepsi commercial recently and the news coverage of his hair catching fire. Teddy says he is the first celebrity to get paid so handsomely, five million dollars, to endorse the beverage. Not only is the financial deal a mind-blowing marketing partnership, but it is significant because the singer is black.

"But Teddy," I argued, "he only half black. I think he mix like coffee and condensed milk. He look like *mỹ lai đen*, like the children in Việt Nam, half black left behind by soldiers. My sister say the war like boiling water, bubbling half Vietnamese babies all time."

Well, for five million dollars, I would not mind being labeled the king of soda either. Hearing Michael Jackson on the radio reminds me of two Christmases ago when Sky gifted Dolly the *Thriller* album. What a good man Skyler is. Had he not been drafted to war, had he not suffered so much, what kind of man would he have become? Katrina and Jean-Adrien said Sky was a good child and at the core of him was someone respectful, kind, and who served others. That loving, innocent little boy is still in there, begging to be found. I see glimpses of that boy. My wonderful friend, Skyler Herrington, could have been a confident and accomplished man, married with beautiful children, and changing the world for the better. I believe he can still be all these things. He had a challenging start on this jagged, crooked road of life with too many dangerous turns, but eventually, the curves will flatten out and the road will straighten. You will see, Sky…and then you will cruise the rest of the way until you grow wings and soar above everyone who pushed you down.

My car burps smoke and coughs as I pull into the parking lot. Without warning, it dies midway into the parking spot. A voice wafts through my window. It is Bình. "Do you want me to call the 'Big Toe' and have your car towed to a mechanic?"

"What are you doing here?" I ask. "Why are you at my work?"

"You will find out soon enough," he says. "Go on in. I'll take care of the car and can pick you up after work."

I thank him and make my way inside the *Seattle Times* building. The past few months have been a flurry of activity for the newspaper. President

Reagan signed a bill two months ago creating Martin Luther King Jr. Day, and then five days later, a bomb exploded inside the United States Capitol. Meanwhile, technology has been advancing and our reporters have been covering Ameritech Mobile's introduction of a cellular network. A man by the name of Bill Gates introduced a system called Windows 1.0, and an Apple company showcased a new Macintosh computer. Teddy says it is revolutionary with the introduction of a mouse and "GUI." He says I will understand when I see it. I told him I did not understand how the gooey parts of mice can produce rainbow-colored apples. Teddy laughed at me. I suppose I will have to wait and see.

For the first time, I watched football this season. The Seattle Seahawks played in the AFC Championship game against the Raiders. Sadly, we lost. The Raiders went on to play the Washington Redskins in the Super Bowl. Teddy, Skyler, and Tree cheered on the Raiders, but I do not understand how they can cheer for a team that just defeated our Seahawks. Dolly convinced me to root for the Washington Redskins because "they are related to us, Mama. They are from Washington too." In any event, I could not cheer for a team that looked like pirates so the Redskins it was.

Amidst all this, there was leaked information about the ARPANET project in which the Department of Defense enabled all military computers to connect. Supercomputing centers at several universities were created and provide network interconnectivity. All of this, of course, is beyond my comprehension, and in my little media coordinator world, the daily routine of positioning advertisements is all I understand. At this juncture, I am tired of seeing Cabbage Patch Kids and Chubby and Tubby war-surplus ads. I want more responsibilities and a promotion.

I make a quick detour to Bill's office before settling in at my desk. Bill looks up with an expression of annoyance but quickly softens. "Snow, come in."

Seeing Bill in his office, concentrating on his work with his brows furrowing, makes me realize how aged he looks since we first met at Ray's Boathouse. I had told Magdaleine about the kiss, and she warned me not to play with fire. "Bill has unfinished business with his ex-wife, and he still has feelings for Katrina. Trust me, you do not want to open that Pandora's box." She filled me in on how Bill had tried to forget Katrina by marrying this woman, but it was a "rebound marriage" that went sour despite his good intentions.

I hesitate at the doorway. "Sorry to disturb. Magdaleine on retreat with Sky, and I…"

"It's all right," Bill says. "I can use a break."

I step past the threshold and close the door. The noise of the newsroom yields to quiet serenity. I have never sat in Bill's office before. I have been inside but always passing through to drop something off or pick something up, never to stay and soak in the smells and comforts of the room. It is well-lit with natural lighting coming in from the big windows. Today's view boasts clear skies with a sprinkle of telephone wires and a chance of good-luck pigeon poop falling on the window washer's head.

The leather chair smells of pine and chocolates. His desk is neat with everything in its place. In the corner is a photo of his ex-wife. She is, to put it bluntly, an ugly woman. Her blemished face is pale with dark sunspots orbiting around her left cheekbone. In her cream-colored wedding gown, she blends in nicely with the background. Even on such a special occasion as her wedding day, in full makeup and styled hairdo, she looks weathered. Her lips smile, but her eyes challenge me to a duel. I once watched Katrina use an iron pole to stoke a fire, and I now have the urge to use that pole to bring the picture to life.

"That's Rebecca," Bill says. "We're divorced, but I keep the picture to remind me what *not* to do ever again." He stifles a laugh.

Behind him are books, framed awards, and a painting of a cow. I point to the painting. "Why you have cow painting?"

Bill smiles. "You mean Barbara?" He swivels his chair around. We both gaze into Barbara's black eyes. "She was my favorite calf. She used to follow me everywhere."

"I have pet in Việt Nam too," I say. "A chicken. Her name *Mông Dơ*. It mean dirty butt, but she die. Communist come to our house, take her, and eat her."

"I'm sorry about your chicken," Bill says. He looks down at his clasped hands on the desk as if he were saying a silent prayer. "Listen, I owe you many apologies and…" His lips quiver, and his voice trails off. I wait patiently for him to speak again. "Snow, I took advantage of you that night. We were both drinking and love was in the air…It was the perfect night despite the blood bath Skyler gave Quang. It was wrong of me to kiss you."

I say nothing. I do not know how to respond. I did not want to admit I enjoyed the kiss—probably more than he did—but since we both came to the same conclusion, that it was not a good idea, there was no need to discuss it further. After a long pause, Bill asks me if I enjoy my job and if there is anything I need. I ask him for more responsibilities and a raise. I remind him my math skills are strong, and I can be persuasive in sales. I tell him I can be of value in accounting or be Jerry's assistant in advertising. Bill agrees I deserve a pay increase and promotion. He will talk to Jerry about transitioning me from media coordinator to advertising account manager. I like the sound of "manager" in my title.

I leave Bill's office and head to my desk. A large vase filled with gerbera daisies and baby's breath grace my workstation. I look around and catch Jerry's eye as he walks from the kitchen with a mug of coffee in his hand. He smiles and points to the flowers with a look of curiosity. I open the small envelope and read the card. *It is best to wash soiled linens at home. Think today and speak tomorrow. I am sorry. Bình.*

The old Vietnamese proverbs about thinking before speaking and not airing private matters for the world to judge has me appreciating Bình's method of apology. Once again, he is an anomaly. A man who surprises me with flowers and apologizes is a man worthy of my time. I will invite him over for dinner tomorrow.

###

Bình stands outside my apartment door soaking wet. "Do you have a dirty floor that needs mopping?" He grins with boyish charm and shakes his hair. Droplets of rainwater sprinkle onto the linoleum floor and on my face. His presence lifts my spirits more than I care to admit. He is like a ray of sunshine cutting through the drizzle of a winter's day. I let him in and offer him a towel.

He wipes his face with my pink washcloth that once was white but somehow snuck into a pile of red laundry. "The towel was for mopping the floors," I tease. "Where is your umbrella?"

He removes his wet shoes and leaves them by the doorway. "A true Seattle native does not use an umbrella, much less own one. I want to blend in like a local."

I take his coat and hang it over the bathtub. "That is absurd. Rain or shine, an umbrella is useful."

"In Việt Nam, maybe," he says, "but not here. The way I see it, the Americans worry more about fashion and trends, not functionality and purpose."

I agree he makes an interesting observation about the culture here. I tell him about Dolly's obsession with Cabbage Patch Kids and how people fight over them like it was their last piece of bread. Hearing my mention of these dolls, Dolly perks up. She tears her attention away from the television screen long enough to greet our guest and tell him she wants a preemie CPK doll.

"Can I help in the kitchen?" Bình asks as he washes his hands.

I decline his offer and invite him to sit with Dolly. They watch *Scooby-Doo* while I prepare a fruit platter. We graze on oranges, persimmons, and pomegranates while the chicken congee simmers to a finish.

Dolly takes her dinner on the couch, in front of the television, while Bình and I sit at the table. Over our meal, he updates me on the status of my car. It will be fixed and ready for pick up in two days. We share parts of ourselves that we remember with fondness, about the good times back home and the dreams we have for the future. Back in Việt Nam Bình's family had been involved with horseracing since the colonial days. His father and grandfather were shrewd businessmen and used their relationships with French military officers to advance their horse breeding program. They belonged to the Saigon Horse Racing Association and owned a few prized ponies. Bình grew up loving horses and found racing thrilling. He admits he was not as savvy as his father or grandfather because he loved the animals too much and cared what happened to the jockeys. Some of the jockeys were as young as fourteen years old, and while they were lithe, they were often naïve about the industry, emotionally immature, and unreliable.

Bình met his wife at the racetrack. She was beautiful, charming, and sophisticated. She came from a wealthy family and was a descendant of the royal family, with a direct bloodline to emperors of the Nguyễn dynasty. She was also a communist, which he did not find out about until after the socialist government took over. Suddenly, racing became unlawful and gambling was prohibited. He had no way of making money.

His wife's family funded his business venture, and he turned to ceramics. He spent his days casting and firing molds of vases, elephants, and dragons, while his wife hand-painted the figures. They would have several kilns going at once, always painting, selling, and meeting the demands of the elite upper class. Their ceramic statues guarded entrances of grand hotels, homes, and buildings or stood over tombstones and graves, protecting the deceased as they passed over to the next realm. Their vases, filled with fresh flowers or silk floral arrangements adorned lobbies and tables of government officials or military officers. Life was good until his wife decided she was bored. She woke up one day feeling sorry for herself, married to a farmer who played with horses and tinkered with clay. She left him.

"When you love someone and then lose them," Bình says, "it is easy to close your heart off to everyone or find someone else to fill the empty void. For me though, I poured my energy into raising my two sons and daughter." Bình dips his *yàuhjagwái*, a fried Chinese doughnut, into the broth and sucks on the crispy exterior until it becomes chewy. "Did you know that the Cantonese word 'yàuhjagwái' means 'oil-fried devil'?" I shake my head.

"It is delicious, which makes it evil." He pops the last morsel into his mouth and smacks his lips as he devours the last bit of this glutinous breadstick.

"And where are your children now?" I ladle more congee into his bowl. The steaming hot porridge is perfect for today's weather. Bình has a third serving of the congee and tells me all three of his kids live in the Bay Area of California. His oldest daughter, Thu, is his biggest joy. She is smart, pretty, and lives in San Jose with her boyfriend, Ken. His second child, Khoi, lives up to his name, which means handsome. He spends his time chasing girls and driving fast cars. He lives in San Francisco and is dating an aspiring Cambodian model named Linh. That leaves Phan, his youngest son, who lives with his mother in Oakland. Bình says Phan is a sweet kid but dull and slow.

"How can you say that about your youngest?" I ask, appalled he would describe his son as such.

"Well, it is true," he says. "Even I can see he is nothing like his older sister and brother. Sometimes I wonder if he is even mine."

My eyes and mouth open wide. "Do you really think so?"

Bình takes a toothpick and spears a piece of persimmon. "Thu and Khoi are good-looking people. They have personality, character, and ambition, even if Khoi's only ambition is to date the most attractive girls and drive the sportiest cars. Phan, on the other hand, has no motivation. His personality is lackluster. He can barely formulate two sentences without shying away. I cannot have a stimulating conversation with that boy. And the way he walks. It's like a gait of a camel, the way he bobs forward and back. It's unnatural. He was coddled too much and was held most of his childhood."

"Maybe I will meet them one day," I say. "After all, Tree and Ngọc are moving down to San Jose."

"Yes, it was my recommendation they go since I have connections there," Bình says. "Ngọc's parents also have a family friend in San Jose who is in the sheet metal industry."

"Tree mentioned he was going to learn machinery. You have many connections."

I share with Bình about my life in Việt Nam and how we came to Seattle. I find it easy to talk to him because he is a good listener. He expresses no judgment, even when I tell him about Sam and the love interests in my life; he does not think less of me. He admires my perseverance and wit. He applauds my resourcefulness. He thanks me for being made of flesh and blood, for having passion, and for not being afraid to love. Above all, he respects my devotion as a mother. He is full of compliments, and I am unabashedly reveling in his attention. I even brag about how I, a single mother with a dying daughter, managed to survive the war and make it this far.

We end our evening together playing the game Connect Four with Dolly. My little hustler suggests we play for money but we settle for candy instead. She is the big winner with fifty-three gummy bears while I come in second with twenty-nine gummies.

"Chú Bình," Dolly says, "do you want to know how I eat my gummy bears?" She sucks on the gelatin candy until it is shiny, then bites the legs off until it is just the head and arms left. She giggles. "Look, the arms look like boobies."

I give my daughter a stern glance and hold my breath for Bình's reaction. He must think my daughter is inappropriate and is second-guessing my aptitude as a mother.

He laughs and copies her. "These fruit bears taste better this way."

I watch Dolly and Bình interact with ease as if they are old friends and listen to them chat about candy and toys. In this new light, I think I can move on. Can I move on with Bình?

22. ROAD TRIP (SUMMER 1984)

I get home from work to find Dolly in tears. She is sprawled on the floor in front of our velour couch, which I have decided I do not like. As soon as I have extra money from my raise, I will buy a new used couch and donate this one. Diệp and her son Hùng need a sofa. Perhaps they will want this one. It is a comfortable couch, but the pattern is anything but calm. The repeating print of barns, pheasants, and daisies does not invite serenity and peace. Instead, it makes me think of the countryside chaos on a farm.

Dolly wails harder and thrashes her body on the floor, writhing like a sidewinder snake on our sand-colored carpet. In her hand is a piece of paper. I kneel beside her and ask her what is the matter. She answers with a moan and curls into a ball. She buries her face into the shag and shoots her hand in the air, waving the paper in my face. It is her report card with her final grades for the year. All A's and one B+ in social studies.

"I am sorry you did not get the straight A's you and I were both hoping for," I say, "but—"

Dolly rolls over and says softly, "It means I don't get my CPK doll." She sits up and hugs her knees, her cheek resting on top of them. One big teardrop makes its final tour down her cheek and stops at the top of her lip.

I clap my hands. "Encore!" She lifts her head and implores with her eyes to explain myself. "That was quite a performance you gave. Am I to feel sorry for you and buy you a doll anyway? Our deal was perfect attendance and perfect grades."

"Mama, I would have gotten straight A's, but—"

"But you did not," I say softly. I scoop her into my arms and hug her. "How much money have you saved from selling our candies and ramen cups to your friends?"

She leaps out of my arms and runs to her bedroom. A moment later she returns with a shoebox of money. She counts the coins. "Nineteen dollars and five cents."

182

"What were you saving the money for?" I ask.

She shrugs. "A sunny day, I guess, for when there is something good at the Circle K."

"How much is a Cabbage Patch Doll?"

She shrugs again. "Do I have enough to buy one?"

My turn to shrug. "It depends on which one you want. I think preemies are more expensive. Since it is not the Christmas season, maybe the prices are better or there is a sale. Do you want to go to Toys "R" Us and see?"

She perks up and gives me the biggest smile. "Can we go now?" I nod. "What if I don't have enough?"

"I will give you a loan, and you can pay me back with the money you earn from pulling my gray hairs and selling candy."

She eagerly accepts the offer. We grab our coats and make it to Tukwila two hours before the store closes.

Dolly and I are the new parents of an adopted CPK girl named Hycinthea Elaine. She has green eyes, brown hair, deep dimples, and a green signature stamp on the left butt cheek. She comes with a blue dress, adoption paperwork, and a birth certificate, which Dolly insists on framing. Jen and Melissa come over often to play "house," and they each mother their dolls like they are real children. It is the cutest thing to watch them feed and clothe the dolls, babysit each other's dolls, have playdates, and even discipline them for bad behavior.

"Hycinthea Elaine," Dolly scolds, "you apologize or get a spanking." She hugs her doll. "All right, I forgive you."

The phone rings. It is Tree. He and Kelly had their baby in April, a little girl they named Holly. They live in a one-bedroom apartment close to his work, so he bikes there every day. He tells me not to worry. They are managing fine, thanks to Bình's, Lan's, and Toàn's connections in the Bay Area.

They have met Bình's daughter, Thu, and her boyfriend, Ken. Both are nice people. "Aunt Eight, you have to meet them," Tree says. "Ken is Chinese. He looks like a movie star. He has thick black hair and is so tall. He is funny, too. Thu is more serious and conservative, but Ken brings out her playful side. They drive a BMW, live in a nice house in a pretty neighborhood, and have Louis Vuitton everything. You need to come down. The weather here is so much better."

I ask about Kelly and the baby. Tree says both are happy, although Kelly wishes she had her mom and sister there to help out. Holly is an easy baby and only fusses when she is hungry or needs a diaper change. She sleeps a lot and laughs a lot. Tree is in love with his child and is amazed at how wonderful fatherhood can be.

"It makes me miss my parents and little brother even more," he says. "I hope we can go back to visit them one day."

"I received a letter from your Aunt Six," I say. "Our country is still at war, fighting the Chinese now at the northern border. China's encroachment to expand its power resulted in a death toll that surpassed six hundred soldiers on the first night of the invasion. It was a massive strike with artillery shells firing into several northern provinces."

Despite Việt Nam being a socialist republic and ruled by the very people I ran from, it does not make it any easier knowing people are still suffering and dying. Year after year of fighting takes its toll, and I worry one day the country will be lost forever. Every fiber, every cell, every neuron in my body yearns for a free and prosperous Việt Nam. I hope one day my country will be surrounded by allies, not enemies, and that the people can live in peace. I dream of the day when my people can recover economically and psychologically from decades of war, live in harmony, and not have to constantly defend our borders and ports.

"How is everyone doing back home?" Tree asks. "Any updates on Uncle Hải?"

Hearing Hải's name weakens my legs and sends a bullet to my gut. I plummet onto the chair and tell Tree that Hải is alive, but he suffered a stroke and is in a wheelchair. The tears fall. "Your father saw him in Sài Gòn on one of his deliveries. He could not believe it at first and thought he was seeing a ghost. They spoke briefly. Hải told him that imagination comes to life when you are in confinement. He saw things that were not there, heard screams that were not his. He tried to rationalize his existence. Oh, Tree, it is terrible. The Việt Cộng cracked him open like an egg and let his guts fry out in the hot jungle. They threw him for the wildlife to pick at. I cannot bear to think of how much he suffered."

I clutch my chest and swallow the lump of guilt and pain in my throat. I feel the knot making its way down into my stomach. The weight is so much to bear. I try to tell Tree more but the words will not come out. A guttural cry of anguish escapes my throat. I hate what they did to him. I hate that he sacrificed himself for my family. I hate that he loved me and made me happy. All this would not be so painful if I did not love him still.

"It was not your fault," Tree says. "You cannot blame yourself." Tree's words flow through me like a salve and soothe my conscience. I did not realize how much I needed to hear those words, that it was not my fault. Still, I wonder if Hải resents me. Years of rotting in a reeducation camp, imprisoned by his thoughts and tormented by dreams that are far out of reach. Eventually, it can break a man's spirit down and build it back up with resentment. Tree strategically steers my attention away from Hải and asks about Doctor Đức and his wife Thủy.

I inhale and breathe out slowly through my nostrils. I blink back the wetness around my eyes and sit back in the chair. I look to the ceiling as if it can give me the strength to speak. "They are well. Their son is three years old now. Your father still gets up at dawn and drives to the city. Your mom is managing her own little tailoring business out of the house. Your little brother is little no more. Tuấn is fifteen now, just a year younger than you when we left Vĩnh Bình."

"Has it been five years already since we left?" Tree asks. "I am almost twenty-two years old, legal to drink in the nightclubs."

I chuckle. "According to your papers though, you're only eighteen. Remember?"

"Oh no, that means I am not old enough to buy alcohol. Wait, that also means I have to work an extra three years before I can retire."

"I am afraid so," I say. We talk for another fifteen minutes about Sister Six and my brother-in-law and how they have been nursing Tâm back to health ever since she came home. Her younger sister, Trinh, has been helping Tâm recover and assimilate back into society. She has been reading to her big sister every day, brushing her hair, and taking her out for walks. Sometimes, they swing on the hammock together or pay their respects at their grandparents' tombstones. It has been a long and slow healing process for Tâm. Her physical scars are gone, and she has gained some healthy weight. There is some light in her eyes again but she does not trust her surroundings. Once in a while, she shares a memory that sparks joy like the time she and I went to the market and the sales lady ate a live cockroach to get a rise out of us.

Sister Six got her hui money and opened a food stand called Six's Kitchen. There is only one thing on the menu and she claims it is the best egg noodle soup in the province, served with your choice of char siu pork, duck, or shrimp wontons. In her letter, she said she will sell me her recipe for one-hundred US dollars. Knowing my sister, she is not joking.

Before hanging up with Tree, I promise to come down to San Jose and visit before Dolly starts the fifth grade.

I stare into my closet and realize most of my clothes are black, brown, or dark blue. I need more colors and prints, bold patterns, and vibrant designs. I can learn a few things from Diệp, Katrina, and Magdaleine about piecing outfits together. In two days, I am going to San Jose to see

185

Tree and meet his baby. Instead of flying, we will do a road trip. It is cheaper and allows me the chance to see Oregon and northern California. Bình has offered to drive. He is anxious to see his children and for me to meet them. Dolly is excited for her first trip down the coast and plans to show Hycinthea Elaine the Pacific Ocean. We decide to take my Honda Civic since it gets good gas mileage and Teddy did a tune-up on it for me.

I dart across to Diệp's apartment to see if she will lend me a few blouses or dresses. Without hesitation, she pulls me into her bedroom and has me try on different outfits. I do a fashion show for her and humor her by putting on every outfit she picks, regardless of how hideous it looks on the hanger. We have a good laugh over the orange tutu dress and banana pants with suspenders and drawstring waist. The palm-print pants have bananas all over them and the way they fit on me, it looks like there is a banana coming out of my crotch. In the end, I settle on a giraffe-print halter jumpsuit in colors of cream and lilac, a yellow maxi dress, a pink V-neck blouse, and blue capri pants.

I ask Diệp if things are going well with Donald and how Hùng did in school this past year. She rolls her eyes and complains her son got B's and C's in his classes. "He has no interest in applying himself and only cares about sports." Donald promises to work with Hùng this summer on his subjects, particularly math.

Things are going extremely well with Donald. He is content to let her boss him around, and he caters to her every whim. His sons, Jason and Ricky, are used to having her in their life, and despite all their differences, they make a happy, blended family. She thinks it is only a matter of time before Donald proposes.

"This Halloween will be the third anniversary of when Dracula met Ronald McDonald," she proclaims. I laugh remembering that night. Donald was a vampire, Jason was Chewbacca, Diệp was in her handmade clown outfit, and Hùng was a hamburger.

"Please promise me your wedding will not be at McDonald's," I say. "What is your dream wedding?"

Diệp giggles. "Have you seen the new Rainbow Brite cartoons?" I shake my head. "You and Dolly have to watch it. I envision my wedding gown to be white like the Western gowns, only I want the train to be in rainbow colors. I cannot decide between a marine wedding or a mountain wedding."

"I admire your spunk and originality," I say. "You have an amazing zest for life."

"What do you think about a summer ceremony in a field of wildflowers near Mount Rainier with me riding a white horse?"

"Can you ride a horse?" I ask.

"Yes," she replies and laughs. "What about inside an aquarium with fish swimming around us, like the world below the waters of camp Kuku?"

"I love that idea," I say, "and that way you do not have to worry about the weather."

"I want to be surrounded by vibrant colors. For party favors, I will have Skittles and M&Ms. I want my cake to be bright and colorful too. Of course, Dolly has to be the flower girl and you my maid of honor."

It amazes me how a woman who survived the Mỹ Lai massacres can have such a positive outlook on life. I suppose the point is not to live in darkness but to seek the light and the rainbows. It is never too late to turn your life around or change your outlook on life, whether you have thirty minutes or thirty years left on Earth.

I thank Diệp for lending me her clothes and leave her in the bedroom daydreaming about her life with Donald. Back home, I pack a suitcase and get ready for the road trip down to San Jose.

By seven-thirty in the morning, Bình, Dolly, and I are on the road heading south on I-5. It takes thirteen hours to drive down to San Jose, but we decide to take the scenic route along the coastline. The three of us have never been to the beaches here and are excited to dip our toes into the Pacific Ocean.

We cut over to US-101 North and stop at a beach town called Ocean Shores. The coastal town sits on Point Brown Peninsula, bordered by the Pacific Ocean and Grays Harbor. It is a charming place, but at ten o'clock the sun is not at its peak yet, so the waterfront breeze is frigid. One toe-dip is all it takes for us to definitively decide the Pacific Ocean is not so hospitable. Dolly finds it amusing we cannot handle the cold water. She tortures us by kicking the salty waves at us and entertains herself by running along the shore looking for crabs and shells.

A few people on the beach fly kites, jog, or ride their horses. Watching the waves roll in brings back so many memories of Indonesia. Out in the distance where the sky meets the water, I imagine there is a tiny shrimp trawler bobbing up and down. Its identity number, 93752, is painted on the outside, but inside are forty-three refugees who fled their homes in search of freedom.

I want to wave the American flag so they can see this land where the colors of red, white, and blue fly high and proud. Today, I am standing on the shores of safety while thousands more are just beginning their journey. How many more will die at sea? How many will find their way to a new home? And how many will forever straddle the realm of life and death because while their heart beats on, their spirit died with the invasion of pirates, the tortures of prison camps, and the disappearance of loved ones?

My regrets are many. Every speck of sand on this beach represents every minute I have drifted through life. Sometimes I catch a good wave and ride it, but it always crashes. When will my life crash again?

The horizon is where both heaven and hell live. Out there, you are in limbo, half lucid, half hallucinating. The only thing you are sure of is the light that cuts through the glassy ripples and the image reflecting at you is not you at all. The face is unrecognizable because it is a mash-up of fear, hope, desperation, longing, and joy. It is a confusing, surreal period in which you see both your accomplishments and your failures. What is waiting on the other side of your escape is unknown.

My daughter runs and laughs with Bình. The two of them have fun outsmarting the sudsy surf. They squat on their haunches and watch a little crab scurry into a hole. I wonder if Dolly remembers much of our journey. I hope she only remembers the good parts of our adventure, like Ommo's kindness, playing the rebab under the coconut trees, and eating sweet sapodillas by the bonfire. I want her to appreciate every sunrise and every sunset because they represent the magic of life. May she look at the moon and the stars and realize so many people made sacrifices so that she can be alive today.

Dolly takes my hand. "What are you thinking about?"

I scoop her into my arms and nuzzle her neck. "I was thinking of how lucky I am and that you are my miracle."

We continue our journey down the coast, taking turns driving every couple of hours. The view from the Oregon Coast Highway is glorious. We see signs for sea caves and other tourist attractions like sand dunes and Crater Lake. Dolly looks for license plates from different states and takes a tally of how many California ones we see. By nightfall, we pull into a parking lot in front of a small motel. We are perhaps an hour's drive from the Oregon-California border. Bình and I get separate rooms for the night and agree to get back on the road early in the morning.

Dolly crawls into the bed and is fast asleep. I curl up next to her and let today's excursion slip quietly under the door and disappear into the night.

Four cups of coffee, two liters of soda, and three rest stops later, we turn into the bedroom community of San Jose in the Silicon Valley, at the southern tip of the San Francisco Bay. The street signs are hard to see in the dark, but we finally pull into the driveway of a two-story home. My back is tight, my legs are stiff, and my mood is questionable. The porch light turns on, and two figures emerge.

Bình's daughter, Thu, and her boyfriend, Ken, greet us in front of the garage. Thu helps me with my luggage while Ken carries a sleeping Dolly out of the car. For a tall man, he moves in and out of my Honda Civic like a ninja. One look at Thu, however, and I feel insignificant. I detect a glimmer of suspicion, probably wondering who her father has dragged in off the streets of Seattle. I am guessing her allegiance is to her mother first and her tolerance for her father is born out of necessity. I remind myself that I am her elder. It is she who needs to earn my respect and trust. I hold my head high with authoritative confidence despite feeling the rocks of travel on my fatigued body.

I forgive Thu's detached demeanor and cold reception of me. It is the dead of night at two-thirty in the morning, and everyone is tired. Tomorrow should be an interesting day. Tonight, however, I only care about blackout curtains and a soft bed.

23. SAN JOSE (SUMMER 1984)

I lift both eyelids to receive the glow of sunshine, but only one eye fully opens. It takes a moment to remember I am in Thu and Ken's house. I survey my room. The curtains are open, letting in all the natural light of the California sun. The walls are painted mint green, the décor and accents inside the room are white, and the bed frame, nightstands, and dressers are dark brown. I cannot help but feel I am inside a mint chocolate chip ice cream container. A large closet with floor to ceiling mirrors stands on the opposite side of the adjoining bathroom. The mirrors make my bedroom feel enormous. On the wall is a large painting of a tan horse with a silver-blonde mane and tail. A man stands beside the majestic beast, holding the reins, and squinting directly at me. It is a young Bình, looking proud, handsome, and aristocratic.

Laughter floats up the stairs. I press my ear against the bedroom door and hear Thu and Ken teasing one another. I smile. The young lovers playfully argue about what toppings are best on Taiwanese shaved ice.

"Strawberries and condensed milk," Ken says. "With lots of tapioca balls."

"No balls," Thu says, "just lots of exotic champagne mangoes."

"You like exotic?" Ken asks. "Nothing more exotic than Ken toppings." Thu squeals with laughter. "If you want me to stop tickling you, you have to declare Ken toppings with coconut cream is best."

"Durian is better." Thu's laughter gets louder as she runs up the stairs past my bedroom. Ken is right behind her. The door slams, and the giggles die down. The noise does not disturb Dolly as she slumbers soundly on the canopy bed that we shared last night. I open my bedroom door and peek out. I hear the lovers moan. The quiet creak of their bed testifies that they are enjoying each other's bodies.

Thoughts of the lovebirds entwined in one another's embrace send hot flashes of desire to my stomach and down between my legs. Bình's face

190

from the painting sparks a light, electric tingle to my breasts. The longer I stare into those dark eyes, the more haunting those eyes become. I have seen those captive eyes before. I recognize how they can inflict fear one moment and show tenderness the next. I see Ommo's eyes looking back at me. Was I wrong not to write to him? What could I have said? I blew the flame out of his candle when I chose America over him. He must loathe me by now. He deserves a woman who is in love with him, who can give him children, and who will devote herself to making him happy.

A great sadness blankets me and smothers me with guilt as I remember Ommo's Adonis face and his minty kiss. Everything about him was primal and male. His athletic physique, his thick forearms, the way he gripped his AK-47, how his uniform sculpted his chest—these characteristics screamed danger—yet his music and smile whispered tenderness.

I miss the embrace of a man's hard arms. I want to feel safe again. I deserve love and need to give someone all my love. How do I open myself to it once more? It was easy with Sam and me. Despite being from different worlds, speaking different languages, having both an age and height difference, none of that mattered. We simply fit together. I swallow the lump in my throat and curl my toes as if that were the cure to my loneliness.

I walk into the bathroom and turn on the shower. The lukewarm water soothes my lamenting thoughts. I watch the stream of water circle the drain at my feet and disappear through the small holes. There goes another piece of Sam, another part of me, another morsel of remorse.

It is a new day. I am in a new place with new people. I must make different choices and live a charming version of my American dream. An exhilarating delight washes over me. I am a survivor. I am going to go after what I want.

What I want is Bình.

It is a beautiful day to explore. The five of us pile into Thu's BMW E28 with Ken behind the wheel and Bình in the front passenger seat. We meet Tree, Kelly, and baby Holly at the San Jose Flea Market at eleven. Thu is all smiles right now having conducted a little tête-à-tête this morning with Ken. She is polite, talkative, and curious. When she smiles, her two dimples make her look innocent. I conclude last night's uncomfortable encounter was due to the poor timing of our arrival. In time, I think we can be friends.

In the backseat, Dolly straps herself in the middle. Thu and Bình do most of the talking, catching up on family affairs, pointing out attractions along the way, and discussing Thu's wedding plans after she graduates from college. She will finish with a BS in economics and a masters in taxation. She and Ken will continue to support each other's aspirations while living under the same roof. The idea of them living together as an unmarried couple having pre-marital relations gives me pause. Of course, in Việt Nam, that is unthinkable and would bring dishonor to the family. Our reputation would be tainted and we would be treated as outcasts in our village. Heaven forbid if there is a pregnancy out of wedlock.

Thu's bold declaration that they will live together and marry after school is admirable. She has great strength which will serve her well. I wish I had that confidence when I was her age. Then again, we live in different times under more liberating and democratic circumstances. What surprises me most is how much Bình takes everything in stride without judgment or contrarian attitudes. I find this attribute in him pleasing and attractive. He is open-minded and supportive of his daughter's life choices. I hope I can be accepting when Dolly tells me one day that she is moving in with her non-Vietnamese boyfriend.

"What do you do?" I ask Ken.

Ken glances at me in the rearview mirror. Tree is right. He looks like a movie star straight out of a Chinese film. Before answering, he changes lanes to take the exit toward Berryessa Road. Ken downshifts to third gear and slowly comes to a stop at the traffic light. "I am a developer at Hewlett-Packard in Palo Alto. The company just introduced an inkjet and laser printer for the desktop computer. I develop the software for printing."

"Impressive," I say. "How long have you all been in California?"

Ken's great-great-grandfather was one of the Chinese immigrants who worked on the railroads in the 1860s. "He built the railroad between San Francisco and San Jose for twenty-seven dollars a month. I am generation five-point-oh, born right here in San Jose."

Thu explains that Bình was among the first wave of men to partake in the offshore pilot program hosted by the US Army and US Air Force. They flew him to Fort Wolters, Texas along with a dozen or so of his fellow countrymen.

"We had intense English language training followed by classroom instructions on how to fly this piston-powered helicopter called the TH-55," Bình says, "and before I knew it, I was on a solo flight. It was the scariest thing I had ever done. It was confusing. They would draw a diagram on the chalkboard and show us how to complete a final approach, tell us where the take-off pad was, and ask us how to identify lane numbers and pad numbers. My English was mediocre, but luckily, I understood the mechanics of how it operated."

"After he came back to Vietnam," Thu says, "my father went through more training on the CH-34. He flew a lot of missions, and after the peace agreement was signed in Paris, the American troops withdrew, and Dad was one of the few who had the opportunity to resettle here."

"Of course, I could not leave without taking my family with me," Bình says. "I convinced my wife that a brighter future awaited us in California, and we could try to be a family again."

"That was 1973," Thu says. "A year later, as you know, the cease-fire was ignored, and war resumed in full force."

Hearing them retell their story makes me realize how many layers there are to Bình. He grew up as a farmer, his family rubbed elbows with the French military and bred racehorses, he married a wealthy woman descended from the Nguyễn dynasty, had ties with her communist family, and then flew dangerous missions into enemy territory for years fighting the Việt Cộng. On top of all this, his wife left him twice, but he still maintains a relationship with his children.

What different lives we lead. While he was making a new life for himself and his family here, I was getting married to Tý and mourning the loss of Sam. While Thu turned fourteen in the summer of 1974 and started high school, Dolly was born fighting for her life. Through all the pain and suffering I witnessed and with the nightmares and flashbacks I still have, I cannot fathom Bình being any less troubled than I am. I wonder if our relationship is already doomed before it even begins. And how in the world did he end up in Seattle?

We arrive at the flea market already bustling with pedestrians and eager to find some bargains, from used tires to emerging artwork. Dolly sees children carrying cheap, shiny, plastic toys, and begs to have one. Another child holds a melting ice cream cone with puddles of vanilla stuck to her shoes. My daughter begs for a cone too, and before I can answer, Ken scoops her up and says, "Of course."

The San Jose swap meet is like nothing I have seen before. Back home there are large blocks of open markets, alley after alley of vendors, all selling food, toys, fabric, and everything in between. This market takes it to another level and stretches so far in every direction that it can swallow a province. Each tent has something wonderful to offer, from enticing foods, electronics, and fashionable clothes, to bicycles, garden accessories, and home décor.

Almost immediately, I spot Tree and Kelly pushing a stroller in our direction. I wave to my nephew. Dolly runs to him and leaps into his arms. She misses her cousin who is more of a big brother than anything. Kelly and I hug. We all say our hellos to one another before Tree, Ken, and Bình take off down the first row of vendors. They agree to return to the hot dog and sno-cone area in an hour.

I squat to take a good look at baby Holly. "Let Great Auntie Eight take a good look at you." I smile at Holly and admire her flawless, pearly complexion. I stroke the damp wisps of hair that curl around her ears and notice the tiny stones in her earlobes. "Your ears are pierced." Holly smiles at me. I melt. "Your birthstone is a diamond, like mine." She smiles again as if she understands. I pick up Holly and gently hug her. "Ngọc, she is beautiful, a darling gem. She is smart, I can tell. Her eyes are alert. I am so happy for you."

We take turns coddling the baby before walking down the same path the men took ten minutes earlier. The market is alive with vendors seducing us with deals. We stop at a few booths and admire trinkets and souvenirs but buy nothing. Halfway down the third aisle, Thu stops at a booth selling ceramic vases and silk flowers. An Asian woman in a straw conical hat sits on a stool behind a small table arranging silk irises, magnolias, and dogwoods into a green foam base. Her helper is a young girl in her teens, half Cambodian, half European, with curly, sandy blonde hair and striking green eyes.

"Hello, Mother," Thu says. "Hi, Claudia."

The woman hovers a quick gaze at her daughter before droning over to me. She scans me like a bar code and makes me feel vulnerable. In just a few seconds, this woman probably knows everything she wants to know about me and has made up her mind whether I am worth her time or should be forgotten on a dusty shelf.

So this is Bình's ex-wife. I imagined her to be a beauty, full of grace and youth, but the woman before me has let herself go. She has weathered a great storm and has come out of it barely alive. There is distrust in her movements, contempt in her eyes, and a low growl in her voice. She makes it very clear I am not wanted here. She may have come from a royal bloodline, but the iron heart before me is bitter and cold.

I take my daughter's hand and steer her toward the booth two spots up where a man is selling volleyballs, basketballs, and other sports toys. Kelly follows us.

"Did you know that was Thu's mother?" I ask.

"No. I have never met her or seen a photograph of her before," Kelly says. "Not what I expected."

"What is her story?" I ask.

Dolly tugs at my shirt. "Can I have a volleyball?" She taps my bottom when I do not respond.

"Fine," I say to appease her. I motion to the salesman. "How much?"

The vendor holds up five fingers. I shake my head and show him two. He grins and dismisses me, refusing my counteroffer. I take a few steps toward another toy booth, and Dolly whimpers. The man calls me back and agrees to two dollars. That was easy. What a thrill to have the upper hand when entering a negotiating zone.

Kelly picks up right where we left off. "Thu looks nothing like her mother. She and Khoi look like Uncle Bình."

"Phan must look like her then," I denote. "I guess you cannot have everything in life. She may have had the wealth and status, but she did not have access to the fountain of youth and beauty."

Kelly nods. "I believe that if you are unfortunate in the first half of your life, you will be fortunate in the second half. I would rather suffer when I am young. What about you?"

I think of something wise to say, but Kelly does not give me an opportunity. She spots Tree and the other two men thirty feet ahead. She calls out to them, and they join us.

"Where is Thu?" Ken asks.

I answer Ken's question but look at Bình when I reply. "She is visiting with her mother."

Bình frowns. "So you met Trang."

"Not really," I say, "but we locked eyes."

Bình tells me they are on friendly terms, but they cannot tolerate more than thirty minutes together. Trang does not know anything about me other than I am the woman in Seattle he is interested in pursuing. Bình laughs when I look shocked. "Do not tease me. Of course, you suspected." I ask him how he ended up in Seattle. "I needed a change of scenery. My children do not need me. I had nothing anchoring me in California. I saw Seattle on TV one day, and it looked so majestic with the mountains and the lakes. Washington also has a lush rainforest and an arid desert. How marvelous to be so versatile and prosperous a state. So I made up my mind to move up there. Washington is also more receptive to the Vietnamese refugees. We are a burden to the Californians. One day I ran into Lan. We were classmates back in Việt Nam, so I took it as a sign that Seattle was meant to be home."

Bình and I split off from the group. Dolly goes with Ken and the others to get ice cream. We agree to meet back at the concession stands in twenty minutes and decide on what to do about lunch. Bình takes my hand, and I shy away at first, uncomfortable with the idea of publicly displaying affection. He reminds me this is the land of the free, and we can hold hands. He points to a couple laughing and hugging and another couple kissing. No one seems to mind they are openly loving. Not a person is staring at them except for me. I relax and feel his fingers dovetail with mine. We stroll up and down the next couple of rows and stop at a record store. People crowd around the tables and milk crates, thumbing through albums from all different genres. I immediately gravitate to Lionel Richie's new album, *Can't Slow Down*, and ask the salesman to play a song for me.

"No scratch?" I ask.

"New," he says. "No scratch."

The man puts on the A side and queues up the song "All Night Long." My hips sway, and I cha-cha to the chorus. Bình takes my hand and twirls me around. He cha-chas with me, and we move perfectly in rhythm back and forth. He takes it up a notch by spinning a full circle and resumes sidestepping the cha-cha without missing a beat. Our audience gets bigger, and another couple joins in. I let go of all insecurities, all pent-up fears of judgment, and focus on Bình's lead. The crowd cheers, and I collapse into his embrace.

"Is there anything you cannot do?" I ask. "You are full of surprises."

"So are you," he says. "Does this mean we are taking Mr. Richie home with us?" I nod, and Bình buys the album for me. He does not even haggle on the price. I object and try to strike a better bargain. Bình says I cannot put a price on something that makes me happy.

With the new album in hand, we meet up with everyone, including Thu, back at the food court. We enjoy a leisurely lunch at the flea market and show each other what we purchased. Tree and Kelly take Holly home for a nap and promise to come by the house for dinner later. Thu plans to extend the invite to her brothers, Phan and Khoi, and Khoi's girlfriend, Linh.

This should be interesting. I am curious about Phan.

###

In Thu's kitchen, I volunteer to be the sous chef and offer Dolly up as the prep cook. Thu glides around the kitchen with ease, and like all executive chefs, she barks her orders and wears her emotions on her sleeves. She is wound up tight today, and I think her mother may have something to do with it.

It does not matter that I am the elder and the guest in her home. Today, I am a crank turner. On one occasion, Thu catches herself from yelling and politely tells me to smash the garlic cloves, not mince them. She shows great restraint from pulling her hair out when Dolly spills the uncooked thread noodles all over the floor. At one point, while I wait for the water to boil, Thu rushes out of the kitchen and returns five minutes later, calmer, more poised, and wearing a different shirt. I notice the bait and switch and wonder if she has a twin I do not know about.

Immediately on her heels is Ken. His presence soothes her. He shows Dolly how to peel ginger and hands her the knife. Under his supervision and encouragement, she slices the knob into thin pieces, then cuts them into strips. My daughter smiles and looks at Ken adoringly. I have a feeling her crush on Mark Hartman at school has been replaced by a new crush on Ken.

We get into a new rhythm and despite having four bodies in the kitchen, we maneuver around each other without getting in one another's way or breaking anything. Before long, everything is cooked, and Thu shoos Dolly and me out of the kitchen so that she can put on the finishing touches. Ken stays back to tidy the kitchen and wash the pots and pans. It is good timing because the doorbell rings.

Bình opens the door. Tree and Kelly are the first to arrive. They look rested and have changed into something more formal. Tree is dressed in black from top to bottom, and Kelly wears a navy polka dot skirt and beige blouse. She compliments me on the giraffe-print halter jumpsuit and says the colors cream and purple suit me.

"I borrowed it from Diệp," I say. "Where is the baby?"

"With our neighbor and her daughter," Kelly says. "We both need a night out without her."

There is a knock at the door, but before Bình can answer it, a young man with slicked black hair walks in. He smiles and displays a pair of dimples identical to Thu's. He is in the middle of a debate with his Cambodian girlfriend and is talking faster than the vehicles on the autobahn. I understand now what Bình meant when he said Khoi is into fast cars and pretty girls. Whereas Thu has her mother's petite stature, Khoi is lanky and tall like his father. Same face, same smile, but with a burst of energy and effervescent youth.

Khoi walks toward me with a confident swagger. He greets me respectfully, "Chào Cô," and leans down to kiss me on the cheeks as if we are family, not strangers. I like him instantly and feel as if I have known him for years. He introduces me to Linh.

Shy and humble, Linh clasps her hands together and gives a slight bow. "Hello, Auntie Snow."

I cannot take my eyes off her. This young raven enchantress before me is a gorgeous femme fatale. I do not think she knows how aesthetically majestic she looks with her long slim legs, voluptuous figure, and full lips shaped like a heart. It is my turn to have a crush, if it is even possible for me to have one. The girl looks like she materialized from an unknown, exotic island.

197

"Dinner is ready," Thu calls out. We funnel into the dining room and encounter a beautifully set table with crystal stemware, fine china dinner plates, and thick cloth napkins. Even Dolly's place setting is arranged with the same expensive dinnerware.

"Wait," Ken says. "Where's Phan?"

Khoi pulls out a chair for Linh. "You know how he is. He'll be here when he gets here." Khoi drapes his arm across the back of Linh's chair. "Okay, sis, what did you make us?"

Thu proudly waves her hand over each dish and explains the cuisine before sitting down next to Ken. "Tonight we have Szechuan pork belly, braised in ginger, brown sugar, soy sauce, and green onions. This is a roasted duck with steamed hoisin baos. This is a fensi salad. And of course, we have jasmine rice cooked in a chicken stock then stir-fried in butter, garlic, and a pinch of sea salt. Last but not least, oyster sauce Chinese broccoli."

"And the watermelon is to cleanse the palate?" I ask.

"Yes," Thu says, "but it is also good with the rice."

Impressive. We all dig in ravenously. No one says grace. I make the sign of the cross and partake in Thu's culinary offerings. Every bite is divine. Dolly's morsels of food get bigger and bigger with every reach. She is a greedy glutton tonight. I could not be happier to see her eat and am proud she is behaving like a proper young lady. She knows how special this is to be sitting at the adult table, dining with expensive dinnerware and stemware and being treated like an adult.

"You should open a restaurant," Dolly says to Thu. "This is yum yum. What would you name it?"

"Well, I almost majored in hospitality," Thu answers, "so that I could open a restaurant, but that is a lot of work. I don't want to be a slave to it. That's why I am getting a degree in economics and taxation. I want the business to work for me!" It is all jargon to Dolly. She repeats her question. Thu gives it some thought. "Well, I guess I would call it *Le Petit Gourmand* for the little greedy eater."

Dolly puts her fork down and looks at Thu seriously. "That is French. You are not French. And all this food is Chinese."

Khoi laughs. "Whoa, she told you!"

Thu cracks a smile. "You are too smart for your own good." She playfully taps the tip of Dolly's nose with her finger.

Like a reverberating earthquake, we rumble with amusement until someone lets out a ripple of flatulent noises. Dolly laughs nervously and says "rut-roh." This amplifies our mirth, and an aftershock of laughter flows around the table.

We are so entertained and thoroughly enjoying our food that we do not notice the slinky figure looming by the archway. A shadow moves, and I turn to see if it is a ghost.

Bình's youngest son, Phan, does not explain his tardiness or apologize for disrupting our dinner. He crosses the room, his head bobbing up and outward until he finds his seat on the far end between Bình and Khoi. He points to a sauce and makes a strange face to express his displeasure. Thu explains it is a hoisin and hot sauce combination for the baos. He waves at it as if to say goodbye.

Dolly leans over and whispers to me, "He reminds me of Willoughby. Do you know who that is, Mama?" I shake my head. "He's a cartoon, a hound dog, and not a very smart one either. He is always chasing after something."

I observe him discreetly and try to figure him out. Bình had said he was shy, but he could just be socially awkward or have a neurological developmental disability. Whatever it is, he is not engaging with his surroundings or conversing with anyone at the table, not even with his siblings and father. It is as if he is sitting at this table alone and none of us exist. Our conversation, our laughter, our lips smacking, our silverware clanging are nonexistent to him.

His personality is uninspiring, and I feel a little guilty for thinking so. It must be challenging to be him. I am guessing he has been teased, bullied, and misunderstood all his life. If he did not look so much like his mother, perhaps I would find myself warming up to him or exercising more patience to get to know him. With only five days in San Jose, I decide it is not the time to take on that herculean project. I want to enjoy my vacation and explore as much of California as I can until our drive home. I will only be disappointed if I try to get him to like me.

As aloof as Phan is with everyone, he seems to be comfortable with Dolly. She is curious about him and is relentless with her questions. She eventually wears him down and bulldozes through his walls. As the evening crawls along, Phan is content to sit with my daughter and play go fish, slapjack, and war with a deck of cards.

Tree and Kelly are the first to leave. We say our goodbyes for the night and make plans to get together again before I return to Seattle. Phan is next to leave since he lost his game partner. Dolly yawns and can barely keep her eyes open. The heat of the day has worn her out, and the food in her belly hypnotizes her into dozing off. She hugs Phan and disappears upstairs to put herself to bed. If she likes him, then there must be more to him than meets the eye.

By midnight, the flow of alcohol slows down and only food crumbs remain, too small to be worth picking at. Khoi keeps us entertained with jokes and stories, and Linh comes out of her shell after two shots of Hennessey. Bình picks up a guitar and strums a song while Ken sings and Linh dances. Bình's talent with a musical instrument is yet another thing to add to his growing list of surprises. He seems too good to be true.

The party fizzles at one in the morning, and we all turn in for the night. Khoi and Linh are too inebriated to drive. They set up camp on the sofa bed.

I take one last look at Lionel Richie, propped up against the lamp on the nightstand, and then it is lights out.

I sleep well and feel energized by the bright sunshine. Dolly is asleep. I watch her little chest as it rises and falls. I am lucky to have her. I love her so much. I resist the urge to blip her lips and slither out of bed in search of coffee.

The house is quiet. I creep downstairs and find Linh and Khoi are gone. In the kitchen, there is a note from Thu. Ken is at work, and she has some business to tend to. I make coffee and sit on the back patio to enjoy the serenity of my surroundings. Today is another sunny day, and I hope to explore more of the Bay Area. My thoughts meander around Phan and how odd he is. He is not unkind, just distant. I will have to ask Dolly what the two of them talked about last night while playing cards.

The patio door opens, and Bình stands before me in his bathrobe and slippers, holding a mug of coffee, and wearing a boyish grin. "What do you want to do today?" He pulls out a lawn chair and sits beside me.

"I want to explore," I say. "Maybe San Francisco?"

"Yes," Bình says, "you will like San Fran. Also, if you are up to it, I want to take you to Orange County, but it is a six-hour drive south of here. A large community of Vietnamese refugees settled there. Being back in San Jose has made me realize how much I miss the weather, the food, and the bonds of family."

"I am up for the adventure," I say. "Tell me, was it hard for you to come here back in 1973? What was it like?"

A minute passes before Bình answers me. I almost think he did not hear my question, but he looks at me, grasping for words, deciding where to start his story. "The American War divided this country. So many were killed, missing in action, or became prisoners of war. The majority of Americans did not want us here. They feared we would take their jobs or dry up their welfare system. On top of that, unemployment rates were high, and the nation was in a recession. Like the American military who came home to hate

200

and resentment, so did I. It was hard. We were called names, kicked at, spat on, and seen as diseased." Bình's voice trembles. He takes a long sip of his coffee.

I squeeze his hand. "Take your time."

"You know, we were at Camp Pendleton for a while before a VOLAG representative from Church World Service found us a sponsor to help us assimilate," Bình says.

"Did you have a good relationship with your sponsor?" I ask.

"Yes," he says, "in Santa Ana, but we were encouraged to be financially independent as soon as possible. Many of us took the first job we could find that did not require fluency in English. I did not want to burden my sponsors, so I took a low-paying job to ease their conscience. There was so much racism in the beginning. The Americans treated us as inferior because we are smaller than they are and do not speak the language or understand their laws and processes."

"Navigating that matrix must have been debilitating on one's confidence," I surmise.

"It did not help that the governor at the time publicly denounced us. Unlike Washington's governor, Dan Evans, who welcomed our people, Governor Jerry Brown tried to prevent planes carrying Vietnamese refugees from landing at Travis Air Force Base. Anyway, my first job was as a gas station attendant and I met other refugees over the years. We all sought each other out for unification and protection. Of all the pockets of refugees who came to the US, I think the solidarity in Orange County grew the fastest. Educated people who were businessmen, teachers, doctors, and lawyers somehow found one another and became resources for one another. A new extended family formed. Small restaurants and markets popped up, and now, it is beginning to look like a little Sài Gòn down in Orange County. Many of the small businesses got started because some families transferred their wealth to foreign banks before Sài Gòn fell, while others joined their trusted friends in a rotating credit system."

"Yes, the hui," I say. "My sister runs one, and she used the money to open Six's Kitchen. There is only one thing on the menu." I chuckle thinking of my sister giving a customer the evil stare and silent treatment if they ask for anything other than egg noodle soup. "So how did your family come to live in San Jose?"

"Thu got accepted into San Jose State University," Bình says. "She is my firstborn. I am protective of her. I also wanted the family to stay together, but my children became independent and more Americanized. They rebelled against our traditions and customs, which caused a divide between Trang and me. We took sides and developed different viewpoints.

201

She was stuck in the old way of life, and because she did not work, she had no social connections or progressive views of American society."

"Do you miss our homeland?" I ask. "I get homesick all the time, and because we came here by boat and survived, I feel guilty. Too many people died escaping oppression, and they risked everything only to lose their life before they could taste freedom."

Bình says he misses his parents and sisters. He hopes to sponsor them over in the next year or two. He is saving money, and once he has nine thousand dollars, he will start the application. The government wants sponsors to prove they can take full financial responsibility for the sponsored family members. He needs a stable job and steady income. His deepest concern, however, is that there will be a huge culture shock for them, and without a thriving Vietnamese community, they will become depressed. Seattle is not exactly tropical weather, and chances are good that their world will be very small once they arrive. They do not know English and cannot drive, so they would be dependent on him. For these reasons, he has thought about moving back to California, to Westminster or Garden Grove.

"My parents are spry for their age. In our village, they are well-respected. There is nothing for them here in the US, but I cannot bear the thought of my parents living the rest of their life in Vietnam. My sisters bring little comfort because they are married and live with their husband's family."

It makes me nervous that Bình is entertaining the idea of moving back to California. I wonder if Seattle will become an enclave for the Vietnamese refugees. Will the community be able to thrive and sustain operations, or will it erode with each new generation and ultimately collapse? I suppose only time will tell. I enjoy our budding friendship. He is easy to talk to, and I know we have feelings for one another. If we dare to scratch harder past the surface and explore this companionship, will we find love or resentment? Bình has been through trials of his own and had his marriage fail twice. I have loved and lost as well and do not know if I can truly love again, even though I desperately want to believe I can.

Can we heal and build a strong foundation together? Can we trust again? Or are we both too damaged?

24. ORANGE COUNTY (SUMMER 1984)

Dionne Warwick's song, "Do you know the way to San Jose," plays on the radio. Her demurring feminine voice coats my troubled mind and cements the distress I have over Bình moving back to California. If there is ever a more slap in the face sign, this is it. I change the station so that any thoughts he may have of moving away sink deep down into his psyche.

Yesterday's visit to San Francisco was amazing. Dolly, Bình, and I walked around the waterfront to Fisherman's Wharf, visiting the open markets similar to Seattle's Pike Place Market and seeing the Golden Gate Bridge. We packed in so much activity, including a visit to a botanical garden and a boat tour around the bay.

This morning's drive to Orange County has me straddling the realms of excitement and dread. The sun siphoned a lot of my energy yesterday. Bình drives so I can relax. The thought of sightseeing the cities of Westminster, Huntington Beach, Anaheim, Irvine, and Santa Ana has me strumming my fingers and tapping my toes to the raspy sounds of Aerosmith and Bon Jovi. Their hard rock sound reminds me a little of the '70s music in Việt Nam when the American soldiers played their boomboxes.

We drive nonstop the 375 miles down to Westminster in six hours, hitting a little bit of traffic on I-5 South near Los Angeles. By the time we exit off the freeway onto Magnolia Street, my stomach rumbles loudly.

"You know what sounds good?" I ask. "*Bánh mì* and iced coffee with condensed milk. I miss this so much."

"If you want good bánh mì," Bình says, "wait until we get back to San Jose. There is a place called Lee's Sandwiches on Santa Clara Street that recently opened."

"I want *phở*," Dolly says, "with a lot of hoisin sauce and no vegetables."

"The herbs are good for you," Bình says. "I will get you a bowl of phở if you eat some of the green stuff."

Dolly agrees without arguing. If I try to strike a deal, she usually pushes back or negotiates. We turn onto Bolsa Avenue, and a surge of nostalgia wraps itself around my heart. On both sides of the street are storefronts and buildings with words written in Vietnamese. Hundreds of people from the Asian community, particularly the Chinese, Cambodians, Laotians, and Vietnamese ethnicities, congregate in small pockets to socialize, shop, and dine. It is incredible. I feel like an archaeologist who discovered an indigenous people living within the deep concrete jungle. My mouth waters. I roll down the window and take in the sounds and smells of Little Saigon.

I lean out the window when we stop for a traffic light and listen to the chatter at the intersection and crosswalks. It is music to my ears. I weed out the different dialects and tune in to the inflections of the Vietnamese language with its singsong diacritics of *ngang, sắc, huyền, hỏi, ngã,* and *nặng*—the six accents of my native tongue. I hear dialects from different regions: the proper north, the incomprehensible central, and the slang south.

The only thing missing is the blaring horn of a thousand scooters zipping in and out of traffic to dodge pedestrians, animals, and other riders. I point to a *phở* restaurant, and Bình signals to change lanes. We pull into the parking lot, and Dolly claps her hands. Unable to contain her excitement, she unbuckles her seatbelt before the engine turns off. Diệp once cooked us this traditional beef noodle soup, but other than that, I cannot remember the last time we had it. The one memory that stands out is my *phở* meal with my niece Tâm at the café in Tuy Hòa. That was thirteen years ago in 1971 when I first met Sky and Sam.

This restaurant is a cash-only establishment, which does not surprise me in the least. The place is a small hole in the wall and packed with patrons slurping their noodles and smoking their cigarettes. Just like Việt Nam. It feels like home. There are two groups before us waiting for a table, but we get seated first at a community table where three seats open up. Hearing everyone speak only Vietnamese fills me with an indescribable feeling of homesickness and pride. I have the urge to hug and talk to everyone like they are long lost brothers and sisters or old friends from a faraway land. The restaurant smells heavenly of beef, fish sauce, charred onions, and ginger. One table has iced coffee and *chè ba màu,* the three-colored dessert made of yellow mung beans, sweet red beans, and green jelly served over a slush of ice and bathed in rich and creamy coconut milk.

The menu is impressive. I have a hard time deciding as everything is delicious. I thought I wanted bánh mì, but the photos of classic dishes like *bánh hỏi* and soups like *bún bò Huế* vie for consideration.

"Oh heaven and earth, they even have *tiết canh*!" I exclaim. This northern Vietnamese cuisine is not for the faint of heart. It is blood soup

204

made from freshly slaughtered duck. The blood is mixed with fish sauce and duck broth to prevent premature coagulation. It is then poured over thinly sliced, cooked duck meat and organs like gizzards. The chef will refrigerate it for a brief period so the blood coagulates to a pudding consistency. Crushed peanuts, lime juice, and herbs, such as mint, cilantro, and basil, top this dish for texture, zest, and flavor when it is ready to be consumed. I have had this once, but I am not adventurous enough to throw caution out the window a second time. I admit it is a popular and tasty dish with beer.

In the end, Dolly orders her phở, Bình gets a broken rice combo plate that comes with grilled pork, egg cake, shrimp, and pickled carrots and daikon, while I choose the delicate, steamed rice cakes called *bánh bèo*, topped with mung bean paste, toasted shrimp, and scallions. After our meal, we walk up and down Bolsa Avenue, exploring shops, food markets, and jewelry stores. Before long, it is dinner time, and we try another restaurant that also does not disappoint.

Tomorrow is Wednesday, and another adventure awaits us in Anaheim at a park called Disneyland. A part of me does not want to go back to Seattle as my people are here. However, I have a community in Seattle, and life would not be the same without Teddy, Catherine, Sky, and Katrina. And it definitely would be dull without Diệp.

Today's Disneyland adventure is expensive, overwhelming, and disappointing. Hundreds of people stand in long, unforgiving lines and wait to strap in on the rides. Dolly wants to buy, eat, and experience everything, but we find out there are height restrictions to some of the rides. The heat and crowded lines bring out the impatience in a lot of people despite this place touting to be the happiest place on Earth. Perhaps it is the happiest place for management and the owner because they are making a lot of money on the overpriced souvenirs and food. The best parts of the visit are the parade and fireworks above the Sleeping Beauty Castle. It is too bad I do not own a camera to take photos as these memories would be nice for us to reflect on one day.

Before we leave, I give in to Dolly's pleading for a Mickey Mouse hat with ears on it. While my daughter and Bình meander off to look at T-shirts, I head straight for the hats. The one I want is perched too high for me to reach. I stand on my toes and stretch but lose my balance and tip over. I bump into a man and immediately feel embarrassed.

"I very sorry," I say to him. "I try get—"

"Watch what yer doin'." The stranger looks down at me. His breath inches from my face. His caustic growl can melt my eyebrows. He takes a step closer to tower over me. I take several steps back. He means to intimidate me and disintegrate any wrought-iron resolve I may have. He is a good eighteen inches taller than I am. I stand dwarfed face-to-chest with him, staring at the red, curly hairs weeding out of his white tank top.

I cannot control the trembling in my body or my voice. "I sorry." My voice is so faint that even I question whether I actually said the words or merely thought them.

"Goddammit, ev'rywhere I turn there's 'nother one of ya. Why don't cha git the fuck outta my country? We don't want yer kind here. Don't ya have a country of yer own? Go home." He runs his fat, hairy fingers through his long periwig hair and mutters, "Damn gooks."

I want to cry but dare not make a scene or give him a reason to mock me again. The airway in my throat constricts. My vision narrows to a peephole view of my surroundings, and all I can see is this intimidating man.

He is a big, heavy-set man with tattoos all over his arms and neck. Everything about him is menacing, even his red mustache and thick sideburns. His nostrils flare, and I can see the thick hair follicles coming out of their cave to join the belittling party.

He points to the door and says, "Git, girl."

I feel like a dog who has chewed her master's favorite shoe.

"You deaf or something? Or just plain stupid?"

My fear of his condescension has me frozen.

He bends down, hunches over me, and grits his teeth. "What's the matta? Cat git yer tongue? Oh, wait, you no speaka Inglish?" He smiles and ridicules me some more. Spit flies out the corners of his mouth and erodes his disingenuous smile.

I am reduced to a child whose hand has been slapped for reaching into the candy jar. The man grabs my wrist and cackles. My fight or flight response kicks in.

Minh-Hoàng's face appears at the forefront of my mind. Remembering that two-faced bastard and what he did to me ignites my adrenaline. Minh-Hoàng had lured me into his good graces so I would trust and depend on him, only to try to collect on the debt when my guard was down. I feel dirty with this man's hand on me. I twist my wrist outward and break free of his grip. I dig my heel into his flip-flop hugging toes and punch him with all my might in his testicles. One punch, two punch. Right fist, left fist. I shudder at the touch of his groin. I cannot believe it. He is not wearing underwear beneath his shorts and his penis is salaciously hard. Is he turned on by the power he has over me? I punch him a third time for good measure.

"Son of a bitch," he bellows in excruciating pain.

"Big man so tough," I say loudly. "No baby for you!"

I scurry out of his reach, feeling half victorious and half terrified, like a Chihuahua who nearly got eaten by a big, bad wolf. I find Dolly and grab her hand. I dash out the door. Bình is right behind me. I look back. The man is not following me. Dolly is crying, no doubt scared, confused, and upset. Bình asks what is wrong. My jog slows to a brisk walk. I peer over my shoulder. Good, he is not chasing me.

I tell Bình what just happened. He wraps his arms around me, and I take comfort in his protective embrace.

Maybe Seattle is where I belong after all.

We are back in San Jose today. Bình remembers to take me to Lee's Sandwiches for a bánh mì. While waiting for our order, we chat with a fellow Vietnamese brother who turns out to be Henry Le, one of the co-owners of the sandwich shop. He tells us he is the second oldest of nine children. Like me, his family escaped the war on a boat. They settled in San Jose, and before too long, what started as a modest catering truck business soon became a permanent sandwich shop. His parents used the truck on the weekends to sell sandwiches near San Jose State University, and with the profits, they opened Lee's Sandwiches.

I ask him why there is an extra E in the name, and he says, "So people know how to pronounce it." He admits business is good, and in time, they hope to expand the store to offer a variety of comfort foods, desserts, and beverages. I am inspired by his family's success and the example they are setting for the Vietnamese community. Henry is a good man. In my brief interaction with him, I find him to be light-hearted, genuinely kind, respectful, and funny. I wish him much success with the business.

Bình picks up our food order and takes Dolly and me to a park. Today is our last day in California and we leave early in the morning to drive back to Seattle. Tree, Kelly, their baby Holly, and Thu join us for a picnic. Ken, unfortunately, has to work.

After lunch, we walk San Jose State's campus and make one last stop at the flea market, the last afternoon together before the vacation is over. I feel good leaving Tree here to fend for himself. He has a job, a devoted wife, a small network of people he can rely on, and a growing Vietnamese community in which to thrive.

25. COBWEBS AND HONEYCOMBS (MAY 1985)

I call Magdaleine to see if she wants to come over. I suggest we rent a movie. "Dolly at Opal's birthday. They have sleepover at Pastor George's house."

Magdaleine suggests we have a girls' night out instead. "I want to see the new *Rambo* movie. Did you see the first one?" She summarizes the storyline of the first movie, which was released in theaters three years ago, of a US Army veteran soldier in the Special Forces Green Berets who returned from the Vietnam War, became a drifter, and faced animosity from deputies in Washington State. The sequel is about John Rambo returning to Vietnam, and he discovers there are still Americans being held prisoner in a remote communist camp deep in the jungle.

I am hesitant to see the movie for fear of it triggering stress and guilt for me. Magdaleine is desperate for me to join her. "Snow, please, I feel like I need to see the movie so I can understand Sky better. He still has episodes of depression and violence. Maybe this movie can shed some light on what he's going through and how I can support him."

"What you mean violence?" I ask. "Sky do something?" Magdaleine is quiet at first and then I hear her crying.

"He was doing great after our couples retreat last year, but..." She trails off and snuffles. I encourage her to continue. "You don't know someone until you live with them. Lately, he has been having nightmares. A couple of nights ago, he rolled over and choked me in his sleep. I had to hit him on the head with the phone to snap him out of it. I don't know what to do. Sometimes he yells and screams orders in his sleep, and last month he took a swing at me because I startled him."

She shares with me some of his stories that were discussed during their counseling sessions. He does not talk about his time in Vietnam unless she asks specific questions. He has mentioned comrades walking into traps, getting hammered with shrapnel, getting killed in front of him in a blink of an eye. Sky's depression can last hours to weeks, and he becomes withdrawn.

"He goes into this dark place where he wants to be left alone, and it gets compounded with stress from work and house chores or family and co-workers." She admits Sky is on six different medications, for back pain, high blood pressure, anxiety, and insomnia. "But, Snow, he's been messing with the dosage and concocting his own remedy to balance himself out. Did you know he can't lift his arm for too long without it going numb? We sometimes have these big arguments, and I want to leave him, but I love him so much, and I know those are the times when he needs me the most. I don't want to give up on him, but…"

I soon drown her voice out and wrap my thoughts in a cocoon. Her frantic, high-pitched voice wearies me. The intermittent words of ambush, kill zone, and booby traps become morse code, dits and dahs for "I am scared."

Perhaps Sky is shutting down because he is finally happy and feels he does not deserve it. Maybe he loves Magdaleine so much that he is self-destructing and self-sabotaging so that she will leave him because he thinks she is better off with someone not as broken as he. It is his way of driving out the light so he can be alone in the dark without dragging loved ones with him. I believe this with all my heart because sometimes I feel this way too.

"Snow? You still there?" Magdaleine's curt voice intercepts my private sojourn.

"Yes," I say. "Magdaleine, the best gift you give to Sky is understand his military service not by choice and his goal was survive. Everything he do in Việt Nam, he do because he told to do. In war, we live minute to minute and worry hour by hour. We have no time to plan, just react and do, then regret later." As I say this, a tear escapes down my face. Will we ever be able to forget the atrocities? How can we self-soothe and heal from the pain?

I do not go with Magdaleine to see the new *Rambo: First Blood Part II* movie. I drive to the house she and Sky share in Renton, a city ten minutes north of where I live. I pull into the driveway. Magdaleine opens the front door and runs to my car before I put it into park and turn off the engine. The tear tracks still mar her beautifully sad face. We hug.

"He will be home soon," Magdaleine says. "Do you want me to stay or—?

"No." I cut her off. "Go see movie. I talk to Sky."

"Thank you," she says. "I know he will listen to you. You're his best friend. You can get through to him when no one else can."

Magdaleine puts on her sunglasses to shield her red puffy red eyes even though it is an overcast day. I wait until her car disappears down the road before letting myself into the house. Now, I wait.

209

Alone with my thoughts, I wonder what I will say to my dear friend. I want to believe he will be receptive to my presence and not see it as an invasion of his privacy, of me overstepping his boundaries.

I walk into the living room, and a stout, muscular dog with a rump as big as his head pounces on me. Magdaleine's dog, a Staffordshire Bull Terrier that she adopted at the shelter, jumps up and down, trying to reach my face. His tail wags wildly and smacks me in the calves, sending sharp stings down to my ankle. I bend down so he can give me canine kisses.

I rub Tank's square face and scratch his back. "Who cutest blue-nose? Huh, Tank? You the cutest staffy?" I give him belly rubs and look around for a toy or treat to give him.

On my way to the kitchen, I pass a few pictures hanging in the hallway and sitting on a console table. I notice there are no pieces of artwork, no eclectic sculptures, no avant-garde paintings, no mid-century modern collections of art anywhere in the house.

Framed photographs of family members, of Sky and Magdaleine as young kids and teenagers, and of Sky in his military uniform catch my attention. There are also two photos on the windowsill that take my breath away—one of Sky and Sam on the beach in Tuy Hòa with their uniform and rifle, and the other, a photo of Sam, Sky, and me. It was taken a month after we met when I bumped into them at my bank. An American reporter had taken our photograph and was writing an article for the publication on the blending of two cultures. The headline on the newspaper clipping says, "One War, Two Cultures, Three Friends." I had forgotten about that photo and never saw the printed work. I am tempted to take it out of the frame and read it. I touch Sam's face with my finger, desperately wishing I could feel his touch and willing him to come to life.

A door creaks open. Tank abandons me and runs down the hall. Sky is home. He calls out for Magdaleine. He stops when he sees me. His flushed face blossoms red. He looks gaunt. His eyes are sunken and hollow. Where is the light behind those kind eyes? Dressed in an oversized fawn-colored trench coat and brown hat, he looks like a southern black mouth cur, a breed of working dogs known for their protectiveness and intelligence. He has not shaved in a few days, and the dark bristles around his lips and chin give him a dangerous burglar vibe. We do not know what to say to break the awkward silence. He cocks his head to one side and asks what I am doing here.

"Forgive me, Sky," I say, "but I want to see you. I want talk alone with you. Magdaleine let me come, and she go see movie. Give us privacy."

"For what?" Sky asks. He takes off his coat and tosses it on the back of a chair. Sky strides to the wet bar and pours himself a drink. He offers me a glass, but I decline. "She told you, didn't she?"

"She worry for you," I say. "Me too. Magdaleine love you so much." Sky shoots his shot of whiskey and pours a double into his crystal whiskey glass. I put my hand gently on his before he lifts the glass to his lips. "I need you not drunk. Sky, you my best friend. I need you, and I think you need me too." I take his arm and lead him to the sofa.

I share my Disneyland story and the encounter I had with the red-haired stranger, hoping my story will invite him to open up. Together we can commiserate. I tell him it was the first time I felt unwanted here in America. Sky tells me the word for what I experienced is racism.

I tell Sky he is all I have, and I need him to pull himself together. For the first time in a long time, I am opening myself to the possibility of love and happiness with Bình. I remind him he has this with Magdaleine and that her gift of love is something he cannot throw away. "Remember what Bill say? If you lucky, you get one chance to find your great love in life. He say you have better chance getting kicked by horse than finding your soul's love."

"Soulmate," Sky says. "How do you remember these things?"

I shrug. "I thought counseling and the retreats go good for you. What happen?"

Sky remembers the glass of whiskey in his hand and takes a generous sip. "I guess I can't shake the compunction from—"

"What mean, 'com-pung-shun?'"

"Guilt," Sky says. "Snow, I destroyed a man's face at Tree's wedding."

"He heal," I say matter-of-factly, having no sympathy for Quang.

"But I reduced him from a man who stands with pride to a beast that slithers on his ass. I can't erase the look on his face and the terror in his eyes. I'm ashamed of how it made me feel, so powerful, and I liked it. Hell, I thirsted for it. I wanted him to die."

We agree that his actions further muddled the relationship between Kelly and Ann. The sisters will be challenged to close the divide between them. The familial rift will take time to bridge, but I tell him it would have happened sooner or later. "Sky, the truth alway come out."

"And I nearly killed Mags," Sky says softly. I cringe hearing Magdaleine's name shortened to something I find unflattering, but Sky does not notice. He stands up to pour another glass. "I can't erase the look of fear on her face. I felt like shit."

I look out the window and notice a dragonfly. Perfect timing for a much-needed sign. Dragonflies symbolize transformation and adaptability. I tell Sky this. "He here to remind us we need joy in our life."

"Yes, we do, but I'm a broken man."

211

"How broken?" I ask. "Like cobwebs or like honeycombs? Like glass or like horse?"

"What?" Sky asks. "I don't understand what you're getting at."

"Webs break but spiders spin more. Honeycombs break, but when they do, it for sharing. Make the honey sweeter when you can share with someone."

"So you are saying that if I share the broken parts of myself with people I love, the rewards will be sweeter?"

"Yes, Sky. Nothing ever really broken. Either it can be fixed or something new is created. A new version of Skyler Herrington can exist. A better version of you."

"And what about you?" Sky asks. "Are you broken?"

I smile. "Maybe."

"I don't see any cracks or broken pieces," Sky says. "Maybe yours are below the surface. Maybe in time or with more pressure, you'll break, but I see you as someone so put together despite the tragedies you've faced. How do you do it?"

"Vietnamese people good with secrets," I say. "Women learn to hide feelings and thoughts and not say anything to dishonor our family."

"Sometimes, I see things on the side of the street, like a plastic trash bag, and I tense up. My body temperature rises and so does my blood pressure. I question whether the bag is a bomb or if it's just garbage. I can't trust my judgment."

"Like you, I get nightmares," I say. "Beautiful sunsets make me cry because I thinking of floating in the sea. Sunrises make me miss my family."

"So what do we do?" Sky asks.

I pan over to the pictures and soak in the smiles on all the people in the photographs. I stare at Sam's face and try to commit it to memory. I yearn to kiss him, hold him, breathe in his scent, and laugh with him. I am pining over a man who is dead and will never come back to me in this life. It brings me overwhelming sadness and brief moments of joy.

I place the framed photos of Sam facedown. "I have idea." Sky implores me to elaborate. "We hurt ourselves with these pictures. We cannot bring Sam back. We cannot change the past. We look at them and we wish to go back in time. How we move forward if we alway look backward?"

"So you are suggesting we get rid of all the photos?" Sky asks.

"Put pictures of past away," I say. The more I think about the idea, the more I am convinced it will help. New energy and optimism surges within me. "Fill our home with new dreams, new inspire pictures."

Sky does not look convinced. He props the photos of Sam back up. He lets out a loud, heavy sigh. "Okay, fine." He gives in. "Let's do it before I change my mind."

We put the pictures in a shoebox and scavenge throughout the house for any trinkets, clothes or souvenirs that weigh Sky down with depression. Dog tags, a throw pillow, and mementos from Vietnam are put away in the attic. We go through photo albums and take out anything that reminds him of Uncle Dawson and the period of molestation in his life. In one of the holiday photos, there is a picture of a woman with long black hair who has her arm draped casually around Jean-Adrien's neck. Sky rips up the photo. It is a family friend who had an affair with Jean-Adrien for six months before Katrina found out.

It takes us nearly three hours to purge everything that brings Sky sadness or madness. We toast our good work with a glass of champagne.

"I feel like a dark cloud has lifted," Sky says. "I feel lighter and unburdened."

"Tomorrow," I say, "you go shop with Magdaleine and buy new, joyful things."

"You know what else I need?" Sky asks. "More photos of Mags."

I wince, and this time Sky notices. I tell him the nickname does not sound feminine and makes me think of a choking duck. I imitate a duck's quack by saying in a nasally voice, "Mags, mags."

Sky roars with laughter. There's the Sky I know, the Sky I want to see more of. I wrap my arms around his biceps and squeeze. He kisses the top of my head. All is right again despite the cobwebs and honeycombs in our lives.

26. LIFE IS GOOD (MAY 1986)

A year has passed since Sky and I had our discussion about cobwebs, honeycombs, and "mags, mags." After I came home that night, I took Sam's photo off the nightstand and put it in a shoebox along with the book *A Separate Reality*. The hardest part was putting away the emerald engagement ring that Sam surprised me with the day he died. I said my goodbyes that night and cried myself to sleep.

Since then, every day has been one step closer to emotional freedom as Sky and I learn to let go of our anxieties. We fill our surroundings with people and things that bring us happiness. We lean into God's teachings and have regular family gatherings. With Bình by my side and Magdaleine by Skyler's, we've learned to hold one another accountable for doing activities that swing the pendulum of joy in the upward direction.

Sky continues to do his meditation retreats, and on occasion, he tries writing poetry since it worked for his friend Charlie Peters. He also started stellate ganglion block injections, and the treatments have been working wonders for him. He is a different man than he was a year ago with a more peaceful mind and spirit.

As for me, I sometimes have setbacks in which I feel sorry for myself or have disturbing dreams of the fall of Sài Gòn, the communists and pirates, and the refugee camp. However, I no longer let myself dwell on them. I joined the Family Fitness Center and have discovered yoga again. Dolly and I often go to the gym to swim in the pool, but when she is not with me, I exercise alone.

I made the mistake of taking Diệp once. She was too disruptive, and I could not concentrate. While I showed up looking Jane Fonda-esque in my matching leotard and tights, she looked like a cross-dressed Richard Simmons wearing neon green high-cut fitness thongs over her multi-colored spandex shorts. Of course, leg warmers, a headband, wrist band, and hair scrunchie completed her outfit. She was a hot mess, sweating, grunting, and falling as she struggled to get into each yoga position. All hell broke loose in the last five minutes of class when the instructor turned off the light and let us relax in child's pose. Diệp was so exhausted and relaxed that she passed gas. Everyone heard it and laughed, but I was the only one who smelled it. It was the last time I took her as a guest.

Dolly is finishing sixth grade and is sad to leave Springbrook Elementary School. Some of her friends, including Nadirah Ahmad, Jackie Osario, and the on again-off again crush, Mark Hartman, will be going to different middle schools. Bình gave Dolly a Sony Walkman as a graduation gift, and she is excited to play it this week at sixth-grade camp. She and her classmates are off to Camp Walkawalka, located at the base of Mt. Si in North Bend, for some bonding with nature and storytelling around a firepit. It has been only two days, but I miss her dearly.

Bình has been courting me the old fashioned way, taking me to the park for picnics or a scenic drive through the Olympic National Forest. We have been to the beach a few times in Ocean Shores and Alki in West Seattle. We hold hands in public comfortably, and on occasion, I let him steal a peck on the cheeks or lips.

Today I call in sick, and Bill tells me not to worry. "Jerry can cover you." He reminds me that I report to Jerry now and should call him in the future when I am sick. I tell Bill he is the big boss, and I prefer to "cut out the middleman," a phrase I learned recently from Katrina, who started her wedding planning business and is in high demand this season. She turned away a high-profile client to squeeze in one important wedding, that of Diệp and Donald. I cannot wait to see how the fairytale wedding planning all comes together. Will it be a Rainbow Brite wedding with Diệp riding a horse or an aquarium wedding under the sea of brightly colored reef fish?

Bình is taking me to Mount Rainier today for a hike and picnic. We leave early in the morning in his Cadillac loaded with blankets and a cooler of food and white wine. During the drive, we listen to the radio until we lose reception and discuss everything from our favorite recipes to what I would do if King Kong climbs the Space Needle and throws up all over the *Seattle Times* building because he is afraid of heights.

He tells me he wants to test for citizenship and change his name from Bình Nguyễn to Ben Yuen. I tell him I like the name Benjamin better.

"If you become a US citizen," he asks, "would you change your name?"

I nod. "Yes, Liz, after Elizabeth Taylor."

"Liz Le sounds funny," Bình says. "Maybe Elizabeth Le is better." Bình slows down the car and pulls into a lookout spot. "Or better yet, how about Elizabeth Nguyễn?"

"Why would I—?"

Bình takes out a small jewelry box and pops it open. I open my mouth and admire the diamond ring. I look at him, excited and nervous at the same time. He takes the ring out of the box and reaches for my hand. "Tuyết, will you be my wife?"

Without hesitation, I say, "Yes!"

We spend a glorious day at Mount Rainier National Park taking in the stunning views of the lakes, groves, wildflowers, and wildlife. I am excited to plan our wedding and our life together. We daydream about the house we will have, the cars we will own, and the vacations we will take.

I tell Bình I want to go back to school. "There is a naturopathic medicine program at Bastyr University up in Kenmore. I want to get a doctorate in acupuncture and Oriental medicine." Bình encourages me to go for it, saying it is never too late. "I do not want to work at the *Seattle Times* forever."

As much as I adore Bill and am proud of the newspaper, I am not mentally stimulated. My boss Jerry is a little prejudiced toward non-white people and women. I tolerate him and perform my assigned tasks, but I have no passion to excel under his leadership. I doubt he would let me soar even if I wanted to climb the publication ladder.

We talk about what Bình wants to do. He thinks he will be good at real estate. I think it is perfect for him. He has a sales background and a business mindset. He also has connections and a knack for influencing others.

The only two questions that remain are where will we live and how do we tell Dolly about the marriage proposal and wedding?

With the exciting engagement news sitting big and bright on my ring finger, I take precautions not to show anyone until I can talk to my favorite person in the world.

My daughter steps off the yellow school bus and runs into my arms. She talks so rapidly I tell her to slow down. Funny how she used to ask me what people are saying and now it is me asking her this same question. The words slingshots from her mouth and ricochets off my ears. "I got to zip line from one tree to another. It was scary, but I did it, and it was so fun. And Jackie and I went canoeing, and she made us fall in because she stood up. But we had lifejackets, so we swam to a patch of dirt. The boys rescued us. I pretended we were on a deserted island. And at night we sang camp songs and told ghost stories. Nadirah didn't get to come because her mom and dad are super strict. I'm glad you're not that strict anymore and—"

Dolly abruptly stops and points to my finger. "What's that?"

I take a deep breath and tell her Bình asked me to marry him. "I said yes." I wait for her reaction. Will she be happy or upset? Will she fight me on this, or want to plan the wedding?

"Can I have a puppy?" Dolly asks.

"What? Why? Are you not happy for me? For us?"

"Sure," she says, "but I would be happier if we got a puppy. You promised to get me a pet."

"I did?" I ask. "When?"

"Well, you did," she says, and gives me the sweetest, undermining smile. That is my daughter, always looking for an opportunity or a profit. I do not say yes, but I do not say no either.

On the way home, we talk and laugh nonstop and share stories of what we did while we were apart. Life is good.

As I walk around downtown in Pioneer Square, new life springs under my feet. It is as if flora and fauna sprout out of the cobblestones and carry me from one block to the next so that I glide over the streets of Seattle. My walk takes me through Occidental Park down to the waterfront by Pier Forty Eight. Elliot Bay looks majestic in its sparkling splendor with the sun rays beaming bright and the breeze seducing boaters to stay awhile longer.

I look at my solitaire engagement ring and take comfort knowing someone loves me, wants me to succeed, and has no expectations in return. A light rain comes down and lasts less than ten minutes. A rainbow appears over the bay, and I think about what Pastor George once said about rainbows being God's covenant with man. In Genesis 9:13, after God sent the forty days and forty nights of rain, flooding the earth and destroying the wicked, he promised Noah that the rainbow would serve as a reminder he would never destroy mankind again.

Let this rainbow be a reminder, too, that I will never let anything destroy me. Let the vast oceans, lakes, and bodies of water no longer bring me sadness and guilt, but instead, be a badge of survival that carried me to the shores of freedom. I have her, the sea, to thank for giving me the strength to persevere and teaching me that I am strong.

For too long, I fought to survive. I kept my mind focused and my body tauter than a piano string. Now, I can relax, be carefree, take chances, and let love claim me. Bình could not have come at a better time when I least expected it but when I most needed it.

The breeze in my hair is now received eagerly as a caress rather than a threatening whisper. The gust of wind and the sideways rain is not here to stop me, but instead, carry me to the next best thing.

I am at peace and ready to rebuild, ready to thrive. Dolly, Tree, and I are safe. Our bellies are full, and our beds are warm.

27. THE RAINBOW BRIDE (OCTOBER 1986)

Seattle Supreme canters from behind the house and toward the wedding guests. She appears from the wet dirt trail that leads to Katrina's yurt. Yesterday it rained rocks, but like typical fall weather in Seattle, the clouds give way to the sun. Now the sky shines so brightly the autumn leaves glow like fire. We knew we were taking a chance with the weather having the wedding in October, but the fortuneteller, Hồng Nhung, assured us October 11 was the blessed date for Donald and Điệp to marry.

What a grand entrance Katrina and her horse make. The new Andalusian beast that Jean-Adrien gave to his wife on their do-over anniversary is tall and agile. Her white-gray coat is brushed and shiny for today's special occasion, and in the October glow, she looks like she is made of sterling silver. Cottonwood flurries run along with them as dandelion flakes swim through the air to guide both horse and rider to the ceremony that is about to start. Katrina slows her down to a four-beat gait and then halts in front of the barn door.

"Oh, Yip!" Katrina exclaims. "You are breathtaking."

Điệp gushes at the compliment. My dear friend is stunning in her ivory A-line wedding gown sheathed with gold silk organza. A rainbow gradient chiffon veil flows from the crown of her head down to the kitty heels of her shoes.

Jean-Adrien takes Điệp's hand. "Are you ready?"

She nods. Katrina gracefully slides off the horse and holds Seattle Supreme steady while Jean-Adrien gives Điệp a leg up. She has practiced getting on and off the horse many times, so today, Điệp hops on like a professional rider.

My dearest Điệp would not be Điệp, however, if she did not have something wacky up her sleeves. In this case, up her dress. As she swings her leg over the saddle, I catch a glimpse of multi-colored spandex shorts. I shake my head and smile to myself.

Pastor George drapes a colorful wreath made of fresh flowers around Seattle Supreme's long, muscular neck and steps back to admire this picture-perfect moment. "Now, I want a Rainbow Brite wedding!"

We all chuckle. Katrina takes the reins and leads our rainbow bride and the horse behind a curtain to shield them from view.

Dolly, Jason, and Hùng appear. Hùng hands his mother a bouquet of gladiolus—magnificent sword lilies in a spring mix of red, pink, white, yellow, and purple. My heart swells with happiness, and I dab the corners of my eyes to erase evidence of tears. The music plays. That is our signal.

Pastor George, as the officiant, walks first. Next is Donald, who steps out from the gazebo looking so dapper, Điệp will probably swoon when she sees him. Katrina and Jean-Adrien walk next and then it is the best man and maid of honor's turn. I take Ricky's arm, and we walk toward Donald. Ricky's arm trembles. He has been as excited about his father's wedding day as Điệp. As we walk, I lock eyes with Bình, who winks at me. Teddy and Catherine are here. Tree, Kelly, and Holly are here. Our friends from Homestead Apartments are also here. I notice Kelly's family, Toàn, Lan, and Ann, but Quang is not with them. I am surprised to see a young man standing next to Ann with his arm around her waist. Good for you, Ann.

There are a few faces on Donald's side whom I do not know, but all in all, it pleases me to see so many of our community here to witness this magical union between two very different people who are made perfectly for one another. At the front of the altar, I turn to watch the ring bearer walk down proudly, the pillow held high at her chest. My daughter sashays along in her satin dress with an exaggerated thrust of her hips and shoulders. She is carrying the important treasures of two gold rings tied with a ribbon. She had insisted she be the ring bearer and Hùng and Jason be the flower boys. Surprisingly, they did not argue, and no one put up a fuss.

The guests giggle, and two people clap—Dolly's friend, Melissa, and her mother Stephanie. Tony sits between them taking in the entertainment that is my daughter. Hùng and Jason follow behind with baskets of flowers. They reach in, take clumps of rose petals in their hand, and throw them on the ground like they are casting Pop-Its.

We all rise and face the barn. The band changes melodies and plays a catchy beat from Daryl Hall and John Oates's song "You Make My Dreams." Seattle Supreme trots out and dances to the beat of the song. She moves playfully and gracefully like she is skipping, and changes her steps as the music changes. Everyone cheers and goes wild with applause. Điệp sits gallantly on top, smiling from ear to ear. I am in awe. She is full of surprises. When in the world did she learn dressage? How many hours of practice? And surely, the countless number of bruises before showtime! What a wonderful secret to keep from the guests.

I look over at Katrina, who is beyond elated and beaming with pride. Dolly tugs at my dress and says, "I want a horse like that one."

Seattle Supreme stops thirty feet from the last row of chairs, and Diệp slides off the horse. A handler takes the reins and leads the horse to the stables. My wonderful friend shimmies the rest of the way. What a character. High on endorphins and adrenaline, she throws her arms around Donald's neck and gives him a loud kiss on the lips.

"Not yet," Pastor George says.

We roar with laughter. Without warning my tears gush out. I cannot help it nor do I try to stop. They are tears of jubilation.

Everyone needs a Diệp in their life!

The band plays the same wedding entrance song to kick off the reception, only this time, with the lyrics to the popular Daryl and Oates song. Not a single person sits at their table. The tune is too upbeat not to get out on the dance floor. Bình tries to swing dance with me, but we look like two jiggly gelatins doing a hybrid cha-cha dance. We laugh at our folly and absorb the romance in the air.

"I cannot wait to start our life together," Bình says. "Imagine, me a real estate agent and you an Oriental medicine doctor practicing acupuncture. We will be rich." I like the idea of not worrying about money.

The music slows down and Bình holds me close. He draws in my scent and grazes my temple with his lips. Electricity runs down my back.

"I want to make love to you," Bình whispers. "Tonight."

I pull him in and close my eyes. His lips find mine and we kiss gingerly. We sway side to side and let the music carry our bodies. Bình's hardness pushes into my soft flesh and I let out a gasp. I clutch him tight and invite him to explore with his tongue. Our kiss is now deep and urgent. I am ready. For him, for peace, for change.

My mind drifts to the future. I cannot compete with Donald and Diệp's colorful wedding, but I know ours will be timeless and perfect.

I open my eyes and rest my head on Bình's shoulder. On the other side of the room, Sky and Magdaleine dance. Magdaleine's cheek rests on his shoulder. It will only be a matter of time before they get married too.

At the wine bar, Tree and Kelly talk to Toàn and Lan, while my daughter plays the auntie role to Holly. Ann and her new beau are enjoying each other's company, feeding bites of food to one another. Love is airborne tonight.

I scan the dance floor and watch Teddy, Jean-Adrien, and Pastor George enjoying their wives' company. Their interactions with their spouses look fluid and easy. Jealousy does not reside here tonight. No love triangles to fight over. No triggers that incite anger and fear. How the mattress flips between Tree's wedding three years ago and Diệp's wedding today.

"I want to move to California," I say to Bình, "after Thủy-Tiên finishes the school year." My words peter out and shock Bình. It surprises me, too, but I go with it. Up to this point, I have not given it much thought but seeing Tree makes me want to be together as a family. He has a daughter now, the second generation of our family. I want to be a part of raising Holly and watching her blossom into a young woman. "What do you think? I know you miss your children and the comforts of the Vietnamese way of life. The community in Orange County is growing, and our culture is there. And when you sponsor your parents and sisters over, they will have an easier transition. We will all be together."

"You would do that for me?" Bình asks. "That would make me very happy."

"Plus," I add, "I am sure we can find an acupuncture school down there. It does not have to be Bastyr University."

"But what about your sponsors and the friends you have here?"

I look affectionately in my fiance's eyes and melt with love for him. "Blood is denser than water, right? I feel good leaving because everyone is in a good place. Family first."

"If you are sure, then California, here we come!"

In the cozy Herrington yurt reserved for lovers, Bình claims me as his. He takes his time exploring my body. It has been so long since I have been touched and tasted by another man. I want him now but my impatience amuses him.

The smells of evergreen trees and the cotton canvas has me feeling like a wild animal tonight. I dig my teeth into Bình's neck and my fingernails into his shoulder blades. I cannot take it any longer.

Bình lets out a groan and I reward him with a massage around his throbbing erection. Every inch of his manhood is mine. I spread my legs and wrap them around his hips, drawing him up until his virility finds my wetness. My body cannot get enough of him. With every thrust of his maleness, I hunger more for his strength and his tenderness.

I arch my back and offer myself to him, wanting him to go deeper. He teases me. His fingers caress the softness between my thighs, gently at first, until I squirm and cry out for more.

28. GOODBYE SEATTLE (JUNE 1987)

I share the news with Bill and Magdaleine at work that I am moving to San Jose and then later to Westminster. Magdaleine cries and promises to visit. She and Sky need a vacation. Bill takes me to lunch and his parting words are, "Go and do *you* in California."

On Sunday after the church service, Pastor George and Dawn host a farewell party for Dolly and me. My daughter and the girls, Olivia, Ocean, and Opal, are in tears. One by one, people seek me out to bid farewell and wish us luck. Word travels fast. My VOLAG agent, Joseph, is here as well. Katrina, Jean-Adrien, and Sky reminisce about my arrival in Seattle, and we laugh about how cold Tree and I were. We walk down memory lane of the times Dolly was in the hospital and how she came out of surgery like a champ. Now, she is healthier, stronger, and feistier than ever, and her command of the English language has surpassed mine. I share fond stories of my immersion into Western culture and divulge Diệp's misunderstanding of canned dog food. We have a good laugh over that one.

Saying goodbye to Teddy, Catherine, and Sky is the hardest. They have shepherded us from the beginning, and I owe them a debt of gratitude. I implore them to come down for a visit and promise to take them to Lee's Sandwiches and Little Saigon.

After the agonizing farewells at the church, Dolly and I come home to find the community clubhouse decorated with streamers and balloons. There stands Donald and Diệp with an army of Homestead Apartments residents, waving ribbons and blowing kazoos. Stephanie, Tony, and the neighborhood kids with their parents show up with platters of food and snacks for the party. Dolly, Melissa, Jason, Ricky, Hùng, and Jen play football and jump rope like it is another ordinary day. At the end of the day, after the food trays are empty and the juice has run out, the children embrace and cry their hearts out. Realization sets in. They make well-meaning promises to call and write often and never lose touch so they can go to each other's wedding one day.

And so another chapter closes, and my story in Seattle will soon come to an end.

Today is the last day of seventh grade. While Dolly is at school, I meet with a buyer and sell my Honda Civic to him at a fair price. I sign over the title and hand him the keys. My heart is heavy. I run my fingers over the hood of the car and give it a loving pat. This car gave me confidence and independence, took me to work, to California, to Canada, and all the roads in between. Dolly will be crushed when she finds out I sold the car. She has been wanting the Honda since the day I purchased it. The new owner backs the car out of the parking space and disappears down the street. I wave to her as if she is an old friend.

Toàn, Lan, and Ann arrive right as I turn to head back up the apartment stairs. They help Bình and me pack up the few remaining items and load up Bình's old Cadillac. We move like robots up and down the stairs of my apartment, dropping items on the sidewalk so that Bình can load our belongings like a game of Tetris into the trunk and backseat. We all keep busy and skirt around the inevitable, tearful goodbye.

Diệp and Donald stop in and offer to scrub the apartment clean so that I can get my security deposit back, even though technically, it was the church that paid my move-in fees seven years ago.

"Chị Tuyết," Diệp says, "you better get Thủy-Tiên from school and be on your way." She does not make eye contact with me for fear of losing control. Neither one of us wants to cry.

"This is not goodbye," I say. "This is 'see you later.'"

I wrap my arms around Diệp, and the walls crumble down. The waves crash in, and our sorrow drowns us. We stand for a long time, crying, shedding tears of pain and love and joy and hope. Diệp tells me a joke, but it makes no sense. In between my sniffles and hiccups and her bursts of wailing, we sound like two alien women about to go to battle, with her pounding my back and me suffocating her with my boa constrictor arms. Donald and Bình pry us apart, and we unwillingly accept what needs to happen next.

I hug Lan and Ann one last time. Bình shakes Toàn and Donald's hand, then opens the car door for me to slide in. I watch my friends wave from the rearview mirror as we drive away. The tears start up again and flood my vision.

"See you later," I mouth to myself.

###

Bình waits in the car while I walk to the front entrance of McKnight Middle School. A swarm of seventh and eighth graders runs out with smiles on their faces, happy that school is over and summer break has begun. Two girls holding hands walk slowly out of the building. Their eyes are moist from the rain pouring from their eyes. Dolly and her new best friend, Marina Ogawa, see me. They stop and hug. My daughter weeps louder.

Marina Ogawa, the girl from Japan who befriended my daughter on the first day of school and shared a bento box with her. Marina, who is a head taller than my daughter and looks sixteen, not thirteen, years old. Witnessing them hold each other tightly is like déjà vu with Diệp and me moments ago.

In nine short months, the girls formed a strong bond and did everything together. They giggled together, rolled their eyes about the same things, shared the latest gossip, and even crushed on the same teen heartthrob, John Stamos.

It is the saddest thing to watch, and I do not rush their farewell. The road to San Jose will still be there in five minutes or five days. When all the promises have been made and after all the exchanges of keepsakes and gifts have been passed, they wave a weak "Ciao, Bella" and go their separate ways.

Dolly wraps her arms around me and gushes another round of angry tears. "I don't want to go!"

I wipe the shimmer from her eyelashes. "My baby girl, you are the sunshine that makes the rivers sparkle. You will make new friends, and you will still have Marina and Opal, Olivia and Ocean, Melissa and Jen…and all your other friends."

Dolly sits down on the curb and hugs her knees. She buries her face and refuses to budge. We sit for a while. She is hurting so much, and there is nothing I can do or say to take the pain away. I cannot pick her up and carry her to the car. I cannot force her to come with me right now and drag her across the parking lot or threaten her to get in the car. I let it take its course.

I sit with her and hold her. I stroke her hair and soothe her with words of encouragement. Bình gets out of the car, but I shake my head. He understands my unspoken cue and gets back in the Cadillac to wait.

"What if I don't make any friends? What if Mr. Bình and I don't get along, or I hate my new school? You are going to have a new husband and new kids—"

"I am too old to have more children," I say.

"No, I mean sister Thu and brother Khoi and brother Phan," she says. "I will have stepbrothers and a stepsister and you'll not love me as much anymore."

225

I squeeze my daughter tight. "Honey, you will always be my one and only. You are my miracle and my hero. You are my number one, and I will always pick you over anyone else, even if you lose your way and break my heart, even if you get jolly fat from all the candies and chocolates." Dolly laughs. "It will always be you and me."

"And our puppy," she says.

"And our puppy."

Dolly sits up straight. "Wait, really?"

"Yes, really."

THE END

Snow and Dolly (early 1980s)

Snow (right) in Vietnam

T. Vuong (Dolly's Father)

"Tree" (November 1978, age 16)

T. Vuong (Dolly's Father)

"Tree" and Dolly (Age 67, Age 45 - Seattle, December 2019)

The Vanzwols (1980s)

"Tree" (San Jose, early 1990s)

Dolly's childhood friend, Melissa

Jackie Osorio
1/6/87

Best Friend in
Elementary
School

Dolly's friend, Jackie (1987)

Dolly and Snow (Seattle, 1980s)

Snow graduated with a Masters of Acupuncture and Oriental Medicine
(California, March 1995)

Dolly's 7th-grade friend, Marina (Evergreen High, Prom 1991)

Snow and Sister Six (Vietnam, (February 2008 – Snow at age 68)

Foreground: Tree and his mother
Background: Sister Six and Tree's wife, Kelly
(Vietnam, February 2008 – Tree at age 45)

Brother Seven with his wife
(Tree's parents - Vietnam, February 2008)

Brother Seven and Brother Six (Vietnam, February 2008)

Foreground: Bình's father and mother
Background: Linh, Thu, Ken, Khoi, and Dolly
(San Jose, 1988 – Dolly at age 14)

Bình and Snow with their classic Citroen car (California, 1988)

Dolly's wedding day (Seattle, September 2008)
Left to Right: George & Tamara (Dolly's in-laws)
Joe (Dolly's husband) & Dolly (author/Amy M. Le)
Snow and T. Vuong (Dolly's father)

Tree and Kelly with their grandkids (Christmas 2014)

Left to Right: Joe (Dolly's husband), Kelly (Tree's wife),
Holly (Tree's daughter), Dolly (author), and Tree
(Vietnam, March 2015 – Dolly at age 40 & Tree at age 52)

Tree and Joe (Dolly's husband
(Vietnam, March 2015)

Tree and Dolly (San Jose, California, late 1980s)

Dolly's son, Preston (11 years old, 2020)

Dolly's son, Preston (6 years old, April 2015)

We hope you enjoyed this book. Please consider writing a review to help other readers enjoy SNOW IN SEATTLE. Thank you!

Want to know more about Amy or her next project?
Subscribe to Amy's monthly newsletter, *Amy's Monthly Yodel!*
https://mailchi.mp/a8bd3ead7647/authoramymle

Follow Amy on social media!
#SnowinVietnam
#SnowinSeattle
#SnowsKitchen

https://www.facebook.com/authoramymle
https://www.facebook.com/quillhawkpublishing/
https://twitter.com/amy_m_le
https://twitter.com/hawk_quill
https://www.linkedin.com/in/amymle/
https://www.etsy.com/shop/QuillHawkPublishing
https://www.instagram.com/amy_m_le/
https://www.instagram.com/quillhawkpublishing/
http://www.amy-m-le.com

About the Author

Amy M. Le was born in Vietnam and immigrated to The United States in 1980 at the age of five with her mother and cousin. She graduated from Western Washington University with a degree in Sociology and worked in the telecommunications and technology sectors for twenty years. Her novels *Snow in Vietnam* and *Snow in Seattle* are tributes to her mother. Amy calls the Pacific Northwest and Oklahoma her home. Her greatest joy is spending time with her family.